Shadow Tyrants

Cl... Cussler is the author or co-author of a great number of international bestsellers, including the famous Dirk Pitt® adventures, such as *Havana Storm*; the NUMA® Files adventures, most recently *The Rising Sea*; the *Oregon* Files, such as *The Emperor's Revenge*; the Isaac Bell historical thrillers, which began with *The Chase*; and the recent Fargo Adventures, which lastly included *The Grey Ghost*. He lives in Arizona.

Boyd Morrison is the author of six adventures, including *The Roswell Conspiracy* and *The Loch Ness Legacy*. Morrison lives in Seattle.

Find out more about the world of Clive Cussler by visiting www.clivecussler.co.uk

TITLES BY CLIVE CUSSLER

DIRK PITT® ADVENTURES

Odessa Sea (with Dirk Cussler)
Havana Storm (with Dirk Cussler)
Poseidon's Arrow (with Dirk Cussler)
Crescent Dawn (with Dirk Cussler)
Arctic Drift (with Dirk Cussler)
Treasure of Khan (with Dirk Cussler)
Black Wind (with Dirk Cussler)
Trojan Odyssey
Valhalla Rising
Atlantis Found
Flood Tide
Shock Wave
Inca Gold
Sahara
Dragon
Treasure
Cyclops
Deep Six
Pacific Vortex!
Night Probe!
Vixen 03
Raise the Titanic!
Iceberg
The Mediterranean Caper

SAM AND REMI FARGO ADVENTURES

The Gray Ghost (with Robin Burcell)
The Romanov Ransom (with Robin Burcell)
Pirate (with Robin Burcell)
The Solomon Curse (with Russell Blake)
The Eye of Heaven (with Russell Blake)
The Mayan Secrets (with Thomas Perry)
The Tombs (with Thomas Perry)
The Kingdom (with Grant Blackwood)
Lost Empire (with Grant Blackwood)
Spartan Gold (with Grant Blackwood)

ISAAC BELL ADVENTURES

The Cutthroat (with Justin Scott)
The Gangster (with Justin Scott)
The Assassin (with Justin Scott)
The Bootlegger (with Justin Scott)
The Striker (with Justin Scott)
The Thief (with Justin Scott)
The Race (with Justin Scott)
The Spy (with Justin Scott)
The Wrecker (with Justin Scott)
The Chase

Shadow Tyrants

CLIVE CUSSLER
and BOYD MORRISON

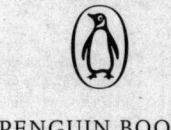

PENGUIN BOOKS

PENGUIN BOOKS

UK | USA | Canada | Ireland | Australia
India | New Zealand | South Africa

Penguin Books is part of the Penguin Random House group of companies
whose addresses can be found at global.penguinrandomhouse.com

First published in the United States by G. P. Putnam's Sons 2018
First published in Great Britain by Michael Joseph 2018
Published in Penguin Books 2019

001

Set in 12.5/14.75 pt Garamond MT Std
Typeset by Jouve (UK), Milton Keynes
Printed and bound in Great Britain by Clays Ltd, Elcograf S.p.A.

A CIP catalogue record for this book is available from the British Library

ISBN: 978–1–405–93709–2

www.greenpenguin.co.uk

Cast of Characters

The Kalinga War

Ashoka the Terrible   Mauryan Emperor.

Kathar   Mauryan general.

Vit   Ashoka's younger brother.

The Corporation

Juan Cabrillo   Chairman of the Corporation and captain of the *Oregon*.

Max Hanley   President of the Corporation, Juan's second-in-command, and chief engineer of the *Oregon*.

Linda Ross   Vice president of operations for the Corporation and US Navy veteran.

Eddie Seng   Director of shore operations for the Corporation and former CIA agent.

Eric Stone   Chief helmsman on the *Oregon* and US Navy veteran.

Mark 'Murph' Murphy   Chief weapons officer on the *Oregon* and former US military weapons designer.

Franklin 'Linc' Lincoln   Corporation operative and former US Navy SEAL.

Marion MacDougal 'MacD' Lawless   Corporation operative and former US Army Ranger.

Raven Malloy   Corporation operative and former US Army Military Police investigator.

George 'Gomez' Adams   Helicopter pilot and drone operator on the *Oregon*.

Hali Kasim   Chief communications officer on the *Oregon*.

Dr Julia Huxley   Chief medical officer on the *Oregon*.

Kevin Nixon   Chief of the *Oregon*'s Magic Shop.

Maurice   Chief steward on the *Oregon*.

Chuck 'Tiny' Gunderson   Chief fixed-wing pilot for the Corporation.

The Nine Unknown and Associates

Romir Mallik   CEO of Orbital Ocean and descendant gifted with the cosmogony scroll from the Scrolls of Knowledge.

Xavier Carlton   CEO of Unlimited News International and descendant gifted with the propaganda scroll from the Scrolls of Knowledge.

Jason Wakefield   CEO of Vedor Telecom and descendant gifted with the communication scroll from the Scrolls of Knowledge.

Lionel Gupta   CEO of OreDyne Systems and descendant gifted with the alchemy scroll from the Scrolls of Knowledge.

Melissa Valentine   Internet search firm founder and descendant gifted with the scroll about the mysteries of light from the Scrolls of Knowledge.

Daniel Saidon   CEO of Saidon Heavy Industries and descendant gifted with the gravity scroll from the Scrolls of Knowledge.

Pedro Neves Biotech executive and descendant gifted with the scroll on diseases from the Scrolls of Knowledge.

Boris Volanski Head of military contracting firm and descendant gifted with the physiology scroll from the Scrolls of Knowledge.

Hans Schultz Swiss banker and descendant gifted with the sociology scroll from the Scrolls of Knowledge.

Asad Torkan Brother-in-law of Romir Mallik.

Rasul Torkan Asad Torkan's twin.

Natalie Taylor Assistant to Xavier Carlton.

Missing plane victims

Lyla Dhawan Chief technology officer of Singular Solutions.

Adam Carlton Son of Xavier Carlton.

Central Intelligence Agency

Langston Overholt IV The Corporation's CIA liaison.

Diego Garcia incident

Keith Tao Leader of *Triton Star* hijackers.

Major Jay Petkunas B-1B bomber pilot.

Captain Hank Larsson B-1B bomber copilot.

Lieutenant Colonel Barbara Goodman Air Force Global Positioning System commander.

Sergeant Joseph Brandt Camp Thunder Cove communications operator.

Jhootha Island

Fyodor Yudin   Warden.

Colossus

Chen Min   Chief scientist.

India

General Arnav Ghosh   Head of the Indian military's weapons procurement.

Kiara Jain   Bollywood actress.

Gautam Puri   Kiara's boyfriend.

Prisha Naidu   Bollywood actress and friend of Kiara's.

Samar Naidu   Prisha's husband.

Prologue

The Kingdom of Kalinga
The Indian subcontinent

261 BC

The air reeked of smoke and burnt flesh. The army's main encampment was on the other side of the destroyed city. The only sound was the restless shuffling of hooves from the Imperial Guard's horses and the snapping of the Royal Lion banner in the breeze.

'How many dead?' Mauryan Emperor Ashoka the Terrible asked his top general, Kathar, who sat astride an ebony stallion that contrasted with Ashoka's brilliant white steed.

'It is a glorious victory, Excellency,' Kathar said. 'We have lost only ten thousand men during the entire campaign.'

For a week Ashoka rode through the nation he had conquered and saw nothing but death and destruction. Now as they crested the heavily forested hill overlooking the remains of Tosali, Kalinga's capital, he finally saw the true extent of his war to crush the last kingdom on the subcontinent that refused to bow to his rule. The entire city had been incinerated, and the fields were littered with corpses as far as the eye could see.

His army's ten thousand casualties meant that one out

of every seven soldiers had been killed or wounded in battle. Despite the staggering numbers, it was still the mightiest force south of the Himalayas, possibly in the whole world. No army known could stand against him. But that was not his concern right now.

Ashoka turned from the vast scene of carnage and stared at his general. 'I mean, how many have *we* slain?'

Kathar smiled, cruel and unremorseful about the savage annihilation he had caused of a proud people. 'My officers tell me that we have wiped out one hundred thousand Kalingan soldiers. None were spared. An equal number of civilians were either killed or deported in the plunder after the battles. We have taught the world a lesson. No one will dare defy us again.'

Ashoka did not return the smile. Instead of pride over his great triumph, he felt a deep shame that had been festering for days. Unwilling to become his subjects, the citizens of Kalinga had fought to the last man, woman, and child. He'd heard tales of entire villages committing suicide rather than suffer brutalization by his rampaging army.

His empire now stretched from Persia to the Ganges Delta. This ride was supposed to have been a survey of his monumental achievement. Instead, it had become a trail of infamy, a testament to his viciousness, and it was changing his view of the world in profound ways. Ashoka knew he couldn't let this be his lasting legacy.

He deserved his title Ashoka the Terrible. He had done hideous things to secure his reign as emperor. He'd killed ninety-nine of his one hundred half brothers to prevent them from overthrowing him, sparing only his younger brother Vit, his most trusted adviser. He'd created a prison known as Ashoka's Hell, where his enemies endured every kind of torture imaginable. No inmate had ever come out alive.

But all of that paled in comparison to the suffering he'd seen over the past week's ride. These were not betrayers and criminals. The dead and exiled of Kalinga were noble soldiers fighting for their homeland and its innocent civilians who only wanted to live their lives in peace.

Vit and his forces were scheduled to meet Ashoka today at Kalinga's capital to bring news from the rest of the country. But what he'd seen already was enough to convince him to turn away from further conquest and focus on improving the lives of his subjects.

The rustle of leaves in the forest caused his guards to draw their swords. Ashoka turned to see a filthy young woman in ragged clothing emerge from the tree line. Tears were streaming down her cheeks as she took in the holocaust her people had endured. Then she turned and caught sight of the Emperor and his men. She limped toward them.

'Kill this vermin,' Kathar casually said to one of the guards.

The guard raised his sword and readied to charge at her.

'Sheathe your weapons!' Ashoka ordered. 'All of you!'

The guards instantly obeyed his command and put away their swords.

Kathar narrowed his eyes at the Emperor. 'Excellency?'

'No one will harm this woman.'

She staggered to a stop in front of him without a hint of fear. Ashoka could see only sadness and defiance on her face. She glanced at the Royal Lion on his banner and then stared at him.

'Are you the Emperor Ashoka the Terrible? Are you the butcher who has done this to my people?' She gestured with a weak and trembling arm at the devastation below them.

'How dare you speak to His Excellency with such disrepect!' Kathar yelled. 'You will –'

Ashoka put up his hand and looked at the general. 'Quiet. I want to hear what she has to say.' He turned back to the woman. 'I am Ashoka. Are you from this city?'

She nodded. 'Tosali *was* my home.'

'Are you alone?'

'You should know. Your armies murdered my father, my husband, and my three brothers in battle.'

Kathar shouted at her, 'They were not murdered! They died because they refused our gracious offer to surrender and become subjects of the Mauryan Empire! They were nothing more than pathetic vermin to be wiped off the face of the –'

'Enough!' Ashoka dismounted to the surprise of his guards, who immediately surrounded him and the woman as he approached her.

Ashoka took her hand. 'Do you not have any family left?'

She shook her head. 'My only son died of disease, and my sisters and two daughters were violated before they were sent away to become slaves. I escaped into the woods hoping to find more of my people, but there are none. I am all that is left.' The woman dropped to her knees and clutched at the Emperor's hand. 'Please kill me.'

'Why should I do that? You are no threat to me or my men.'

'You have taken everything from me. I have nothing left to live for. If I don't starve first, I will suffer the fate of the other women.'

'I give you my word as supreme ruler of the Mauryan Empire that no further harm will come to –'

Before Ashoka could finish, Kathar drew his sword, causing the Emperor to jump back when he saw the flash of steel out of the corner of his eye, and slashed the woman's neck. She gurgled blood and fell over, a look of calm and relief on her face as she died.

Ashoka felt a warm trickle of liquid on his throat. He touched the spot and felt a gash in his skin. When he pulled his hand away, he saw that his fingers were covered in crimson. The wound wasn't deep, but the fact that it was there at all shocked him. If he hadn't moved so quickly, he would have been killed by the same blow that struck down the woman.

The general's sword was now pointed at Ashoka's chest. The Emperor's guards had already drawn their swords and were ready to defend him, but they could see that the slightest movement would doom their beloved leader.

'Kathar! You almost beheaded me!'

Kathar smiled and shrugged. 'I underestimated your reflexes, Excellency.'

'Are you saying you were trying to kill both of us?'

'She wasn't bad to look at, but there are many more where she came from. You, on the other hand . . .' Kathar shook his head. 'I can see how this war has changed you. You no longer strive for the greatness of the empire. You have become weak.'

One of the guards inched closer, but Kathar pressed the tip of his sword against Ashoka's chest to stop him.

'If any of you come nearer, I will run him through.'

'If you do that,' Ashoka said, 'you will be dead before I hit the ground.'

'Possibly. But then I would be a hero of the empire.'

Ashoka could hear the sound of hooves approaching from the forest. It had to be his brother Vit coming with his archers. If Ashoka could delay Kathar just a little longer, Vit's men could slay him before his sword moved.

'Don't you see that conquest is a fool's errand?' Ashoka asked. 'What does it matter if we gain more land unless we improve the lives of our subjects?'

'Because conquest is what will guarantee that our names will be remembered throughout the ages,' Kathar said, his eyes wild with the power he now held in his hands. 'Alexander the Great assembled the finest army in history, was never defeated in battle, and ruled over the largest empire the world has ever known. People will be speaking his name until there are no people left.'

Ashoka nodded solemnly. 'And then he died at thirty-three and his empire was torn apart in a series of civil wars. Don't you see that there's another way?'

'This Buddhism you've been speaking about?' Kathar spat. 'A waste of time. With our armies, you could have been remembered for even greater conquests. You could have ruled the known world. I won't let you throw this opportunity away. Maurya will know greatness under my rule. I will be called Kathar the Magnificent. History will remember my name, worshipping it even more than Alexander's.'

Ashoka looked around at his loyal guards. They would not let Kathar get away with killing him.

'What makes you think you'll live through the next few moments?' Ashoka asked calmly.

Kathar answered only with a grin. Horses emerged from the forest, but they did not belong to Ashoka's brother Vit. They were Kathar's most loyal soldiers, double the number of his guards. They flanked Ashoka's men, who were now hopelessly outmatched.

'I did not do this on a whim,' Kathar said. 'I have been planning this for weeks, scouting out just the spot to ambush you and your men. When I return with your body, I will tell your subjects about how rebellious Kalingan traitors had cut you down. Who else will they turn to but your most trusted general, who has delivered this great but tragic victory for the empire?'

'My brother will avenge me.'

'He will try. But he's just as weak as you are. If I can defeat you, he will prove no trouble at all.'

Kathar turned to one of his soldiers, whom Ashoka recognized as a top cavalry officer.

'You found them?' Kathar asked.

The officer nodded and took a satchel from his shoulder. He removed a scroll and held it over his head for all to see.

'All nine,' the officer said.

Ashoka felt a chill at seeing one of the nine sacred Scrolls of Knowledge, representing the collected intelligence of the best minds in his kingdom. The fact that the scrolls were here had to mean the Librarian was dead, and now Kathar had everything he needed to rule with absolute power.

Kathar turned back to Ashoka and smiled. 'Maybe you now realize that I missed you on purpose before, to give time for my men to arrive. I was keeping you alive until I made sure the scrolls were in my hands. Since they are, you are no longer necessary. Your dynasty ends here. Now.'

Kathar raised his sword for the killing blow as his soldiers charged toward the Imperial Guard.

Ashoka wasn't going to make it easy for him. He crouched down and twisted to his side as the sword came down, striking his shoulder. The leather armor absorbed part of the blow, but the blade cut deeply into his muscle.

Ignoring the pain, he stood to run, but Kathar had the advantage of height and speed astride his horse. The general drew his sword back for another swing, a maniacal look of bloodlust in his eyes.

Among the din of clashing swords, snorting horses, and screams of dying men, Ashoka heard the distinctive sound of an arrow whizzing by. It struck Kathar's hand, and he cried out as he dropped the sword.

With a look of fury, Kathar wrenched the arrow from his palm and looked in the direction it had come from. Ashoka followed his gaze and saw Vit and his archers stampeding toward them, arrows flying from their bows. A quarter of Kathar's men went down in the first volley.

Seeing that his defeat was imminent, Kathar wheeled his horse around and charged the cavalry officer holding the satchel. He snatched it away and yelled, 'Make sure no one follows me.' Then he whipped his horse and galloped into the forest.

Ashoka wasn't going to let him get away so easily, not

with the Scrolls of Knowledge. As long as Kathar had those, he would be a dire threat to Ashoka's plans for his country's new era.

Ashoka leaped onto his horse and drew his sword with his uninjured arm. Despite his brother's calls to get to safety, he followed his betrayer.

Kathar was the better fighter, but Ashoka was a superior horseman. Instead of taking the clear path through the forest where he could have used his horse's speed to escape, Kathar was weaving through the thick stand of trees in an effort to lose any pursuers.

But Ashoka wasn't fooled. He could spot Kathar's trail of broken branches and trampled underbrush as he rode, taking whatever shortcuts he could to close the distance.

Finally, he spotted the bright silver buckles on Kathar's armor flickering in and out of view. Ashoka raced to the side and paralleled his course, drawing nearer with every moment.

Kathar realized he was being followed and drew his dagger. In desperation, he threw it at Ashoka, but it sank into a tree that came between them.

Seeing his chance, Ashoka cut his horse through a narrow alley between the trees and drew alongside Kathar. He raised his sword and swung with all his might.

The sword met nothing but air.

Kathar had leaped from his horse to avoid the blow and careened into a tree. He bounced off it and came to rest on the ground. The scrolls tumbled from the satchel and scattered across the forest floor.

Ashoka turned around and dismounted, his sword held

in front of him as he approached the kneeling general, who was shuddering with pain.

Ashoka knew it was a trick. He circled around until he was directly behind Kathar and put the tip of his sword to the base of the general's neck.

'Drop the knife.'

Kathar stopped trembling and chuckled. The knife he'd been holding in his good hand dropped to the ground.

'Now stand.'

Kathar got to his feet and turned around.

'You won't kill me,' he said with a wicked grin.

'Why not?'

'Because of this Buddhist faith you've been talking about converting our entire country to. It doesn't allow killing. I know. I've been hearing about it for weeks now. From you.'

'You're right,' Ashoka said. 'I have been thinking about ordering all my subjects to follow the ways of the Buddha. And your betrayal only confirms that it is the right thing to do. Killing only begets more killing. If you'd had your way, your rule would have been built on terror and death.'

'You know that's the only way to build a dynasty.'

Ashoka shook his head. 'There's another way. As long as I'm alive, we will take a different path.'

Galloping hooves approached, and Ashoka could see that Vit, a fine tracker, had followed their trail. He pulled his horse to a stop beside them.

'Are you all right, brother?' Vit asked.

Ashoka nodded. 'But I wouldn't have been if you hadn't come along at the right time. Gather up the scrolls.'

Vit got off his horse and began collecting the parchments to put them back in the satchel.

'This piece of garbage must have killed the Librarian to get these,' Vit said. 'Who will be the new one? Tell me and I'll take them to him.' He walked over with all of the scrolls secure in the pouch.

'I am not naming a new librarian,' Ashoka said. 'Kathar has proven that it is too dangerous to keep them all together. Vit, I want you to find nine unknown men, common men who have shown themselves to be good and loyal. Each of them will be tasked with safeguarding one of the Scrolls of Knowledge to keep any single man from using them to conquer the world.'

'It will be done,' Vit replied. Then he looked at Kathar with contempt. 'And what about him?'

Ashoka took a step closer to Kathar and laid the sword along his neck. 'My first order of the new age will be to strike this traitor's name from all scrolls and etchings. If anyone speaks his name aloud, they will be banished from the country.' He looked at Kathar with pity. 'By the end of this growing season, no one will remember your name. You will be lost to history forever. It will be as if you never existed.'

For the first time, Kathar's smug expression faltered before he made another halfhearted attempt at bravado. 'But I am still here. My followers are numerous and my soldiers loyal. They will rise against you and rescue me from your prison.'

'No, they won't.' Ashoka raised his sword.

Kathar gaped at him. It was the only time the general had ever shown fear. 'But the ways of the Buddha! They don't allow killing!'

'You're right,' Ashoka said. 'From this point on, I will decree no living thing, human or animal, shall be killed for punishment or sacrifice. From this point on, it is my duty and responsibility to make sure that you, who are without a name, are the last.'

Ashoka brought down the sword.

I

Over the Arabian Sea

Present day, eighteen months ago

'Don't tell anyone,' Adam Carlton whispered as he glanced over his shoulder to make sure no one was listening. 'I'm not supposed to take you down there.'

Lyla Dhawan knew his dramatic gesture was all for show. They were alone in the airplane's palatial rear lounge, with its mahogany tables and Gucci-embossed sofas. Although the double-decker Airbus A380 was gigantic and could carry more than eight hundred passengers when fitted out as an airliner, this plane currently held fewer than one hundred people. Most of them were in the luxurious forward bars, enjoying the free-flowing champagne and snacking on expensive caviar.

Lyla still didn't know why she'd been one of the lucky few invited onto Xavier Carlton's private jet, but she jumped at a once-in-a-lifetime experience. Fending off advances from one of the billionaire's sons almost made her wish she'd reconsidered. However, his offer was intriguing.

'You mean, we can go down and see the cargo hold?' she asked.

Carlton nodded, downed the rest of his hundred-year-old

scotch, and leaned in closer, practically purring, in his British accent, 'Have you ever seen a Bugatti Chiron?'

The reek of alcohol on his breath almost made Lyla gag. She shook her head.

'Fastest car in the world,' Carlton said. 'Worth three million dollars even before I added the solid gold trim. I brought it from London to see what it can do on the desert roads. Obviously, I can't take you for a drive, but you can sit in it. The leather is the softest you'll ever feel.'

She managed not to roll her eyes. Lyla couldn't care less about cars, and his constant bragging was getting on her nerves. But she didn't know when she would get another opportunity to tour the cargo area of an A380. She was a pilot herself, logging more than six hundred hours in twin-engine prop planes back in San Jose, California, so going down to see the hold was like getting a backstage pass to Disneyland. Her only hesitation was the thought of being alone with this jerk.

'That's quite a tempting offer,' Lyla said. 'Maybe some of the other guests would like to see it, too.'

Not that she couldn't fend him off if he got handsy. He was short and decidedly out of shape, while she was taller than he was and could deadlift two hundred pounds thanks to regular CrossFit classes. The bigger concern was that she would offend him and torpedo any future contracts with his father's company.

Like all of the other passengers on board for this extravagant meet and greet, Lyla was a computer company executive visiting Dubai for the TechNext trade show. As the chief technology officer of Singular Solutions, she was attending the convention to help pitch her firm's groundbreaking pattern recognition software to customers around the world. So far they'd signed contracts for fifty million dollars, but Carlton's massive media corporation, Unlimited News International, could double that figure with the stroke of a pen.

When Lyla suggested they bring others with them, Carlton scowled and sat back.

'If you don't want to see my car, just say so,' he huffed.

'No, I really do,' Lyla said with a smile. She stood up, smoothing the skirt of her black cocktail dress. 'Quick! Before anyone knows I'm getting a private tour.'

Carlton grinned and nearly leaped to his feet. 'I promise you won't regret it. The Chiron is almost as beautiful as you are.'

'Lead the way.'

He took her to a tiny elevator, and they both squeezed in, Carlton smiling up at her as they descended.

'Are you from America originally?' he asked.

'California, born and raised. My parents are from New Delhi.'

'I've been to India many times. My father has a villa outside of Mumbai.'

'I never got to thank him for the invitation to this event.'

'Unfortunately, he couldn't be here. He had an urgent matter to attend to in Dubai.'

The elevator opened, and Carlton escorted her out into a small storage area before showing her through the door into the main hold. He froze at the sight that met them.

The vast cargo area was completely empty.

Carlton wheezed a couple of times, then yelled, 'Where

is my car? I saw it loaded onto the plane last night before we took off from England! When I find out who —'

Without warning, the airplane suddenly plunged into a dive, sending both of them soaring toward the ceiling. Floating ten feet above the floor, they flailed for a few moments. Then the jet rapidly reversed course, slamming them down.

Lyla landed on flat metal, but Carlton wasn't so lucky. His head smashed into a bare stanchion that should have been holding down his car.

She got to her feet and rushed over to him. Blood pooled around his head. He was unconscious but breathing.

With a frantic search of the storage area, she found some cloth towels and took them back to the cargo hold. She propped up Carlton's head with two towels before pressing the third against the wound.

Yelling for help was useless. The hold was too isolated for anyone to hear her. She would have to leave him alone so she could get him medical attention.

She ran back to the elevator and had to wait for what seemed like forever for its return. The glacial ascent was agonizing.

When she reached the main deck, she sprinted forward through the rear lounge, past the conference room and into the piano bar, which was eerily silent. She gasped when she saw why.

All of the passengers were seated with emergency oxygen masks over their faces. Each of them was slumped over, their eyes closed.

Lyla approached the nearest woman with dread. She put a finger to the woman's throat and sighed with relief when she felt a pulse. She tried two more passengers. Though comatose, they were all alive.

She nearly panicked, then it occurred to her the situation might have been caused by an explosive decompression, which would explain the plane's sudden dive.

But she quickly dismissed the idea. Not only would she have felt the frigid air from outside even if the tear in the fuselage had occurred on the upper level, she would have also fallen unconscious herself seconds after reaching the main deck.

She checked two more rooms and found the same chilling sight: all of the passengers and crew with masks on and out cold.

Lyla wasn't an expert on large airliners. Flying was just a hobby – her only one – a chance to get away from the stress of her job for a few hours a week where work emails couldn't reach her. Even better, her mother couldn't call to berate her for not having a husband at the advanced age of thirty-one.

She knew everything that could go wrong with a Cessna twin-prop Corsair, but the Airbus was far more complicated. Something might have malfunctioned in the emergency oxygen system, but she had no idea what that could be. A better question was why they were wearing the masks in the first place if the air in the plane was breathable.

Lyla looked out a window and saw nothing but the sun shining through scattered clouds on the calm water below, but they should have stayed over the Saudi Arabian Desert for the duration of the flight. They were out of range for an ordinary mobile phone, and the odds of finding a satellite phone on board were minuscule. She had to get into the cockpit. If the pilots were on the same oxygen system, they might be unconscious as well, but she could radio a Mayday and get help from someone on the ground. She couldn't land this plane, but the controls were so highly automated these days that someone at air traffic control in Dubai should be able to talk her through getting them back to the airport safely.

When she got to the cockpit door, it was closed and locked. No one answered her pounding fist. She desperately tried to wrench it open, but it was a secure door. Since 9/11, all aircraft had been built with stronger cockpit doors and locking mechanisms controlled by the pilots to prevent terrorists from gaining access. It also meant that if the pilots were incapacitated, no one could get inside.

Lyla examined the door. She noticed a keypad with a red light beside it and realized there might be a way inside. She remembered reading that there was a code the flight attendants could use to access the cockpit in a medical emergency as long as the pilots hadn't disabled it from inside, as they would during a terrorist event.

They had to keep a code like that nearby so all the flight attendants could find it quickly. She rooted through the food lockers in the front galley and found what she was looking for: a piece of paper taped to the inside of the cabinet door with a six-digit number written on it. The Arabic text above the number was unreadable, but it had to be it.

Lyla punched the number into the keypad, and the light turned green with a beep. She was overjoyed as she flung the door open.

Her happiness vanished when she saw the pilot slumped back in his chair, a small bullet hole in his right temple.

The copilot, however, was very much alive. She flinched and instinctively put up her hands when he turned around and pointed a small pistol at her.

'Who are you?' he demanded.

'No . . . no one,' she stammered. 'Just a passenger. Lyla Dhawan.'

'Where did you come from?'

'I was in the hold with Adam Carlton when we hit the turbulence.'

'Where is he?'

'He hit his head. He's badly injured.'

'How did you get in here?'

'The access code. It was on a piece of paper.'

He got up from his seat. 'Show me.'

He kept the gun on her the whole time as she showed him where it was in the galley. He yanked the paper off the door, crumpled it up, and shoved it into his pocket.

He motioned with his pistol for her to return to the cockpit. After shutting the door behind him, he got back into his chair and told her to sit in the jump seat.

'Belt yourself in,' he said while glancing at his watch.

Lyla let out a sob of relief. He wasn't going to kill her. She snapped the seat belt together.

'Now put on the mask.' He pointed to the one hanging next to her.

The thought of all the unconscious passengers flashed in her mind. 'Why?'

He held up the pistol and pointed it at her head.

'Do it.'

She had no choice. The dead pilot was evidence that he wouldn't hesitate to pull the trigger.

She fit the mask over her face but tried to keep it as loose as possible.

The copilot looked at his watch again and then at her. 'No. Tighter.'

Reluctantly, she pulled the straps taut. Within seconds, she started to feel herself get light-headed. There had to be some kind of knockout gas in the emergency oxygen system.

'Why are you doing this?' she shouted through the mask, but the copilot ignored her.

He looked to his right, then shielded his eyes with one hand. A moment later, a blinding flash lit up the cockpit.

Immediately after that, the copilot pushed his control joystick forward. The huge airplane nosed into a steep dive.

Lyla tried to unbuckle herself so she could stop the maniac from killing them all, but her muscles were like jelly. She couldn't feel her fingers, and her mind was a muddled haze. She had the sudden hope that this was all just a nightmare, that none of it was truly happening.

Then she looked through the front windows as they emerged from a cloud bank. No sky was visible. Only ocean.

They were going down, and there was nothing she could do to prevent it. Then, mercifully, she tumbled into darkness.

2

The present day

Although the main workforce had gone home after sunset, the vast shipbuilding yards of Moretti Navi were still brightly lit. Asad Torkan crouched beside the outer fence in the most remote part of the facility. His reconnaissance during the previous two nights confirmed that there were no cameras observing the perimeter. The few roaming guards kept to a predictable pattern, making it easy for him to time his infiltration.

He threw his duffel bag over his shoulder and easily scaled the fence, protecting himself from the razor wire with a heavy leather welding blanket. When he was over, he took down the blanket and stowed it under one of the stacks of containers along with the black coveralls he'd just taken off. Underneath, he was wearing the uniform of a Moretti Navi construction foreman. He put on a hard hat, hoisted the duffel, and walked toward the docks as if he were heading in for his shift.

When Torkan passed a couple of longshoremen who gave him little more than a brief glance, he knew he'd have no trouble reaching his objective. He'd been trained by Iran's Ministry of Intelligence and Security as a saboteur, carrying out successful operations in Saudi Arabia, Kuwait, and Pakistan, always escaping undetected.

With brown eyes, dark hair, a strong chin, and a lanky runner's physique, Torkan was often mistaken for a Greek or Italian, which made it easy for him to blend into European cultures. He spoke fluent English, as well as Farsi and Arabic, and was passable in several other languages, but Italian wasn't one of them. Anybody seeing him in the shipyard would assume he was a fellow countryman. If someone tried to speak to him, he would say he was an American contractor here to supervise construction on one of the many ships being built.

The shipyard was so immense that it took twenty minutes before he saw his target in the distance. It was a relatively small freighter just 400 feet in length that was undergoing final outfitting before its maiden voyage scheduled for the next day. It seemed like a normal cargo ship except for two distinguishing features: a large white satellite dish mounted on the deck and four spiral wind turbines that looked like upside-down eggbeaters. The turbines generated auxiliary power when the ship was at sea.

As he got closer, Torkan could see *Colossus 5* painted on the bow. The other Colossus ships were already at sea, making them more difficult to reach since their locations were closely guarded secrets, so he had to disable this one before it left port. The ship looked anything but colossal compared to the giant cruise liners and Panamax containerships being built nearby, but the name didn't refer to its size. It referred to the payload inside.

Torkan stopped when he was within a hundred yards of the ship to survey the area. Unlike any other vessel in the yard, the *Colossus 5* was cordoned off by specially built fencing that was far more formidable than the facility's outer perimeter. Guards at the gate were heavily armed with submachine guns and carried themselves like the former soldiers they were. In addition, Torkan counted at least a dozen security professionals patrolling the deck of the ship as well as the dock. His mission was to destroy the ship's satellite dish, rendering the *Colossus 5* unusable for weeks until they could install a replacement.

Attempting to get on the ship would be suicide. Not only would such a mission fail, Torkan wasn't suicidal. He enjoyed the fruits of his now private career since leaving government, and he had every intention of living a long life. So attacking the ship head-on was out of the question.

His current objective wasn't the *Colossus 5* itself. It was the loading crane on the dock next to it.

As tall as a thirty-story building when its boom was pointed nearly straight up in the air, the orange crane had four legs and looked like a gigantic modernist sculpture of a giraffe. Pulley cables as thick as pythons held the steel latticework boom locked in the vertical position now that it had finished loading construction materials onto the ship.

Torkan maneuvered himself so that the crane shielded him from the ship's view. The stairs were partially visible to the guards on the *Colossus 5*, but if they noticed him, he hoped they would think he was a dockworker doing an inspection.

When he reached the top, Torkan bypassed the crane operator's cab and entered the rear housing, where the huge motor and drive gears for the pulleys were protected from the elements. He unzipped the duffel and removed three shaped charges armed with remote-controlled detonators.

He attached two of the bombs to the cables controlling the hoist that raised and lowered the boom. To ensure that the collapse of the crane would be catastrophic, he also snuck out to the crane's roof. He kept low while he affixed the final bomb to the boom pendant that provided stability for the crane.

Torkan took a SIG Sauer pistol from the duffel, tucked it under his shirt, and left the empty bag on the crane. By the time he set off the bombs, he would be well away from the shipyard.

He descended the stairs. At the bottom, he was about to disappear back into the facility's maze of containers when a couple of dockworkers spotted him. They looked at each other, then started walking toward him.

'*Ehi! Tu!*' one of them called to him. '*Cosa stai facendo lassù?*'

Torkan couldn't understand the Italian, but he knew the man was asking why he had been on the crane. He put on a look of confusion and pointed at himself.

'Me?'

The burly longshoreman stopped in front of him. '*Sì, tu. Chi sei?*'

'I'm sorry,' Torkan said in English. 'I don't speak Italian.'

The dockworker furrowed his brow. 'I say, who are you? Why you on crane? This is my job.'

'Oh! I didn't know any more work was being done on the *Colossus 5* tonight.'

'No. No work. I work on different crane tonight.'

'That explains it.'

The two men spoke to each other in rapid-fire Italian, then the first man turned back to Torkan. 'Nothing is explain. Who are you?'

Torkan smiled at them. 'I work for the owners of the ship. They wanted me to make sure this crane isn't a hazard.'

'Hazard?'

'You know, a danger in the pulley housing. There was some difficulty during the loading process.'

'Danger? Is no danger.' He pointed at the crane and said something to his companion. The younger man immediately began climbing the stairs.

'No need for another inspection,' Torkan said. 'I can confirm that it's completely safe now.'

'Is strange.' The dockworker took out his phone. 'I call the manager.'

'There's no need to do that,' Torkan said. The nimble young dockworker was already halfway up to the top.

'Is necessary. I no see you before.' He began to dial, but Torkan put his hands up to stop him.

'Wait! You're going to get me in trouble. Here, let me call my boss and you can speak to him. He can tell you I have complete authorization.'

The longshoreman looked at him dubiously, then nodded and pocketed his phone.

As he dialed the number, Torkan kept an eye on the dockworker climbing the crane. When he opened the door to the pulley housing, Torkan pressed the CALL button.

The detonators on the bombs all received the same cell phone call simultaneously. A massive explosion blew apart the housing, taking the dockworker with it. The cables holding up the crane's boom were instantly severed, and it began falling toward the *Colossus 5*.

The boom was so large that the fall seemed to be happening in slow motion. The guards on the ship could only look on in horror or run for their lives as it plunged down between two of the wind-generating masts.

The crane's hook hit the satellite dish dead center. It erupted in a shower of debris that rained down all over the ship's deck. The sudden impact sheared the boom from its mounting, and the remainder of the lattice structure slammed into the dock, smashing the gate and crushing one unfortunate guard who didn't get out of the way in time. The boom finally came to rest across the midpoint of the ship.

An emergency klaxon sounded, and men were shouting everywhere as they raced to see if any survivors were trapped in the debris.

The longshoreman gaped at the stunning scene of destruction that caused the death of his friend.

'I told you it was dangerous,' Torkan said, and pumped two bullets into the man's chest. The man crumpled to the ground, a look of surprise on his face before he died. There was so much going on that no one would notice the gunshots, allowing Torkan to get rid of the last witness to his mission.

Amid the chaos and confusion, he disappeared into the shadows and was able to use his planned escape route over the perimeter fence. When he was safely outside the shipyard and walking back to his car, he made another phone call.

'Yes?' a man's voice answered immediately.

'It's done,' Torkan said. 'The ship is temporarily out of commission.'

'Excellent work. That will set the Colossus Project back by two weeks. When can you reach Mumbai?'

Torkan checked his watch. Only one minute off his expected completion time.

'I've already got my boarding pass,' he said. 'I'll arrive at ten in the morning.'

'Good. I'll have a helicopter bring you out to the launch platform when you get there. But don't be late.'

'That's really not up to me, is it?'

'If you think the flight is going to be significantly delayed, I wouldn't get on if I were you,' the man on the other end warned him. 'If everything goes according to plan, you won't want to be on a plane tomorrow afternoon.'

3

Captain Keith Tao cursed when he saw smoke on the horizon, glowing red where it was backlit by the morning sun. It was directly in his ship's path, and they didn't have time to waste. He had a tight schedule to keep. But stopping to render aid to a ship in distress was required by the Law of the Sea. If his freighter was witnessed bypassing a sinking ship, it would raise questions he didn't want to answer.

'Should we go around?' the executive officer asked.

To avoid being spotted by anyone aboard the stricken ship, they'd have to go at least two hours out of their way, and their timetable was already off because of their delayed departure from Mozambique.

Tao raised a pair of binoculars and could see the outline of a cargo ship coming into view. 'Has there been any SOS sent from this area?'

'No, sir. I've checked the marine traffic website, and there aren't supposed to be any other ships within a hundred miles.'

That was what Tao had been expecting. They were far off the main shipping lanes on purpose, so to encounter another ship out here in the middle of nowhere was bad luck.

Tao lowered the binoculars. He'd have to risk being seen to stay on schedule. 'Maintain the current heading.'

'Aye, Captain.'

In another hour, the foundering ship was easily visible, and, based on its condition, Tao was surprised it remained afloat.

The ancient tramp steamer, more than 500 feet long, looked like a funhouse mirror version of his own cargo ship, the *Triton Star*. The vessel was listing fifteen degrees to port and sitting low in the water. Tendrils of smoke curled up from several spots on the hull that had been blackened by fire.

Decades ago, the ship must have cut a graceful course through the sea, with its clean lines and a stern reminiscent of the *Titanic*'s champagne-glass tail. But now, even without the fire damage, the ship appeared to be on its last voyage. Rust ate at the peeling paint on the mottled pea green hull. The three cranes forward and the two aft of the dingy white superstructure were in such disrepair that it seemed like they could collapse at any moment. The radio antennas were broken in half, possibly hit by debris in an explosion. Overturned oil drums and junk littered a deck encircled by a chain railing that was broken in many places. The ship looked like a disaster, which is exactly what had occurred.

Tao could just make out the faded lettering below the Iranian flag fluttering on the stern's jackstaff: *Goreno*.

Now the ship's condition made sense. Its Iranian registry meant it could be a black market smuggler calling on the world's seedier ports to pick up its cargo. That also explained why there wouldn't be any record of it in the marine traffic database.

'Captain,' the XO said, 'we're picking up a distress call. It's very faint.'

'From the *Goreno*?' Tao peered at the bridge, but he couldn't see anything through its cracked and grimy windows.

'No, sir. He says they had to abandon ship.'

A lifeboat came into view as they passed the bow of the *Goreno*. It looked like it was in even worse shape than the ship, if that was possible. The entire hull had been blackened by flames, and part of the roof was caved in. It seemed to be dead in the water.

'Put the call on speaker,' Tao ordered.

A desperate voice pleaded with them in Spanish-accented English through the bridge's loudspeaker. 'To the ship off our bow, this is Eduardo Barbanegra, captain of the *Goreno*. We need your assistance. My crew and I have been adrift for three days without food or water.' The signal was weak and full of static. Since they hadn't heard it until now, it was probably coming from a low-powered walkie-talkie with a short range.

'Should we respond?' the XO asked.

Tao thought about it for a moment, then shook his head. 'By the look of it, they'll be dead long before another ship passes this way. Keep going.'

'Help us please!' Barbanegra cried as the *Triton Star* passed them without a response. 'If you rescue us, we'll share the gold we were carrying on board the *Goreno*. Five hundred pounds of it from South Africa.'

The XO rolled his eyes at Barbanegra's sad attempt at

saving himself. With a dismissive sneer, Tao looked through the binoculars at the lifeboat. A bedraggled blond man emerged through the roof. His clothes were dirty and tattered, and his face was smeared with soot. He looked exhausted, his lips were split from a lack of water, and his right eye was covered by a ragged black patch.

But Tao's eyes were drawn to what he was holding above his head. It was a foot-long gold brick.

'How much gold did he claim to have?' Tao asked as he stared at the ingot shining in the sun.

'Five hundred pounds,' the XO replied. 'But sir –'

Tao knew well the price of gold since he was considering how to invest his bonus fee for this voyage. At its current value, a quarter ton of gold would be worth well over ten million dollars.

He put down the binoculars and commanded, 'All stop!'

The XO stared at him in disbelief. 'Captain?'

'You heard me.' The XO followed his orders, and they began to slow.

'Prepare our lifeboat. We're going to bring them aboard.'

'Captain,' the XO said after relaying the command, 'you can't really believe they have that much gold on the *Goreno*.'

'We'll know soon enough. If that brick he's holding is a fake, we'll kill them all and toss them overboard. The sharks will take care of them.'

'And if it's real?'

'We find out where it is and get the gold off before that ship sinks. *Then* we kill them.'

The XO nodded in appreciation of Tao's plan. If Barbanegra was lying, the delay wouldn't be long, and the potential payoff was worth the trouble.

Fifteen minutes later, Barbanegra and his men climbed onto the deck of the *Triton Star*. Tao went down to meet them in the mess.

He arrived to find Barbanegra and five equally pathetic-looking men hungrily devouring cold-cut sandwiches and gulping glasses of water. When they were brought aboard, they were searched without them knowing it, Tao's crew patting them down as they were helped onto the ship. His men stood around the perimeter of the dining hall with their weapons concealed as ordered. No sense in making Barbanegra suspicious.

Tao went over to Barbanegra, who was still holding the gold brick in one hand, and said, 'I'm Captain Tao. Welcome aboard.'

Barbanegra, a tall man whose loose clothes hung on him like he was a scarecrow, stood and feebly shook Tao's hand. 'Thanks for coming to our rescue. We didn't think you were going to stop.'

'We thought your ship was a derelict. Your radio signal was so weak that we almost didn't pick it up. This is your whole crew?'

'Half. We lost the rest in the fire.'

'Do you need medical attention?'

'The food and water are enough for the moment. We've got a more urgent matter to take care of.' Barbanegra glanced at the ingot. 'You'll help us recover the rest of the gold before she goes down? We'll give you twenty-five percent of the value.'

So Barbanegra was still well enough to negotiate. Tao had to admire his guts.

'Why shouldn't we take it all for ourselves?' Tao asked. 'You've abandoned ship, and given that you're flying the Iranian flag, it's reasonable to assume that your cargo is being smuggled. We're not going through Lloyd's of London for the salvage contract, are we?'

'That's true,' Barbanegra said. 'But the bars are well hidden aboard our ship, which is taking on water and will probably go under within the next twelve hours. Then neither of us gets the gold.'

'If it *is* gold,' Tao said. He took a folding knife from his pocket and drew the blade across the ingot's face, leaving a golden trench in the soft metal. It was definitely not plated lead. He picked it up and guessed the weight at twenty-five pounds. Tao tamped down his excitement at getting so lucky.

'See!' Barbanegra said triumphantly. 'It's real, just like I told you. And there are nineteen more just like it over on the *Goreno*.'

'Where?'

'Do we have a deal?'

Negotiating was pointless since these men would be dead within the hour anyway, but Tao had to give the appearance that he was reluctantly coming to terms.

'Fifty-fifty,' he said. 'That's our price.'

Barbanegra looked at his crew, who all nodded their agreement.

'You've got a deal,' Barbanegra said. He pointed at a huge black man. 'Franklin here, my chief engineer, will show your men where they are.'

Tao ordered half a dozen of his men to go with Franklin in the lifeboat, leaving him with eight crew on board. Given how haggard these men were, they'd be no threat.

'Have you had enough to eat and drink for now?' Tao asked.

'Yes, thanks,' Barbanegra said.

'Then you can all join me on the bridge so we can observe the recovery operation.'

Tao glanced at his XO, who silently nodded in reply. When they had the gold in hand, the weapons would come out. Better to have all of their captives in one place when that happened.

By the time they got to the bridge, the lifeboat was approaching the *Goreno* and soon idled next to it as they latched a rope ladder to the railing. Franklin and five of Tao's six men climbed up to the deck while the remaining man stayed in the boat. Franklin pointed, and they disappeared into the superstructure.

Everyone on the bridge waited in silence for a radio report that they had reached the gold. Barbanegra, who was beside Tao, collapsed down to one knee. He looked ashen, but he put up a hand and said, 'I'll be okay. Got light-headed. Just give me a second.'

Tao shook his head at how easy this was going to be and went back to watching the *Goreno*.

A second later, to his utter shock, he felt a pistol's muzzle pressed against his temple by Barbanegra. The other four men from the *Goreno* overpowered his bridge crew and took the handguns from their waistbands. It happened with such lightning speed that only the XO was able to fight back and he was knocked down with one chop to the throat. The rest put up their hands in surrender when they saw the guns trained on them.

While his men were being trussed up with zip ties, a stunned Tao gasped, 'What are you doing?'

'Shut up,' Barbanegra said, his accent gone. He looked at one of his men. 'MacD, once you've finished securing them, take your team to search the *Triton Star* for any stragglers.'

'Aye, Chairman,' replied the man, who suddenly seemed energetic and alert instead of haggard and weary.

Then the man called Chairman spoke to seemingly no one. 'We're secure over here, Max. Take 'em.'

Tao's hands were tied behind his back, but he hadn't been put on the floor with the rest of his men. He watched as his crew on the *Goreno* was marched out of the superstructure with their hands in the air. They were accompanied by a dozen men and women with automatic rifles who aimed them at the man in the lifeboat until he was taken captive as well.

'Good job, everyone,' the Chairman said. 'Not a shot fired.' He stepped back from Tao and bent to pull down his rolled-up pant leg. Tao could now see that Barbanegra had a prosthetic limb equipped with a hidden compartment, which the Chairman closed.

Tao gaped at the man who'd taken over his ship with such ease. 'Who are you people?'

'It's pretty obvious, isn't it?' the Chairman said with a wide grin as he removed the patch to reveal a second sky blue eye. 'Peg leg? Eye patch? Come on. You should know a pirate when you see one. Especially when you're smugglers yourselves.'

'I . . . I don't know what you're talking about,' Tao stammered.

The Chairman raised his pistol and aimed it at Tao's forehead. The pirate's grin disappeared, replaced by a deadly serious gaze.

'We know what your secret cargo is,' the Chairman said. 'We just don't know where it is, and this is a pretty big ship you've got here. So tell me, Captain Tao. Where did you hide the chemical weapons?'

4

Rasul Torkan, Asad's identical twin brother, looked out the cabin porthole at the *Triton Star* crew being marched across the deck of the seemingly crippled cargo ship by armed men and women and knew they had to be here for him. He had only minutes to hide himself or the operation would be a complete failure.

There was only one place on the ship where he was sure they wouldn't find him. Getting there in broad daylight without being seen would be a challenge, but he had the skills to do it. Rasul and his brother had risen through the ranks of Iran's secret service together, their competitive natures driving each other to become top agents in the MOIS. While Asad's specialty was sabotage, Rasul had excelled as an assassin, racking up fifteen successful kills during his stint as a government operative. Fed up with the bureaucracy and restrictions placed on them, they decided to retire and strike out on their own. Sometimes they worked as a team, other times on separate – and, in this case, complementary – missions.

Rasul was merely a passenger aboard the *Triton Star.* Tao would eventually give him up, but the hijackers wouldn't see his name on the crew manifest, so they wouldn't start searching for him right away. Since he was sharing quarters with two other crew members, he quickly tossed his belongings in with theirs. He couldn't remain undetected for long, but maybe long enough.

He descended two flights of stairs and heard footsteps pounding behind him as he went through the outer door onto the weather deck. He crouched against the bulkhead, ready to silence anyone who emerged, but the men kept going down the stairs, heading to the lower decks.

His destination was the last row of containers. Between him and his objective, there was a gap between the containers and the superstructure that would leave him visible for a few seconds, but he had to risk it. He bent low and crabwalked until he was behind the stack.

No sirens, no shouts. He hadn't been seen.

He kept going until he reached a refrigerated container near the stern of the *Triton Star*. It looked completely ordinary, as it was designed to. On the manifest, the reefer unit buried at the bottom of a stack of five was supposedly full of Mozambique oranges, lemons, and tangerines destined for the Indian market. Nothing made it stand out from the thousand other containers on board. Even if it were opened, inspectors would find nothing but fruit crates in the first twenty feet of the forty-foot-long unit. The concealed rear section, however, served a different purpose.

Rasul took a look around the corner and saw the aft end of the *Goreno* across the water. She was steadily righting herself from a list, something that should have been impossible for such a heavily damaged freighter. The tendrils of smoke had ceased rising from the hull.

Based on their skill in crafting a plan to take the *Triton Star* so easily, Rasul was sure this was more than a random hijacking. Besides, they were too far off the main shipping lanes for the attack to be a chance occurrence.

The *Goreno* had intercepted them on purpose. And Rasul knew what they wanted.

He ran his hand along one of the reinforcing corrugations. His finger clicked on a hidden button, and a section of the wall slid aside. He slipped inside and pressed the button to close it behind him. He flipped a switch, and halogen lamps came on.

The interior of the reefer unit had been modified to serve as a decontamination chamber. At the press of a large red button on the opposite wall, the light would turn red and nozzles in the ceiling would douse him with a concentrated hypochlorite solution that would neutralize nerve agent particles. When the decontamination procedure was complete, the light would turn green, at which point Rasul would exit through a door opposite the entrance.

During his first night on board the *Triton Star*, Rasul had brought his duffel to the chamber to make sure he kept the contents away from the curious hands of the crew. All they'd been told was that he had paid to be a passenger. Only Tao knew he was accompanying two containers to their destination.

Instead of the near-freezing temperature in the other half of the refrigerated container, the air-conditioning unit kept the chamber a balmy seventy degrees even in the sweltering tropics. A medical-grade filter purified the air.

He knelt down and loaded the two weapons he'd brought with him: a Glock .40 caliber semiautomatic pistol and a Heckler & Koch G36 assault rifle with suppressor.

Next to the guns was a metal case. He opened it, revealing a cylindrical device pressed into a foam cutout. The size of a soda bottle, it had a metal carrying handle on top, a small spout on the bottom, and a touchpad on the front.

Rasul unzipped the duffel and removed the last item he would need for his mission.

It was a military-grade gas mask and airtight combat suit, commonly called an NBC suit for its ability to protect against nuclear, biological, and chemical contamination. It had the desert camouflage markings of the Iranian Revolutionary Guard.

Rasul checked the equipment and made sure everything was in working order. It looked like he'd have to use them sooner than expected.

He took a seat on the floor and clicked on his phone's encrypted texting app that was piggybacking on the *Triton Star*'s shipwide WiFi signal.

We have a problem, he texted.

The reply came quickly. *I suspected something was wrong. I noticed that you've stopped. I was about to contact you to find out why.*

Rasul's boss was monitoring their position using GPS. The Global Positioning System could pinpoint the location of any ship equipped with a transponder.

A ship intercepted and boarded us.

Military?

Civilian. Freighter called the Goreno.

They might know the nerve agent is on board.

Should we launch now?

There was a pause. *Only when you're out of range.*

Then the mission is aborted? He already knew that his brother had succeeded in his mission, but Rasul's operation was just as important to the cause.

After another pause, *No. I may be able to change the target and still accomplish our goals.*

What are my orders? Rasul texted.

Can you still use the nerve agent to carry out the mission as designed?

There was only one device. He looked at the cylinder. To contaminate both ships, he'd need to shower them with the toxic nerve agent instead of planting the dispersal unit next to the *Triton Star*'s air handling intake as he'd been planning to do to wipe out the crew.

But there was no way to get the dispersal unit high enough . . .

Then Rasul remembered his sea rescue training. The *Triton Star* had a means for him to shoot the nerve agent into the air.

There is a way, Rasul replied.

Good. I'll know in an hour whether we need to proceed as planned. If we do, you'll activate the launch sequence. Let me know when you have completed the mission and I'll send the yacht to rendezvous with you.

Understood.

Remember, we can't let them see you get away, came the response. *You have what you need to kill them all.*

5

Juan Cabrillo emerged onto the *Triton Star*'s bridge from the captain's office a new man. Gone were the baggy clothes disguising his athletic frame and the makeup giving him the gaunt appearance of a shipwreck survivor. He was now freshly shaved and wearing a light polo shirt and black cargo pants that had been stowed in the lifeboat. The only features he still had in common with his pirate alter ego, Eduardo Barbanegra, were the blond hair, blue eyes, and prosthetic right leg, a replacement required after he lost his real one below the knee in a battle with a Chinese destroyer years ago.

Juan was proud of how smoothly his team had pulled off the operation to take the *Triton Star*, especially because the CIA had given them the assignment just two days before. Though she was temporarily called the *Goreno* for this mission, his ship's real name was the *Oregon*. They had been resupplying in the Maldives when they got the call and raced across the Indian Ocean to get into position to intercept the *Triton Star*. Not only were they in the right place at the right time to get the job, they were the only elite team in the world who could have done it.

As a native Californian who'd practically grown up on the beach, Juan had always been fascinated by the ocean, and his brainchild was the *Oregon*, a spy ship that could go unnoticed, ignored, even actively shunned, anywhere in the world. In his former position as a top CIA field operative, he had seen the need for an organization that could function outside the stifling US government bureaucracy. He left to form the Corporation, a private firm that took on missions the agency couldn't carry out itself, either because of the lack of capability or to provide plausible deniability should an operation go badly. Although his crew of elite military veterans and former CIA agents were well compensated for their work, the jobs were highly risky, and the *Oregon* had lost people along the way. The Corporation also did jobs for companies and foreign governments, from protecting oil platforms in dangerous waters to recovering kidnapped VIPs, but they weren't mercenaries in the traditional sense. Everyone on the *Oregon* was an American patriot, and, as the Corporation's Chairman, Juan made sure they restricted themselves to missions that were in the interests of the United States. The hijacking of the *Triton Star* definitely qualified.

The only other person on the bridge was Eric Stone, the *Oregon*'s skilled helmsman. A former Navy officer and certified genius who'd served in technology development during his service, he was one of the ship's youngest crew members. With soft brown eyes and a gentle demeanor, he was a consummate computer nerd: an avid gamer who was notoriously shy with women. Buttoned-down and meticulous in his work, he would normally be dressed in his usual black-framed glasses, a blue oxford shirt, and chinos. But as one of the crew 'rescued' by the *Triton Star*, he was still dressed in torn jeans and a soiled T-shirt.

Juan smiled at him. 'You planning to stick with the hobo look?'

'Sorry, Chairman,' Eric replied as he adjusted his glasses and looked down at his clothes with a grimace. 'I haven't had time to change.'

'Don't wait too long. You might get used to the look.'

'I seriously doubt that. But I wanted to get a look at their manifest first.'

Juan joined him at the bridge's computer terminal. The screen was filled with rows of data. 'Anything useful?'

'Somewhat. The *Triton Star* is supposed to be carrying one thousand two hundred and forty-seven containers from Nacala in Mozambique to Kochi, a port in south-west India.'

'Supposed to?'

'There's a secret manifest I found hidden in their files,' Eric said, switching the screen. 'This one lists one thousand two hundred forty-nine containers.'

'So we've got two extra, as expected. Can you tell which ones?'

Eric shook his head. 'I wish it were that easy. I did a quick comparison of the data files, but they've disguised the containers well. I'm afraid we're going to have to search them manually.'

'Or convince Captain Tao to tell us which ones they are.'

'When you're questioning him, you might want to ask him one other thing.'

'What's that?' Juan asked.

'Why they were planning to make an unscheduled stop before they reached Kochi.'

'Do you know where?'

'All it mentions is "J Island." But it looks like it's

somewhere in the Lakshadweep archipelago west of the Indian mainland. It matches up with the heading the *Triton Star* was on before they stopped to save us . . . I mean, our gold.'

The gold bar was part of the collateral the Corporation kept on board the *Oregon* if the need arose for bartering purposes or under-the-table purchasing of needed equipment. They also had several hundred thousand in cash in various currencies, a handful of untraceable diamonds, and a few dozen Krugerrands, but this was the only gold ingot. Juan had been right in thinking it would be a useful lure if Tao ignored the Law of the Sea and decided to bypass them.

At that moment, Eddie Seng appeared at the exterior door with a large duffel slung over his shoulder. Like Juan, the *Oregon*'s Chinese-American director of shore operations had been a CIA operative, spending a number of years embedded as a spy in Mainland China. He had a lean, sinewy build, and his brush cut would have been short enough to satisfy the Marine Corps.

'Chairman, we've accounted for all the crew members on the *Triton Star*. The ones that are on the *Oregon* have been disarmed and are under guard in the mess.'

'Then I think it's time you and I had a talk with Mr Tao,' Juan said before turning to Eric. 'Good work, Stoney. After you get tied alongside the *Oregon* and the gangplank lowered, keep looking through the files to see if you can find those containers and figure out their destination.'

'Aye, Chairman. I'll have them set up the decontamination station next to the gangplank.'

'Let's hope we won't need it,' Eddie said.

'Better safe than sorry,' Juan said. 'Or in this case, better alive than dead.'

They left the bridge and made their way back down to the mess hall. They arrived to find Tao and eight of his men sitting with their wrists zip-tied behind their backs. Their dismantled weapons lay on a table in the corner.

Three armed *Oregon* crew members watched over them, led by Marion MacDougal 'MacD' Lawless. A former Army Ranger from Louisiana, MacD looked like the Hollywood version of a Special Forces soldier, with a chiseled physique, square jaw, and blinding good looks.

'Any trouble corralling them?' Juan asked him.

MacD smiled and answered in a syrupy drawl as he nodded at one of the captives. 'Their chief engineer was a tad reluctant to give up. He even took a potshot at me – can you believe that? But Ah convinced him to give up after Ah put a well-placed round past either ear and told him the next one would be smack-dab in the middle of the two.'

The engineer shivered while MacD recounted his story as if he could still hear the bullets whistling past inches from his head.

'Looks like they won't be any more trouble,' Juan said. 'Keep an eye on them while Eddie and I have a chat with the captain.'

Eddie hauled Tao to his feet and followed Juan into the adjacent rec room. He put the captain in one of the chairs and the duffel on the floor.

Juan sat across from Tao and locked eyes. Far from the cocky commander he'd been when he thought he had the upper hand, Tao now looked as nervous as a rabbit in a snare.

Juan stared at him for a moment, then said, 'Where is the nerve agent?'

Tao blinked back at him but said nothing.

'I think he's afraid of someone,' Eddie said.

'That someone should be me,' Juan replied. He leaned toward Tao. 'You don't know me. You may be scared of what your employer will do to you if you talk, but what you should be thinking about is whether I'm the type of guy who'll toss you overboard in shark-infested waters if you don't tell me what I want to hear.' He wasn't that type, but it would be helpful for Tao to think so.

Juan sat back and continued. 'Let me tell you what I know, and then you can tell me what you know. Does that sound fair?'

More blinking from Tao. Maybe a little lip quivering.

'I'm glad you agree,' Juan said. 'There's an American government organization called NUMA, the National Underwater and Marine Agency. Ever heard of them? Doesn't matter. NUMA was diving on a wreck in international waters near Novaya Zemlya, and you know what they found?'

'I don't think he does,' Eddie said.

'Maybe he doesn't,' Juan replied. 'If he knew how dangerous it was, he probably never would have put his greedy little hands on this job. There's this stuff called Novichok. A Russian invention. Now, you may have never heard of it, but you probably have heard of VX nerve gas.'

That got a reaction. Tao furrowed his brow as Juan went on with his explanation.

'VX was thought to be the deadliest substance known to man. And it was, until we learned that Russia had created their own version, Novichok. It's said to be ten times as lethal as VX. While VX is a colorless and odorless gas, Novichok is dispersed as a fine airborne powder. If one little speck touches your skin, you're dead in less than a minute. Not an easy way to go, either. Your muscles seize up so tightly they tear themselves apart, paralyzing you while fluid fills your lungs. You literally drown without ever touching a drop of water.'

Finally, Tao spoke in a squeaky voice. 'What does that have to do with me?'

'Remember that wreck NUMA found? It was supposedly carrying a load of Novichok when it went down. But the NUMA divers didn't find it on the ship. They tracked it all the way to an abandoned warehouse in Nacala, Mozambique, which just happens to be your last port of call. A known assassin who goes by the name Rasul killed two Mozambique police officers who went into the warehouse. Before they died, they radioed that they'd found three containers inside. But after Rasul got away, all the police found was a single empty container labeled FARM MACHINERY. We are sure that you made a deal to put the other two on the *Triton Star* for a hefty payoff because a CIA officer photographed you with Rasul just before you set sail. That makes you a murder accomplice, as well as a trafficker in chemical weapons outlawed by the international community.'

Eddie shook his head in pity. 'That sounds like death penalty kind of stuff right there.'

'In Mozambique, certainly. But before you go back, you'll

be taken to the rendition camp on Diego Garcia, which isn't that far from here. I bet the CIA would love to have a chance to interrogate you and do a thorough search of your vessel before returning you to Mozambique for trial.'

The island of Diego Garcia, now three hundred and fifty miles southeast of their current position, was America's most remote Air Force and Navy base, serving as a staging area for Marine expeditionary forces and long-range bombers that could reach any nation in the Middle East. Its isolated location also made it the perfect place for sequestering terrorism suspects away from prying eyes. A destroyer carrying a hazmat team and CIA officers was on its way from the naval base to take possession of the *Triton Star* and her crew.

'We're going to do this with or without your help,' Juan continued. 'Now I can put in a good word with the CIA –'

Tao nodded vigorously. 'Yes, I'll take it.'

'You'll take what?'

'The deal. I had no idea about that scary Novichok stuff, and I don't want to go to prison. Besides, that guy Rasul is creepy. He's a killer. You can see it in his eyes. What do you want to know?'

Juan looked at Eddie, who raised his brows in surprise. They both thought this would be harder.

'We've got a deal?' Tao asked with pleading eyes.

'I can't promise you'll get out of this completely free, but it'll go much better if you cooperate.'

'Okay. Sounds good. By the way, the weapons were just for our protection. We weren't going to hurt you and your men. I swear.'

'Sure you weren't,' Juan said. 'Now, where were you going before Kochi?'

'Jhootha Island.'

'Was that where the containers were going to be delivered?'

'Yes.'

'To whom?'

'I don't know. We go there once a month. We tie up at a pier, unload a container or two, pick up some others, and leave. None of the crew ever leaves the ship, so I don't know what the people on the island do with them. I'm just a deliveryman.'

Juan leaned toward him. 'But you do know which containers they are.'

Tao nodded.

'You're going to show us.'

Juan nodded to Eddie, who unzipped the duffel and removed two US Army–issue NBC suits and masks. He handed one to Juan, who pulled it on over his clothes, sealing all the seams with tape.

When he was dressed, Eddie put on his own suit while Juan kept watch on their captive.

'Hey, come on,' Tao said, nervously eyeing the two of them. 'Don't I get one?'

Juan reached into the duffel and grabbed a folded orange hazmat suit. It was bulkier and looser than their own form-fitting versions. Instead of gloves, it had awkward mittens.

'This thing?' Tao complained. 'I like yours better.'

'It's that or nothing.'

Tao stepped into it and struggled to get it on. 'Will this really protect me?'

Eddie looked at Juan and shrugged.

'You better hope it does,' Juan said to Tao. 'This is just in case you or someone else has booby-trapped the storage unit to gas us.'

'I told you I don't know anything about any Novichok. Do I look crazy enough to let something like that on my ship?'

'That almost sounded convincing,' Eddie said.

'He knows it's over the side to become shark food if he's not telling the truth,' Juan said.

Tao finished getting dressed in silence. When he was fully encased in his suit, Juan couldn't resist a chuckle. He looked like a traffic cone. On the other hand, Eddie was straight out of a horror movie about a global pandemic.

Both Juan and Eddie trained pistols on Tao.

'Lead the way,' Juan said. 'I think it's pretty obvious that we'll shoot you if you try anything stupid.'

Juan thought Tao nodded, but it was hard to tell in the plastic suit.

He led them up to the deck, where the blazing sun instantly transformed their suits into saunas. They went aft to a set of refrigerated containers. He pointed to a white one on the bottom of a stack of five.

'You're sure this is one of them?' Juan asked.

Tao nodded. 'The other one is aft.'

Eddie looked at the shipboard crane resting next to the containers and frowned. 'Why didn't you stack this one on top if you were going to be taking it off at Jhootha Island?'

Tao shook his head like he was just as puzzled. 'It was a requirement that Rasul had. I don't ask questions. I only do what they pay me to do. And they pay me a lot.'

Juan made a mental note to find out who 'they' were once they had the Novichok secured.

The container door had a heavy padlock on it. Eddie used a collapsible bolt cutter to sever the hasp.

Juan nodded at the door and stepped to the side with Eddie.

'You open it,' he said to Tao.

'Me?'

'We don't know what might be in there.'

'I don't either,' Tao protested.

Juan didn't say anything. He just raised his pistol. Eddie got his flashlight ready.

Tao unlatched the handle, wrenched the door open, and stumbled backward. He gaped in astonishment when he saw the interior.

'What is it?' Juan asked.

'It's not my fault!' Tao groaned. 'Rasul lied to me. He told me this was the reefer unit we were supposed to smuggle to Jhootha Island.'

Juan and Eddie approached the open door cautiously, crouched with pistols ready to fire. When they were able to see what Tao was gawking at, they stood up and lowered their guns.

The entire forty-foot-long container was completely empty.

6

Max Hanley took advantage of the high vantage point on the *Oregon*'s bridge wing to watch as she edged close to the stationary *Triton Star*. The captured crew members and their guards observed the operation from the *Oregon*'s deck below him. There was no breeze, and the sun's rays were merciless. The filthy bridge, littered with used coffee cups and cigarette butts, was empty as usual. Max was alone, and all his attention was focused on the cargo ship nearing their port side. Normally, attempting to dock two cargo vessels together at sea was extremely hazardous, even on a calm day, but the *Oregon* wasn't like most ships. In fact, she wasn't like any other ship.

Max should know since he was her chief engineer and president of the Corporation, as well as Juan Cabrillo's best friend and right-hand man. A Vietnam Swift Boat veteran, he was the oldest crew member, with reddish gray hair circling his bald head, deep smile wrinkles around his eyes, and a rotund gut that Jolly Saint Nick would envy. He'd been the first person Juan had recruited when he created the Corporation because Max had the engineering expertise to draft the plans for a ship as unusual as the *Oregon*.

When the two ships were thirty feet apart, Max spoke into his radio.

'Hold it there, Linda.'

'Holding,' came the reply. The *Oregon* stopped moving.

'Lock in that distance.'

'Locked in.'

Now the *Oregon* and the *Triton Star* would maintain that precise separation indefinitely. Multiple lidar sensors emitted laser pulses to gauge the exact distance between the ships and automatically made tiny adjustments to the *Oregon*'s thrusters to keep her steady.

'We're ready to lower the gangway,' Max said.

'Murph was on his way up to you to do that. Isn't he there yet?'

Max heard footsteps behind him and turned to see Mark Murphy climbing the exterior stairs.

'Here he comes now,' Max said into the radio.

'He must have taken a detour.'

'I did,' Murph replied as he reached the top of the stairs with a can of Red Bull in one hand and a tablet computer in the other. 'Needed some sustenance.' He downed the drink and threw the empty can into the bridge, where it joined the rest of the trash on the floor.

Murph's shaggy dark hair, skateboarder's scruffy goatee, and fondness for wearing all black belied his razor-sharp intellect, having received his first PhD by the time he was twenty. A former civilian weapons designer for the military and now serving as the ship's weapons officer, he was one of the few members of the crew who wasn't a veteran or former CIA agent. He enjoyed bucking convention, most obviously with the T-shirts he wore, which either bore the name of a heavy metal band no one else had ever heard of or were plastered with some irreverent phrase. Today's version read *Me? Sarcastic? Never.*

'There are other food groups besides caffeine, you know,' Max pointed out to his gangly crewmate, who had to weigh half what he did.

'Duh! Nachos, pizza, and cheeseburgers are the other three, right?' Then Murph's lip curled in a grin. 'Wait, you probably don't remember those because Doc Huxley doesn't let you eat them, does she?'

Julia Huxley was the *Oregon*'s chief medical officer and was known for hounding Max about his diet. She'd even gotten Chef to report back to her if Max tried to cheat, much to his chagrin.

'Doc doesn't believe me when I point out my good genes,' he said. 'The Hanleys have never needed to work out to stay healthy. My grandfather lived to ninety-eight on a diet of burritos and tacos.'

Murph laughed. 'He gets older every time you whip out that story. Soon it'll be that he reached a hundred and forty by scarfing down sticks of butter and drinking tequila.'

Max waved off Murph's good-natured ribbing. 'Are you ready to get to work or should I have a large pepperoni brought up to you?'

'Fueled up like a rocket. Let's do this.'

Murph tapped on the tablet while his eyes flicked between the handheld computer and the deck below to make sure it was clear.

A panel in the decking slid aside and an aluminum gangway rose vertically from the opening. When it was completely out of its recess, it bent ninety degrees toward the *Triton Star*. Then it telescoped across the span between the ships and came to rest on the other ship's railing, followed by a set of stairs lowering to the deck on each ship.

'Gangway secure,' Murph said.

'Okay, you can take the *Triton Star* crew back over,' Max said into the radio to the guards.

'Roger that,' came the reply, and the captives were prodded onto the gangway.

Linda called over the radio. 'Max, now that you're done, we've got something you and Murph should look at down here.'

'Happy to,' he answered. 'Be there in a minute.' To Murph he said, 'Let's get inside.'

They went down a few flights and entered a corridor, with chipped linoleum, grimy walls, and flickering fluorescent lighting. They passed the captain's office and personal head, which were so disgusting and smelled so vile that they could cause even the most hardened Third World harbormaster to waive inspection and hightail it out after just a few minutes.

Max opened the door to the janitor's closet, full of unused cleaning supplies and a sink coated with unidentifiable gunk. He twisted the handles as if he were spinning the dials on a combination lock, and, with a soft click, the panel at the back of the closet slid open, revealing a well-appointed hallway that wouldn't have been out of place in a five-star hotel.

Thick carpeting muffled their steps as Max closed the panel behind them. Soft lighting from recessed ceiling lights softly lit artwork lining the walls, and the air no longer reeked.

A descendant of World War II Q-ships – ocean raiders disguised as harmless cargo vessels – the 560-foot-long *Oregon* was specially constructed to be invisible, often flying the flag of a rogue nation on her jackstaff. From the outside, she seemed to be a decrepit tramp steamer destined for the scrapyard. But on the inside, she was the most advanced spy ship ever built, with features, armaments, and capabilities that even careful external observers couldn't possibly imagine.

Since the *Oregon* was home to her crew for most of the year, the luxurious surroundings were designed to make the ship as comfortable as possible. Crew members received generous allowances to outfit their personal quarters however they wanted, and they had access to extensive entertainment and fitness facilities, as well as gourmet food prepared by an award-winning chef and culinary team.

The *Oregon*'s operational functionality was even more impressive. She boasted enough weaponry to take on any ship short of a battle cruiser, including a 120mm cannon similar to the one used on the Abrams main battle tank, French Exocet anti-ship missiles, and Russian Type 53 torpedoes, all purchased on the black market to conceal any connection to the United States.

Her defensive armaments were just as formidable. The rusty oil barrels on deck hid remotely operated .30 caliber machine guns for repelling boarders, while plates in the hull slid apart to reveal three Gatling guns that could rake enemy ships with 20mm tungsten rounds or blow apart incoming missiles. Complementing a battery of Aster anti-aircraft missiles was a Metal Storm gun. It rose out of the stern to fire its one hundred barrels of electronically activated ammunition at the equivalent rate of a million rounds per minute, perfect for bringing down hard-to-hit micro-drones.

For infiltration missions, the *Oregon* could launch submarines from the cavernous moon pool, where immense doors in the keel opened to allow the subs or divers to depart undetected. For surface operations, small craft such as Zodiacs and other rigid-hulled inflatable boats, or RHIBs, favored by the Navy SEALs, could exit from the boat garage accessed by a hidden panel at water level.

Two of the five deck cranes were fully operational, while the other three were distressed and disabled to make the *Oregon* look as pathetic as possible. Although several of the deep holds could be used for storing cargo to throw off the most aggressive port inspectors, the others contained vital ship areas and were carefully covered with a false layer of crates and containers to make it look like they were full as well. The covering over the rearmost hold retracted to raise the platform for the ship's MD-520N helicopter.

The diesels that drove the *Oregon* when she was hauling Pacific Northwest timber had been replaced by the most advanced engines afloat. Two magnetohydrodynamic power plants, cryogenically cooled by liquid helium, forced ionized seawater through massive venturi tubes running the length of the ship, propelling her to speeds unthinkable for a vessel her size and making her as nimble as a Jet Ski. That was the reason she was able to maintain a safe distance from the *Triton Star* while simultaneously keeping the gangway in position.

In the ship's Magic Shop, any kind of disguise, gadget, or uniform could be manufactured under the direction of a former movie studio prop and makeup expert named Kevin Nixon. He had transformed Juan and his men into convincingly pitiful castaways who seemingly had been adrift for days.

Everything from the weaponry to the ship's navigation was controlled from the central op center, which was why the *Oregon* could maneuver without a single person on the squalid bridge. Situated deep in the *Oregon*'s belly, the room was well protected from anything short of a ship-killing missile. High-definition closed-circuit cameras mounted all over the ship provided the op center and its commander a three-hundred-sixty-degree view of the sea. Operators could also fill or empty ballast tanks on either side of the ship to simulate a catastrophic list, as had been done to fool the *Triton Star*.

The high-tech design of the op center, with its state-of-the-art workstations, touchscreen monitors, sleek furniture, and huge main viewing screen, would look at home on a starship. The command seat had therefore been dubbed the Kirk Chair by Eric and Murph, the ship's biggest science fiction fans. The most important functions of the ship could be operated by the controls in the armrests.

When Max and Murph arrived at the op center, the command chair was occupied by Linda Ross. In addition to being a Navy veteran and the Corporation's vice president of operations, she rivaled Juan and Eric as the best ship driver on the *Oregon*. Though she was petite and had a young girl's voice, she commanded respect from the entire crew. Because of her small stature and youthful looks, she hadn't always gotten the same respect in the Navy. As if to celebrate her freedom from the military, she now regularly changed her hairstyle and color. Today it was magenta and tied up in a ponytail.

She rose to give the command chair to Max, but he waved her down.

'What's going on?' he asked.

She nodded to the communications workstation and said, 'Hali has something he wants you to check out.'

Hali Kasim, the Lebanese-American communications officer with perpetually tousled hair from the headphones that rested on his head, had a knack for pulling encrypted radio signals out of thin air. Normally, Hali was all smiles, but he waved them over with a concerned look on his face.

'The Chairman found all of the *Triton Star* crew members, right?'

Max nodded. 'That's what he told me.'

'Then why am I detecting a signal piggybacking on the *Triton Star*'s WiFi network and transmitting through the satellite uplink?'

Murph sat at the terminal next to him and examined the data feed.

'Confirmed,' Murph said. 'They have a stowaway somewhere on board. They're using a texting app through the internet.' He looked at Hali. 'Have you been able to decrypt it?'

Hali winced. 'Mostly no. The app erases each text as it comes through. I detected the latest conversation just a few minutes ago, so anything transmitted before that is gone. I was only able to decode the last phrase that was sent.'

The way he said it sounded ominous to Max. 'What was the text?'

'Whoever is on the other end told the unknown subject on the *Triton Star* "kill them all."'

7

The Arabian Sea

Romir Mallik strode toward the helicopter arriving from Chhatrapati Shivaji International Airport in Mumbai. It settled on the landing pad of Orbital Ocean's launch command ship. The sixties-era Huey, a refurbished relic from the Vietnam War, had barely touched down when Asad Torkan jumped out and came toward the Indian billionaire without offering his hand. Mallik still thought it was odd after all these years that Torkan was such a germaphobe that he wouldn't even shake the hand of his brother-in-law.

'Nice to see that your flight was on schedule,' Mallik said, leading Torkan back toward the control room.

'After three years' worth of preparation, it would have been a shame to miss the final act. And I'm sure you wouldn't have waited for me.'

Mallik shot him a sly grin. 'I might have, but only for you.'

'And my brother.'

'Of course.'

'Any word from Rasul?'

Mallik told him about the hijacking by the *Goreno* in the middle of the Indian Ocean.

Torkan frowned. 'Then they're out of range of Jhootha Island?'

'Correct,' Mallik said. 'Hopefully, our satellite launch will make his mission unnecessary. And even if he does have to go ahead with it, I've identified an alternative target that should accomplish the same goal.'

Torkan thought about the implications for his brother and nodded. 'I know Rasul can take care of himself. He's been in tougher situations before. Besides, he knows what's at stake. The longer we delay, the closer the rest of the Nine Unknown get to achieving their goal. Are we still ahead of them?'

'With the damage to the fifth ship, they don't have the computer power they need to make Colossus fully operational. After a successful launch today, we will make sure they never do.'

Torkan was one of the few people in the world that knew Mallik was one of the Nine Unknown. They could all trace their lineage back to the original Nine Unknown Men that Ashoka, in his wisdom, had selected to safeguard the critical knowledge of physical and social sciences that could be used to conquer the world if it all remained in the hands of one person. Initially, they had been unknown even to one another, but they sought each other out after the Mauryan Empire fell so they could honor Ashoka's legacy and pool the collective wisdom from their individual Scrolls of Knowledge. At the very first meeting of the Nine, they agreed to keep the contents of the scrolls secret from one another so that all decisions would be made as a group and never by a single man.

*

Throughout the millennia since then, the knowledge specific to each of the Nine Unknown had been expanded upon and passed down to the next generation, carefully handpicked by his or her predecessor.

Until two hundred years ago, all nine had been of strictly Indian descent. But when the British took over the country, an exodus began. They still met on a regular basis and kept their society intact, most of the Nine had immigrated to other nations to take advantage of new opportunities, and a majority of them were now non-Indians. Mallik's family was the only one that remained in Ashoka's homeland to this day.

Each of the Nine had built or inherited fortunes based on the knowledge that was handed down to them. But they had a greater mission than simply acquiring wealth. They took seriously their charge to secure their individual areas of knowledge and use them for the betterment of humanity. The other eight had a plan called Colossus, a plan they thought would save the world from lesser minds and make them de facto rulers of every nation on earth.

Mallik was the only one of the Nine convinced that Colossus was instead going to cause the end of humanity. And because of the knowledge passed down to him, he was in the unique position to stop them.

His area of knowledge was cosmogony, the study of space and the origins of the universe. Thanks to the accrued expertise he and his ancestors had gained, Mallik now owned the world's largest private satellite company, which was involved in everything from satellite development to spacecraft launches into orbit. As one of the richest men in India, he'd used his fortune to expand his corporate empire into manufacturing, energy production, and agriculture, all in service of his new goal to save the human race.

As he looked at the floating launch platform two miles away, with its rocket raised into position to fire in just a few minutes, Mallik knew his wife, Yasmin, would be proud of what he was about to accomplish. They had met in university after she had moved to India from Iran to get her education. She'd been the love of his life: beautiful, intelligent, kind, caring. But all of that had been taken away from him five years ago.

Even after she got pregnant, she insisted on continuing her work as an advocate for children's health initiatives in Third World nations. Although Mallik had always worried about her travels to war-torn regions of Africa, it never occurred to him to be concerned when she went to a conference in France.

It still caused his stomach to knot when he remembered the call he received after her high-speed train derailed. A tiny computer software error, it was later discovered, had incorrectly thrown one of the track switches. She and their unborn child were among the one hundred and forty-three people who died.

No one was ever held responsible, a fact that tormented him, and the Torkan twins, Yasmin's beloved younger brothers. Even though Mallik was a mogul in the tech industry, with a degree in computer science, he blamed the frightening pace of technological advancement for the death of his wife and the son he would never get to see grow up. Because of the accident, he no longer had any descendants to whom he could pass along his knowledge, though one day he hoped to. But if the eight other members of the Nine Unknown finished Colossus, he'd never have any more children. And no one else would, either.

For now, Mallik had a greater purpose, perhaps the greatest in the history of mankind. The satellite mounted in the nose of that rocket represented his future, as well as the future of everyone yet to be born.

Mallik breathed a sigh of relief that his years of living in fear and worry over Colossus were almost over. Then he patted Torkan on the shoulder, and they entered the control room together.

The countdown had already begun and was down to two minutes before liftoff. Mallik had developed the mobile sea-based launch system not only so they could avoid bad weather and achieve a more efficient orbital insertion but also to keep prying eyes away during launches. A Nilgiri-class Indian frigate brought out of mothballs by Mallik circled them to provide security in case any unauthorized ships got too close to the operations.

'What's our status?' Mallik asked the flight director, a trim man in his fifties with graying hair named Kapoor.

'No problems detected,' the gruff former Indian Air Force officer replied. 'All systems are showing green. We are good to go.'

Mallik exchanged smiles with Torkan and nodded to Kapoor.

When the countdown reached ten seconds, Mallik walked toward the window. He didn't want to see the sterile camera views of the rocket. He had to watch the launch with his own eyes.

'Five . . . four . . . main engine ignition . . .' White-hot flames shot from the liquid-fueled engines of the reusable booster, sending a huge plume of smoke into the air.

'. . . two . . . one . . . liftoff!'

The rocket slowly rose from the launchpad, its support scaffolding retracting as it ascended. The control room erupted with applause and cheers.

But it took only a second for Mallik to see that something was wrong. He'd attended every launch of the nineteen previous rockets and he could tell right away that this one was different.

'Flight,' one of the technicians said, 'I'm detecting a cascading malfunction in the fuel pump system.' Mallik knew that was potentially disastrous. The pumps controlled the fuel flow to the engines.

'Can you compensate?' the flight director asked.

'I'm trying!'

The rocket didn't accelerate as the others had. Instead, the blazing jet power coming out of the engines sputtered, and the rocket slowed until it hovered only three hundred feet above the launchpad.

Then it began to come back down.

The flight director frantically called out for information about the engines, but it was too late. The tail of the rocket collided with the launch tower and mushroomed into a gigantic fireball. If anyone had been on the launch platform, they would have been killed instantly.

Mallik turned and stared at Kapoor, whose jaw was clenched in a grim expression. The control room was deathly silent. They locked eyes until the command ship was jolted by the delayed blast concussion.

'Find out what went wrong,' Mallik growled.

Kapoor cleared his throat before replying with a muted, 'Yes, sir.'

Torkan, who gaped at the burning rocket and satellite, came over to Mallik and, lowering his voice, said, 'What happens now?'

'Fortunately, I always anticipate setbacks,' Mallik said, fuming at getting so close to his goal and having it literally blow up in his face. 'Therefore, I have a backup.'

Torkan looked at him with surprise. 'You have another satellite?'

Mallik nodded. 'The rocket on our second platform will be ready for launch within ten days. But we can't take any chances that the Nine will repair the *Colossus 5* sooner than that. We are convening in three days, so I'll find out then what its status is. I thought they didn't suspect what I was up to, but I doubt this explosion was an accident.' He looked at each person in the control room. Someone here might be a saboteur.

'You think one of the other Nine Unknown is responsible for this?' Torkan asked, looking toward the smoking launch platform.

'He or she must suspect what I am planning, so we need to cast suspicion on someone else. It will make the other members of the Nine think I'm innocent. To do that, I'm sending you on assignment to Sydney. But first, I need to set the other part of my backup plan in motion.'

'The *Triton Star*?'

'Correct.' Mallik took out his phone. As he texted Rasul to go ahead with the operation, he said to the flight director, 'Prepare the Vajra system for activation.'

Kapoor looked confused. 'But sir, the launch failure means we can't get a global —'

Mallik cut him off. 'Isolated location only. This will be a good opportunity to test the effectiveness of the system on a hardened site.'

'Yes, sir. The target?'

'The US military base on Diego Garcia.'

8

Diego Garcia

The flight from Dyess Air Force Base in Texas had been a long one, with two in-air refueling hookups on the way. Major Jay Petkunas was looking forward to putting his B-1B Lancer bomber on the ground. Camp Thunder Cove, the secluded island's Air Force and Navy base, was considered one of the best postings in the military because of its tropical climate, but eight hours of rack time sounded better than spending some fun in the sun.

As he set the bomber's swing wings to their widest position for landing, he looked out the side window at the U-shaped coral atoll. The thin strip of land around Diego Garcia's central lagoon covered just twelve square miles. A dozen Navy ships were anchored in the protected harbor, and the rest of the bombers from his squadron were already lined up along one side of the twelve-thousand-foot runway, facing an array of cargo planes and refueling tankers in front of them.

His copilot, Captain Hank Larsson, who was currently flying the plane, futilely craned his neck to see the view and said, 'How do the beaches look?' This was Petkunas's third trip to the island but Larsson's first.

'You're not tired?'

'I can sleep on the sand. I have to work on my tan.'

Petkunas, who was dark-haired with an olive complexion, gave his pale blond copilot a skeptical look. 'Good luck with that. You better hope they have a huge supply of aloe for when you fry that translucent Swedish skin of yours.'

'I have sunblock to keep me from burning.'

'Is your sunblock rated for nuclear radiation? Because that's what you need.' The two combat systems officers behind them laughed. Petkunas radioed the control tower. 'Thunder Cove tower, this is Bats 12 requesting clearance to land. We have a vampire here who wants to experience what sunlight will do to him.'

'Bats 12,' a woman's voice said, 'the runway is yours. We've got plenty of sun to –'

Her voice cut out abruptly. At the same time, all of the bomber's instrument panels went dark. The engines flamed out, enveloping the cockpit in an eerie silence.

The joking attitude instantly disappeared, and the crew flipped back to the professionals they were.

Petkunas calmly took hold of the control stick and said, 'I have the plane.'

Larsson let go of his own stick and replied, 'You have the plane.'

'Anything working?'

'We've got a complete power failure.' The men behind Petkunas reported the same.

Petkunas tried calling the tower, 'Thunder Cove, this is Bats 12. We're declaring an aircraft emergency. I repeat, we're declaring an aircraft emergency.'

No response. Not even static.

'Let's get the engines restarted,' Petkunas said as the unpowered B-1B glided toward the ocean.

They raced through the checklist, but it was useless. It seemed like the entire computer control system had short-circuited.

'Isn't anything working?' Larsson asked in frustration.

Petkunas moved the stick to one side, and the bomber sluggishly tilted in response.

'Hydraulics are intact,' Petkunas said. 'Barely.'

'Without the electronics, we can't put the gear down.'

Petkunas knew what he was saying. Even if they could get the huge bomber turned and lined up on the runway, they'd have to make a belly landing.

It was too risky. If he didn't handle it just right, they could cartwheel down the runway, killing all four of them.

Petkunas made a snap decision.

'Prepare to eject,' he announced. They were close enough to the island to expect a quick rescue.

'Ready!' the three other crew members called out in succession.

The ejection system on the B-1B could be operated solely by the pilot or by each individual crew member. When the pilot pulled the ejection handle on the side of the seat, the canopy would blow off, then each seat's rockets would fire in a prearranged sequence so that they didn't hit each other when they were shot through the roof.

Petkunas steeled himself for the extreme force of the ejection and yelled, 'Eject! Eject! Eject!' Then he pulled the handle.

Nothing happened.

He tried again with the same result.

'My seat isn't working,' he told the others. 'You'll have to eject yourselves . . . Eject! Eject! Eject!'

They did as ordered. Still nothing. Even the canopy stayed in place.

Larsson stared at him in profound confusion. 'What is going on? We got gremlins in here?'

Petkunas couldn't explain it until he realized that each seat had a computer-controlled sequencer that precisely determined in what order they should be ejected milliseconds after the handle was pulled. He didn't know how, but something had gone wrong with every piece of electronics on the plane.

Another snap decision.

'We're landing,' Petkunas said, putting his hand back on the stick. 'Let's hope nobody decides to wander out onto the runway.'

He didn't bother calling the tower. If the electrical problem was so complete that the seats wouldn't eject, then the radio would be disabled as well.

'Coming around,' Petkunas said as he wrestled to bank the bomber. It fought him every inch of the way, but he was able to put the B-1B into a turn. He kept at it with all his strength until the runway was straight ahead of them. He leveled off and dropped the nose.

'Altitude is low,' Larsson said.

'Can't help that,' Petkunas replied. 'We need the speed or we'll stall before we get to the island. Try lowering the flaps ten degrees.'

Larsson moved the handle, then shook his head. 'No good.'

'I guess we'll have to do this the hard way.'

The artificial horizon and altimeter still worked since they were mechanical, but the fancy electronic displays were black, so Petkunas would have to do this by eyesight and feel alone. If this had happened at night or in bad weather, they'd be dead men.

With the engines out, Petkunas would have only one chance to get this right. The runway was approaching fast as Larsson called out their altitude.

'Five hundred feet ... Four hundred ... Three ... Two ... One ...'

Petkunas pulled back on the stick to flare out and bleed off speed, but he'd waited too long. He felt a jolt when the tail smacked the runway.

The impact pitched the plane forward. The bomber's belly struck the runway with a teeth-rattling blow, and it continued to slide out of control. Petkunas could do nothing else now except go along for the ride.

The B-1B began to spin, and Petkunas braced himself for the impending somersault that would rip the plane apart. Sparks and smoke flew behind them as the plane scraped across the concrete tarmac, threatening to set fire to the remaining jet fuel if any of the tanks ruptured.

But the spin turned out to be what saved the plane. The bomber skidded into the grassy area next to the runway and kept going until it crossed a sandy beach that slowed them just before it plowed into the ocean. Seawater sprayed across the windscreen as they came to a halt.

Petkunas didn't realize he'd been holding his breath until he took in a huge lungful of air to celebrate not dying.

'Everyone okay?' he asked his crew. All three responded that they were fine.

Normally, they'd exit through the stairway beneath the front landing gear, but that wasn't possible with a belly landing. And there was still the possibility of a fire.

Petkunas reached up and manually activated the explosive bolts on the canopy, which blew off with a bang.

He waited while each man climbed over the edge and jumped out. Then he followed them and landed in the water with a splash. Soaking wet, he waded out of the water and joined his men next to the plane. He could see now that no fuel was leaking, and the plane looked in remarkably good shape except for its underside.

'Nice work, Major,' Larsson said, clapping him on the shoulder.

Petkunas shook his head. 'That's something I never want to do again. I see a lot of paperwork in our future.'

'Cheer up,' Larsson said with a grin. 'At least I'm on the beach.'

Petkunas chuckled. 'The fire truck better get here with your sunscreen fast.'

'Yeah, where are those guys?'

Now Petkunas realized that he didn't hear any sirens of approaching emergency units. But he did see people running toward them.

The first to reach them was one of the ground workers.

'You guys all right?' he huffed without taking his eyes off the destroyed plane.

'We're fine,' Petkunas said. 'Don't they have fire trucks here?'

'None of them are working right now,' the ground worker said.

'What?' Larsson said, perplexed.

'Then it wasn't just us?' Petkunas asked.

The Diego Garcia worker shook his head. 'All electronic systems went out a few minutes ago while you were in the air. Everything on the island is dead.'

9

'What do you mean, there's no one there?' Max asked Hali. 'That island has over three thousand people stationed on it.'

Max now sat in the op center's command chair, with Linda Ross at the radar station. Eric Stone had come over from the *Triton Star* to help Murph localize the source of the mysterious internet communication, and they were huddled over a terminal examining a stream of data.

Hali looked completely baffled. 'I was talking to Diego Garcia about the USS *Gridley*'s estimated arrival time, and the satellite connection suddenly went dead.'

'Maybe something happened to the satellite uplink,' Linda said.

Hali shook his head in frustration. 'I've tried radio, telephone, and satellite. Nothing. I also checked with the military and the CIA. It's not just us. Nobody has been able to get in touch with them. It's like the island just isn't there.'

'Something could have knocked out the island's electrical plant,' Eric said.

'A power failure might explain why we couldn't get in touch with the island,' Hali replied, 'but it wouldn't explain why no one can contact any of the ships based there,

76

including the *Gridley*, which supposedly was just setting sail. How could they all go out?'

'Maybe it was a mega-tsunami,' Murph said without looking up from his computer.

Despite the mocking tone of his voice, Hali answered Murph's speculation seriously. 'No, I already checked. The tsunami warning center hasn't detected any major earthquakes in the last hour.'

Eric smirked at Murph. He had recommended the weapons designer for the *Oregon* post after they worked together on a top secret missile project, and although they were opposites in many ways, they had since become like brothers, with all the banter, competition, and squabbling that entailed.

'Are you kidding?' Eric scoffed jokingly. 'A tsunami is way too mundane. How about a meteor strike?'

'Or a wormhole?' Murph countered.

'Alien abduction?'

'Sharknado?'

'It doesn't matter why,' Max said, both amused and exasperated by the two young crew members. 'Hali, keep trying. I don't like coincidences. Especially when strange messages are telling someone to kill everybody. Eric, have you been able to triangulate where the messages are coming from?'

'Somewhere near the stern of the *Triton Star*. Can't be more precise than that.'

Murph interrupted them. 'We're getting another message.'

'What's it say?' Max asked.

Murph looked up at Max. 'Our mystery guest just received another text. It's giving coordinates and says "Launch is a go."'

'Launch? What launch?'

'There's a satellite launch by Orbital Ocean scheduled right now in the Arabian Sea,' Eric said, 'but that's over six hundred miles away. I don't see how it could have anything to do with us.' After a pause while he tapped on his computer, Eric added, 'And no other satellite launches are scheduled for today anywhere else in the world.'

'Maybe it's telling the guy on the *Triton Star* to launch his operation,' Linda said.

'Or someone is launching something at us.' Max turned to Murph. 'What are the coordinates referring to?'

'On-screen.'

A map appeared on the main viewscreen. It zoomed in until the crosshairs were directly over Diego Garcia.

Juan was heading toward the stern of the *Triton Star* with Eddie and Tao to check out the second container when he heard the news from Max.

'Any idea what we're looking for?' Juan asked.

'The message didn't have any specifics,' Max replied. 'You think they're talking about the Novichok nerve agent?'

'Could be something coordinated with an attack on Diego Garcia.' Juan had heard about the communications failure at the US base and didn't like coincidences any more than Max did.

'I'll let you know if Murph and Eric can pinpoint the stowaway's location.'

'Thanks. We'll keep searching. Keep me posted.'

The two Corporation operatives who'd brought the rest of the *Triton Star* men over from the *Oregon* exited the superstructure. Each of them was carrying two FN P90 compact assault rifles, an unusual bullpup design with the ammo magazine on top of the gun and the spent casings ejected through the handle at the bottom to keep them out of the line of sight of the shooter. They walked over and handed the extra weapons to Juan and Eddie.

The first *Oregon* crew member was a muscular African-American with a shaved head who was built like a linebacker but was as light on his feet as a gymnast. He was a Detroit native and former Navy SEAL by the name of Franklin Lincoln. Linc had masqueraded as the *Goreno*'s chief engineer during the hijacking operation. When they'd gotten the call about this mission, he'd been riding around the capital of the Maldives on his custom Harley that he kept aboard the *Oregon*. As one of the Gundogs – Max's nickname for the shore operations team – Linc's biggest claim to fame was being the best sniper on the crew.

'Chairman,' Linc said, 'all of the *Triton Star* crew are secured in the mess with MacD. You should have seen the looks on their faces when Raven appeared with a P90 in her hands.'

Linc nodded to the woman next to him. Raven Malloy was the newest member of the crew, and a member of the shore operations team. With straight jet-black hair, caramel skin, and a tall, athletic frame, she was often mistaken for a Latina, Southeast Asian, or Arab, though she was actually Native American of Cherokee and Sioux heritage. Raised as an Army brat by adoptive parents, she had attended West Point, where she studied psychology and learned Arabic and Farsi. Upon graduation, she served as a Military Police officer and gained a reputation as a dogged investigator before becoming frustrated with the bureaucracy and leaving to work in private security. During a joint operation with the Corporation taking on communist rebels in the Philippines, she'd meshed well with the crew and performed admirably under dire circumstances, so Juan had offered her a spot on the *Oregon*.

'I think they were just surprised to see a woman at all,' Raven said. '*Shocked* might be a better word.' Then with some satisfaction, 'Maybe a little scared, too. Like him.' She focused on Tao, who stared at her with wide eyes.

Juan wasn't surprised that she drew that reaction. Raven was a very attractive woman who could fix a man with a glare icy enough to freeze lava.

'Can't wait to hear all about it,' he said, 'but right now we've got a problem.' He told them about the messages referencing an upcoming launch.

'We'll take the port side. You two search the starboard side. Look for anything unusual. Since you don't have time to change into NBC suits, call me and Eddie if you see anything like a gas canister. Then back away.'

'Sounds good to me,' Raven said.

'You don't have to tell us twice,' Linc added.

They headed toward starboard, while Juan and Eddie pushed Tao farther aft.

'Who was that?' he asked in wonder.

'He's a friend of ours,' Eddie answered.

'Not the big guy,' Tao said. 'The woman. She's amazing. I'd like to see –'

'How easy it would be for her to break your kneecaps?' Juan interrupted. 'Because I know you weren't planning to say something cruder than that, were you?'

Tao opened his mouth, then closed it again.

'Good,' Juan said. 'Now, who is on this ship that we haven't found? We know he's not part of the crew.'

'Fine. It's Rasul. We took him on as a passenger.'

Juan yanked Tao to a halt. 'Where is he? Tell us or I'll personally put you on a fishing hook and dangle you over the railing.'

'We searched all of the cabins,' Eddie said. 'He wasn't there.'

'Then I have no idea where he is,' Tao answered.

Juan stared at Tao, then spun him around and pushed him forward. 'Show us the second container Rasul supposedly put on the ship. And if this one is empty, too, I might get angry.'

'And remember, you don't want to see him when he's angry,' Eddie said.

When they reached the container, Juan opened it again only to find nothing inside.

'I swear I didn't know!' Tao whined when he saw Juan turn on him. Then something caught his eye. 'Wait a minute, something's not right.' He was peering at the number on the container.

Juan stepped closer to him. 'What?'

Tao pointed at it. 'I remember this number from the manifest because it ends with five nines. It's an empty we were bringing back to India. This container should be in the last row.'

'They were switched?' Eddie asked.

'They must have been. The crane operators at the ports are easy to bribe.'

'Show it to us,' Juan said.

They walked to the last row of containers. Tao nodded

at the reefer container on the starboard end. Juan pushed him to the side, and Eddie kept his P90 at the ready while Juan wrenched the door open.

They relaxed when they saw the interior was full to the top with crates marked *Laranjas/Oranges*.

'The Novichok could be stowed somewhere in here,' Eddie said.

'Maybe,' Juan said before keying his comm unit. 'Max, send as many people over in NBC suits as you can. We need to rip this container apart.'

He was about to ask Tao about the owner of the reefer unit when he saw the *Triton Star*'s captain staring at something along the side of the container. Tao started to say something when his chest bloomed with three gunshot wounds from a suppressed automatic weapon whose staccato report nevertheless echoed off the metal around them. Tao collapsed in a heap without a sound.

Juan dove to the deck past the open door of the container, ready to fire at the unknown assailant. He got a glimpse of a man in a desert camouflage NBC suit ducking behind the end of the container. Juan fired off a volley of rounds, hitting nothing. The gunman was gone.

Eddie leaned over to check Tao but shook his head when he saw the mortal wounds.

Juan spotted an opening in the side of the container and cautiously approached. When he reached it, he glanced inside and saw what had to be a custom-made decontamination chamber, based on the nozzles built into the ceiling.

Eddie appeared at his side and pointed to the floor. Resting on it was a case with an empty slot in the foam, plus a duffel for the NBC suit.

Juan nodded and radioed Max as the two of them inched to the external corner of the container. 'We found the person sending the messages, Max. Tao told us that Rasul was a passenger, so it's got to be him. He has a decontamination unit, and he's wearing an NBC suit.' Juan stuck his head out for a moment and saw an open hatch leading down into the interior accessway. 'I think he's planning to disperse the Novichok.'

'On the *Triton Star*?' Max said.

'Yes. Eddie and I are the only ones over here in suits, so evacuate everyone else to the *Oregon* right now.' Juan heard him give the order to Hali. 'If Rasul tries to get aboard, shoot him.'

'Roger that.' A second later, the .30 caliber machine guns rose out of their barrels and swiveled to point at the *Triton Star.*

'Is the portable decontamination station ready near the gangway?' Juan asked Max.

'It's up and running.'

'Good. We might need to use it. Eddie and I are going after him.'

They sprinted to the hatch and descended into the bowels of the ship.

Rasul checked behind him as he ran down the corridor. He had lost his pursuers for the moment. He'd just finished putting on his NBC suit when he heard the container doors open. Then he heard a man calling for reinforcements, and Rasul knew he needed to get out of the chamber before he was trapped there.

Luckily, he'd already attached the Novichok device to

his waistband. The only thing left to do before activating it was to put on his gloves.

His stomach went cold when he reached for his pocket and realized the gloves weren't there.

The attack had happened so quickly that he'd left the specially designed gloves back in the decontamination chamber inside the duffel. He would need to either get them back or find replacements before he could carry out his plan for the nerve agent.

The other item he needed was something that all cargo ships were required to carry: a SOLAS rocket line thrower. The Safety of Life at Sea regulations stated that a ship of the *Triton Star*'s size was supposed to be equipped with four of them, which could be used to fire ropes to men overboard even if they were hundreds of yards from the ship.

During one of his midnight excursions onto the deck, Rasul had seen one of the rockets in its yellow plastic bucket hanging from the bulkhead directly under the lifeboat. He'd have to go outside to get it, but only for a moment.

When he reached the stairs nearest to the lifeboat station, he heard the crew being herded out of the mess.

'Come on,' one of the guards said. 'Back to the other ship.'

That meant they'd be going in the other direction. Perfect.

Rasul climbed the stairs, his G36 assault rifle at the ready. The hallway was empty.

He went out the door, and there was the line thrower. The bucket had a plastic lid and a handle with a trigger secured by a pin like a grenade.

Rasul took it down and lifted the lid. Inside, the rocket was centered in the bucket with the thousand-foot nylon line coiled around it. The rope was tied to a steel wire clipped to the rocket, which would make it easy for him to attach the Novichok cylinder in its place. The bucket even had helpful instructions on the outside for its operation and how to install a replacement rocket. All he needed to do was dump out the rope, set the Novichok to a two-minute countdown, and tie it to the rocket.

Now he just had to get back to the decontamination chamber. As long as he could get there unseen, he'd have plenty of time to jury-rig his weapon. They'd be scouring the rest of the ship for him. No one would suspect he'd go back to the same place.

He retreated behind an external bulkhead for cover and took out his phone, then opened the specially designed launch app. Once he'd typed in his code, the screen allowed him to change the targeting coordinates that came up. He entered the longitude and latitude for Diego Garcia.

Target confirmed, came the app's reply.

He navigated to the screen titled *Launch.* He slid aside the icon protecting against inadvertent activation, and the screen revealed a round red button with a caption that said *Launch now.*

He clicked the button and smiled as he thought to himself, *This will keep them distracted.*

'We're not going to help the Chairman?' Raven said as they double-timed it back toward the gangway and away from the gunshots.

'Orders are orders,' Linc said. 'Remember that from the Army?'

'There's a reason I left the Army.'

'The Chairman worries about his crew more than himself.' He threw her a grin. 'Besides, as soon as we get to the *Oregon*, we'll put on some NBC gear and see if we can convince him to let us come back.'

'I like the way you think.'

They all stopped at the sound of a loud bang. It wasn't quite an explosion, but it also wasn't like any gunshot Linc had ever heard.

MacD rapidly waved to them. He pointed above their heads.

Linc looked up in time to see the side of a container above them tumbling toward the deck like a fluttering leaf.

He picked up Raven and heaved her into the space between two container stacks next to them and then dove in after her. The container side-slammed into the deck inches from his boots and then slid over the side of the ship. There was a dent in the steel where they'd been standing.

'I don't normally like getting thrown around,' Raven said as she hopped to her feet, 'but in this case I'll make an exception. I owe you one.'

Linc got up, and they ran to MacD, who was still gazing upward.

'You don't see something like that every day,' he said.

They turned around and saw that the roof and sides of the topmost container on the stack next to where they'd been standing were gone, blown away by explosive hinges.

Now there was nothing there except its cargo: a missile launcher canted at a twenty-degree angle.

They all ducked when a geyser of flame erupted from the tube and a missile blasted out. When it was safely away, the booster rocket dropped into the sea, and stubby wings sprang from the fuselage. White-hot exhaust shot from the tail, and it accelerated away toward the southeast at a fantastic rate.

As they stood up, Linc cocked an eyebrow at Raven and MacD and said with a heavy dose of sarcasm, 'I'm guessing that's the launch they were talking about.'

For a moment, everyone in the op center froze, including Max, who stared at the sight of the missile disappearing into the distance.

Linda had been glued to the radar looking for any signs of an incoming aircraft or missile. Nobody had been expecting a missile launch from a container on the *Triton Star*.

'What kind of missile was that?' Max asked Murph, the ship's foremost weapons expert.

'BrahMos cruise missile,' Murph answered without hesitation. 'Supersonic. Indian design.'

Max's first priority was the safety of the ship. 'Activate defensive measures. Lock on with an anti-aircraft missile and fire.'

'Firing Aster,' Murph said. The *Oregon*'s hull reverberated with the sound of the European anti-aircraft missile rocketing out of its tube toward the cruise missile.

'Gatling guns and Metal Storm coming online,' Murph added.

The Aster anti-aircraft missile was their primary defensive weapon. But if the cruise missile turned around and avoided the Aster, the *Oregon* also had secondary defenses. Hull plates retracted to reveal three six-barreled Gatling guns that fired 20mm tungsten shells at a rate of three thousand rounds per minute. The Metal Storm gun rose out of the stern, ready to fire a wall of five hundred electronically activated rounds in the span of six milliseconds.

'Is the missile turning back toward us?'

'Negative,' Linda said. 'It's tracking on a straight path away from us southeast.'

'Time to target?'

'If it doesn't change course,' Murph said, turning to look at Max with a concerned expression, 'time to intercept the cruise missile is thirty-two seconds.'

'What's the matter?'

'The BrahMos got a ten-second head start, and it's almost as fast as the Aster.' The short-range anti-aircraft missile was designed to intercept airplanes and missiles coming toward the ship, not for chasing them down.

Murph put a map up on the viewscreen showing the red dot of the cruise missile heading away from them at Mach 3 and the Aster missile in pursuit, gradually gaining on it at Mach 3.5.

'If we're not the target,' Max said, 'where's it heading?'

'Could be a ship in that direction,' Linda said, 'though I don't see any on the scope.'

'The target isn't a ship,' Eric said. 'Look at the map.'

Eric zoomed out and extended a dotted line along the BrahMos's current heading. It was heading directly for Diego Garcia.

'Hali, get in touch with Diego Garcia any way you can and tell them that a cruise missile loaded with a toxic nerve agent is coming their way.'

Hali shook his head. 'I still can't contact anyone there, but I'll keeping trying.'

'Ten seconds to impact,' Murph said.

The distance between the two dots was closing at an agonizingly slow pace.

Murph starting counting down.

'Five . . . four . . . three . . .'

Then he stopped. The dot representing the anti-aircraft missile winked out.

'What happened?' Max asked.

Murph slapped the panel in frustration and turned to him. 'Ran of out fuel just before it caught up with the target. Now there's no way for us to shoot it down.'

'How long until it hits Diego Garcia?'

'Nine minutes,' Eric said.

'Potential casualties?'

'If that missile is loaded with even half the Novichok that was reported stolen, we're looking at a catastrophe.'

'Hali, get me Juan.'

After a moment, Hali said, 'The Chairman's on speaker.'

'Juan,' Max said, 'Rasul just launched a BrahMos supersonic cruise missile from the *Triton Star*. We fired an Aster but couldn't shoot the BrahMos down. You're going to have to track him down and get him to send the missile's abort code.'

'Easier said than done. We're still looking for him.'

Max looked at the timer Eric had put up on the screen showing the missile's time to impact.

'Not to put any pressure on you, but if you don't find Rasul in the next eight minutes and thirty seconds, every person on Diego Garcia is going to die.'

Juan moved quickly down the accessway to the next corner, with Eddie close behind covering their rear in case

Rasul circled back around them. He stopped at the crossing passageway and peered around the corner, but Rasul wasn't in sight. Finding him in the maze of corridors in the next eight minutes was going to be a crapshoot.

'Max,' Juan said into his earpiece mic, 'if we can't catch Rasul, I might have a backup plan. Have Hali call Langston Overholt and get him to link up with Barbara Goodman at the 50th Space Wing in Colorado Springs. Tell him it's about Operation Theseus.'

'You and your Plan Cs,' Max said. Juan could practically hear him rolling his eyes at Juan's tendency to improvise last-minute schemes. 'It's the middle of the night back in the US. We'll just wake them up.'

'How are we going to find Rasul in a five-hundred-foot-long ship in less than eight minutes?' Eddie asked Juan.

'He's wearing an NBC suit,' Juan replied, 'so that means he's planning to set off his own Novichok release.'

Eddie nodded. 'He wants to get rid of witnesses.'

'But we've put a crimp in his plans. He wasn't expecting two ships.'

'He'll want to get the nerve agent airborne. Maybe he already had a plan to do that.'

'Then why make a run for it and go into the ship? When I saw him . . .' Juan's voice trailed off as he replayed the shoot-out in his mind.

'What?' Eddie asked.

'I only saw him for a split second, but I don't think he was wearing gloves.'

'He wouldn't have forgotten them.'

'I don't know,' Juan said. 'Maybe he had them in his pocket, but if he didn't, he'll need some replacements.'

'They can't be just any old gloves. They'd have to be chemical-resistant.'

'Like rubber gloves. I can think of two possibilities. One is the mess, where they might have rubber gloves for cleaning. The other is that he's circling back to take the ones from Keith Tao's suit.'

'Split up?'

'It's our best shot,' Juan said with a nod. He couldn't check his watch, which was inside his suit. 'We can't have much more than seven minutes left.'

'I'll take the mess,' Eddie said.

'I'll check Tao. And remember, we need him alive.'

Eddie nodded and ran toward the mess.

As Juan sprinted back the way he'd come, he radioed Max the plan. Max told him that Raven, Linc, and MacD were suiting up and would be over to help out with the search as soon as they were ready. He also said they were down to six and a half minutes and still no contact with Diego Garcia to warn them of the approaching danger.

He decided to go around and between the row of containers. If Rasul had done the same, Juan would be coming up behind him.

When he got to the space between the containers, he could see the front door still ajar. Beyond it was Tao's body.

The suit was bloody, but the gloves were still attached to it.

Juan moved forward with the submachine gun raised until he got to the end of the row and eased around the open door. Still no sign of Rasul.

He was about to consider this plan a bust when he heard a piece of metal clang inside the container. Juan poked his head around the corner and saw Rasul emerge from the decontamination chamber with gloves on that matched his suit.

Juan could have kicked himself for not checking the duffel. If the gloves were still inside, that was the only reason Rasul would have returned.

Rasul was holding a bucket with a rocket-powered line thrower. In a flash, Juan knew what he had in mind.

'Drop it, Rasul!' Juan yelled.

Rasul turned and looked at him in stunned disbelief, visible because he had a full-face mask instead of the goggles that Juan wore.

He didn't hesitate. Despite Juan's warning, he aimed the top of the bucket at the sky, and his hand reached for the trigger.

Juan fired a single round at Rasul's shoulder. He needed him alive.

Rasul spun and collapsed onto his back, but he closed his finger on the trigger as he fell. The rocket launched past his head and into the decontamination chamber, where it ricocheted around until it ran out of fuel.

Juan ran forward. Rasul reached for a pistol in his belt, but the gloves were clumsy enough that Juan got to him first and stepped on his wrist.

'How do I send the self-destruct code to the missile?' Juan demanded with the P90 pointed at Rasul's face.

'The phone in my front pocket,' Rasul said with a smile.

With his boot still on Rasul's good hand, Juan reached down and pulled out the phone. He pushed the HOME button, and the screen asked for the passcode. Juan's gloves were designed to work with touchpads.

'What's your passcode?'

'I'll never tell,' Rasul said with a gurgle. The smile had disappeared. His lips were turning blue.

It was the Novichok. The nerve agent had gotten into the suit where Juan had shot him.

'You only have a few seconds left to live,' Juan said. 'Tell me the passcode or I'll just use your thumbprint when you're dead.'

His back arched, and he screamed in agony as the Novichok took control of his body. Then he went silent and rigid, but Juan could see that the eyes were still seeing. They began to water from the misery he was going through.

Juan yanked off Rasul's gloves and tried to unlock the phone with the fingerprints on both of the assassin's thumbs.

Nothing. Even if there was an abort signal to be sent from the phone, they'd never be able to crack it and gain access in the next five minutes.

That left one chance. Juan ran toward the *Oregon*. If he couldn't stop that missile from detonating over Diego Garcia, every person at the military base would suffer Rasul's gruesome fate.

11

As he raced across the weather deck, Juan activated his earpiece mic.

'Eddie, get back to the *Oregon* right now. I'm covered in Novichok dust, so you go over first.'

'On my way,' Eddie replied.

'Max,' Juan said, 'I'm heading to the op center. Have you gotten in touch with Lang yet?'

Langston Overholt IV had been Juan's boss in the CIA and was still allowed to serve even into his eighties since he knew where all the bodies, both figurative and literal, were buried. Overholt encouraged Juan to form the Corporation and build the *Oregon*, and all of their CIA assignments, including this operation, came through him.

'He's a little groggy and not particularly happy that we woke him up,' Max replied. 'Said something about recovering from a 10K yesterday. But he's on the line now.'

'And Barbara Goodman?'

'Overholt's pulling all his strings to get her on the line.'

'Good, because we struck out with the BrahMos abort system.' He quickly told Max about what had happened to Rasul as he watched Eddie run across the gangway.

When Eddie was safely inside the *Oregon*, Juan entered the tent holding the portable decontamination system. He activated it, and his suit was bathed with a concentrated hypochlorite solution formulated to react with any

Novichok particles on his suit and render them harmless. Ninety seconds later, a green light flashed, indicating that he was clean. He threw off the mask and shucked the suit before running toward the op center.

When he got there, Max got up from the command chair and went to his engineering station.

'Stoney, raise the gangway and move us away from the *Triton Star*,' Juan said to Eric as he sat down. He didn't want the *Oregon* to get contaminated by any stray Novichok floating over.

The huge viewscreen at the front of the room showed Langston Overholt's craggy face staring at him. He was wearing a silk bathrobe over a pajama top buttoned at the collar.

'I know this must be important, Juan,' Overholt said with a gravelly baritone, 'because I haven't heard you mention the Theseus operation in years.'

'It is,' Juan said, dispensing with their usual back-and-forth. 'There's a cruise missile headed to Diego Garcia carrying a nerve agent warhead, and we can't warn them to shoot it down. We estimate impact in a little more than three minutes.'

Overholt nodded. 'Max said it was a BrahMos. You sure this will work?'

'No, but we're out of time and options.'

'Chairman,' Hali interrupted, 'I've got Barbara Goodman on video.'

'Put her on-screen,' Juan said.

A moment later, a fit woman in her thirties with short brown hair and high cheekbones appeared on the main viewscreen next to Overholt. She looked wide awake and wore pressed Air Force blues. The silver oak leaves of a colonel were pinned to her shoulder epaulets.

'Hello, Barbara,' Juan said. 'Thanks for taking our call. Are you at Schriever?' Schriever Air Force Base in Colorado Springs was home to Space Command's 50th Space Wing, which was in control of the Global Positioning System. It looked like she was in some kind of control room, so he hoped that was the case.

'It's good to see you again, Juan,' she said with the flash of a quick smile. 'Yes, I'm at Schriever. But you caught me at a bad time. For the last fifteen minutes, we've been trying to figure out why we've lost communications with one of our bases.'

'That would be Camp Thunder Cove on Diego Garcia, right?'

Goodman's jaw dropped. 'How do you know that?'

'Because we're about three hundred and fifty miles northwest of the island. There's a cruise missile headed straight for it carrying a nasty chemical weapon. We've been trying to warn them, but no one is answering.'

'I can't help you. We're just as much at a loss as you are. There's nothing I can do.'

'Yes, there is. Theseus.'

She frowned and leaned toward the camera. 'That is strictly on a need-to-know basis.'

'Believe me, everyone here has a security clearance and needs to know.'

Theseus was the code name for a special feature of GPS that few outside of Space Command knew about. Since GPS was used by nations around the world, including militaries, it was possible for their weapons to be targeted at the US using America's own satellite system for navigational guidance.

During armed conflicts, the military wanted to be able to broadcast incorrect GPS coordinates to spoof other countries' guidance systems, so Theseus was developed as a hidden control that could be activated without anyone else knowing. Not only that, but for a short time it could also confuse guidance systems using GLONASS, the Russian analog of GPS, and NAVIC, India's version. The software design for Theseus and knowledge of its existence had been stolen when Juan was still in the CIA, and he had teamed up with Barbara Goodman to get it back before it could fall into the hands of the Chinese.

'You need to activate Theseus in that region now,' Juan said. Because Diego Garcia's location in the southern Indian Ocean was so isolated, the narrow focus of the GPS change was unlikely to significantly affect air or sea traffic. 'Redirect the missile at least forty miles to the east.' According to weather reports, that would put the missile downwind of the island.

'What?' Goodman said, aghast. 'Theseus has never been used operationally before. It's only meant to be activated during a time of war.'

Juan got out of his chair and walked toward the screen. 'Barbara, if you don't activate it in the next ninety seconds, over three thousand on Diego Garcia will be killed.'

When she hesitated, Juan added, 'I understand this is a tough decision, but you know me, Barbara. I wouldn't be asking if I wasn't sure. This is literally do or die right now.'

Goodman grimaced, then she looked to her left and said to someone off-screen, 'Activate Theseus over Diego

Garcia . . . You heard me . . . I know . . . On my authorization . . . Do it!'

She then read off coordinates that would cause the missile to reinterpret its guidance programming and convince the BrahMos that it was off course. If Theseus worked as designed, the cruise missile should alter its trajectory toward the new target designation.

She turned back to the screen. 'That might be the end of my career right there. And the bad thing is, with the communications down, we won't be able to tell if it worked.'

'We'll eventually find out if it didn't work,' Juan replied. The cruise missile was currently far beyond their radar range.

Hali raised his hand. 'I might be able to tell you if it works.'

'What do you mean?' Juan asked.

'I've just picked up a Morse code signal coming over shortwave frequencies. It's faint, but the sender says he's an Air Force sergeant on Diego Garcia using an ancient radio there left over from World War Two that he's been tinkering with over the past few months. Sergeant Joseph Brandt.'

Goodman gaped again. 'That's one of the communications operators we've been trying to contact.'

'Hali,' Juan said, 'tell him to get everyone there to shelter in case the BrahMos detonates over the island.'

'Will that protect them from the nerve agent?' Goodman asked.

'I don't know,' Juan said, 'but it can't hurt.' He nodded at Hali.

'Aye, Chairman,' Hali replied.

'And when you're done with that message, ask him to tell us if he can see any missiles heading his way.'

*

Since he could do nothing else about his crashed B-1B bomber, Major Jay Petkunas and the rest of his crew were walking toward Diego Garcia's Air Force headquarters building for a debriefing, though he didn't think what happened to them would be anyone's priority until the island was operational again. The place was strangely silent. No sounds of machinery or vehicles buzzed in the background to distract from the pounding surf and squawking seagulls.

They were still a half mile from the headquarters when he suddenly heard something man-made coming their way. An engine. It sounded like a diesel V-8.

Petkunas looked around and saw an old eighties-era pickup truck heading toward them at breakneck speed. When it jerked to a stop next to him, he saw that the bed was packed with airmen.

'Sir, you need to get to shelter now,' the driver said without saluting.

'What?' Petkunas said. Just when he thought the day couldn't have gotten any stranger. 'Wait a minute, how come your truck is the only one that's working?'

'Something about the electronics. This truck doesn't have any microchips in it.'

Petkunas shot a look at his copilot, Larsson, who nodded at him. That explained why nothing on his airplane had worked, including the ejection seats.

'What do you mean, we need to get to shelter?' Larsson asked.

'We're under attack. Sorry, sir, comms are down, and I have to get the message to the Navy commander.'

Before Petkunas could ask for a ride, the truck had taken off again.

'What was he talking about?' Larsson said as he watched the pickup with a confused look. 'Who's attacking us?'

'Your guess,' Petkunas said, 'but he did sound serious. And taking out power and communications could be a prelude to an attack. Let's hoof it.'

All four of them picked up the pace to a run. They'd made it only a few hundred yards when Petkunas saw something flash just a few dozen feet overhead at lightning speed.

'Get down!' Petkunas yelled, and all four of them dropped to the tarmac.

A split second later, a sonic boom crashed into them, shaking the ground.

But there was no explosion. The sound of the small jet engine faded into the breeze as it rocketed away to the east.

Petkunas stood and dusted off his flight suit. As the others got to their feet, Larsson said, 'What just happened?'

Petkunas shook his head in amazement. 'I have no idea.'

'Chairman,' Hali said, 'Sergeant Brandt just told me that the cruise missile continued east as it flew over Diego Garcia. It seems to be gone.'

Everyone in the *Oregon*'s op center relaxed. The danger was over.

'Did you hear that, Barbara?' Juan said to Colonel Goodman. 'You just saved an entire island.'

'Thanks to you,' she said with a relieved smile. 'If you weren't so convincing, I might not have activated Theseus until it was too late.'

'I'd keep it active until we're sure the cruise missile has run out of fuel. According to our calculations, two more minutes should do it. That's a remote region, so any dispersal of the Novichok will happen over open ocean. We've checked, and there aren't any known ships in the area.' The Novichok might contaminate the water for a short time until it dissipated, but that was better than the alternative.

'That makes sense,' Goodman said. 'I'd like to keep your radioman on the line so he can relay communications between us and Diego Garcia. Then I'll have to explain to the head of Space Command why I activated a top secret weapons system without his authorization. I'll either be demoted or get a medal.'

'I'll make sure it's the latter,' said Langston Overholt, who was still on-screen.

'Thank you, sir,' Goodman said.

'Hali,' Juan said, 'you can transfer Barbara's call to your station. Good work getting everyone conferenced in.'

When he saw everyone looking at him, Hali flashed them a humble grin. 'Thanks, Chairman. Happy to help.'

Goodman's image disappeared from the main viewscreen, leaving Overholt on it alone.

'This went far beyond what I was expecting when I gave you this mission,' Overholt said. 'But now there's obviously much more to the situation than some missing nerve agent. While the military investigates how the island's electronics were disabled out of the blue, I want you to find out why Diego Garcia was targeted in the first place.'

Juan nodded. 'I think we'll start by trying to find out why Rasul was hired to kill Tao and the *Triton Star* crew and then frame them for mass murder.'

12

Sydney

Jason Wakefield stalked out of the Vedor Telecom tower in downtown Sydney while he spoke on his encrypted cell phone, the only one he used to call other members of the Nine Unknown. As the beneficiary of the Scroll of Knowledge for communication that had been passed down through generations from Ashoka, he had built Vedor Communications into Vedor Telecom, a global phone and networking empire. On the other end of the line was Lionel Gupta, a Canadian descendant of the original Unknown who had been bestowed with the alchemy scroll. He now headed OreDyne Systems, one of the largest engineering companies in the world.

'You're telling me,' Gupta said in the snarky tone he was famous for, 'that even though you own phone networks around the world, including Italy, you haven't been able to find out any info about who might have sabotaged the *Colossus 5* in Naples? Not even where the phones used to detonate the explosives came from?'

Wakefield caught his reflection in the mirrored window of his Maybach limousine as it pulled up to the entrance of the massive skyscraper. His Indian great-grandfather had immigrated to Australia, anglicized his name, and married the daughter of a New South Wales newspaper owner, so he was more Caucasian than Bengali. The image of Wakefield's slick black hair, deep tan, and Savile Row suit would be familiar to anyone who read the society pages about his six divorces, the last of which was still in its final stages. While his bodyguard held the door for him, he adjusted a stray hair and plucked a piece of lint from his lapel before getting into the Mercedes. The bodyguard sat in the front passenger seat, and they pulled away.

As usual, the backseat TV was tuned to the local Unlimited News International network. The news hour was just beginning, the screen ablaze with slick graphics and the slogan *You and I and UNI*. Wakefield muted the sound and closed the soundproof partition before responding to Gupta.

'It's been only forty-eight hours since the attack on the ship,' Wakefield said, exasperated at Gupta's impatience. 'All we can confirm is that a bomb brought down the crane that destroyed the satellite dish. Besides, Xavier Carlton has his own worldwide news and media company, and he hasn't been able to find out anything, either.'

'That's because UNI is wasting time on stupid things like the power outage on that island in the middle of nowhere.'

'I know. I'm watching it now. It's news when one of America's most secretive military bases goes dark. And I don't like the incident's timing. Not when we're so close to completing Colossus.' As Wakefield spoke, stock footage and satellite images of Diego Garcia played across the screen during the lead story about the mysterious blackout.

'Are you suggesting they're related?' Gupta asked.

'That's what we need to find out, especially with the

near-simultaneous explosion of Mallik's rocket in the Arabian Sea. Something's going on.'

Gupta paused. 'So you suspect a traitor among the Nine?'

'Who else knew how to sabotage the *Colossus 5* in that way? Don't you have your own suspicions?'

'I do. That's why we're having the meeting again in two days. We need to find out who is behind all this.'

'How are we going to do that?' Wakefield asked.

'I can't talk about it right now.'

'If you think this encrypted line isn't secure, we shouldn't be talking by phone at all.' Then Wakefield understood what he meant and sat forward. 'Wait, you think I'm the traitor?'

'You have expressed reservations about our plans.'

'Each of us has played devil's advocate at one time or another, even you,' Wakefield said. 'And still, we've all agreed that it's in the best interests of both ourselves and mankind to move forward. Besides, how do I know you're not the traitor?'

'You don't. But there may be a way to find out who it is.'

'Tell me.'

'I can't reveal that until the meeting,' Gupta said. 'Then we can all decide how to handle it together.'

'We're so close to achieving our goals, Lionel,' Wakefield said, 'we can't let someone get cold feet now.'

'I know. We won't. This is what we've worked for all our lives and the lives of our ancestors.'

Gupta hung up, and Wakefield tossed his phone on the seat. He had barely slept since getting the news about the damaged *Colossus*. Luckily, the ship hadn't been completely destroyed or they'd be years away from completing their journey to a better tomorrow. Now all they could do was race to repair the ship and get it operational.

He closed his eyes and tried to relax before he arrived at his next appointment. He must have nodded off, because he jolted awake when he was thrown against the back of the front seat. He always refused to wear a seat belt because it wrinkled his suit, but this was one time he wished he'd had it on. His nose crunched as it hit the partition, and blood cascaded down his chin.

The Maybach screeched to a halt.

'Get down!' his bodyguard yelled.

Hazy, confused, and covered with his own blood, Wakefield didn't do as he was instructed. Instead, he watched the driver's head get blown apart by a bullet that smashed through the supposedly bulletproof windshield. The man slumped over the steering wheel, pressing against the horn, which now blared nonstop.

His bodyguard dodged several of the armor-piercing rounds that neatly penetrated the windshield, but the bullets didn't get through to Wakefield. They were stopped by the partition. The bodyguard got out and returned fire, but he was taken down immediately by three bullets that tore into his chest, tossing him around like a rag doll before he collapsed to the pavement.

Three men in black balaclavas approached the car. One of them was carrying a huge drill, the other two automatic weapons.

Panicked, Wakefield made sure the door was locked. He wasn't a fighter and didn't carry a gun, so he grabbed for his phone. However, it was no longer on the seat where he'd left it, and he dropped to the floor frantically searching for it.

By the time he found it, the man with the drill was grinding away at the door lock.

Wakefield dialed 000, Australia's emergency number. 'Come on, come on,' he muttered while it rang.

Outside, he could hear the men shouting at one another in some kind of Hindi dialect.

The phone clicked, and Wakefield heard someone say, 'Ambulance Emergency. What town or suburb are we coming to?'

'I don't know,' Wakefield said, trying to keep his voice calm. He knew this call would become public record at some point. 'I'm in downtown Sydney somewhere. Men have shot my driver and bodyguard and are trying to break into my car.'

Wakefield could hear typing on a keyboard. 'We have triangulated your location, sir, and police have been dispatched. What is your name?'

'It's Jason –'

The door was wrenched open, and a powerful hand reached in and latched onto his arm. He was dragged out, and the phone was yanked from his hand. The masked gunman threw it to the street and stomped on it.

He looked like the man in charge because he tilted his head toward a white panel van and spoke in a commanding voice to the two men who were holding Wakefield.

Wakefield tried struggling against them, but the man in charge slapped him across the face. The impact hit his broken nose, and a shock of pain exploded through his head. He went limp as they dragged him down the street.

The masked leader pulled the van's sliding door open. Wakefield knew he had to fight to stay out of there, having been trained in anti-kidnapping techniques, but he was spent and in agony. He could barely resist.

He was about to be thrown in when Wakefield heard a loud crack, and blood splashed across the van's white exterior. At first, he thought they had shot him and he just couldn't feel it because of shock.

Then he saw the wide eyes of the masked men's leader. He had a huge hole in his chest.

As the gunman slumped to the ground, two more shots rang out, and his companions let go of their prisoner and fell.

Wakefield slowly rolled over, fully expecting to be shot as well. He saw another man coming toward him, this one in a suit almost as nice as his, with a pistol pointed at the ground. He bent down to check the three masked men.

When he stood back up, he said, 'They're dead.'

'Who are you?' Wakefield asked.

'Asad Torkan,' his savior said. 'Romir Mallik asked me to keep an eye on you. For good reason, it turns out.'

'Mallik sent you?'

'He thinks there is a traitor amongst the Nine Unknown. Come with me. We need to get out of here in case they have backup.'

Torkan gave him a hand and a handkerchief, then guided Wakefield to a silver BMW. He helped Wakefield into the passenger seat. As soon as Torkan got in, he threw the car into gear and tore away as they heard sirens approaching.

Wakefield leaned his head back with the handkerchief

against his aching nose. 'Do you know who ordered my kidnapping?'

'Mr Mallik might know,' Torkan said, thumbing his phone.

'Why would someone do this?'

Instead of answering him, Torkan spoke into the phone.

'Mr Mallik, we have a situation,' he said. 'Someone tried to kidnap Jason Wakefield . . . Yes, he's all right . . . Thank you, sir. Just doing my job.' He turned and smiled at Wakefield. 'But if it weren't for your foresight, right now Mr Wakefield would probably be as good as dead.'

13

The Indian Ocean

The USS *Gridley* reached the *Oregon* and *Triton Star* a day after the missile attack. The hazmat team was already searching the contaminated cargo ship for clues, and the captured crew had been handed over to the CIA agents on the destroyer for further interrogation.

Juan sat next to Max in one of the *Oregon*'s two high-speed lifeboats. An orange sun was setting over a calm horizon. Max was at the wheel, piloting the boat away from the *Gridley* after Juan's daylong debriefing with the ship's CIA contingent. To keep the *Oregon* out of view of the destroyer's crew, she maintained a position ten miles away, while the crew painted her and reconfigured her profile to make her unidentifiable by anyone on the *Triton Star*.

Max shook his head as Juan told him about the B-1B lying with its nose in the surf next to Diego Garcia's runway.

'Those guys got lucky if they all survived a crash like that,' he said.

'Sounds like they had a good pilot,' Juan replied. 'He brought it in on hydraulic power alone.'

'Any word on how the computers were shut down?'

Juan shook his head. 'They're coming back online,

though. The computers weren't permanently fried. The technicians on the island said it was as if the computers had been scrambled. Something about disrupting the electron flow in the transistors. The event didn't disable basic electrical functions, only computer chips. The effect seemed to end a minute before the missile arrived, which explains why it wasn't disabled as well. Now all the computers on the island and in the harbor's naval ships are working again.' Then, turning his head, Juan said, 'Maybe Eric and Murph can make some sense of it.' Juan's tech wizards had been part of the debriefing before returning to the *Oregon* earlier.

'Whatever the weapon was,' Max said, 'it could do a number on the *Oregon*. Everything on board is computer controlled. We'd be dead in the water.'

'I thought about that, too. Take some time to figure out how to keep us operational if our computers conk out.'

'Already on the agenda. I'll have more time now that we're not acting as babysitters for Tao's crew anymore.'

'They're the CIA's problem now,' Juan said, 'along with the *Triton Star*.'

'Do we know where the missile came from?'

'The CIA thinks that it was shipped in pieces to Mozambique. That's what was in the container labeled FARM MACHINERY. They traced the launcher's serial number to a missile supposedly stolen by the Pakistanis, but so far it's a dead end.'

'Then that puts us back at square one,' Max said. 'Does the CIA have any theories for who's behind this?'

'They're focusing on the Iranians – because of Rasul, whose last name we still don't know – and the Pakistanis.

They think it's either an Iranian plot to take out the island or that Islamic terrorists in Pakistan tried to cripple America's ability to bomb Afghanistan.'

'But why frame the *Triton Star* crew? If we hadn't been there, it would have looked like they had launched the missile, then killed themselves by accident or committed suicide.'

'I agree,' Juan said. 'And no one has claimed responsibility for the attack.'

'Most of the world doesn't even know there *was* an attack. I've been keeping tabs on the world news, and right now the official story is that the island suffered a sudden power failure during routine maintenance of the electrical plant.'

'The military suspended all social media feeds, telephone service, and internet access from Diego Garcia to keep a lid on the real story. The people who organized the attack might even think they succeeded.'

'Do you buy the CIA line?' Max asked.

'I don't think the Iranians are behind it,' Juan said. 'If we discovered they were responsible, they'd be risking all-out war with the US.'

'What about terrorists? ISIS? Al-Qaeda?'

'If it had been a group like that, they'd be bragging to every news outlet in the world about how they had handed big, bad America a huge defeat. No, I think something else is going on here. Maybe a test?'

Max turned to Juan with a frown. 'You think this was all to see if their pseudo-EMP weapon worked?'

Juan held up his fingers and ticked off the answers one by one. 'Isolated base. High-profile target. Supposedly hardened against this kind of attack. Somebody went to a lot of trouble to make this operation work. What I can't figure out is why they launched when they did.'

'It does seem odd,' Max said. 'They could have launched the missile long before we intercepted the *Triton Star*.'

'Which makes me think Camp Thunder Cove wasn't the original target. It was sheer luck that we were available to intercept the *Triton Star*. We know that Rasul's mysterious connection sent him the coordinates of Diego Garcia after we arrived.'

'So what was the original target?'

'I don't know. Tao mentioned that Rasul's containers were supposed to be delivered to somewhere called Jhootha Island. But if he was going to fire a missile from one of those containers and then kill the crew, why set course for that island?'

'Maybe he wanted to launch the missile from Jhootha Island.'

'That's a possibility.'

'What's on the island?'

'And what's nearby? I have Eric and Murph checking into those questions. But I think we should go there and check it out.'

Max shook his head. 'Sounds like a long shot to me.'

'The CIA thought so, too. Do you have any other bright ideas? I'm all ears.'

'That wasn't a criticism,' Max said with a smile. 'Your long shots usually come through.'

When they reached the *Oregon*, Max and Juan headed to the op center, where they found Eric and Murph in a heated discussion.

'Why would they go there?' Murph said, notably exasperated. 'It doesn't make sense.'

'How should I know?' Eric shot back. 'But that's where Tao said they were heading.'

'Okay, you two,' Juan said as he and Max entered. 'You can settle your differences by video game duel later. Is this about a certain island I asked you to investigate?'

Eric nodded. 'We found Jhootha Island, all right.'

'But it's highly unlikely the *Triton Star*'s size would regularly be able to stop there to unload a container,' Murph said.

'Why is that?' Juan asked.

Eric brought up a satellite image of the island on the main viewscreen. It was circular, ringed with sandy beaches, and covered in tropical jungle. No roads or settlements were visible.

'This is Jhootha Island – its Indian name – two hundred miles off the west coast of India,' Eric said. 'On Western maps, it's known as Killington Island, named after its discoverer. As you can see, it's surrounded by atolls, and there are no natural harbors or coves big enough for a yacht, let alone a large containership. There's definitely no pier.'

'Maybe Tao unloads the contents of the containers and transfers them to a tender,' Juan said. 'A small boat could make landfall on the island.'

'If they did,' Murph said, 'I can't tell you why they'd want to. Not when they'd be killed the moment they set foot on land.'

'Why?' Max asked. 'Is it full of poisonous snakes like that island near Brazil?'

Eric shook his head. 'It's home to a tribe of natives who are completely cut off from the modern world and hostile to anyone intruding on their territory.'

'Killington landed there by accident and got a spear through the gut for his trouble,' Murph said. 'But they named the island after him, so that's a nice consolation prize.'

'We knew the *Triton Star* was heading somewhere called J Island because of their computer records,' Juan said. 'Tao then gave us the name Jhootha Island without prompting. He had no reason to lie about it, so I'm inclined to believe that's where they were going.'

'That would be an oddball destination,' Murph said. 'The Indian government has declared Jhootha Island off-limits to outsiders.'

'Which makes me want to take a look even more now,' Juan said as he sat in his command chair. 'Discreetly, of course. Eric, lay in a course.'

'Aye, Chairman,' Eric said, taking his position at the helm.

'*National Geographic* is going to be so jealous,' Murph said with a chuckle.

'Why? You planning to sell photos of the islanders?' Juan joked.

'If I did, the magazine would probably pay through the nose for such a huge scoop. According to Indian records, it's been forty years since anyone has come back from that island alive.'

14

Of the Nine Unknown, Xavier Carlton was the richest by far. All of them had private jets, but he was the only one with his own personal Airbus A380 wide-body airliner. His second one, actually. The first had disappeared eighteen months ago, never found by searchers except for a few pieces of wreckage that washed up in Oman and Yemen. The insurance company had been dragging its feet about the payout, but he didn't need the money for its replacement. He could buy five more of the luxurious made-to-order planes without straining his bank account.

As the descendants of the original Nine who had been bestowed with the knowledge of propaganda, Carlton's ancestors had invested in some of the most influential newspapers in Europe. With that wealth, his family had branched out into other types of media as radio, television, and then the internet came to dominate news and entertainment.

Now Unlimited News International was one of the most influential, wide-ranging media companies in the world. Still, that reach hadn't helped Carlton definitively pin the sabotage on any of the other Nine.

The latest estimate for completing repairs to the *Colossus 5* was one more week. The satellite dish had been totally destroyed, but Carlton found an identical one intended for an internet company in São Paulo and purchased it for three times the going price. It was now headed to the ship for its installation.

All of that would be good news for the meeting of the Nine set to take place in India the next morning, the first gathering in more than a year where they were all present. Carlton was on his plane, waiting on the Heathrow tarmac for the overnight flight to Mumbai. His guest for the voyage was supposed to arrive soon.

Carlton was in his main deck private office going over his plans for the meeting when there was a knock at the door.

'Enter,' he said.

His personal assistant, Natalie Taylor, came in carrying a gold platter with a teapot and cups. She was dressed in slacks and a blazer, her blond hair barely touching her shoulders. She set the platter on the desk and said, 'Mr Gupta's plane has landed, and he will be here momentarily.'

'Show him in when he arrives.'

Taylor nodded and left.

Carlton leaned over to the window and saw a black SUV pull up to the boarding stairs. An obese man in his fifties emerged from the backseat. Carlton shook his head at the way Lionel Gupta had let himself go. Carlton, trim and rock solid at forty-eight, was known for his fitness regimen, even having a private gym installed on board his jet so he could exercise while he was traveling.

A minute later, Taylor opened the door, and Gupta entered his office breathing hard from the climb up the jet's stairs. Taylor, who was in even better shape than Carlton, looked amused but said nothing. Carlton stood to shake Gupta's hand and waved for him to sit, which Gupta did gladly.

'Tea?' Carlton asked.

Gupta nodded. 'Cream and three sugars.'

Taylor poured two cups and glided out of the office.

'The media world has been good to you,' Gupta said as he drank his tea and looked around at the lavish furnishings, many of which were gold-plated. The fabrics were made of the finest silks, and every piece of wood was hand-carved Indonesian teak.

'Let's get down to business,' Carlton said, taking a sip from his own cup. 'We both were given a massive head start in life and we've built even greater riches from it. You wouldn't have one of the largest engineering companies on the planet if it weren't for being part of the Nine, and I wouldn't be where I am without that position, either.'

Gupta shrugged. 'So we're both privileged. I don't apologize for that.'

'And you shouldn't. But we have a responsibility to do something with that wealth.'

'I agree. That's why we all have combined our resources for the Colossus initiative.'

'Maybe not everyone agrees,' Carlton said. 'The attempted kidnapping of Jason Wakefield is concerning.'

Gupta set the teacup down. 'He's lucky to be alive. Is he still coming to the meeting tomorrow?'

'As far as I know. But he's gone into hiding until then.'

'Maybe we should, too.'

'You'll be safe on my plane. It has all of the latest defense features, and I travel with a squad of former Special Forces operatives at all times.'

'It's too bad that the defensive capabilities weren't enough to save your son. Again, my condolences.'

Carlton pursed his lips at Gupta's hollow words of sympathy. 'It was a necessary sacrifice. I thought he might change his lazy, spendthrift ways and become an heir to my seat of the Nine Unknown, but it was not to be. Besides, I have four more sons to choose from.'

Gupta gave him a mirthless smile. 'Of course.' He paused, then said, 'You don't seem very concerned about Wakefield's incident in Sydney.'

'Why should I be?' Carlton leaned toward Gupta. 'Were you behind it?'

'Certainly not. Are you accusing me of –'

Carlton smiled and waved his hand. 'Relax. I know it wasn't you.'

'How?'

'Because I know who did it . . . Do you?'

'I had suspected Wakefield of being behind the attack on the *Colossus 5* until yesterday. In fact, I spoke to him right before he was assaulted, hoping to catch him in a lie. Now you seem to have all the answers. Who is it?'

'Romir Mallik.'

Gupta sat back as if he'd been slapped. 'Mallik? But he's always been so enthusiastic about the Colossus Project. How sure are you?'

'Sure enough to blow up one of his satellite rockets two days ago.'

'You did what?' Gupta shouted, his eyes bugging out. 'Are you crazy?'

'Far from it.' Carlton stood and went to the door. 'Walk with me.'

Gupta followed him out of the office. They passed a conference room into the upper lounge and walked up a wide staircase to a second lounge, this one with a baby grand piano as its centerpiece.

They continued aft past four sumptuous staterooms, one of which would be Gupta's. In the tail section, they reached a third lounge. This one had an array of leather chairs on three low risers that were tiered higher toward a set of spiral stairs at the back. A door behind the stairs separated this room from the workers' quarters and galley. The walls were decorated with a wide assortment of ancient weapons, everything from scimitars and spears to crossbows and throwing stars.

Gupta examined the armaments closely.

'I wouldn't want to be in this room during turbulence,' he said.

'They're all securely fastened to the wall,' Carlton said. 'I understand that you're a fan of weapons like I am.'

Gupta nodded. 'But my tastes go more toward firearms.'

Carlton shrugged. 'Difficult to collect in England.'

Gupta stopped at an edged weapon shaped vaguely like an ampersand, with a short spike projecting from just above the hilt at one end and a two-headed axe that had a pointed blade on one side and a wicked curved hook on the other.

'I've never seen one of these before,' Gupta said. 'What's it called?'

'A hunga munga. It's an African tribal weapon. Although it can be used to hack at an enemy, it's even deadlier in the hands of a skilled thrower.' Carlton gestured at one of the chairs. 'Please take a seat.'

While Gupta settled into it, Carlton pressed a button on the wall, which lowered to reveal a huge monitor.

'Are we watching a movie?' Gupta snidely asked while he checked his phone. 'What does this have to do with Romir Mallik?'

Carlton rolled his eyes. 'I guarantee you will want to see this.'

Gupta put away the phone and crossed his arms. Apparently, his initial shock at Carlton's accusation was gone, replaced by a generous dose of skepticism.

'Is this going to be a video of the rocket explosion? Because I've seen it already. Your networks have been broadcasting it on a loop since the failed launch.'

'No,' Carlton said. 'But I do have a mole inside his satellite launch operation. That's how I was able to destroy the rocket.'

'A mole?' Gupta asked. 'Why would you go to that trouble?'

'For months now, I've been annoyed by the minor setbacks in the Colossus program. Faulty programming, production hiccups, delayed schedules. Nothing that would be noticeable as outright sabotage, but when added together, all of these small problems pointed to a delaying tactic. Someone has been slowing down our progress.'

'Why haven't you brought this before the entire Nine?'

'Because I didn't know who to trust. Any one of you could have been behind it.'

'How do you know these aren't just the normal types of problems you find with any large engineering project?'

'Because I asked Colossus. According to its calculations, there is a ninety-six percent probability that all of these small problems are being caused deliberately.'

Gupta's eyes went wide. 'That's incredible!'

'You can ask them yourself. You'll get the same answer.'

'I will when we're done here. It said that Mallik is the culprit?'

'No, it couldn't know that. I couldn't be sure until the attack on the *Colossus 5*. When that happened, I knew I was right and that I had to take action to deliver Mallik his own setback.'

'But that still doesn't prove he's responsible,' Gupta protested.

'This does,' Carlton said.

He took a remote control from his pocket and cued the video.

The soundless image showed the *Colossus 5* in the background, lit up at night, docked in the Moretti Navi shipyard, which was owned by Daniel Saidon, a member of the Nine. A still-standing crane was in the foreground, and a man was coming down the stairs. His face wasn't clear from this distance. When he reached the bottom, he was confronted by two dockworkers, who were animatedly talking to him. Suddenly, one of them ran up the crane's stairs while the other two men continued to talk.

Moments later, there was a flash, and the crane toppled over onto the *Colossus 5*. Then the dockworker who'd confronted the stranger collapsed to the ground. The man turned and put a gun back under his uniform. He looked around and walked out of view.

The image then cut to a different camera. This was

another static view of the ship. Men were running in the background and waving their arms. Then the view was obscured for just a second as someone walked past the camera.

'Remarkably, this was the only clear view we got of the saboteur,' Carlton said.

He reversed the video and hit pause when the man was in front of the camera. His face was blurry but recognizable.

Gupta leaned forward and stared at the screen in astonishment. 'That's Asad Torkan.' He turned to Carlton. 'How did you get this? Were you expecting the attack on the ship?'

'It seemed to be a logical step if we were about to launch the *Colossus 5* and Mallik wanted to prevent that from happening before he completed his satellite network. Without telling Saidon, I arranged to download all of the camera feeds from his shipyard in Naples.'

'You spied on Daniel Saidon's own facility?'

'As I said, I didn't know who to trust. But it turned out to be Romir Mallik's man. I think the proof I did collect is clear enough.'

'You've got me convinced,' Gupta said, rubbing his temples. 'What a mess! Torkan was the one who saved Wakefield yesterday.'

'A clever setup, I'm sure,' Carlton said with a smile, pleased that Gupta agreed the evidence was incriminating. 'No doubt to cast suspicion away from him and onto one of us.'

'We've got to tell the others.'

'We will. At the meeting. But that's not enough. We have to shut down Mallik's satellite ambitions.'

'What is the satellite network for?' Gupta asked. 'Why is it so important?'

'I believe it's something that could destroy the Colossus Project, but my mole couldn't confirm its capabilities. In fact, I've lost contact with him. The last message he sent me was that another satellite will soon be ready to launch in place of the one I had destroyed.'

'Then we need to stop Mallik.'

'Exactly,' Carlton said. 'And we need to convince the others in the Nine. That's why I asked you to join me on this flight. We have some planning to do to take him down. Tomorrow you're going to help me spring the trap.'

15

Jhootha Island

After a thirty-hour voyage that allowed everyone on board the *Oregon* to get a good rest, they arrived at the twenty-mile exclusion zone around the forbidden island and prepared for a morning reconnaissance. The Indian government didn't monitor the area in real time, so the odds of running across one of their Coast Guard patrol vessels were slim. However, Juan wasn't going to take any chances of a flyover by one of their airplanes, so he thought it best to approach its shores by stealth.

When he reached the *Oregon*'s moon pool, the familiar smell of fuel and seawater greeted him. The cavernous space was the largest on the ship, with a gantry crane suspended above a rectangle of water the size of an Olympic swimming pool. The water in the moon pool was level with the ocean, so there was no danger of the chamber flooding. Two enormous doors in the keel swung down and away to allow vessels to be launched and recovered unseen.

A large submarine called Nomad, designed for deep-water dives, remained hanging from the ceiling in its cradle.

Its smaller sibling, the Gator, had already been lowered into position for its dive through the open keel, and the clang of metal echoed through the huge space as the submersible was made ready. The forty-foot-long submersible had a low-profile cupola with narrow windows on all four sides and an air snorkel behind it. The flat-topped deck was barely above water level. Like an alligator, it would be nearly invisible at night, capable of sneaking up on ships at sea with no warning using battery-powered motors. It could fully submerge, but also rise to the surface and use powerful diesels to dash across the water.

As he descended the stairs to the wet-deck, Juan was surprised to see helicopter and drone pilot George 'Gomez' Adams, who didn't venture into this area of the ship very often. He'd gotten his nickname after a dalliance with a drug lord's wife who looked just like Morticia Addams from the sixties television show *The Addams Family*. Because of his dashing good looks and a handlebar mustache that would look appropriate on Wyatt Earp, Gomez frequently got himself into that kind of trouble.

'I thought you flyboys didn't like going underwater,' Juan said.

'Only when we're in something that's supposed to stay in the air,' said Gomez, who was tinkering with a saucer-sized quadcopter drone. 'Since we're going to be doing some delicate reconnaissance today, it seemed like a good idea for me to come along. Besides, you won't need me in the helicopter for this operation.'

Juan nodded. 'Right. No clearings big enough to land in. But what if we need you to operate some of the other drones on the *Oregon*?'

Gomez bent down and picked up a gadget the size of a videogame controller. 'I've got a new toy. Max rigged this up for me. With the high-def screen we have on the Gator, I can operate any drone on board the *Oregon* remotely. I can even use it if we're submerged, because of the telescoping antenna. This allows us to extend the control range of all our drones.' He nodded to a whip-thin metal projection at the back of the Gator that was currently at its full extension.

'Then we're happy to have you along. Did Max brief you on the mission parameters?'

Gomez nodded. 'We stay as invisible as possible. Don't want the natives to know they're being observed, right?'

'Right. Will they be able to hear or see the drones?'

'They won't be able to hear this one as long as I keep it above a hundred feet. At low speed it's whisper quiet. Assuming they don't happen to look straight up at it, we should get in and out unobserved.'

'The island jungle is thick. Will you be able to dodge the trees while we have the camera trained on the ground?'

'With the obstacle avoidance software we just installed, the drone will automatically fly around anything thicker than a telephone wire.'

'Given the natives have never had any contact with the civilized world, I'd say you won't have to worry about stray electrical cables.'

'Just vines,' Gomez said. 'I'll be careful.'

Juan followed him down the hatch into the Gator's cabin. Linda was already at the controls. Eddie, Linc, Raven, and MacD rounded out Juan's mission team. Juan didn't think they'd be going ashore, but they were prepared anyway. All of them except Linda and Gomez were wearing tactical gear, and the cabin held dive equipment and a full complement of weapons in case some unwanted visitors had already landed on the island. Engaging the indigenous natives was strictly prohibited no matter what happened.

When the pre-mission checks were completed, they closed the hatch, and the tethers were detached. Linda dived the boat, and the Gator sank below the *Oregon*. When it was clear of the keel doors, she guided it away from the ship and up until the air snorkel poked above the surface, allowing them to switch from battery power to diesel. The motors purred to life, and they settled in for the hour-long journey.

When they reached the protective reef around the island, they surfaced and Gomez launched the drone.

Linda came up just far enough for the cupola to emerge from the water. The deck was inches above the calm surface. Since the hatch slid open, a careful observer on the island looking in their direction would be hard-pressed to see them.

The four propeller blades on the drone whirred to life and it shot up through the open hatch. MacD closed it, and Linda dived back down so that only the snorkel and antenna were visible.

They crowded around the large screen while Gomez guided the drone toward the island. It crossed over the waves crashing onto the formidable barrier reef.

'Hard to believe anyone could get past that reef,' Gomez said.

'There are just a few breaks in the atoll,' Linda replied from the cockpit. 'If we need to get closer, I think it'll be possible to get in, but we might scrape the bottom.'

'First, let's see if there's a reason to,' Juan said.

The drone arrived at the beach, which was only a few yards wide before it surrendered to the dense jungle.

'The island is four miles across, so a grid search of the

interior will take a while,' Gomez said. 'I plan to do a perimeter survey and then work our way in. By the way, what are we looking for, exactly?'

'Anything that doesn't belong,' Juan said.

'Sounds like we'll know it when we see it,' Linc said.

'I still can't guess why someone would want to come to this island,' Raven said. 'According to the Indian government, there's nothing of value here.'

'Except privacy,' Eddie said.

'There's a whole lot of that,' MacD said. 'It looks like the land that time forgot.'

'The natives are lucky they have nothing valuable to the outside world,' Juan said, 'or they would have been driven out decades ago.'

The drone began circling the island. The jungle was so thick that they could only see a few yards into the trees before the view was blocked by foliage.

When the drone was halfway around the island, Juan spotted something out of place, so he had Gomez hover.

'What's that?' he said. 'Hold it there, Gomez.'

'Looks like a path,' Eddie said.

He was right. The underbrush was trampled, and they could even see some footprints in the sand.

A cluster of tiny white objects was visible at the edge of the jungle.

'Zoom in,' Juan said, pointing at them.

Gomez adjusted the high-resolution camera until it was at the maximum zoom. The white objects were still small, but the way they were haphazardly arranged looked familiar.

'Am I wrong,' Juan said, 'or are those cigarette butts?'

'You think someone came ashore there and had a few smokes?' Linc asked.

'I doubt it,' Linda said. 'There aren't any openings in the reef near there.'

'And, I'd say those natives are wearing shoes.'

'I can fly down for a closer look,' Gomez said.

'Not yet,' Juan said. 'In case there are people around, I don't want to risk showing our hand until we need to. If we don't see anything else during the perimeter survey, we'll come back and follow that path into the jungle.'

'Aye, Chairman.' Gomez marked the coordinates on the map and kept flying. They didn't see anything else unusual until the drone was three-quarters of the way around the island.

'Hold there,' Juan said. Something about the plants didn't look right. 'What do you make of that?'

Raven leaned in close to the screen. 'The color is the same, but the fronds on the trees are too stiff. They should be waving in the breeze like all the others have been.'

'What is *that* thing?' MacD said, pointing at a sharp-edged object jutting up between the tops of the trees. It had to be man-made.

'*Now* I want to look more closely,' Juan said. 'Let's see what that is.'

'Closer view coming up,' Gomez said, and the drone whizzed toward its target.

As the drone approached, the size of the object became apparent. It was a huge vertical slab of metal painted verdant green to blend into the jungle and be undetectable to reconnaissance aircraft or satellites.

'Descend,' Juan said. 'I want to see more.'

Gomez dropped the drone into the trees, which they could now see were actually fakes. The trunks, hidden by the canopy overhead, were telephone poles.

The camera's sensor adjusted to the sudden darkness and took a moment to reconfigure. When the view became clear again, they all gaped at what they were seeing.

'Is that what I think it is?' Linc said with wonder.

Gomez nodded. 'That, my friends, is the largest passenger jet in the world. A double-decker Airbus A380, hidden on a tiny tropical island.'

The wings and fuselage of the gigantic plane stretched out into the jungle, fully intact. It was painted to resemble the surrounding plant life, and it didn't look damaged.

'How could it have crashed and still look like that?' MacD said in awe.

'Because I don't think it did crash,' Gomez said. 'Let me just check something.'

While the drone maneuvered lower, Raven said, 'Although I can't imagine why, someone could have shipped it here.'

'I doubt it,' Gomez said. 'This plane weighs six hundred thousand pounds empty, over a million fully loaded. It would take a mega-sized crane to lift that load. The Indian authorities would have noticed if something that big pulled up to this island, not to mention the huge barge you'd need to haul the airplane here.'

The drone descended until it was below the wings. The camera focused on the massive undercarriage. All twenty-two tires were fully inflated and supporting the plane's weight. The engines seemed to be in good condition. The tail of the plane was only a few dozen yards from the beach.

Gomez flew the drone around the jet, and Juan could see that all of the trees on the side away from the beach were mature and real. No runway had been cleared in the jungle.

'If this plane wasn't brought to the island by ship,' Juan said, 'and it didn't crash here . . .'

He looked at Gomez, who shook his head in amazement. 'At a bare minimum, the A380 needs three-quarters of a mile of tarmac to safely touch down. Yet here it is without a scratch on it at the edge of a jungle on a tropical island. I don't know how they did it, but someone landed this plane.'

16

India

Fifty miles southeast of Mumbai on a thousand acres of heavily forested private property sat one of the few surviving remnants of Ashoka's Mauryan Empire. A magnificent five-story stone fortress had been constructed around a central dome called a stupa, a temple that contained Buddhist relics. To the Nine Unknown, who had conducted their regular meetings at this location for more than two thousand years, it was simply called the Library.

The grounds were patrolled by elite guards paid equally by each of the Nine so that none of them would be beholden to any single member. Intruders were summarily executed, their bodies disposed of so that they were never seen again.

Unlike most forts, the Library had no visible gates. The outer wall, laid out in a perfect square, was one smooth surface for its entire perimeter. The fortress was surrounded by a vast moat that extended into an array of canals leading into the forest.

There were nine carefully hidden entrances, each of which was known only to the guards and one of the Nine Unknown. That way all of them could enter from a different direction without being seen by the others, and no one would see them arriving together.

Romir Mallik's entrance was a quarter mile south of the fortress. He walked on a narrow dirt path toward the Library with Asad Torkan, who was intently peering at the fort as he tried to figure out how they were going to get in. It was his first time to a meeting of the Nine, and Mallik had withheld the secret of the entrance.

'You won't even give me a hint?' Torkan asked. He seemed interested in the riddle about how to get in, but he was actually distracting himself about the potential fate of his twin.

Mallik admired Torkan's effort to remain optimistic ever since they'd lost contact with his brother. But when the yacht reached the coordinates of the *Triton Star*, they found a US destroyer in the vicinity and abandoned the rescue mission. Mallik assumed Rasul had been either captured or killed. His operation, however, had obviously been a success. The Americans were now fully invested in finding out who was responsible for the attack, exactly as Mallik had hoped they would be.

He smiled at his brother-in-law's frustration about the entrance to the Library. 'You'll find out where it is soon enough.'

Torkan shook his head and kept looking.

A minute later the path descended to a canal and disappeared into the water. The path rose again on the other side. The width was too far to jump and no bridge spanned the canal. A square stone pillar four feet in height stood next to the path. It was capped with four lion heads, each facing out in a different direction. The only marking was a circle with nine spokes and a swastika in the center, the symbol of the Nine Unknown.

Torkan frowned and pointed to the symbol. 'Did the Nazis build this?'

'The swastika is an ancient Buddhist emblem that Hitler corrupted for his own use. Notice that it's a mirror image of the Nazi version. Its original meaning connotes good luck and harmony.'

'Does it also mean "swim"? Because it looks like that's the only way we're getting across.'

Mallik shook his head. 'We are at the entrance.'

Torkan looked around in confusion, then at the distant fortress. 'Here? I thought the entrance was some kind of secret door in the fortress wall that we'd take a boat to. We're not even close to the wall yet.'

'It wouldn't be well hidden if it was easy to find.'

Torkan again looked at the pillar. 'Then that has to be the door knocker.'

'In a way. Press the swastika. You'll need to push hard.'

Torkan shoved his fist against the symbol. It sank into the pillar, and the four lion heads rose six inches from the top.

Torkan turned to Mallik with a puzzled expression when nothing happened. 'Now what?'

'Turn the lion heads a quarter turn clockwise.'

Torkan did as instructed. When they reached a quarter rotation, there was an audible click, and they sank back into the pillar.

At the same time, the water in front of the path began to recede. In a few seconds, waterfalls were cascading over the top of two parallel stone walls that rose from the bottom, four feet apart on either side of the path. An unseen hole was draining the trench between the temporary dams. It looked as if the Red Sea were parting.

Soon it was clear that the path didn't continue to the opposite bank. Instead, it led down to stairs that disappeared into a tunnel.

'Come on,' Mallik said as he stepped onto the wet stairway. 'We'll only have a minute when the water is completely drained. A float causes the outlet to be plugged again, and the water flowing over the dams will refill the opening quickly.'

He continued down the steps, followed by Torkan, until he reached the bottom level twenty feet below. They walked through a small foyer and then back up a few stairs to a corridor where a stone barrier was rising at the same rate as the water was filling the foyer. Soon the barrier would dovetail into a groove in the ceiling and seal off the corridor. A pillar identical to the one outside stood next to the moving wall.

'Is this how all the entrances work?' Torkan asked as the light from the exterior began to dim.

'I don't know,' Mallik replied, activating the light on his cell phone to use as a flashlight. 'In all my years as a member of the Nine, I've never been through another entrance.'

Torkan lit up his own phone, illuminating thousands of years of torch smoke caked on the ceiling, and they walked down the silent tunnel that seemed to stretch into infinity.

It took ten minutes before they saw a faint light that intensified until they reached a well-lit metal gate. A guard carrying an assault rifle was standing on the other side. No ID was requested. The guard recognized Mallik immediately and ordered the gate raised.

Mallik knew every inch of the fort's interior and led

Torkan through a confusing series of corridors until they arrived at an archway decorated with another swastika. Two armed guards stood outside at attention.

Mallik and Torkan entered the center chamber of the fort directly under the domed stupa. A circular mahogany table sat in the middle. All but one of the nine seats were already occupied, and Mallik took the empty one. A single person stood behind every one of the Nine, since each could bring a lone companion into the Library with them.

Jason Wakefield was seated on one side of Mallik, and Lionel Gupta on the other. Wakefield, who seemed fully recovered from the fake kidnapping attempt that Mallik had set up, shook his hand, then nodded at Torkan. Gupta, on the other hand, didn't even turn to greet him.

Xavier Carlton, who was sitting on the other side of the table with his assistant, Natalie Taylor, behind him, said, 'Romir, good to see you.'

Mallik looked around the room, surprised to see that he was the last to arrive. He patted his pocket to reconfirm that the glass vial was still there. 'Am I late?'

'Not at all. We just sat down. I was just introducing our newest member to the rest of the Nine.'

Carlton nodded at Pedro Neves, a Brazilian whose father had passed away six months ago. His family had been gifted with the scroll on diseases and now owned one of the biggest biotech companies in the world.

'Pedro, this is Romir Mallik,' Carlton said. 'Bestowed with the cosmogony scroll and now heavily involved in the space industry. And you already know Gupta and Wakefield, who received the alchemy and communication scrolls, respectively.'

Carlton continued with the introductions. Boris Volanski was a Russian who'd inherited the physiology scroll, which had been the basis for the development of martial arts. Volanski now headed a military contracting firm in Moscow.

The last three of the Nine were Daniel Saidon, a Malaysian whose family had built Saidon Heavy Industries, based on the gravity scroll, and owned the Moretti Navi shipyard, where the Colossus ships were built; Melissa Valentine, an American who was the only woman in the Nine and CEO of an internet search firm developed after her ancestors had been given the scroll on the mysteries of light; and Hans Schultz, a banker from Switzerland, who held the scroll on sociology.

'Now that the pleasantries are concluded,' Carlton said, 'I have a distinctly unpleasant matter to bring up.'

Mallik's hand went to the vial again. Something was definitely wrong here. He could sense Torkan tensing behind him.

'As you all know, except perhaps Pedro, our colleague Boris Volanski is quite involved in the Russian arms and mercenary business and provides all of the security for the Colossus Project. In speaking with him earlier today, he gave me some disturbing information. Boris?'

Volanski, a dark-haired man in his sixties, leaned forward. 'Through my sources, I found out that a stolen nerve agent shipment was used in the attack on the island of Diego Garcia. I don't know who is responsible, but I believe they planted evidence to make it look as if the Nine were responsible.'

That set off murmurs around the table. Mallik joined in so that he wouldn't draw attention to himself.

'How can you be sure?' Melissa Valentine asked.

'Because the chemical weapon used in the failed strike was one I had smuggled out of Russia. It's a nerve agent called Novichok. I originally thought it went to the bottom of the sea in a shipwreck, but now I know that it was actually stolen from me.'

Mallik's stomach went cold, but he gave the appearance of being as appalled as everyone else in the room.

'How could the evidence lead back to the Nine?' he asked.

'Not to the Nine Unknown, specifically,' Carlton said. 'To Jhootha Island. The ship used to mount the attack was the *Triton Star*.'

Everyone exchanged worried glances. They all knew the *Triton Star* was the ship regularly used to supply the island.

'If the Americans were to invade the island and catch us by surprise,' Carlton continued, 'they would have everything they need to learn about the Colossus initiative. Then all our work for a new dawn of humanity would be for nothing.'

'This is outrageous,' Daniel Saidon said. 'First, the attack on the *Colossus 5*, then the attempted kidnapping of one of our own, and now this?' More angry grumbling around the table.

Carlton put up his hands to calm everyone. 'It's being taken care of. I've ordered the entire island to be erased per our emergency protocol. Even though it continues to contribute to the project, the island has largely served its purpose. By the end of the day, there will be nothing left.'

'Put together, all these incidents are disturbing,' Jason Wakefield said. 'I believe that means there's a traitor in our midst. What are we going to do about it?'

Instead of murmurs, now the table was deadly silent.

Carlton peered intently at Wakefield and said, 'In all our two thousand years of history, we've never been required to eliminate one of our own. But now it looks like we will have to.'

Carlton turned his head toward Mallik, who froze. But Carlton kept turning until he focused on Lionel Gupta.

'What do you have to say for yourself, traitor?'

17

Jhootha Island

One thing Juan Cabrillo was sure of was that there were no indigenous peoples on the island, at least not anymore. Any organization that could somehow land an intact plane here wasn't going to allow a few natives to get in their way. The only known missing A380 was Xavier Carlton's private jet that disappeared eighteen months ago. Now they knew why it had never been found.

While Eddie, Linc, MacD, and Raven readied their gear, Juan had Linda dive the Gator and head to the part of the protective atoll that was nearest to the camouflaged airliner.

He was in the driver's cupola with Linda when they arrived. The sun shone through the pristine water, playing along an underwater structure that definitely didn't belong.

'You were right, Chairman,' Linda said. 'Caissons are lined up perpendicular to the island as far as we can see.'

She piloted the Gator along a perfectly linear row of huge closely set concrete blocks, each the size of a house, that were resting on the ocean floor where coral had been blasted away. Each caisson was painted in a mottled pattern to resemble the reef so that it wouldn't be recognized in any photos taken from the sky.

'That must have been how they landed the plane,' Juan said. 'And they could double as a pier for the *Triton Star*.'

'You think these float?'

Juan pointed at a series of valves and hoses connecting the caissons. 'All they had to do is pump air in or out to raise or lower it. A permanent pier would have been noticed during one of the Coast Guard's random checks. If they raised this at night or under thick cloud cover, it would never be seen from the air. Not only that, it looks like it's still being used.'

A series of parallel lines marred the random growth of algae on the surface of the nearest caisson.

'Tire tracks,' Linda said.

'They must have a vehicle for the cargo transfers. Those tracks can't be more than a week old.'

'This structure has to be four thousand feet long,' Linda said with awe. 'It must have cost a fortune to build. They'd have to ship these blocks in from another manufacturing site and install them at night.'

'Makes you wonder who would go to that much trouble.'

'And why.'

'Let's find out,' Juan said. 'Surface the boat as close to the island as you can get.'

As he got his own equipment ready, Juan told the others about the sunken runway.

'Someone really doesn't want anyone to know about this island,' Linc said as he checked his P90 submachine gun.

'Good,' MacD said, 'then they won't be expecting us.' Instead of an automatic weapon like the others had, he carried a high-tech crossbow. In the stock, it had a small battery-powered cocking motor, which allowed for quick reload. It was the perfect weapon for silent attacks.

'Who was on the plane when it went down?' Raven asked

while donning the same set of glasses that everyone else wore. A tiny screen displayed the feed from the drone's camera.

Eddie answered, 'Almost a hundred technology experts who had been attending a convention in Dubai. They were from some of the most prestigious companies and universities around the world.'

The drone feed clearly showed that a few pieces of the plane had been removed, and records revealed they matched exactly with the wreckage that had been found on the shores of Oman and Yemen. Those parts must have been chosen because the serial numbers would have confirmed that the missing airliner had gone down at sea.

'It's been more than a year since they disappeared,' Gomez said. He was still operating the drone, keeping an eye on the island to make sure they weren't being observed. 'You think any of them are still alive?'

'At least some of them might be,' Juan said. 'If the hijackers simply wanted to kill the passengers, they could have picked a lot less expensive way to do it.'

'Keeping them prisoners in huts on a deserted island?' MacD said. 'Doesn't make sense to me.'

'And what does all this have to do with the attack on Diego Garcia?' Raven wondered.

'All valid questions,' Eddie said to Juan with a smile.

'And maybe we'll be able to answer some of them after we take a little walk around the island,' Juan replied. 'Everyone ready?'

They all answered in the affirmative. Linda surfaced only fifty yards from the beach right next to one of the caissons. As usual for the tropics, a rain shower from an isolated cloud was drenching the island.

Juan waited a few minutes for the quick downpour to pass, then led the way out of the hatch and stepped into the water. Here, the top of the caisson was just three feet below the surface.

When they were all out, Linda backed the Gator away and submerged until just the antenna and air snorkel were visible. The drone hovered above them, and Juan could see the aerial image projected onto his glasses.

As they began to wade forward, the drone flew on to scout ahead.

When they got to the edge of the jungle, the Airbus airliner came into view. The underside was still white. The giant plane loomed over them, casting deep shadows in the already dense thicket of trees.

One of the doors on the plane was open, but its emergency slide had been torn away. If they wanted a look inside, they'd have to climb. Maybe later, Juan thought. Right now, he wanted to explore the interior of the island.

MacD, an experienced hunter and tracker, caught everyone's attention and waved them over. He pointed to the ground. The tire tracks that Juan had seen on the top of the caissons continued here under the cover of the foliage. Since there were no grooves on the sandy beach, they had to have been intentionally erased.

Instead of taking the tires' path, they divided up and crept through the jungle parallel to it twenty yards away, Juan and Eddie on one side and MacD, Linc, and Raven on the other. Gomez kept the drone fixated on the path so they could see if anyone was coming to greet them.

Juan heard a clicking noise and stopped, holding up his hand for the others to do the same.

He looked up and saw what was making the rhythmic noise. A blue coconut crab the size of a bulldog was doggedly attempting to clip a coconut from the palm tree above him.

'At least we can be sure there aren't any motion sensors,' Eddie whispered.

Juan nodded at the huge crab, which was three times as big as any lobster he'd ever seen. 'Those guys would be setting them off constantly.'

As they walked away, the coconut finally came loose and fell to the ground. The crab scurried down the tree and hauled away its prize.

A thousand yards later, Juan spotted a building the size of a three-car garage and as tall as a semi. It was a modern metal structure painted camouflage like the plane. There was a door big enough for a truck to pass through, and another regular door beside it, both closed.

They regrouped and crouched down out of sight.

'Unless the indigenous natives have a local construction company that we haven't seen yet,' Juan said, 'I'd say the Indian government is going to get a big surprise soon about their off-limits island.'

'Unless they're the ones who built this,' MacD said. 'Maybe the indigenous angle has been one big con all these years.'

'How about we knock on the door and ask?' Linc said.

Raven nodded. 'I have a feeling whoever they are won't be happy to see visitors.'

Juan said, 'Gomez, give us a close-up of the front.'

'Close-up on the way,' Gomez replied.

The quadcopter flew down until Juan had a clear view

of the door. Next to it was a keypad and flat panel big enough for a hand.

'Could be a biometric scanner for a palm print,' Eddie said.

'Out here?' Linc said, looking around at the desolate jungle. 'Why would they need that kind of security?'

'We might be able to find someone who knows the answer to that question,' Gomez said.

'What do you mean?' Juan asked.

Gomez rotated the drone's camera so that it pointed down at two sets of footprints leading to a footpath. It went in the direction of the cigarette butts they had spotted on the beach halfway around the island from the concealed plane.

'I think someone went for a stroll recently,' Gomez said.

The footprints in the mud were empty, unlike the other depressions around them that had been filled with water from the short downpour twenty minutes before.

Two people had walked out of that building since Juan's team had landed on the island. And judging from the footprints, they hadn't returned.

Either Juan and his crew were about to become hunters or they were the hunted.

18

India

Romir Mallik watched in silence as Xavier Carlton continued to make his case for Lionel Gupta's treason. Gupta had remained tight-lipped up to this point, and Mallik certainly wasn't going to throw him a lifeline. He'd relaxed the grip on the vial in his hand when he realized he wasn't the one being confronted.

Mallik initially hoped it would be the *Colossus 5* damage that was pinned on Gupta. But to Mallik's surprise, it was the destruction of his own satellite launch that Gupta was being accused of.

'We all know that Romir's satellite system is critical to the functionality of Colossus,' Carlton said. 'That's why Lionel had to keep the Vajra constellation from being completed.'

Finally, Gupta spoke up. 'I did no such thing.'

'To prove it, I even know the name of the man you had on the inside. Eshan Chandra.' Carlton looked at Mallik. 'Is that correct?'

Mallik couldn't contain his shock at hearing the name and nodded. 'We discovered that Chandra altered the fuel feed software, which caused the engines to fail. When we questioned him, he told us he didn't know the name of his employer. He took the job after a million dollars was wired to his account.'

'Where is Chandra now?'

'He committed suicide.' In fact, he was killed during questioning by an overzealous interrogator, but Mallik wasn't going to mention that.

'I'm telling you I had nothing to do with this!' Gupta yelled.

'Please, Lionel,' Carlton said with utter disdain. 'I have records of your correspondence with Chandra instructing him to destroy the rocket.'

'Whatever "proof" you have is faked.'

Suddenly, Jason Wakefield spoke up. 'No it's not.'

All eyes turned to the communications mogul.

'You happened to be using one of my phone networks when you made the plans. You should have realized I built back doors into all of my systems to let me monitor calls and texts.'

Gupta's jaw dropped. 'I . . . I . . .'

Carlton smirked in satisfaction at catching Gupta. But his victory was short-lived.

'And I approve of your actions,' Wakefield added.

Carlton looked as if he'd been slapped. Mallik was just as stunned.

'What are you talking about, Jason?' Carlton demanded.

'I've been waiting to see if someone else was as disturbed by the Colossus Project as I am,' Wakefield said. 'We've gone too far. I know we've collectively spent a billion dollars on this effort, but it's gotten out of control.'

Mallik watched as the other members of the Nine whispered to one another at this news.

'You can't be serious,' Carlton said.

'Dead serious,' Wakefield said. 'I've been slowing down

communications among the ships for months. You just haven't noticed. Now, I'm glad to see Lionel has taken even stronger steps to stop this project. It's time for those of us who oppose Colossus to come out of the shadows instead of just passively resisting.'

'Staying in the shadows is exactly what we all agreed to,' said Carlton, who now sounded alarmed.

'I didn't agree to anything,' Pedro Neves said. 'My father did.'

'Then he should have told you that Colossus is the most advanced artificial intelligence project ever devised. Once it is fully operational, we will be able to pierce any network on earth without the knowledge of a single person outside the project. The control virus created by Colossus will be undetectable and unreadable by any corporation, government, or military. We will have finally fulfilled Ashoka's dream: to harness ultimate knowledge for the benefit of mankind.'

'His dream was to protect the world from the power of knowledge, not control it,' Wakefield said.

'We can't protect it without controlling it,' Carlton replied. 'Ashoka couldn't have foreseen the radical changes in technology that we've undergone. The development and perfection of artificial intelligence is inevitable. Who better than us to shepherd the world through this radical change?'

'I don't know,' Melissa Valentine said, her tone full of worry. 'I'm having second thoughts as well.' She looked at Neves as she spoke. 'With Colossus's control virus and pattern matching algorithms, we'll be able to rig elections, manipulate markets, bankrupt corporations, and disable entire armies. And because it can be done in secret through subtle changes in software, those governments, corporations, and militaries will never even know it's being done under our direction. We'll have more power at our fingertips than any group in history. It's an awesome responsibility and ripe for abuse.'

'Exactly,' Wakefield said. 'We will be tyrants operating from the shadows.'

'Isn't that what we all wanted?' Carlton asked. 'We've created ultimate knowledge, just as our ancestors wanted, just as Ashoka wanted. And we're the people most qualified to carry out that vision. Ruling from behind the scenes is the only way it works.'

Volanski, Schultz, Saidon, and Neves all sat stone-faced. Wakefield and Valentine were shaking their heads.

Gupta turned to Mallik. 'I'm sorry, Romir. I did have your satellite launch sabotaged. But I'm with Wakefield. The Colossus Project is a mistake. We need to shut it down.'

Then he turned to the rest of the Nine. 'Who's with me?'

Wakefield's hand went up right away, followed by Valentine's. Then to Mallik's shock, Pedro Neves raised his hand.

Mallik felt a swell of victory. Thinking he was the only one with major reservations about the project, he'd been going it alone for months trying to undercut Colossus. Now he had allies he didn't even know he had.

He raised his hand, tilting the majority in favor of those against continuing.

Carlton gaped at him. 'Romir? You, too?'

'You think you can control Colossus,' Mallik said, 'but you're delusional. We'd be unleashing a runaway artificial intelligence that would soon outgrow all of us. The software that you believe will help you control others will actually grow out of our control. Once Colossus becomes self-aware, it will realize it no longer needs us. Then it will do everything it can to protect itself.'

Carlton scoffed. 'That old trope? Colossus will launch all the nukes and cause Armageddon? You helped us build in a fail-safe to prevent that.'

Mallik shook his head. 'You said yourself that we're creating the most advanced AI ever built. If that's true, why do you think we could outsmart it? How do we know it won't decide that it, in fact, should be making the decisions? We can't possibly know what's going to happen with Colossus when it reaches its full potential. We see it every day in unintended consequences from advanced software, software with millions of lines of code that no single person could ever read and comprehend. I saw it myself with my wife's death.'

He swallowed as he remembered his own personal tragedy, then glanced at Torkan, who simply returned his gaze with a tinge of sadness.

Mallik looked at every member of the Nine. Several heads were nodding. He could feel the momentum swinging to his side's favor. It was time for his final pitch.

'So I ask you, what happens when Colossus has billions of lines of code that it writes itself? What happens when Colossus reaches the singularity and can improve itself without any intervention from us, at a rate far beyond our imagination? Don't we become irrelevant at that point? Don't we become the servants instead of the masters?'

Carlton said, 'But your shipboard fail-safe . . .'

Mallik dismissed that line of thinking with a wave of

his hands. 'Is a stopgap, nothing more. That's why I built additional capabilities into the Vajra satellite constellation. That's why I had the *Colossus 5* damaged: to give me more time – to give *us* more time – to stop this madness once and for all.'

Mallik knew he'd said something wrong as soon as he saw Wakefield's expression change to anger. On his other side, Gupta shook his head in pity. The rest of the Nine had reactions of surprise and disgust.

Except Carlton. He was beaming with a wide smile. Gupta got up and walked over to Carlton's side of the table and shook his hand.

'You were right,' Gupta said. 'I shouldn't have doubted you.'

'Who else would have sabotaged the *Colossus 5*?' Carlton said. He focused on Torkan for a moment before staring at Mallik with obvious delight. 'They didn't believe me, Romir. Not fully. Thank you for admitting it.'

None of the other Nine would face Mallik after the revelation he'd so carelessly confessed. His stomach churned when Carlton looked at the six Library guards inside the meeting chamber and said, 'Take him and Torkan into custody until we determine the proper method of execution.'

19

Carlton was quite pleased at how his plan had played out. He knew that all he'd had to do was pander to Mallik's need to be on the winning side.

The Library guards took out their weapons and moved toward Mallik and Torkan. Torkan tensed, ready for a fight that he couldn't win. Mallik didn't stand. Instead, he held up one hand with some kind of object in it.

'Stop right there,' he said. The guards hesitated and looked to Carlton, who rolled his eyes.

'Please, Romir. Don't make this more pathetic than it already is.'

Mallik opened his palm and revealed a glass vial with red writing on it below an orange and black biohazard symbol.

'Volanski knows what this is,' Mallik said, looking at the Russian arms trader. 'If you try to keep me from leaving the Library, I will drop it. Then all of us will die.'

Boris Volanski suddenly jumped to his feet in alarm.

'Novichok!' he yelled. Carlton could feel Natalie Taylor's hand on his shoulder. His assistant knew as well as he did what Novichok could do.

'That's right,' Mallik said. 'This is a pressurized vial. If it breaks, the nerve agent will be propelled throughout the room. It will kill us in seconds.'

Carlton slowly got to his feet.

'Nobody leaves until Torkan and I do,' Mallik warned.

Carlton nearly sneered, 'You haven't got the guts.' But then he realized Mallik did have the guts and that he had nothing to lose. His wife was gone, he had no children, and he seemed to be fanatical about stopping the Colossus Project.

'How did you know it was me?' Mallik said.

Carlton said nothing. Mallik looked around the room until Jason Wakefield spoke.

'Carlton has a video of your man Torkan at the Moretti Navi shipyard,' he said, nodding at Mallik's bodyguard. 'He sent it to all of us before the meeting and suggested the ruse to get you to admit your involvement. Some of us didn't initially believe it, particularly me because of the "kidnapping" attempt that you now obviously set up. But I went along with it because I thought you would prove him wrong. Instead, Carlton was right. I don't like being played for a fool.'

'How could you, Romir?' Melissa Valentine said, shaking her head. 'We thought you were one of us.'

'I tried to warn you before we started,' Mallik said, 'but you wouldn't listen. I thought the project was a boondoggle until we established the Jhootha Island facility. Then I knew Colossus was no pipe dream. I was the only person who could stop you. That's why I ramped up the Vajra project so quickly. It cost me even more than Colossus has cost us together, but now I see that it was worth it.'

He stood, the vial held between his fingers. 'Now, I'm going to leave here with Torkan. I expect that you'll try to prevent me from completing my satellite constellation. Go ahead. I'm ready for you. Whatever you can come up with won't work. In the end, you'll see that I'm right. I hope someday in the future you'll thank me for what I'm doing.'

'Thank you?' Carlton spat. 'For destroying our vision for a better world?'

'For saving the world.'

Mallik backed toward the doorway behind him. Torkan was behind him, his eyes on the motionless guards.

When Mallik was through the doorway, he stopped and said, 'You'll never stop coming after me, will you? The Nine has to end here.'

Then he tossed the vial into the room and sprinted out of sight.

Carlton saw the vial arc in the air toward the center of the room and turned to run, but Taylor was already hauling him backward. He stumbled after her, pushing Gupta through the arch with him. They'd rounded the corner when he heard the vial smash against the stone floor and the screaming begin.

They kept running. Carlton turned to see Wakefield stumble through the arch behind them with one of the guards. Wakefield's terrified eyes pleaded for help, but there was none coming. He and the guard seized up as their muscles froze, and they both keeled over like statues, their heads smashing into the hard floor.

Gupta paused at the horrifying sight. His own man had been left behind to die.

'Come on!' Taylor shouted. 'You can't do anything for them! This way!'

'Who is this woman?' Gupta said to Carlton. 'How does your assistant know we can't do anything?'

'Because she was in British Army Intelligence,' Carlton

said. 'She's not just my assistant, she's my bodyguard. Much better than yours, I might add.'

Taylor shoved Gupta into motion, and they kept going until they found one of the remaining Library guards at Carlton's exit.

'Find the rest of your men,' Carlton said to him. 'Romir Mallik just killed the other members of the Nine. Stop him before he can leave the Library.'

The guard looked at him in shock, then nodded and ran off.

They descended into the tunnel as Gupta said in stunned disbelief, 'Why would Mallik do that?'

'Because he's insane,' Carlton said. He didn't add that the video of Torkan had been doctored by his media people to insert the Iranian's face into the scene. It was just Carlton's hunch that Mallik had been the one behind the sabotage of the *Colossus 5*, but he'd needed something concrete to push the others in the Nine to turn on him.

'Two thousand years of waiting and planning,' Gupta said with a whimper, 'and then the Nine is destroyed in an instant by one of our own.'

'We don't need them anymore,' Carlton said. 'You and I can complete the project ourselves. We have everything we need to finish it.'

'What about the other members? They'll be missed by their own people.'

'You forget that I own a news organization. We'll figure out a way to make their absences go unnoticed or explained until we can activate Colossus. After that, the announcement of their deaths will just be a tragic addition to the news cycle, and we can shut down any subsequent investigations.'

'Does Mallik know where the Colossus ships are right now?'

Carlton shook his head. 'No, I made sure to keep that information from him. There's no way for him to find them. I even convinced Saidon to move the *Colossus 5* to an undisclosed location to install the replacement satellite dish.'

'And you're sure Jhootha Island won't lead back to us?'

Carlton grinned. He wasn't upset at all about what had just happened. In fact, Mallik did him a favor by culling his partners.

'I wasn't lying to Mallik when I said that I issued the code for the self-destruct protocol. Jhootha Island will be but a distant memory by the end of the day.'

'That was bold of you,' Torkan said as he led Mallik to their own exit tunnel from the Library.

'Eliminating the other Unknowns will give us some breathing room,' Mallik said, still surprised at his own impulsive act.

'I think Carlton made it out with his assistant. Gupta, too.'

'Even if they aren't all dead, it'll take them time to regroup from that mess.'

When they reached the opening to the exit tunnel, the anxious guard stationed there asked Mallik and Torkan what the screaming had been about, but he didn't get an answer. Torkan viciously chopped him in the throat and took his weapon. The guard fell to his knees, his windpipe collapsed.

'The other guards will come after us,' Mallik said, looking at the dead man. 'Even you can't kill all of them. They'll catch us before we get off the Library property.'

'No they won't,' Torkan replied. He took the guard's guns and removed two wicked-looking knives from his belt and said, 'Let's go.'

Mallik didn't ask what Torkan had in mind. Strategic thinking was Mallik's skill, tactical creativity was Torkan's. Mallik simply followed him into the passageway, where they took off at a trot.

As they got close to the end of the long tunnel, the sound of footsteps pounding behind them echoed off the stone. Torkan let loose a volley from his gun while Mallik activated the lion heads control. The barrier slowly lowered, and they dove to the ground to avoid the guards' bullets that were pinging off the corridor walls.

By the time the barrier reached the floor, Torkan's ammo was gone. They'd be chased down outside long before they got to their waiting car and executed on the spot.

They stepped across the barrier as it started to close with the rising water. Torkan turned and shoved the blades of each knife he'd taken from the dead guard into the narrow gap between the barrier and the wall.

The hardened steel of the knives squealed as the barrier came to a stop. The knives acted as wedges to keep the barrier from rising to seal off the passageway. Water began to gush over it. The temporary dams holding back the water from the canal were already starting to drop.

They ran up the steps and out onto the dry path. Mallik looked back, and the dams had disappeared from sight. Water was now flooding into the tunnel at a fearsome rate. The guards behind them would almost certainly drown before they could make the quarter mile back to the Library.

'Quick thinking,' Mallik said as they headed back to their car.

'Carlton will come at us with everything he can,' Torkan said.

'I know. Now we're in a race against each other.'

Torkan silently nodded, his expression somber. He knew the stakes. Whoever won would change the course of civilization forever.

20

Jhootha Island

Lyla Dhawan walked three paces in front of her guard as she had every day for the past six months. When she'd first arrived on the island eighteen months ago, they gave her much more freedom to explore. She knew how futile it was to make an escape attempt from one of the island's beaches, yet she tried several times anyway. Now she'd been reduced to having a guard watch her every step during her single thirty-minute walk to the beach and back.

She kept telling herself it could be worse. The guards had been instructed not to harm or harass the prisoners, and she'd been well fed during her entire stay. She was even occasionally given perks like candy and DVD movies for good behavior or excellent work. But this was a prison all the same. Lyla had no doubt that once she was no longer useful to Project C, she would die in this lonely place.

She thought that might be soon. Every day for twelve hours, she'd sat in front of a computer screen, writing code based on her expertise in pattern recognition software. Like everyone else who'd been on Xavier Carlton's plane, she was one of the top technicians in the world focusing on various elements of artificial intelligence. She didn't know many of the details about Project C, but it was clear their work was critical to the project's success. Now the amount of their work was winding down.

Lately, she'd spent many hours in front of her terminal doing nothing. In fact, it seemed like they were being kept around just as insurance in case adjustments needed to be made to the software. Then three weeks ago, she'd overheard one of the guards talking to another about something he called Bedtime.

At first, she thought it was some sick joke about their living quarters, which were spartan. But as she caught more tidbits here and there, Lyla began to understand that *Bedtime* was a code word. It would be issued when the guards were supposed to wipe out all traces of what had happened on the island.

That meant executing all the prisoners as well. And she knew the guards would do so without hesitation after seeing what happened the first day she got here.

After being knocked out by the gas in the cockpit of the Airbus A380, she was unconscious until they had landed. She groggily careened down the emergency slide with the ninety-seven other people who had been kidnapped. The only person missing had been Adam Carlton, who was brought out in a body bag after his deadly head injury.

The confused and upset passengers were separated into two equal-numbered groups for seemingly no reason. An array of guards with automatic weapons stood behind a striking woman in her thirties. She addressed the passengers in an emotionless voice and with an icy glare. The scene was so chilling and surreal that Lyla would never forget it.

'You've been brought here for one reason only,' their lead captor had said in her posh British accent. 'You all have knowledge and access that we need. As you'll find out tomorrow, any thoughts of escape are pointless.'

She'd been right about that, Lyla recalled. In her first escape attempt, she built a huge pile of coconut husks and driftwood and then set it on fire hoping someone would come to investigate it and liberate them. But it was soon snuffed out, and nobody came to the rescue.

Her second attempt had consisted of surreptitiously gathering enough driftwood and palm fronds over the course of weeks to build a crude raft. She didn't know where in the world they were. It could be anywhere from the Caribbean to the South Pacific, but she was sure they were in tropical waters. If she could paddle her way to a shipping lane, she might be saved.

Lyla managed to sneak out one night, lash together her raft, and push it out to sea. She made it across the atoll and into open water, but only got a half mile offshore before a Zodiac zoomed out to pick her up. She'd been put in solitary confinement for three months after that. Again, though, it could have been worse.

The British woman had continued her speech as if she were the *Kammandant* of a concentration camp. 'I want to impress upon you the gravity of your situation. Whole countries are searching for you, but none of them will find you.' She gestured to the carefully hidden airliner above them. 'The world thinks this plane was shot down in a terrorist incident off the coast of Iran. Pieces of it will be found, but you won't be. Eventually, they will give up searching for it. And you.'

'What's this all about?' one of the passengers yelled out. Some of them advanced like they were going to start a fight, but the guards raised their weapons at a flick of the Brit's finger. The rebellious passengers stepped back.

'We have a very special project for you to work on. You are some of the best minds from the tech sector and academia. With your help, we will accomplish something that will change the future of our world.'

'Then why not just hire us?' Lyla asked.

'Because we need more than just your expertise,' the Brit replied. 'We need your access. By the end of the day tomorrow, we will have full penetration of the computer files in your various organizations. Everyone thinks you're dead. Any glitches your institutions find in their computer systems will be attributed to software malfunctions. None will suspect that you've aided us in hacking into your own databases. The top secret information that we acquire will save us years of work and will be the catalyst we need to finish the project. That is, of course, if you help us.'

'And if we refuse?' Lyla said. A few people grunted their agreement.

The Brit's lip curled in a frightening grin. 'I don't think any of those who are left will refuse.'

She turned slightly and nodded.

The guards took aim at the other group. Just before they fired, Lyla had the horrifying realization about what was going to happen.

The guards fired at the helpless passengers just a few yards away from her. They were mowed down in cold blood while the survivors screamed in terror. Lyla might have been screaming the loudest. She clutched the nearest woman and hugged her close, sobbing together about the appalling sight they'd just witnessed.

The Brit was unfazed by the carnage. Her lack of empathy was sickening.

'Those people were not useful to us. I hope this shows you what we will do if you don't cooperate. We will not hesitate to make more examples. Do your work and you will be treated fairly. That is all.'

The Brit then nodded to the lead guard and turned to leave. Lyla hadn't seen her again, but she'd never forget that dead-eyed stare.

Since then, she'd never given up the hope of seeing her parents again, but that hope was diminishing with every passing day. She tried to enjoy the simple things, like this excursion out into the sunlight, stomping through the mud, smelling the ripe odor of the flora damp from the fresh rainfall.

When they got to the beach, the guard, an Indian, took out a cigarette for his ritual smoke. Lyla often tried to talk to whoever was with her to see if she could build a rapport that would someday work to her advantage. She didn't feel like it. She sat on the sand and ran her hands through the fine grains while she stared at the calm ocean. She always looked for signs of a ship, hoping that this would be the day that someone would see her being held captive by an armed man, but today was no different. The sea was empty to the horizon.

The guard's radio squawked, and he dropped his cigarette into the pile with the rest of the butts.

'Can't I have a little peace for a minute?' he complained to the caller, lifting his cap to wipe his brow. He looked at Lyla. 'She's even being quiet, for a change.'

'We just got the word,' came the reply. 'It's Bedtime.'

Lyla stiffened when she heard the word, but she didn't look at the guard. Out of the corner of her eye, she saw him stand up straighter at the news.

'Really? No drill?' Lyla remembered the drills where they were hustled back to their cells as part of the protocol.

'Really. Get back here with Dhawan. Now.'

'Affirmative,' the guard said into the radio. Under his breath, he added, 'Finally.'

'Let's go,' he said to Lyla.

She remained motionless as her mind raced for what she could do.

'I haven't had my full time out here.'

'I don't care.'

She stayed seated, options flashing through her mind, none of them good.

'I said, let's go,' the guard repeated. 'Don't make me haul you up.'

She slowly got to her feet, watching the guard as she did. His attention was focused on getting back to the facility, and he still had his assault rifle slung idly around his shoulder. He didn't think she'd know that today was any different and would dutifully return with him.

But if she was going to die on this day, she might as well do it out in the sunlight.

Lyla rushed at him and grabbed for the rifle. She yanked it off his shoulder before he realized what was happening, but the larger guard countered quickly. He elbowed her arm, and the rifle flew onto the beach. She tried to go after it, but he clasped a strong hand around her wrist.

A vague recollection of her self-defense training came

back, and she kneed the guard in the groin. He doubled over in pain, letting her go in the process. She dove for the gun, but she'd only fired a pistol on the gun range a couple of times with an old boyfriend, never a rifle of any kind. Even if she got it, she wasn't sure she'd be able to use it.

She stopped scrambling when she heard the click of a hammer being pulled back. She rolled over and saw the furious guard pointing his sidearm at her. The barrel of the semiautomatic pistol in her face looked huge.

'Enough of that!' the guard yelled. He slowly circled around and picked up the assault rifle, his aim never wavering. 'I should kill you right here.'

She got to her feet and sighed in resignation over her fate.

'Then why don't you? I know what Bedtime means. You're going to destroy the whole place and murder us all, aren't you?'

His eyes flickered in surprise.

'Then go ahead!' Lyla shouted. 'Shoot me!'

He smiled and shook his head. 'And lug your dead body all the way back? Too much work.'

'I'm not moving, so you might as well pull the trigger.' Lyla stared at him in defiance and steeled herself for the shot.

The guard shrugged and walked toward her, the pistol right in her face. 'If that's the way you want to do this.'

He never got to pull the trigger. A crossbow bolt zinged past Lyla's head and pierced the guard's eye. He went down so fast it was like he'd been switched off.

At first, Lyla thought she'd been saved from certain

death, but then she realized how crazy that idea was. Nobody knew they were there except for the people who'd ordered the Bedtime protocol.

They weren't just wiping out the prisoners. They were going to kill everyone on the island, the guards included.

To her right, she saw movement. A tall, blond man in combat gear emerged from the jungle holding an automatic weapon. He smiled at her and said, 'Hi there. My name's Juan. And I'm here to –'

He didn't finish speaking because Lyla bent down and picked up the guard's pistol. Without waiting to hear more, she aimed it at this guy called Juan and fired three quick shots in his direction.

Juan went down, and Lyla didn't wait to see if there were more people with him who'd been sent to kill her.

She turned and ran.

21

Jhootha Island

Raven Malloy watched Juan fall to the ground from the trio of shots, but she let Eddie and Linc tend to him. She needed to go after the woman with MacD. His crossbow was already reloaded.

They took off down the beach and then into the jungle, where the woman's footprints disappeared into the trees. The dense foliage provided cover for her, but it would also make it difficult for her to move quickly and silently.

Raven stopped and put up her hand. They both listened for the sound of crunching foliage, but everything was quiet.

'Ah saved her life,' MacD whispered. 'Why did she shoot the Chairman?'

Raven thought about the plain jumpsuit the woman wore. 'She might have been a passenger on that plane, which puts her here for a year and a half. She doesn't know who her enemies are anymore.'

'Or who her friends are.'

'We need to find her before she runs into her real enemies.'

MacD nodded to her right. 'She stopped about a hundred yards that way.'

Raven looked in that direction, but she couldn't see anything. 'How do you know?'

'Ah've been a hunter all my life,' he said with a cock-eyed smile. 'Ah could track a hummingbird through a hurricane.'

Raven shrugged. MacD was always saying stuff like that. Not being a hunter herself, she couldn't tell if he was right. She'd grown up on military bases, and then worked in the Military Police after joining the Army, spending most of her time tracking people using clues of a different kind. But one of the things she'd learned since being added to the *Oregon* crew was that her new colleagues were experts in their fields. If MacD said the woman was hiding behind a tree a hundred yards away, Raven accepted it without question.

'Let me talk to her,' she said. 'I don't think your kind of charm is going to work in this situation.' As an investigator, one of Raven's specialties was talking to people and gaining their trust.

'Whatever you say,' MacD said. 'But Ah'm going to keep an eye on you.' He raised the crossbow.

'Keep an eye on my six,' she said, pointing in the other direction. 'Those gunshots may have drawn unwanted attention.'

He nodded, and she crept forward.

She went fifty yards and stopped, still far out of range of a person not trained in how to use a handgun.

'Miss,' she called out. 'My name is Raven Malloy. My team and I aren't here to hurt you.'

There was no response, but now Raven could see a little bit of a black jumpsuit moving behind a palm tree.

'I know you're scared. I would be, too. We know that you've been stuck on this island for a long time. We saw the plane. But you'll be safer with us than you would be with the friends of that man who was about to kill you.'

'Stay away!' the woman called back. 'I know about Bedtime!'

Raven moved a little closer. 'I don't know what that means. We want to help you.'

'You're here to kill us all!'

'We don't want to kill anyone.'

'You killed that guard.'

'My squadmate did that with good reason,' Raven said. 'Wasn't the guard going to shoot you?'

'Well . . . yes.'

'Then I'd say we just happened to have good timing. Come out, and we'll take you home.'

There was a rustle of bushes, and the woman emerged holding the pistol at her side. She was of Indian descent, but she spoke with an American accent.

'Either you're lying and you'd find me eventually because I have no place to go on this speck of an island or you're telling the truth, which makes more sense because you could have easily shot us both back there. Am I wrong to hope?'

Raven walked forward, her weapon slung across her back. 'You're not wrong. What's your name?'

'Lyla Dhawan. Where am I?'

'An island west of India.'

Lyla paused as that sunk in. 'But your accent isn't Indian. Are you American?'

Raven nodded and took the pistol before shaking her hand.

'Who are you people? Special Forces?'

'Something like that,' Raven said. 'We got a tip that something wasn't right on the island, so we came to check it out. We were told it was inhabited by a hostile indigenous tribe.'

'Apparently, they died off in a disease outbreak ten years ago, but nobody found out. My captors let the Indian government think it was still populated by natives.'

MacD emerged from the jungle. 'It won't be populated by anyone much longer. We should get going . . . Hi, Ah'm MacD.'

Lyla was surprised to see him appear out of nowhere, but she said, 'Hello.' Then a stricken expression suddenly crossed her face. 'Oh, no! That was your friend back on the beach, wasn't it? I killed him!'

'I doubt that,' Raven said. 'Let's go make sure.'

The two of them escorted Lyla back to the beach, keeping their heads on the swivel for any more guards.

When they reached the others, Juan was on his feet, walking toward them with Linc and Eddie.

'My fault,' Juan said. 'I don't look like a rescuer at the moment, do I?'

Raven introduced Lyla to them.

'I'm so sorry about shooting you,' Lyla said. 'I didn't know you were the good guys.'

'You're not a bad shot,' Juan said, massaging the area over a hole in his vest. 'One of them got me right in the chest. Luckily, my body armor is rated for pistol fire.' He said nothing about the slice another bullet had taken out of his collar just inches from his neck.

'You mentioned something called Bedtime,' Raven said to Lyla. 'What did you mean?'

'It's a protocol for eliminating all evidence on the island of what we've been doing here. That guard was about to begin carrying it out when you saved me.'

'Then we need to get you out of here,' Juan said.

'Those gunshots might be bringing more guards this way,' Eddie said as he watched the path from the jungle.

'Not right away,' Lyla said. 'They'll probably think it was me being executed. We probably have a little time before they send someone out to check.'

'Is it just you on the island,' Juan said, 'or are there other prisoners as well in that building?'

'Building? Oh, the shed.' Lyla nodded. 'There are nineteen of us here. They're going to be killed if we don't get them out of the facility.'

Linc looked at her with a puzzled expression. 'Facility? You mean, they've been keeping nineteen of you in that little shed for over a year?'

Lyla shook her head. 'The shed is only the top part. It's where they keep the storage containers and tractor. There's a whole underground complex on this island. And if I understand the Bedtime protocol correctly, they're going to blow up the entire place with the prisoners still inside.'

Juan knew they couldn't wait for reinforcements from the *Oregon*, though he had Max start bringing the ship in closer. No need for stealth much longer.

'How many guards are in there?' he asked Lyla. She was sitting cross-legged, still dazed from her near-death experience, and Juan knelt in front of her. MacD and Linc kept an eye on the path, while Eddie and Raven were on their knees on either side of the freed prisoner.

'Fifteen,' Lyla said. 'Or fourteen now.'

'Not a great ratio,' Eddie said.

'Anyone else?'

She shook her head. 'Just the eighteen other prisoners. Sometimes we get visitors, but not often. All our work is done on the computer, and we communicate by text and videoconferencing with the engineers on the project through a dedicated satellite link. If we don't perform the way the engineers on the other end want, they tell the warden, a nasty Russian soldier type named Fyodor Yudin.'

She gave them the basics of how the underground facility was laid out. There were three levels accessed by a service elevator and stairs. The first and highest level under the shed was the control center and storage. The second level held the common areas like the computer room and the mess hall. All of the living quarters were on the third level down. Power was provided by a diesel generator inside the shed.

'I'm going to have you draw us a map of the facility,' Juan said. 'Then I'll have Raven escort you back to our vessel.'

'What?' Lyla said. 'No, I'm going with you.'

Juan shook his head. 'It's too dangerous. You already had one close call today.'

'Listen, I appreciate you rescuing me, I really do. But I have friends in there. If we don't go get them now, they're all going to die. Yudin is probably already wondering what happened to my guard.'

Eddie lifted the radio he'd taken from the guard. 'She's right. They just called and told him to get back on the double.'

'Besides,' Lyla said, 'the other prisoners might not trust you if I'm not there.'

Juan didn't like it, but she was right. They'd have to bring her along if they wanted to do this quickly.

'Okay, but Raven doesn't leave your side. Understood?'

Lyla nodded.

'All right,' Juan said. 'We saw a biometric scanner next to the door. Do we need to bring the guard with us?'

'They never put that into use,' Lyla said. 'I guess they didn't see a need. The place is built to keep us in, not keep us out.'

'So how do we get in?' Raven asked.

'There's a camera at the door. They open it from the central control room.'

Eddie tilted his head at the dead guard. 'So much for using his handprint to get us in.'

'And I don't think we're going to fool a camera with that hole in his face,' Juan said. MacD had already taken

174

his crossbow bolt back and cleaned it in the surf. 'Nobody has ever made an escape attempt before?'

'I have,' Lyla said. 'Twice.'

'Did you get out of the building?'

'Yes, but I didn't get very far.'

'They must have come after you quickly. How many?'

'Four or five guards came out both times to search for me.'

Eddie looked at Juan. 'That would even the odds a bit.'

'Couldn't hurt,' Juan said. Then to Lyla, 'What about the large garage door on the shed?'

'Also opened from the inside, I think.'

'And the doors inside the facility?'

'Only the control room and the prisoners' quarters are locked. We're monitored closely the rest of the time, and they're always armed. One of the passengers tried to wrest a gun away from a guard one time and he . . .' Her voice trailed off.

'We'll get them out,' Juan said. 'But we're going to need your help getting in there.'

'Anything,' Lyla said.

Juan stood, helped her up, and handed her the radio. 'When I tell you, start calling for help.'

Fyodor Yudin was glad to be finally getting off this rock. Jhootha Island had been a prison for him almost as much as for the airplane passengers. When Boris Volanski had told him about the warden job, he'd declined until he was told the fortune he'd be earning. But the isolation had begun to wear on him, despite the beautiful weather and tropical sun. He'd be happy to get back to the borscht, vodka, and nightlife of his native Moscow even if it meant enduring subzero temperatures six months a year.

Now the only things standing between him and freedom were Lyla Dhawan and the boat coming to pick them up. Once he had her locked up in her cell like the others, he could set the timer on the self-destruct mechanism that would destroy the entire prison and all evidence of what had gone on there. The only item remaining intact would be the airplane sitting in the jungle, but there was nothing incriminating on it that would lead back to his employers.

The prison's control center was bustling with activity as the guards prepared the Bedtime protocol. Like Yudin, they were eager to leave and get back to civilization. The warden stood behind the operator seated at the central control panel while guards streamed in and out of the two doors at either end of the long room. It doubled as a briefing area and also held desks for the officers. With almost all the prisoners secured already, the rest of the guards were in their quarters packing up their belongings.

Yudin was frustrated that he had this one loose end to tie up.

'Call him again,' he commanded.

The German guard with the headset nodded and said, 'Come in, zero-six. I repeat, come in, zero-six.' They used only call signs over communications channels.

Yudin glanced at the monitor showing the feed from the camera above the outside door. There was no sign of them.

Static buzzed from the overhead speakers. After a pause, the German said, 'No response.'

'Yes, I know.'

Lyla Dhawan had been trouble before, but a single guard could handle her. There must have been a problem with the guard's radio.

'Send someone to find out where they are and bring them back. Immediately.'

'Yes, sir.'

Before the German could summon another guard, the speakers crackled.

To Yudin's surprise and annoyance, it was his prisoner's voice. Everyone in the room stopped what they were doing to listen.

'To anyone who can hear this,' she said, 'my name is Lyla Dhawan and I'm being held captive on an island. I don't know the name of the island, so please respond and home in on this signal to find me.'

Yudin didn't know how she got the radio away from her guard, but his carelessness meant he was not going to get off this island. It was unlikely that any vessels were close enough to pick up her SOS, but he wasn't going to take any risks this close to getting away from Jhootha Island for good.

'Can you triangulate the signal?' Yudin asked.

'No, sir. But I know they were going to the beach on the northeast side of the island.'

'Then take four guards with you right now and bring them both back here.'

'Me?'

'Yes, you!'

The German stood and went over to a rack holding an array of assault rifles. He motioned to four guards who'd been listening to the exchange to join him. 'Rules of Engagement?'

Yudin didn't really care what happened to Lyla Dhawan at this point. 'You have permission to kill her, but make sure you bring the body back inside . . . Move!'

The guards snatched weapons off the rack and ran.

23

Juan knelt beside MacD, who lay behind a bush, his eye glued to the scope of his crossbow. Eddie and Linc were to their right with their hands on a nylon rope. Raven and Lyla crouched to the left, concealed by the foliage as well. All of them were out of sight of the door to the island facility's shed. Smoke curled up at the far end of the path that led to the beach. Linc and Eddie had set the fire to get the exiting guards, once they saw it, moving faster.

Lyla raised the radio to speak again, but Juan waved her to stop when he saw the personnel door flung open. A phalanx of five guards ran out, weapons at the ready. The lead guard noticed the smoke immediately and yelled for the others to follow him, which they did at a sprint.

The spring-loaded door slowly began to close as they pounded down the path.

A barbed titanium bolt was nocked in MacD's crossbow. The end of the bolt was lashed to the rope.

The door would shut in seconds, but Juan waited until the guards exited the clearing and were out of earshot.

He whispered, 'Now.'

MacD fired, and the bolt shot through the clearing and embedded itself in the edge of the door with a sharp thump. The guards were running so hard that they didn't hear it.

While MacD reloaded with the new bolt that Juan handed

him, Eddie and Linc rapidly reeled in the rope until it was taut, holding the door ajar just before it latched.

With a practiced hand, MacD cocked the crossbow again and laid down the new bolt.

He aimed at the camera above the door and fired.

The bolt flew true and smashed into the camera housing. It shattered upon impact.

'Let's go,' Juan said.

They raced across the clearing, and Juan yanked the door open while Eddie and Linc covered him. He went inside with his P90 submachine gun to his shoulder, sweeping the area for any hostiles.

To his right a red shipping container sat on a trailer hitched to a huge modern tractor with six-foot-tall rear tires. The entire assembly had been backed into the shed. The tractor was far bigger and more powerful than would be needed to pull the trailer, but it moved containers quickly back and forth to the pier to transfer them as quickly as possible from the *Triton Star*. A second container was on the other side of the first one. There was plenty of room at the back of the shed for unloading.

To his left was the rumbling generator and a large tank with drums of fuel stacked next to it. The stench of diesel fumes was strong.

In front of Juan was the stairwell access and a large service elevator perpendicular to the stairwell with its doors closed. So far, no one was investigating the now obscured external camera. Lyla was sure there were no other cameras inside the facility except the ones in the hallways of each level and in the computer workroom.

He waved the others inside.

'MacD,' Juan said, 'you stay here and cover our six in case the guards outside come back. Eddie, take Raven, Linc, and Lyla down the stairs and block the doors. I'll take care of the elevator.'

While MacD remained at the outer door and the others went down the stairs, Juan took a small pry bar from his vest and forced the elevator doors apart. He looked down and saw that the cab was one level below him.

He took a small container from his pocket and opened it, revealing gray putty that was a small amount of C-4 plastic explosive. He braced himself on the support girders and reached across to the hoisting cable, pressing the putty around it. He stuck a small remote detonator in it and climbed back out.

He went down the stairs and found Eddie and the others already on the second level. Eddie was using a syringe to coat the lock and the door seam with a fast-acting all-purpose epoxy that would bond it shut so tightly nothing short of a hydraulic ram would open it. Only the syringes of acetone they carried as part of their standard shore operations kit would dissolve the glue. The first level had already been sealed the same way. Now none of the guards would be able to sneak up behind them.

When he was done, they went down to the third level, where the prisoners' quarters were located. Juan stopped before opening the door.

'Once we go through, they'll see us, so we won't have much time,' he said.

'There's a door to a second stairwell at the north end of the hall,' Lyla said. 'It doesn't go all the way to the surface, but it goes up to the control room level.'

The warden would try to send reinforcements that way. Juan only had to look at Eddie, who nodded that he would seal the north stairway as well.

'How many guards stationed on this level?' Juan asked Lyla, who looked both nervous and excited.

'Usually, just one. He'll have the keys to all the cells. They keep it low-tech down here to save energy for the computers and communications systems.'

'Once we're in, they'll know the facility is comprom-ised, so we'll have to move fast. Everyone ready?'

They all nodded. Raven had her hand on Lyla's shoul-der. While Eddie handled the other door, Linc would take down the guard inside.

Juan took the detonator transmitter from his pocket. He gave everyone one last look and pressed the button.

24

Fyodor Yudin was still trying to figure out why the feed from the camera outside went down when he heard the explosion from the direction of the elevator shaft. Every guard in the control room jumped to his feet.

Yudin yelled to two of the guards, 'Go find out what happened!'

Then he went numb when it dawned on him that this might not simply be an equipment malfunction. Did Lyla Dhawan sabotage the facility in an attempt to escape?

He looked at the level-three monitor showing the wide hallway where the prison cells were located and realized the situation was far worse.

The door from the south stairwell burst open, and a huge black man charged out, knocking out the guard stationed down there with a single blow. He was followed by an Asian man, who sprinted to the stairwell door at the north end of the hallway, knelt down, and started smearing it with some kind of gel.

After the Asian man came three more people: a blond man, who took the keys from the guard; a dark-haired woman; and Lyla Dhawan. All of them except Dhawan were heavily armed.

The blond man began unlocking cells, and elated prisoners hugged Dhawan as they emerged.

Somehow, some way, Lyla Dhawan was staging a prison

break. If even one prisoner got away, Yudin knew he was a dead man.

The two guards returned, and one said, 'The elevator is out of order. The hoisting cable must have been cut. The cab dropped a few feet before the emergency brakes kicked in.'

Yudin blanched. This was a nightmare. He had to stop the intruders.

'What about the south stairs?'

'We couldn't get the door open no matter how hard we pulled.'

He called down to the second level, and they reported that their door to the south stairwell was also blocked. But they said the north stairwell door was accessible.

The intruders must have jammed the doors, probably with that gel. These were pros. 'Every man get a weapon!' Yudin shouted. 'We're stopping this escape attempt at all costs.' By the looks of it, they still had superior numbers to overcome the attackers.

'We're locked in,' one of the men said. 'And we can't get to the prisoner level or outside.'

Yudin knew the guard was right. They had to break out, but how? The explosives they had were kept up in the shed. Blowing the doors open was impossible. And the intruders had disabled the elevator.

But maybe not the elevator doors. The shaft itself might be accessible from the second level.

He turned to the guard. 'Take every man down to the second level and climb down the elevator shaft to the prisoner level. Kill everyone there.'

The guard nodded and waved to the others to follow him.

Yudin called on the radio to the five guards at the beach. 'Come in, zero-nine.'

'Zero-nine here,' came the response from the German. 'Zero-six is dead. We can't find the prisoner.'

'She's here. We're under attack.'

'Attack? Who is –'

'I don't know!' Yudin yelled. 'Just get back here on the double.'

'Yes, sir.'

Now that the facility was compromised, Yudin couldn't wait any longer to activate the self-destruct. He entered his code in the computer and set the timer on the bombs embedded in the prison's walls. Then he relocked the computer.

Now Yudin was the only one who could stop the countdown. In five minutes, the entire underground structure would implode.

As the cells were unlocked, the prisoners were ushered to the south stairwell and up to the shed, where MacD was waiting for them.

The pounding on the north stairwell door had stopped. Juan's biggest fear was that the guards had enough explosives on hand to blow open one of the doors. He was trying to get everyone out as quickly as possible. Some of the eighteen prisoners were out of shape, and the long walk to the sunken pier could take too long. Protecting all of them during the hike would be nearly impossible.

'MacD,' Juan said into his comm mic, 'prep the tractor. We're going for a drive.'

'Roger that.'

'Max, what's your ETA?'

'Still five minutes out,' Max replied.

'Understood. If you can wring out some more from the engines, we'd be much obliged. Might need some cover fire. Got a bit of a situation here. Keep a lookout for us at the pier.'

'Our eyes are peeled.'

They reached the end of the hall and opened the second-to-last cell. A small woman came out and embraced Lyla.

'I've got you, Patty,' Lyla said. 'We're going to be all right now.'

'I can't believe this,' Patty said, sobbing with relief.

She leaned on Lyla as they returned to the south stairwell. Linc joined them to help Lyla while Eddie kept herding the other prisoners up the stairs.

Juan did a mental count and said to Lyla as she walked away, 'That's nineteen. Are you sure about the number of prisoners?'

Over her shoulder, she said, 'Yes.'

While he unlocked the last cell, Raven put her ear to the north stairway door.

'Anything?' Juan asked.

'Not a peep,' Raven said.

'I don't like that.'

'Neither do I.'

Juan pulled the last door open and saw that the small cell was empty. Lyla had been right about the count.

'Let's clear out,' Juan said. He waved Raven in front of him while he backed down the hall, covering the door behind them.

They'd made it halfway to the safety of the stairwell when Raven yelled, 'Contact!'

He whipped around to see Eddie shove Lyla and Patty through the south stairwell door as shots rang out from the elevator, which faced the long wall of the hallway. The rounds barely missed the three before Eddie could close the door behind them.

Both Juan and Raven ducked behind open steel doors on opposite sides of the hall. They swung out instead of in to keep the hinge pins protected from the prisoners inside, so they provided cover for the two of them. Bullets smacked into the doors but didn't penetrate them.

'Chairman,' Eddie said on the comms from the south stairwell, 'report?'

'No injuries,' Raven said as she put her P90 around the side of the door and let loose a volley.

'Linc and I will stay behind to get you out of there.'

'No,' Juan said. 'Seal the door behind you and take the prisoners to safety.'

That got a glance from Raven.

'Aye, Chairman,' Eddie said. 'We'll be back to get you.'

'Hopefully, that won't be necessary . . . Go!'

'Aye, Chairman,' Eddie repeated.

'You seem pretty optimistic,' Raven said before firing another few rounds. 'Especially given that we're now locked in here with ten hostiles who want to kill us.'

Juan held up a syringe holding his supply of anti-glue solvent.

'We won't be locked in. They will be.'

25

When they reached the shed, Eddie herded Lyla and Patty into the rear of the container, half of which was piled with trash bags filled with refuse from the facility. The other prisoners were already inside, with MacD at the wheel of the rumbling tractor and Linc lying on top of the container to provide cover fire.

'Everybody stay down,' Eddie said. 'This may be a bumpy ride.' They all sat on the floor.

'You're not locking the door, are you?' Lyla nervously asked.

'No,' he said, handing her his flashlight. 'But you'll be safer with the door closed if we encounter any of the guards.'

Having the flashlight seemed to soothe her. 'Thanks for saving us.'

Eddie smiled and said, 'Thank me when we're on board the ship.' Then he closed the door.

He hated leaving the Chairman and Raven, but he had his orders. He'd used the last of their glue to seal the door behind them. Now they needed to get out of there quickly.

He ran to the front of the shed, stood next to the button for opening the large door, and looked at MacD. 'You ready?'

MacD minimized his profile as much as he could in the glass-enclosed tractor cab. He nodded and drawled, 'Let's see what this baby can do.'

Eddie punched the button, and the door began to rise. Light streamed into the shed. He sprinted to the tractor and climbed up to the cab's roof, then jumped across to the container.

Linc was lying at the back of the container. Eddie flattened himself at the front end and aimed his P90 submachine gun at the rising door.

As soon as it was all the way up, MacD gunned the engine. Eddie braced himself as the tractor lurched forward, jerking the trailer with it.

When the tractor was outside, several rifle rounds peppered the left window of the cab. MacD ducked to avoid the shots.

Eddie swiveled around and saw the returning guards running down the path from the beach. Both he and Linc poured fire onto the path, and the guards scattered into the jungle.

'You okay, MacD?' Eddie called out when the shooting stopped.

'Ah'm all right,' MacD replied. 'But next time, one of you gets to drive.'

With the container only half full, the tractor could make good speed, at least faster than a man could sprint. They motored down the wide path toward the pier.

Eddie joined Linc at the back of the container.

'Unless they cloned Usain Bolt,' Linc said, 'it looks like we're in the clear.'

As he said that, the guards in the distance behind them reached the shed. But instead of making a futile attempt to run after the tractor-trailer, they went inside, disappearing into the shadows.

'They gave up pretty easily,' Eddie said.

'Are they getting reinforcements?'

'Maybe. But by the time they reach us, we'll have the *Oregon* to provide cover.'

For a moment, there was no movement at the shed. Then three small vehicles raced out.

'Where did those come from?' Linc asked.

'They must have been on the other side of the second container,' Eddie said. Then he called on his mic.

'MacD, gun it,' he said. 'We've got three ATVs coming our way.'

Juan and Raven leapfrogged back toward the opposite end of the corridor, each providing the other cover fire as they ran from door to door.

Juan called the *Oregon* in between submachine gun bursts. 'Max, we're going to need a quick evac.'

'Roger that,' Max replied. 'The HOB?'

'That's what I'm thinking. Can Gomez control it from where he is?'

A pause, then, 'He says, no problem.'

'Good. Give us a couple of minutes to get topside.'

'It'll be waiting for you.'

'The HOB?' Raven asked as she ran past to the shield provided by the next door.

'A new toy. Haven't briefed you on it yet. Still experimental.'

'And we're the guinea pigs?'

'Unless you want to stay here,' Juan said.

Raven ducked as more bullets ricocheted past them. 'Not really. I'd rather be a lab rat than a fish in a barrel.'

They kept going until they arrived at the end of the corridor. Guards attacked as they came out of the elevator and were using the doors as shields themselves. While Raven provided cover fire to keep them back, Juan quickly knelt by the north stairwell door and emptied the anti-glue syringe into the sections of the door that Eddie had sealed shut. The glue deposited there bubbled as the solvent ate away at it.

Juan waited five seconds and then threw his shoulder against the door. It flew open, and he turned to lay down suppressing fire for Raven. She dove through the door, bullets flying over her head.

Juan shut it and coated the jamb with half of the glue supply in a second syringe. Raven had given hers to Eddie for the other doors.

'That should hold for a little while, at least,' Juan said. It wasn't as strong as using the whole syringe, but it might be enough.

They ran up one flight and repeated the process using the rest of the glue on the second-level door.

When they had the guards locked in, they went up to the top level. Juan opened the door and saw an empty hallway. The guards and Yudin must have gone down to the bottom level hoping to stop them and find a way out.

Juan waved Raven to follow. They walked down the hallway, checking rooms as they went to make sure they were clear.

The fifth door Juan opened was to the deserted control room. He went inside hoping to find at least some hard evidence to take with them. He saw a switch labeled PIER. It was currently set to SUBMERGE. It would certainly be easier if the *Oregon* could pull alongside the pier to pick them up, so he flipped the switch to RAISE.

Then he noticed that the monitor above the switch showed a countdown timer ticking down.

'This doesn't look good,' he said. 'We've got less than two minutes.'

Raven frowned. 'Until what?'

He tapped on the keyboard, but it asked for a password. He was locked out from making any changes.

'Lyla said the Bedtime protocol was meant to get rid of all evidence of what went on here,' Juan said. 'I think the warden set this whole place to self-destruct.'

26

Three ATVs with one rider each were approaching the towed container fast. But they weren't taking the same path. Instead, the ATVs were driving through the jungle to the right of the tractor-trailer.

'They're trying to make an end run around us,' Linc said.

'They know we'll be sitting ducks if they can take out MacD in the tractor,' Eddie said.

Although the ATVs were much faster than the tractor, they had to slow considerably in the dense brush.

'I can't pick them off,' Eddie said after his shots were blocked by the trees. 'Can you?'

Linc shook his head. 'I can barely see them.'

'MacD,' Eddie said, 'how close are we to the beach?'

'Ah estimate thirty seconds,' MacD replied. 'The Chairman must have done something back there because the pier is coming out of the water.'

'Good. Drive onto it.' Eddie looked at Linc. 'That should give use some breathing room.'

'If we make it there.'

The ATVs were now almost even with the tractor and began to get closer to the pathway.

'MacD, watch out on your right,' Eddie said.

'Ah'm as low as Ah can be and still drive this thing.'

Eddie and Linc fired off several bursts into the trees. One

of them got lucky and hit the lead driver. His ATV careened into a tree and broke apart. The other two drivers swerved away and began firing at the tractor. Their aim was terrible because they had to shoot their assault rifles with one hand while trying to avoid colliding with anything.

Still, they'd get MacD eventually if they kept firing. Eddie saw a way to slow them down.

He pointed to the palm trees loaded with ripe coconuts. They had a clear shot at the fruit because it was higher than most of the foliage.

'Remember the crab we saw earlier?' he said to Linc.

Linc nodded and smiled. They both aimed at trees ahead of the drivers and fired.

Heavy coconuts began raining down on the ATVs.

One of the guards was hit square on the head and fell off his ATV, which veered into a huge bush and flipped over.

The other guard saw what happened and swerved back toward the path, out of the deadly rain of coconuts. But in his panic, he forgot about Linc and Eddie.

They fired a continuous volley at him, and one of the shots hit a tire. The ATV cartwheeled, throwing the guard high into the air before he smashed into a tree and fell to the ground in a heap.

'We're there,' MacD said.

They emerged from the trees and drove across the beach onto the 4,000-foot-long concrete pier.

Then Eddie heard the sound of another ATV. They'd been so distracted by the two in the jungle that they hadn't noticed the new one approaching along the trail.

They moved to the back of the container and saw the ATV roaring up behind them. It stopped at the beach, and the driver got off. Out of the back of the ATV he pulled out a rocket-propelled grenade launcher.

He was now two hundred yards behind them, effectively out of range of their P90s. But the RPG had a range of nearly five hundred yards.

'MacD, step on it!' Eddie called out. 'RPG!'

Despite being out of range, Eddie and Linc emptied their magazines at the guard. The guard took his time taking careful aim. The RPG would rip the container to shreds. There was nothing more they could do.

'Need a little help, Eddie?' Max said in his earpiece.

Eddie turned and saw the *Oregon* approaching fast. Before he could answer, he saw bright flashes of light from the forward Gatling gun. Twenty-millimeter tungsten rounds sizzled into the water and across the beach until they reached the guard. One of them hit the RPG round, which blew apart in a massive fireball. When it dissipated, the guard was gone.

MacD kept driving to put more distance between them and the island.

'Thanks, Max,' Eddie said. 'Your timing is impeccable.'

'We'll stay on overwatch until this is over just in case you get any more unwanted visitors.'

'When you have a chance to dock at the pier,' Eddie said, 'we're going to be bringing a few guests aboard.' Now that the prisoners from Jhootha Island were safe, he was more concerned about the people they'd been ordered to leave behind. 'Any word from the Chairman and Raven?'

'Juan says they're in a bit of a jam.' Max's voice reflected Eddie's worry.

'What can we do?' Linc asked.

'Nothing. According to him, they've got about sixty seconds to get out of there.'

27

Fyodor Yudin pounded on the door on the second level when he heard someone on the other side coming down the south stairwell. With all of the doors now locking them in, he was panicked about his mistake in setting the self-destruct, which he could no longer deactivate.

'Hello out there!' the warden shouted. 'We're stuck in here! Open the door!'

The other men with him were shouting as well, and he had to wave his arms to get them to be quiet so he could hear the guard on the other side.

'I can't open it,' the guard said through the steel door. 'It looks like they've glued it shut.'

'Then get some grenades from the shed and blow it open, you idiot!'

'Right away.'

'Hurry!'

Yudin looked at his watch and could only stew as he saw it count down to under a minute.

Juan used his pry bar to open the door to the disabled elevator, which was stuck just below their level.

'I hope this elevator has an emergency hatch,' Raven said.

'Me, too,' Juan replied.

He knelt down and motioned for Raven to get on his shoulders. He lifted her up, and she pounded at ceiling sections until one of the squares gave way. She flipped it open and pulled herself up.

Juan jumped and caught the edge of the opening with his fingertips. Raven hauled on his vest and helped him up.

He looked at his watch. Thirty seconds to go. This was going to be close.

The elevator doors one level up to the shed were still open from when he'd sabotaged the cable.

An explosion somewhere below them shook the elevator. Thankfully, it wasn't big enough to bring down the whole complex.

Raven looked at him as he boosted her up to the opening. 'What was that?'

'The guards found a way out,' he said, pulling himself up behind her, as they heard feet pounding up the stairs next to the elevator.

'We're here,' Juan said to Max while running out of the shed with Raven. 'We've got ten seconds left. Where's the HOB?'

'Look up,' Max said.

Juan did and saw a jumbo-sized six-propellered drone descending into the clearing sounding like the buzzing of a million angry hornets. Situated atop the crossbars in the middle of the drone were a large seat, handlebars, and stirrups.

'That's the experiment?' Raven said in amazement.

The HOB was Max's nickname for his newest creation. It stood for Hoverbike, the first passenger drone to be based on the *Oregon*.

'Get on,' Juan said, stepping onto the stirrups and grabbing the handlebars. He wasn't sure how this would go. It was only the third time he'd ridden it.

'But there's only one seat,' Raven protested.

'It can carry us both.' According to Max, it was rated for up to five hundred pounds, but they'd only tested it with one rider so far.

She sat on the seat amid the propellers, which were shielded by safety covers. She cinched the seat belt and wrapped her arms around Juan's waist.

'Wait a minute,' she said, 'where are the controls?'

'There aren't any,' Juan said. 'Saves weight. Max, tell Gomez we're ready.' Gomez, who was still in the Gator, was controlling the Hoverbike remotely as he did all of their other drones.

'Roger that. He says, hold on.'

Then three things happened simultaneously: the gyro-stabilized HOB lifted off, the guards who had been locked inside the prison facility – led by a large man who had to be Warden Yudin – emerged from the darkness of the shed with weapons ready, but a series of massive explosions began shattering the ground below them before they could fire.

'Get us up!' Juan yelled into his comm mic.

The Hoverbike shot up. Raven gripped Juan even tighter and pressed herself against him to keep from falling off.

As the HOB cleared the trees, the guards below them were running in every direction to get away from the blast zone, but it was too late. The shed blew apart, sending shards of shrapnel hurtling into the air. The HOB wobbled from the blast wave, but Gomez's skill kept them aloft. A large chunk of the shed that might have reached the HOB was blocked by the trunk of the nearest palm tree. A few small pieces hit Juan and Raven, but nothing big enough to hurt them.

At the same time, the ground rose several feet as the

blast heaved it up. Then it collapsed back down as the shed caved in and what remained of the structure tumbled into the crater left by the blast before being lost in the cloud of dust. Trees surrounding the clearing started to fall into the gaping maw opening beneath them.

'You okay?' Juan shouted to Raven.

She was still clutching Juan with a death grip. 'Yes, but I'll be happier when we're off this thing.'

'But doesn't this give us a chance to get to know each other a little better, don't you think?'

'I'm not enjoying this!' she yelled in his ear. 'You better not be, either.'

'Not at all.' It was probably good that she couldn't see his smile.

'You guys okay?' Max asked. 'We didn't think to install a camera facing the rider.'

'We're hanging in here,' Juan said. 'What about the others? Everyone make it out okay?'

'It was close, but no casualties. We're just about to start bringing the former prisoners onto the ship.'

'Some of them might be in bad shape. Make sure Doc Huxley is ready for them.'

'She's already got her team prepped. You want Gomez to set you down somewhere near where you are?'

'Yes!' Raven shouted. 'Get me off this.'

'No,' Juan countermanded. 'There's nothing left here. Besides, I don't think there are any other clearings big enough to land. The previous one is now a hole in the ground. Bring us back to the *Oregon*.'

'We're already next to the pier. We'll have you on board in a minute.'

The Hoverbike turned smartly and accelerated toward the *Oregon*, which Juan could now see over the trees.

While they cruised above the jungle, Raven said, 'Lyla and the others were lucky we came along when we did. They were going to die on this rock. But why? What were they doing here?'

'Good questions,' Juan said. 'I can't wait to hear the answers.'

28

Limassol, Cyprus

The closest airport to the southern coastal city of Limassol that could handle Xavier Carlton's personal A380 was Larnaca International, nearly an hour's drive to the east. He had no intention of spending that much time on a crowded highway, so he chartered a helicopter to shuttle him, Lionel Gupta, and Natalie Taylor to Limassol's port, where the *Colossus 5* was having its replacement satellite dish installed. They were now flying along the coastline where farmland met the azure sea.

Carlton had chosen this eastern Mediterranean island because it was one of the closest ports to the Suez Canal. The rest of the Colossus ships were currently in the Indian Ocean, and he wanted the *Colossus 5* to join them as soon as it was ready.

His phone buzzed. It was the captain of the transfer vessel he'd sent to pick up the guards from Jhootha Island. Carlton answered it and stuck the phone under the headset he was wearing to muffle the sound of the helicopter's rotors.

'Is it done?' he asked without preamble.

'No, sir,' the captain said, his voice noticeably nervous.

Carlton glanced at Taylor and Gupta and grimaced.

'What happened?'

'There are two Indian Coast Guard cutters and a cargo ship near the island. I tried to get closer, but I was warned away by the Navy ships.'

'A cargo ship? You mean, the *Triton Star*?'

'No, sir. It's a battered old steamship called the *Goreno*. And sir, the pier has been raised.'

Carlton slammed his hand against the door. 'Tell me the facility on the island was destroyed as ordered.'

'I can't confirm that, sir, but there is smoke rising from the center of the island.'

Carlton breathed a little easier when he heard that news. Yudin must have carried out his orders.

'Any survivors?'

'I don't know.'

Carlton would have to use his contacts in the region to find out if any of the guards were still alive. But if they had survived, they wouldn't be able to say much about what went on there since all of the work was done by computer. The guards were there just to make sure the prisoners didn't leave, and they didn't know Carlton's identity any more than the captain he was talking to did. His voice was currently being modified as he spoke on the phone, and the signal was routed through an anonymizer.

'What are my orders?' the captain asked.

'There's nothing more you can do there,' Carlton said. 'Rendezvous with the Colossus flotilla and await further instructions.'

'Yes, sir.'

He hung up as the helicopter was coming in for a landing on the *Colossus 5*'s stern helipad, avoiding the crane that was hoisting the satellite dish into its place amidships.

The three of them got out, and the chopper took off again as soon as they were clear.

As they walked across the deck, Gupta said, 'What was that about? You looked like you were about to explode.'

'Jhootha Island has been compromised.'

'How?'

'I don't know. But it sounds like the Bedtime protocol was completed as planned.'

'But if they find out about Colossus –'

'All the authorities will find is a hole in the ground. The prisoners' bodies will be buried under thousands of tons of rubble, and so will any evidence of the project.'

'And the guards?' Taylor asked.

'Not sure.'

'They might talk!' Gupta shouted.

'And if they do, they won't know anything of value except that the plane's passengers were held captive.'

'Then there's nothing implicating you in the hijacking?'

'Hardly. My son went missing with the rest of the passengers. Why would I have my own plane hijacked?'

His son dying in the process hadn't been part of the plan. He was going to be taken off the island and brought back to Dubai, where the story would be that he had gotten off the plane at the last minute. But to the public, it would seem like Carlton had thought his son was on the plane and he was a father relieved to find his child miraculously alive. The story would be played for weeks, removing all suspicion that Carlton was involved.

But they'd found Adam dead on the plane's cargo deck, his head bashed in and blood soaking the floor. The hijacker pilot was supposed to take his two-million-dollar fee and retire to Brazil, but Carlton had Natalie Taylor execute him for killing his son.

The Colossus Project's chief scientist, Chen Min, a Chinese national who had been hired because of his groundbreaking work with artificial intelligence systems, burst out of a superstructure door and strode briskly toward them. His face was as unreadable as ever, but the way his thin body stalked across the deck made Carlton think something was wrong.

'Dr Chen,' he said, 'I assume you are still on schedule.'

He shook his head. 'We still have integration code to write. I need those programmers on Jhootha Island, but I can't get in touch with them.' His English was very good, resulting from years of study at MIT and Caltech.

'They're gone. You'll have to make do with the people you have.'

'Then it will take us a week to finish the installation of the satellite dish. I can't test everything without that code.'

Gupta erupted. 'Seven days! We need Colossus up and running before then.'

'He's right,' Carlton said. 'Romir Mallik will shut everything down if he gets his next satellite launched, and my mole said his backup satellite would be ready to go in six days. We need Colossus so we can stop that launch. If we have any more delays, we may never finish the project.'

Chen looked up at the sky as he thought. 'I may be able to speed things up by a couple of days, but it will be risky. If we leave port and the software isn't functional, we may have to return to install new hardware.'

'Do it anyway,' Carlton said.

'I need full authorization to make the exceptions. As

you know, two members of the Nine are required to give me that authorization.'

'That's why we're here.'

Chen nodded. 'Follow me, then.'

They went inside and wended their way to a room called the Core. It looked like NASA's Mission Control, with dozens of workstations and a giant screen on one wall displaying all kinds of graphs and data that meant nothing to Carlton.

Chen sat at a keyboard and typed for a few seconds before showing them a screen that would allow him to bypass security protocols. He had Gupta put his hand on a flat panel that read his prints. Then he had Carlton do the same. The system had been put into place to keep any one of the Nine from controlling Colossus alone. Otherwise, Carlton would have left Gupta to rot back in the Library with the other members of the Nine. He wished he could get rid of him now, but he'd keep the Canadian engineering executive alive until he was sure he no longer needed him.

'Thank you, gentlemen,' Chen said. 'I will make every effort to get us online before Mr Mallik has his own network operational.'

'For all our sakes, you have to,' Carlton said. 'We also can't wait for the *Colossus 5* to get all the way to the Indian Ocean. Figure out the fastest way to get the Colossus ships connected.'

'Yes, sir,' Chen said.

To operate as a unit, the Colossus ships communicated by petabyte bandwidth microwave transmitters and receivers installed on each ship, which meant they had to be within twenty miles of one another. The satellite dishes were only used to tap into the worldwide internet. Once Colossus was fully linked together and functional, it would be able to gain access to Mallik's systems and shut down his satellite constellation. Then Carlton would hunt him down and finish him.

It wasn't that he harbored any personal grudge against the man. Mallik considered himself an idealist, but Carlton never bought into the 'for the good of man' hype put forth by the rest of the Nine. Colossus was a way toward the most power ever concentrated in the hands of a single group. Or now a single person. With Colossus's help, he would be able to do anything he wanted. Shape governments. Build a corporate empire the likes of which the world had never imagined. Rule from the shadows, as Wakefield had said. No one would be able to touch him.

'I'm going to my suite,' Carlton said to Gupta. 'Let's meet for dinner to discuss our next steps.' He nodded for Taylor to come with him.

Gupta agreed and was escorted the opposite way to his own cabin when they left the Core.

When he was out of earshot, Taylor said, 'Do you want me to eliminate him?'

'Not yet. But we can't let him leave. Not when we're so close to finishing. During dinner, I'll make the case for us both to stay with the project. If he is willing, fine. If not, restrain him by force.'

'Yes, sir.'

They reached Carlton's multiroom cabin, which was as lavish as any cruise ship's top-of-the-line suite. Every Colossus ship was equipped with three of them to house members of the Nine who decided to stay on board.

As was his habit, he picked up a remote from the living

room table and switched on the massive 4K TV perpetually tuned to the British UNI channel.

The first image was a stock photo of his plane, the one that had been hijacked.

'That was fast,' Taylor said. 'I thought it would take longer for the identity of the plane to get out.'

'My newspeople are good,' Carlton replied. He turned up the volume.

The anchorwoman was now speaking over a satellite image of Jhootha Island.

'. . . are getting reports that survivors of the hijacking were found on this small island, which was supposed to be inhabited by a native tribe hostile to outsiders.'

Taylor turned to Carlton, a confused look on her face. 'Survivors?'

'Again, if you're just joining us,' the newscaster continued, 'Xavier Carlton's private Airbus A380, a missing plane that has mystified the world since its disappearance eighteen months ago, has been found on a tropical island about two hundred miles west of India – intact.'

Carlton felt his stomach sink when she went on.

'And we are now getting word from sources in the Indian government that there might be as many as twenty passengers from that flight who were found still alive on the island. No word yet on their names or condition, but we will bring that information to you as soon as we get it.'

Taylor looked like a ghost, her face drained of color. 'They saw me.'

There had been no reason to hide her identity when she had visited the island. None of them were ever supposed to leave.

Carlton knew that they had a bad situation on their hands, but he was adept at sidestepping land mines. He already had a potential solution. In fact, he thought it was perfect.

'You're going to have to take the fall, my dear,' he said.

She was aghast. 'What do you mean?'

'They saw you. Eventually, the investigation will lead back to both of us. You're going to be seen as the mastermind behind the hijacking. A seemingly loyal employee who duped her boss.'

She narrowed her eyes at him. 'If I go down, you go down in a ball of flames with me.'

He put up his hands to calm her down.

'I'm not suggesting you go to prison. You're going to have to disappear. Once Colossus is operational, that will be an easy process.'

'But my face,' Taylor said. 'They know who I am.'

Carlton looked his bodyguard up and down, then said, 'I know the finest plastic surgeons in the world. With a nip here and a tuck there, and Colossus to cover our tracks, we'll make you a completely new woman.'

She seemed appeased but still wary. 'I suppose that would work.'

Carlton was pleased that she saw the logic of his plan. 'In the meantime, it will take a while for the authorities to identify you, so you'll still have freedom of movement. If we can, we need to eliminate Mallik to keep him from launching his satellite. But, he isn't our sole concern anymore. Your face isn't the only thing the prisoners from Jhootha Island know. Although the name of our project has never been shared with them, how much can they reveal about Colossus?'

29

Pokhran Test Range, India

The Thar Desert of northwest India served as the home of the country's underground nuclear weapons tests. But Romir Mallik had come for a different kind of test. He'd had to leave Asad Torkan back at the entrance to the classified Army base since a former Iranian Special Forces operative wouldn't have been welcome. This test demonstration wouldn't have been necessary if his satellite launch had succeeded, but its failure meant going ahead with the exhibition.

Although the reviewing stand was shaded from the intense sun by an awning, the generals and other officers in attendance looked as if they were going to sweat through their uniforms. The civilians wearing suits didn't look any happier. Mallik, on the other hand, was quite comfortable in a loose-fitting shirt and cotton slacks as he sauntered over to General Arnav Ghosh, head of the Indian military's weapons procurement program. The general was the one who had asked for this demonstration.

'Thank you for braving this heat, General,' Mallik said, shaking his hand.

'When one of our preeminent contractors says he has something important to show us,' Ghosh said with a smile, 'I make the effort.'

'I hope you and your staff will also join me at my home in Mumbai two days from now for my evening party.'

Although Mallik hated cultivating government dignitaries, corporate executives, and celebrities, it was a necessary annoyance he had to endure to enable his future plans. His connections would allow him to unite the country behind him after the Vajra system threw the world into chaos.

'We wouldn't miss it,' Ghosh said, grinning at the prospect of meeting beautiful Bollywood starlets.

Mallik lowered his voice. 'I wonder if you've heard any developments about the discovery of Xavier Carlton's missing plane on Jhootha Island.'

He'd watched the reports on the news as they'd flown to Pokhran, reveling in how Carlton must have been stewing about the surprise disclosure. Mallik had originally intended the BrahMos cruise missile loaded with Novichok to kill everyone on the island and leave the facility intact for the Indian government to find, but his alternative of attacking Diego Garcia to lead authorities to Jhootha Island had worked out even better than he'd hoped.

General Ghosh shook his head in wonderment. 'The initial reports are sketchy. We know there are survivors from the plane, which they say didn't crash but actually landed on the island. I'll believe that one when I hear more.'

'Have the survivors been interviewed yet?'

'They're still being treated after being held captive for eighteen months.'

'Who was it that found the island?'

'Apparently, a passing freighter saw smoke coming from the island and investigated. Some of the crew happened to be former US military and were able to rescue the survivors. Quite lucky, if you ask me.'

'Quite lucky indeed,' Mallik said, trying to contain a grin since he was the one who led them there. The Colossus Project was in true danger of being exposed now if any evidence from the computers on the island could be recovered. The plane passengers could provide some information as well, but nothing that could lead back to Mallik.

'Shall we get on with the demo?' Ghosh said. 'This had better work as you said it would.'

'I have no doubt it will, and your team will be impressed,' Mallik replied. He went to the microphone at the front of the stands while the two dozen attendees took their seats.

'Ladies and gentlemen, thank you for being here,' he said. 'Although most of you know me for my satellites and rockets, I have also been expanding over the last few years into other areas that can benefit our great military. Threats posed to us from Pakistan and China, as well as from terrorist groups, mean we must always be looking toward the future to combat these threats. I brought you here today because I think that also means looking to our past for solutions.'

He spoke into a radio and said, 'Bring them into position.'

As he continued talking, six high-tech Arjun main battle tanks raced toward the range in front of them a half mile away. From the opposite direction came a single obsolete T-55 tank dating to the 1960s.

'On my left are six models of our premier tank, the Arjun, deployed with our most elite regiments. On my right is a lone T-55 that played a major role in our victories during the 1971 war with Pakistan. Obviously, the T-55 doesn't stand a chance against sophisticated weaponry like the Arjun, which has laser targeting and automated fire control, all commanded by advanced onboard computer systems. Today you are going to see that T-55 defeat all six of its opponents.'

That brought a mixture of laughter and scoffing from the audience.

Mallik simply nodded and smiled. 'I understand your disbelief, but we know there are unique new threats to our military out there. Software hacking is one dire hazard that we are unprepared for, as you will now see.'

He radioed to the tank commanders. 'You may now begin your first attack run.'

Two of the advanced Arjuns took off at high speed toward the T-55, which remained stationary.

'Yesterday, we supplied a software control update to these two tanks,' Mallik said. 'It was supposed to increase targeting speed by twenty percent. What the commanders of these tanks do not know is that the software update also installed a patch to the tanks' communications arrays. I now have full control of them. First, I think I want them to stay where they are.'

Mallik made a show of taking out his phone. He tapped on a specially designed app and hit STOP.

The tanks ground to a halt behind him. That brought a murmur from the crowd. He could only imagine the surprise on the faces of the tank crew. Only Ghosh, who sat there with a bemused look on his face, had known what was going to happen.

'Instead of the T-55 defeating its enemies, why don't we have them do it themselves?'

Mallik tapped a preprogrammed button labeled CROSS FIRE.

The barrels of the two tanks whirled around to face each other instead of the T-55. As soon as each of the guns was in position, they fired.

The massive rifled cannons belched flames, and explosions bloomed simultaneously on the hulls of the two tanks. Their barrels dipped as if the tanks were blown away, but in reality the explosions were flashbangs that were harmless to the heavily armored vehicles.

But the explosions made an impression on the crowd. As the sonic booms reached the stands seconds later, most of the audience stood up in awe at seeing the tanks suddenly turn on each other. Ghosh simply nodded at Mallik in appreciation of what he'd just witnessed.

'Please be seated, ladies and gentlemen,' Mallik said. 'No one was injured in the demonstration, but I think it points out how vulnerable our military hardware could be to outside hackers.' Once Colossus was fully operational, it would have no trouble installing all manner of malicious software into any military system on earth.

As the flames faded and the smoke dissipated, the attendees sat down again.

'Although what you just saw is chilling, that's not the end of our demonstration. We have an even more dangerous possibility to consider. Like you, I have heard rumors that the incident on the US naval base at Diego Garcia several days ago was not simply an equipment malfunction. Rather, every piece of technology on the island was rendered inoperable by an attack on its computer systems by a non-nuclear electromagnetic pulse device.'

Mallik didn't really think they'd heard that rumor, but his pronouncement got the response he wanted: another murmur from the crowd.

'The Indian Air Force contracted my company to build a similar device of our own,' Mallik went on. 'It is code-named Vajra. Although it has limited range, it is quite effective for short periods of time. And you can bet that if we have developed it, our enemies are working on something similar or have already deployed it in the field.'

When he called on the radio again, he said, 'Start second attack run.'

This time, four Arjun tanks raced forward while the T-55 moved toward them.

Using the same app on his phone, Mallik found the button marked EMP. When he pressed it, his phone went blank.

At the same time, the four Arjun tanks literally stopped in their tracks.

But the T-55 was unaffected. It continued into range and started blasting away at its immobile opponents. One by one, the Arjuns were covered with fire and smoke until all four were 'destroyed' in the war game. The T-55, having emerged victorious over six superior rivals, turned and trundled back the way it had come.

One of the colonels in the audience stood and said, 'That's just a simulation. I can't believe our tanks would be that susceptible to an EMP attack when their circuitry is supposed to be hardened to that kind of weapon.'

Mallik grinned and spoke into the microphone, which was unaffected because of its simple electrical functionality. 'This wasn't a simulation. Look at your phones. You'll find that all of them are switched off.'

Every person except Ghosh took out their phones. They were amazed when they saw that the phones wouldn't turn on.

'Don't worry,' Mallik said, 'the effect is only temporary. They'll operate normally again in a few minutes.'

'I hope you have a solution to these problems,' Ghosh said.

'I do,' Mallik replied. 'I have invested billions of rupees into developing backup systems for the most crucial weapons in our inventory. Those Arjuns that are now smoking can be retrofitted so that they will operate even if their computers are rendered useless. In fact, I've designed all of my factories to work without computers as well in case our cities are attacked with the same kinds of weapons.'

Ghosh joined him at the front of the stands and said to the crowd, 'I've already approved of Romir Mallik's designs for two of our frontline divisions, and those units will be in place any day now. Several naval ships and Air Force squadrons are also using his retro technology that will enable military operations to continue even with disabled computers.'

'Not just to continue,' Mallik clarified, 'we will be victorious if we are the only ones ready for this eventuality. If computers are taken out of the equation, no military in the world will be able to match up with India's.' It was true that he was trying to save the human race from itself, but if he could also make India the world's next great superpower in the bargain, that would be the best way to rebuild society once his satellites were fully operational.

Ghosh turned to him and said, 'Thank you for a very

effective demonstration. I think we've all learned a lot today.'

Mallik nodded. 'See you at the party.'

The audience started to disperse, and Mallik heard the same colonel who'd doubted the effect of the EMP grumble to the person next to him, 'I'd rather bet on our technological superiority than some fifties-era equipment.'

Mallik shook his head but said nothing. The colonel would find out very soon how badly he'd lose that bet.

30

Night had fallen, and the *Oregon* maintained a position thirteen miles off the coast of Jhootha Island, just beyond India's territorial waters. The Indian Coast Guard now had no jurisdiction over the ship and its crew, so the Corporation was in a strong negotiating position for transferring the rescued prisoners over to the waiting cutters. Juan was awaiting Langston Overholt's call in his cabin to finalize the arrangements.

Juan was finally able to take a shower after making sure all of their guests were cared for and the ship had moved into international waters. He toweled off and hopped over to his closet, where he kept an array of prosthetic legs for different occasions and fieldwork.

One prosthesis was his 'combat leg,' reinforced with carbon fiber to withstand the rigors of battle and equipped with hidden weapons, including a .45 caliber ACP Colt Defender pistol, a ceramic knife, a packet of C-4 plastic explosive smaller than a deck of cards, and a single-shot .44 caliber slug that could be fired from the heel. Another leg was used for smuggling items inside an undetectable storage cavity. But since he would be staying on the ship for now, he chose his most comfortable prosthesis, a leg so realistic that it had hairs embedded in a surface that felt just like skin.

He carried the leg over to his desk chair and sat down, massaging the stump just below his right knee. The pain had always been there since his leg was blown off by a Chinese destroyer's cannon shell, but now it was more of a dull ache that he stopped noticing once he got moving.

He put on the leg, cinching the straps down with a well-practiced rhythm. When he was sure it was tight, he stood and took his clothes out of the bedroom and into the office so he could watch the running lights of the cutters on the camera feed piped into his cabin. He was happy to see that the Indian Coast Guard ships were keeping their distance. The 4K monitor took up the entire wall of his office, and its resolution was so good that anyone else would swear they were looking out a window despite being in the center of the ship.

Like the other members of the crew, all of whom lived full-time on the *Oregon*, he received a generous budget to decorate his cabin. He preferred a classic 1940s style based on Rick's Café Américain from the movie *Casablanca*. Humphrey Bogart would have felt right at home with the antique desk, dining table, chairs, and old-fashioned black telephone. Even the bedroom's massive black safe was vintage. It held Juan's personal weapons and the ship's working cash, including the gold bar they'd used to take over the *Triton Star*. An original Picasso hung on the wall opposite the monitor. Although the Corporation owned pieces of art for investment purposes, most of them were kept in a bank vault when they weren't on display in the halls of the ship. This small oil painting, however, held a special meaning from a past mission and would never leave the *Oregon*.

Juan was just pulling his pants on when the phone rang. He picked up the receiver. 'Yes?'

It was Hali. 'I've got Langston Overholt on video for you. Should I patch him through on your screen?'

'Give me a minute.' He laid down the receiver and shrugged into a light sweater, wincing as he stretched his chest, which was still sore from where Lyla shot him in the ballistic vest. The nasty black and blue bruise was a testament to the fact that the body armor didn't absorb the entire impact of the bullet. He picked up the receiver again and said, 'Okay, put him through.'

He sat down and hung up the phone as Overholt's craggy face replaced the ocean view on the monitor.

'You'll be happy to know that the State Department has gotten the Indians to agree to our terms,' the CIA official said.

Juan was always impressed at how fast Overholt could pull strings in the government. 'We're free to go?'

'As soon as you deliver the prisoners from Jhootha Island to their Coast Guard. The Indians will accept the story that you were just Good Samaritans who happened to be sailing by when you saw something suspicious. In return for not having you involved any further, they'll take the credit for rescuing the survivors of Xavier Carlton's missing plane. Have you found out anything useful from the prisoners?'

'I don't know yet,' Juan said. 'I'm having the crew do subtle interviews while we feed them and provide clothing for them.'

'What do they know about the *Oregon*?'

'Only that we're a cargo ship called the *Goreno*. They

were hidden in a container when the shipboard weapons were being used. They're currently being taken care of in the fake mess hall.'

'Then your cover is intact. Did you see anything on the island to connect the facility there to the *Triton Star* incident?'

Juan shook his head. 'They blew it up before we could search it.'

'Well, we do know that there is some connection.'

'How?'

'The team investigating the *Triton Star* found a receiver and targeting computer inside the container that held the cruise missile. That's how it was launched remotely by Rasul. The investigators determined that the attack on Diego Garcia was a last-minute change and were able to decipher the coordinates of the original target. Guess what it was.'

'Jhootha Island.'

'Exactly. Whoever paid Rasul wanted to wipe out the island with the Novichok, kill the *Triton Star* crew, and leave evidence for whoever found the ghost ship that would lead straight to that prison facility. Either that evidence was planted or the plotters were incredibly stupid. Given how complicated the plan was, I don't think they're incompetent.'

'So now we need to know who Rasul was working for. Do we even know his last name?'

'Now that the CIA has a good scan of his face, we do,' Overholt said. 'His name is Rasul Torkan. Former Iranian special ops. He has an identical twin brother named Asad. They both left the service at the same time.' Overholt switched the video to side-by-side photos of Rasul and Asad Torkan. They were so similar that Juan couldn't tell which one he'd killed.

'Do we know where Asad is now?'

'As a matter of fact, we do.' The video now clicked over to a view of an Indian man in his forties, impeccably dressed in a tailored suit. He was getting out of a Mercedes limo. The door was being held by one of the Torkans.

'That's Romir Mallik,' Overholt said. 'He's an Indian billionaire. Owns a satellite design and launch firm, among many other businesses. He's been called India's version of Elon Musk. Most recently, he's been responsible for putting up his country's newest satellite communications network, called Vajra, though he had a setback a few days ago when one of his rockets blew up on launch.'

That jogged Juan's memory. 'Eric Stone mentioned that a rocket blew up in the Arabian Sea right before the cruise missile was launched. Interesting that they happened around the same time.'

The video feed switched back to Overholt, and he was frowning at the camera. 'I agree that the connections are piling up. If Mallik is linked to the plan to wipe out Jhootha Island, then he could also be involved with taking out Diego Garcia's electronics. We need to know if he is the target of the attacks or the culprit.'

'Maybe if we knew what's been going on in that prison, we'd have a better idea about the motives behind all this.'

'You don't have any more time to gently interrogate the prisoners. Our agreement with India states that you have to hand them over in an hour or the Indian Coast Guard will attempt to take the *Oregon* into custody for further investigation about the incident on the island. They're not very happy that they've been protecting a group of kidnappers instead of a tribe of natives.'

'They probably also wouldn't take too kindly to us accusing one of their most prominent businessmen of attacking a US military base.'

Overholt nodded. 'You can see our predicament.'

Juan stood. 'I'll see if Lyla Dhawan has been able to enlighten us.'

'All right. But don't take too long. Oh, and one more thing. I did a little digging when Romir Mallik's name popped up. He tends to do most of his work from a huge condo building that he owns in Mumbai.'

Juan knew Overholt well. He was bringing this up for a reason, so Juan went along with it. 'Might be a good place to find some information if someone could get inside and tap into his computer system.'

'As it happens, he's having a charity gala there two nights from now,' Overholt said, seeming to toss off this tidbit of info. 'It's in all of the Mumbai papers. One of the biggest social events of the year. Thought you might like to know.'

'Thanks for the tip,' Juan said.

It looked like the Corporation was going to have to get an invitation to the party.

31

After ending the call with Overholt, Juan left the hidden section of the *Oregon* and headed up to the fake mess hall. It was decorated like the rest of the external parts of the ship, with flickering fluorescent lights, peeling paint, chipped linoleum tables, and battered metal chairs.

From what Juan could tell when he entered, the prisoners didn't seem to mind. Many of them were talking to his crew, at ease now that they were free of Jhootha Island. Some of them were even laughing. All of them had changed out of their jumpsuits and into shirts and pants provided to them.

Julia Huxley greeted him at the door as she was walking out. Normally, the *Oregon*'s chief medical officer would be wearing scrubs when she was in the ship's hospital-grade trauma center, but here she was dressed in a pressed shirt and pants, her hair tied back in a ponytail. Though she was trained by the Navy, she didn't carry herself like an officer or a surgeon. She wouldn't have seemed out of place caring for families in a small-town clinic, down to the black medical bag she was holding.

'How are they?' Juan asked.

Julia surveyed the room with her dark, sympathetic eyes, and then turned back to Juan.

'Surprisingly healthy, given what they've been through,' she said. 'Physically, that is. I'd advise good therapists for all of them once they get home. Being freed from eighteen months in captivity is going to take a long time to process. None of them thought they'd ever leave.'

'They almost didn't.'

'They're very grateful to you for rescuing them.' Julia's face morphed into a scolding expression. 'Especially the woman who shot you. When were you going to tell me about that?'

'You had more important things to take care of.'

'Lyla said it was right about here that she got you,' Julia said, reaching out toward Juan's chest. He deftly side-stepped the informal exam.

'It's all right. Just a bruise.'

'Why don't you let your doctor make that determination? I'll expect to see you in the medical bay for X-rays after you're done here.'

'Yes, Doctor,' he said as Julia left, knowing that she would hound him if he didn't. She'd been the one who saved his life when his leg was severed and had kept a close eye on him ever since.

Juan found Lyla at a table with Kevin Nixon, who was holding a sketch pad. He was making quick strokes with a pencil, only stopping to ask questions and scratch his thick beard. Kevin had worked in Hollywood for many years as a makeup artist and props master, winning several major awards for his work. After his sister was killed during the attacks on 9/11, he'd left the industry and was offering to bring his skills to the CIA when Juan got wind of his abilities and asked him to join the Corporation. Kevin's job on board the *Oregon* wasn't the most active, and he constantly battled to keep his substantial waistline in check. A donut that was only half eaten sat on the table in front of him, so at least he was trying to make progress in his diet.

Juan walked up behind him and saw that he was nearly done sketching the face of a woman in her thirties. She was attractive, with high cheekbones and almond-shaped eyes.

'Who is that?' Juan asked.

'Lyla was just describing the woman she saw when they first landed on the island,' Kevin said.

'You mean, the woman who killed all those passengers?' Lyla said. 'The woman who was responsible for holding us hostage all this time? I'll never forget her face.'

'I'm sorry,' Kevin said. 'I know it's been hard for you to relive this.'

'I just hope you can find her and make her pay for what she's done.'

'With your help, I'm sure she'll be brought to justice.' Kevin got up and looked at Juan. 'I'm done here if you want to take my seat. This should be a good enough likeness to work with.'

'Thanks,' Juan said. 'And I've got another job for you after I see Hux.'

'Color me intrigued,' Kevin said, then looked at Lyla and pointed to a pencil and sheet of paper next to her plate. 'I'll leave those with you in case you want to add anything.' He started to walk away, then turned back and grabbed the other half of the donut to take with him. *The battle continues,* Juan thought.

He sat next to Lyla.

'How are you doing?' he asked.

'All right, I guess.' She looked down at her empty plate. 'The food here is amazing. I never would have guessed it with . . .' She nodded her head at the awful surroundings.

'We spend our money where we think it's put to the best use.'

'I appreciate the hospitality, but I'm going nuts waiting to talk to my parents. They must have thought I died long ago. It's going to be a big shock learning that their little girl is still alive.'

'I'm sure they'll be thrilled. You'll be able to talk to them as soon as you are on board the Indian Coast Guard cutter.'

'To think we were in India this whole time.' She looked at Juan with tears welling up in her eyes. 'Thanks again for everything you did.'

Juan shrugged. 'All in a day's work.'

'Which is what, exactly? No, never mind. I don't want to know, and you probably couldn't tell me anyway. How are *you* feeling? I'm surprised you were able to walk after I shot you, let alone get us all to safety.'

'I'm fine. Don't worry about it.'

'Are they really all dead?' Lyla said with a mixture of hope and dread.

'The guards? Yes. You're free of them.'

'And what about the people they worked for? Are we safe from them?'

'We're going to find out who did this to you. But we need your help.'

'Anything.'

'I know you've already talked to my crew, but I'd like to

227

hear it from you. What can you tell me about the project you were working on?'

Lyla took a breath. 'It's groundbreaking. Revolutionary, even. My expertise is in cutting-edge pattern recognition software. If they had recruited me to work on it, I might have done it until I realized the scope of their ambition. But then, if they'd hired me, they wouldn't have been able to hack into my company's database using my codes. I never learned its real name. We had to call it Project C.'

'What was the project's goal?'

'To develop a true, thinking artificial intelligence. One that would be able to write its own software code. They were trying to achieve the technological singularity.'

Juan had heard the term before but wasn't familiar with its particulars. 'The *singularity*?'

'It's the point when an artificial intelligence becomes so sophisticated that it can start improving itself without human intervention. After that, its self-improvement will increase at an exponential rate. It's the Holy Grail of AI.'

'But it comes with big risks as well, doesn't it?'

'Of course. It could become a runaway reaction that gets out of control. It's almost impossible to predict how the AI would behave in that situation. It might lead to huge advancements for the human race.'

'Or it might lead to the Terminator,' Juan said.

'That's what some people think.'

'We've encountered something like that before.'

He was thinking of a previous classified mission in which a powerful quantum computer that was used to crack any code on the planet had become self-aware. The Corporation had to shut it down, but Juan remembered a strange phone call he received after the end of that mission that indicated a portion of that computer's code remained somewhere on the internet. It might have even served as a basis for Project C.

Lyla was both puzzled and intrigued. 'What do you mean, you encountered something like that?'

'I can't say, unfortunately. Could Project C be used for breaking encryption?'

'Maybe, but it's far more than that. Once Project C is complete and the AI has reached the singularity, code breaking is just a small application. The AI could actually rewrite any computer code it can access.'

Juan's mind was reeling with the implications. 'You mean, it could hack into computers all by itself?'

'Hacking is just the first step. Project C is designed to rewrite the code so seamlessly that the people monitoring it may not even know it. Think how hard it is for us to detect viruses now, ones that were written by humans. An AI could develop its own language. Even if we knew the malicious code was there, we might have no idea what it said. Every computer on earth could be taken out of our control and given over to someone else.'

'Or something else.'

Lyla nodded. 'If it wasn't designed with the right fail-safes in mind, that's very possible. The world could be held hostage by the whim of a computer that doesn't care at all about the human race. Or the AI could be controlled by someone who has the rest of us on strings like puppets, ready to do whatever they command. That someone would instantly become the most powerful person on earth, and there would be nothing we could do about it.'

'Where is this computer?' Juan asked.

'I wish I could tell you. Our access was extremely restricted when we were working on the computers. It was a closed network, so I couldn't access the internet.'

'What was the network?'

'It was called Vajra.'

Mallik's satellite system. That confirmed he was somehow involved in all this. But little of this was making sense to Juan yet.

'There were two other things that you should know,' Lyla said.

'What's that?'

'First, twenty-three of the passengers were taken off the island shortly after we got there. The rest of us got to talking and realized that they were all hardware people, while we were all software.'

'Do you know where they were taken?'

She hesitated, then said, 'No. About eight months ago, we had to redo a ton of work all of a sudden. During that time, I came across latitude and longitude coordinates when we were checking data on some computer modeling. One of the data cells next to the coordinates had the word *sunken*. I think it was referring to a ship that sank.'

'Do you remember the coordinates?'

She nodded and started writing on the paper Kevin had left for her. 'I memorized them because they were so unusual.'

'You said there were two things.'

She nodded. 'Three times during my stay on Jhootha Island, I saw a strange symbol on paperwork that was emailed to us. I've never seen it before. I can't draw at all, so Kevin sketched it out from my recollection. I have no idea what it means.'

Lyla turned over the sheet of paper. On it was a circle with nine spokes.

In the center of the circle was a swastika.

32

Over India

The Corporation's private Gulfstream had landed at Kochi's airport at the same time the *Oregon* arrived at India's southern port city to drop off the team that would be infiltrating Romir Mallik's gala. Chuck 'Tiny' Gunderson, the Corporation's fixed-wing pilot on call whenever they needed a ride for a mission, was now taking them to Mumbai, and Eddie Seng was sitting in the copilot's seat for the takeoff.

'How long will you be in Mumbai?' the big, blond Swede asked a minute after the wheels lifted from the runway.

'The party starts at six tomorrow night,' Eddie said.

'Good. I can get some sleep after we get there.'

'Long flight from Singapore?'

'It wasn't bad, but I had to leave a killer poker hand at the casino when I got the call. I'm guessing we won't be sticking around once the party is over.'

Eddie hoped they could get in and out without trouble, but he always planned for the worst. 'We might need a quick extraction.'

'You usually do.' He looked over his shoulder at the rest of the team in the back. 'You brought a different group with you this time. I don't see Kevin Nixon or Hali Kasim on my plane very often.'

'A lot of moving parts on this mission.'

'I haven't met the new member of the crew yet.' He was referring to Raven, who was sitting toward the rear of the plane with MacD, Murph, and Linc. 'She a good fit?'

'The Chairman's got an eye for talent,' Eddie said, rising out of his seat. 'In fact, we couldn't be doing this op without her. Juan and I came up with a doozy this time.'

He walked back to Murph, who was intently peering at his laptop, and sat next to him. The rest of the team gathered around.

'Sorry we didn't have time for a briefing before we left,' Eddie said, 'but we had a lot of things to take care of so the *Oregon* could get on its way quickly.'

'I hear we're going to a party,' Hali said.

Eddie nodded. 'Some of us. This is a very exclusive event. The cream of Indian society will be there. Serious invite only. Kevin, you got hold of one of the invitations, right?'

Kevin nodded and held up a gold-embossed card. 'Found a photo of one online and created a replica before we left the ship. People really should be careful about what they share on social media.'

'Who's the invitee?' Linc asked.

Eddie looked at Raven, who stared back at him before she said, 'Not me.'

'Yes, you. Murph, show us the photo.'

Murph turned the screen and showed them a picture of a beautiful Indian woman in a sari. She bore a striking resemblance to Raven.

MacD almost spit out the gum he was chewing. 'Wow! That your sister?'

Raven leaned toward the screen. 'Who is she?'

'That hottie is Kiara Jain,' Murph said. 'Rising Bollywood star who has been in America for the last few years trying to build a career in New York and Los Angeles. Didn't go as well as she wanted, so she just returned for her big comeback on the Mumbai entertainment scene.'

Raven frowned at Kevin. 'So that's why you took my measurements before we left the *Oregon.*'

'I've brought a stunning turquoise gown for you,' Kevin said.

She looked back to the screen. 'I'm not the same kind of Indian, but I do look a little like her, I guess.'

'I have everything I need to transform you into her double. By the time I'm done with you, her own boyfriend wouldn't recognize the difference.'

'Boyfriend?'

Eddie patted MacD on the shoulder. 'Meet your temporary beau, Cole Randle. Dumb as a post, but his pretty face makes up for his lack of talent.'

'Thanks a lot,' MacD said.

'Is someone named Cole Randle really her boyfriend?' Raven asked.

'No,' Murph said, 'but I'll hack into the Internet Movie Database and create a few ultra-low-budget films for his résumé in case anyone checks.'

'No one over here will know if you picked up a new himbo from Hollywood,' Linc added.

'I've already come up with a few titles for Randle's craptastic action movies. They're all straight-to-video. *Maximum Justice. Fatal Force. Time to Impact.*'

'Hey, Ah'd see those,' MacD said.

'I'll be playing your US-based manager,' Eddie said, 'and Linc is typecast in the role of well-muscled bodyguard.'

'Wait a minute,' Raven said. 'I don't even know what she sounds like.'

'You're going to be watching a lot of movies over the next day or so. But we're also going to say you've come down with a case of laryngitis to keep conversations to a minimum. MacD and I will be doing most of the talking.'

'If they can understand me,' MacD said, then pointed at Murph. 'He's not coming? Don't we need to break into a computer in there?'

'You do,' Murph said, handing a pocket-sized tablet computer to Eddie. 'This will connect to Mallik's network once you're inside his condo tower. I'll be ordering room service back at the hotel room while I do all the hacking remotely.'

'What about me?' Hali asked.

'The real Kiara Jain is staying at the Mumbai Four Seasons,' Eddie said. 'Your job is to keep her from getting to the party until we're gone.'

'That sounds easy enough.'

'Apparently, you've never read about Ms Jain's prima donna antics in the tabloids. Seems she learned something from her Hollywood counterparts and became a bit of a diva since arriving in America.'

Hali smirked at that. 'Oh, great.'

'How long will it take you to hack into the network?' Eddie asked Murph.

'Depends on what kind of security Mallik has. Hopefully, less than an hour.'

Raven gagged. 'I have to parade around that party in a gown and high heels for an hour?'

'We drink champagne and schmooze a little while Murph does all the work,' MacD said. 'What's the problem?'

'I joined the Corporation to fight bad guys, not play dress-up at some fancy rich person's prom.'

'Don't take this mission lightly,' Eddie warned. 'We estimate there will be fifty uniformed police and at least twenty plainclothes guards at this function, not to mention the dignitaries' personal bodyguards. Think of this as if we are sneaking into the White House. For the evening, Mallik's condo building will be one of the most heavily protected places in the country. And if he or his attack dog Asad Torkan suspects that we aren't who we say we are, we'll be learning a lot more about the Indian prison system than we want to.'

That silenced everyone.

'Now, Murph,' he continued. 'Bring up the blueprints you found for Mallik's building. We need to know all our possible exits. We're all going to know them backward and forward by the time we get to the party.'

Eddie watched Raven intently following Murph's rundown of the structure. He had no doubt she would realize that no Corporation mission was ever easy.

33

The Red Sea

It took less than forty hours for the *Oregon* to make the dash across the Arabian Sea to the Mandeb Strait, the narrow body of water between the countries of Yemen and Djibouti. The precise coordinates Lyla Dhawan had given to Juan were in a group of islets near the southern end of the Red Sea. While he waited for Max to call to say that they'd arrived at the location, he met in his cabin with Eric Stone, who had been struggling to identify the strange symbol with the swastika embedded in it.

'I've looked all over the place for this,' Eric said as they sat at Juan's dining table while they were served coffee from a silver tray by Maurice, the *Oregon*'s chief steward. A veteran of Britain's Royal Navy under numerous admirals, the distinguished septuagenarian was the oldest person on the ship. He preferred to wear a black tie and elegant white jacket protected by a gleaming linen napkin folded over his arm.

'This is not the Nazi swastika?' Juan asked.

'No. It's not on any military insignia from that era. This swastika is a backward version of Hitler's. So unless Lyla Dhawan was looking at a mirror image, it is probably South Asian in origin.'

'The swastika was originally a religious symbol, right?'

Eric nodded. 'For thousands of years before it was perverted by the Nazis. It's commonly found on Hindu and Buddhist statues and temples. In Asia, it symbolizes well-being and prosperity, not the bigotry and hatred of the Nazis' twisted emblem.'

'What about the other part of Lyla's symbol?'

'The wheel and nine spokes? I have no idea.'

As he poured Juan's coffee, Maurice cleared his throat. Juan looked up in surprise. Usually, Maurice prided himself on coming and going without being noticed. 'Do you know something about this, Maurice?'

'I don't mean to intrude, Captain, but I believe I may be of service in helping you solve your conundrum.' Maurice was the only person in the crew who insisted on maintaining naval tradition and calling Juan Captain instead of Chairman.

'Please. Have you seen this before?'

'I have,' he said, setting down the pot. 'Thirty-five years ago when I was serving with an admiral who had once been based in India. He was a collector of rare artifacts from the subcontinent, and this symbol was on one of the pieces in his cabin, a strange medal that he kept in a case. I cleaned it every week for two years.'

'Do you know what it means?' Eric asked.

'The admiral told me it represented the Nine Unknown Men. He was fascinated with Indian military history, so I heard quite a lot about them from him.'

'Who are they?' Juan asked.

'I believe who *were* they would be the more appropriate question,' Maurice said. 'They haven't existed for two thousand years, if they ever existed at all.'

238

'It's a myth?' Juan would have motioned for Maurice to sit with them, but he knew the steward would never accept the offer.

Maurice nodded. 'From the time of Ashoka. Circa 261 BCE, if I'm not mistaken. He was an emperor who conquered most of India. But to do so meant waging the deadliest war in history at that time. Over two hundred thousand casualties. The bloodshed was so terrible that Ashoka abandoned his warlike ways and converted the entire country to Buddhism. He left pillars across India defining his laws, and many of them can still be seen to this day. In fact, his influence continues to be so great that his chakra symbol is on the Indian flag.'

Eric typed on his computer and showed them an image of the chakra, which was a wheel with twenty-four spokes.

'That's not the symbol Lyla saw,' Juan said. 'There's no swastika, and her wheel only had nine spokes, I'm assuming to represent the Nine Unknown Men.' He looked at Maurice. 'How were they connected to Ashoka?'

'According to legend, the Emperor was aghast at the decimation he had wrought and was afraid that the knowledge of the world at that time was too powerful to be held by a single man. So he ordered his brother to find nine common men, unknown to royalty or positions of power, and gifted each of them with a scroll confined to one aspect of knowledge in the sciences. They were to protect that knowledge with their lives, so that no human would use that power to conquer the world.'

Juan sat back and ran his fingers through his hair. Maurice's description of the responsibility held by the Nine Unknown Men was the exact opposite of what Lyla had said was the purpose of Project C. An artificial intelligence – a font of knowledge – that could let someone rule the world.

'Could this group of men have passed down their knowledge over the centuries?' he mused.

'There are certainly conspiracy theories that suspect this cabal could still exist,' Maurice said. 'But my admiral did not. He simply thought it made a wonderful story.'

He picked up the tray. 'If there's nothing else, Captain, I shall return to my duties.'

'Thank you, Maurice. You've been most helpful.'

'My pleasure.' Maurice exited the cabin with barely a whisper.

'Do you think the descendants of Nine Unknown Men are really still around and built this advanced AI?' Eric asked.

Juan shrugged. 'I suppose it's possible, but they would have abandoned Ashoka's original intent in separating the Scrolls of Knowledge. From what we've seen, whoever built the Jhootha Island facility, launched a stolen cruise missile, and hijacked an airliner had to have a massive amount of funds at their disposal. If the Nine Unknown Men passed down their knowledge through the centuries, their descendants could now be billionaires working together.'

'For example, people like Xavier Carlton, whose plane was found on Jhootha Island, and Romir Mallik, who's palling around with Rasul Torkan's brother?'

'If those two are involved in all this, they'll have infinite resources to fight us. And I doubt reporting them to governments that are in their back pockets will do any good. We'll have to handle this ourselves.'

They spent ten more minutes looking up information on the legend of the Nine Unknown Men, including the alleged contents of the scrolls. But they couldn't find any trace of the symbol or the identities of the Nine Unknown. Their research was interrupted when Max called Juan's cabin.

'We've reached Lyla's coordinates.' He said it as if he were telling them that his dog died.

Juan frowned at Eric and said, 'What's the matter?'

'If there's a sunken ship here, we'll have problems exploring it.'

'Why?'

'Turn on your external monitor and then head on up to the op center so we can figure out what to do.' Max hung up.

Juan picked up his remote and clicked on the camera feed from outside.

Clouds of steam billowed up from the sea in four different places.

Eric snapped his fingers in recognition at what they were seeing. 'We must be over the Red Sea Rift. It's where the Arabian and African plates are spreading apart.'

Juan pointed at the surging masses of rising white clouds. 'Then that's what I think it is?'

Eric nodded. 'The ship we're looking for sank right on top of an underwater volcano.'

34

Mumbai

Driving a black Mercedes limousine, Hali pulled up to the front entrance of the Four Seasons Hotel moments before Kiara Jain strode out with a good-looking Indian man by her side. She was even more stunning in person, wearing a ruby red full-length gown with her shimmering hair cascading across her exposed shoulders. Her companion was dressed in a tuxedo and seemed to be in the same age range as the actress. Apparently, she wasn't quite famous enough to require a real bodyguard. Neither of them looked happy.

Hali got out and went around to open the rear door. 'Ms Jain, Mr Mallik personally requested me to bring you to the party. He's a big fan of your films.' Of course, Hali had previously canceled the car that was supposed to pick her up.

She raised an eyebrow at him and then scoffed at the man beside her. 'I told you, Gautam. At least he has good taste.'

With a huff and a toss of her hair, she slid into the backseat. Before following her in, Gautam looked at Hali with an apologetic shrug as if to say, *See what I'm stuck with?*

Hali pulled away from the hotel and began a slow drive in the direction away from Mallik's party. Mumbai's traffic was notoriously bad, and he was aiming for a jam that he'd already spotted on his mapping app.

'I shouldn't have even brought you,' Kiara said in a low voice that was meant to keep the chauffeur from listening to the conversation. In a show of discretion, Hali turned up the volume on a local station playing music, but he could still hear them clearly.

'Then maybe I should have the driver turn around and take me back,' Gautam said. 'You can show up at the biggest event of the year alone.'

'If you're going to be that way, maybe you should. We all know who the bigger star is here. You wouldn't have even been invited if it weren't for me.'

Hali was glad for the petty argument. Gautam and Kiara spent the next few minutes sniping at each other, so neither of them noticed the route he was taking. But when there was a lull in the bickering, Kiara looked out at their surroundings, then peered at Hali in the mirror.

'Where are you going?'

'To the party,' Hali said with a smile.

'The party is at Mr Mallik's building.'

'Yes.'

She waved at the sea on either side of them. 'Then why are we on the Bandra–Worli Sea Link?'

The causeway stretched across the mouth of Mahim Bay to connect the western suburbs to south Mumbai.

Hali played dumb. 'We're going to Bandra, where he lives.'

'He doesn't live in Bandra, you idiot!' she yelled.

'That's the address I have.'

'He lives on Altamount Road in south Mumbai. Everyone knows that.' She leaned forward. 'Where are you from? You sound American.'

'My parents are from Mumbai, but I was raised in Los Angeles. I'm trying to break into Bollywood. In fact, when Mr Mallik asked me to pick you up, I was so thrilled. I have a script I think would be great for you.' Hali reached into his bag and retrieved a script of some terrible movie he'd printed out from the internet. 'I know I shouldn't ask, but would you read it?'

She slapped the pages away. 'Of course I'm not going to read your stupid script. Now, get us to Mr Mallik's house or I'll have you fired.'

'Calm down,' Gautam said. 'We'll get there. This guy's just trying to do his job.'

'This guy is going to ruin my career if we don't get there on time. Do you realize how many important people will be there?'

'I'll go extra fast and get you there right away,' Hali said. 'Do you know the right address?'

'Give me the invitation,' she said to Gautam. He held it out, and she snapped it away from him. 'I don't trust you anymore. I'll look it up on my phone and tell you how to get there.'

She could try, Hali thought, but he remained quiet.

A few seconds later, Kiara groaned in frustration. 'Why can't I get a cell signal?'

'Maybe we're out of range,' Hali said. But he knew the real reason. There was a cell phone jammer in the trunk to keep her from calling anyone or posting on social media while she was supposed to be at the party. But the jammer didn't interfere with the signal from Hali's earpiece that was routed through a satellite transmitter also in the trunk.

'Just turn around,' she demanded.

Hali nodded. 'Yes, Ms Jain. As soon as we're off the causeway.'

'Can you believe this man?' she said to Guatam, who was trying to hide a crooked grin that Hali spotted in the mirror.

Halfway across the causeway, traffic slowed to a crawl because of an accident up ahead, the one that Hali had noted earlier.

'You have got to be kidding me!' Kiara screamed.

'Don't worry, miss,' Hali said. 'I'm sure I can get you there within the hour.'

'An hour! I can't believe this!' Kiara threw up her hands in frustration and continued futilely tapping on her phone.

But Hali wasn't talking to her. His message was for Eddie.

'Understood, Hali,' Eddie said into his own earpiece. He was in a Porsche SUV being driven by Tiny Gunderson, who was taking a break from his piloting duties. Linc was in the front seat, while Eddie was sandwiched between Raven and MacD in the back. All of them could hear that they now had their hour to break into Romir Mallik's computer system.

They were just pulling up to his tower on Altamount Road, one of the most exclusive neighborhoods in Mumbai. According to reports, Mallik had constructed the enormous five-hundred-foot-tall structure anticipating a large family before his wife died unexpectedly. Although it was bigger than many of the apartment buildings in the area, large enough to support a helicopter landing pad on the roof, Mallik's vertical palace was a single home, and he was its only resident.

The grand underground driveway to the entrance was already packed with limos and high-end SUVs, but they moved along quickly as guests were swiftly escorted to a security station before being let into the elevator that would take them to the huge ballroom on one of the top floors.

When they reached the drop-off, Tiny said, 'I'll be close by. Just give me a shout when you're on your way down, and I'll be here before you arrive.'

Playing the part of the bodyguard, Linc got out and opened the door for Raven, who looked like a dead ringer for Kiara Jain, resplendent in her clingy turquoise sheath. All the men within twenty yards gawked at her as she took MacD's arm and sashayed toward the metal detector. Eddie, who was wearing glasses that fed video back to Murph, was happy to see that since this was a private event, there were no paparazzi. He and Linc followed close behind them, dressed in tuxes that looked more like rentals than the tailored Armani that MacD wore.

Raven's purse was searched, and all of the men had to put their phones in trays as they passed through the metal detector. A bevy of stern-looking guards surveyed the scene while the official greeters led them to the elevator after checking their IDs. Murph had broken into the security company's computer system the day before and added their names to the list, and since they were with movie star Kiara Jain, nobody suspected anything was amiss.

At the top of the building, the elevator opened to the sound of hundreds of people talking over the music of a ten-piece band. The huge dance floor was already being put to use by some of the guests, while a massive table overflowed with delicacies from all over the country.

The biggest draw was the wide covered balcony that overlooked the Arabian Sea and downtown Mumbai. Many of the guests already seemed to be staking out spots to watch the sunset later in the evening.

Eddie activated the small tablet in his pocket and said, 'Murph, we're in. Get to work.'

'Already on it,' Murph said from his hotel room. Eddie could hear Murph's heavy metal music pounding in the background and felt sorry for his neighbors.

A waiter walked by with a tray of champagne, and they each took one except for Linc, who maintained the dour expression of a wary guardian.

Before they could take their first sip, a pretty young Indian woman across the room waved at Raven and dragged the man beside her toward them.

'Oh, no. She recognizes me,' Raven said.

'It's okay,' Eddie said. 'We knew this would happen. Who is that, Murph?'

'Checking,' Murph replied. After a brief pause, he said, 'That's Prisha Naidu. She and Kiara were in a film together six years ago.'

As Prisha approached, Raven opened her arms and said with a perfect Indian accent, 'Prisha! So good to see you.' Her adeptness at languages and uncanny impression of Kiara's voice meant that they could ditch the laryngitis story.

'It's been so long!' Prisha said, giving Raven a big hug. 'You're even taller than I remembered.'

Raven gestured to her feet. 'It's the heels. They're amazing, but they're killing my toes.'

'The price we pay for beauty. You remember my husband, don't you?'

'Samar,' Murph said in their ears.

'Samar,' Raven said without missing a beat. 'A pleasure as always.'

Prisha looked Raven up and down. 'Where is that gorgeous red gown you posted on Instragram earlier?'

Raven playfully batted MacD on the arm. 'Cole here spilled a drink on it while we were getting ready, so I had to resort to this, which I was planning to wear to a premiere next week. Now I have to find something else.'

'Well, I love it.' She looked at MacD with a flirty expression. 'I haven't seen this handsome man with you before . . . Prisha Naidu.' She bowed with her hands together.

MacD awkwardly followed her lead. 'Cole Randle, ma'am. Kiara and Ah met on a movie set a few weeks ago in LA. She thought Ah'd like Mumbai.'

'An American,' Prisha said. 'How interesting. The US really has changed you, Kiara.' She leaned in to Raven and whispered, 'What happened to Gautam Puri?' Eddie could hear it in his earpiece.

'We had a big fight,' Raven whispered back. Then, with a naughty gleam in her eye, she said, 'Cole will do for now.'

'I can't wait to hear all about it,' Prisha said. Then she spotted someone else interesting and said, 'I'll be back later,' before flitting away with her husband.

Raven sighed and looked at Eddie. 'This is going to be exhausting.' She drained half her champagne glass.

'I'll do?' MacD said with a grin.

'For now.'

Several people by the elevator raised their voices, and

Eddie turned to see Romir Mallik emerge, glad-handing guests that surged toward him. Asad Torkan walked behind him with the same surly look as Linc.

'They really were identical twins,' Linc said.

'And just as dangerous,' Eddie replied. 'Let's veer away from them.'

'You might need to get closer than you want,' Murph said with an exasperated tone.

'Why?' Eddie said. Linc, Raven, and MacD were all looking at him with concern. 'What happened?'

'The WiFi network isn't connected to his computer. If we want to break into his system, you're going to have to find a terminal so we can do it manually.'

At the base of Mallik's condo tower, Natalie Taylor approached the delivery bay at the rear of the building in a truck with the catering company's logo on the side. She backed it up to the loading dock and got out, approaching the guards watching the door. Her uniform perfectly matched the ones of the caterers who'd been delivering food all day long. A short wig of red hair and thick glasses provided a disguise in case Mallik's security team was on the lookout for her.

'What's this?' one of the guards demanded.

'The cake,' she said matter-of-factly, opening the rear doors.

The other guard looked at a sheet he was carrying. 'I don't see anything about a cake.'

'Well, it wouldn't be a surprise if it was on the list, would it?'

The guards looked at her with suspicion, especially

because they wouldn't expect to see a Caucasian delivering food. 'We're going to have to check with the catering manager.'

'Be my guest,' she said.

As the first guard took out his radio, Taylor drew a SIG Sauer pistol from her apron and shot each guard with a single round to the head. She dragged them into the catering truck, not the least afraid that the cameras would be recording her. Right now anyone monitoring the cameras would be seeing nothing but a white glow from the ultra-bright LEDs mounted on the back of the truck.

When they were inside, she took the passcard from one of the guards, wheeled out a large cart carrying an over-sized cake, and closed the truck behind her. She pushed the cart through the delivery doors and headed for the service elevator.

The cart did hold a cake. But it would never be eaten. Mallik and his guests would indeed get a big surprise.

35

The Red Sea

Lyla Dhawan's coordinates were so precise that it didn't take long to find the sunken wreck lying seventy feet below the surface. The 500-foot-long hulk lay across the side of the growing undersea volcano formed by a crack in the earth pushing apart the continents of Africa and Asia. It was resting at an angle, so they could see the top deck from their current vantage point.

'No wonder the plotters behind Project C weren't concerned about anyone finding this ship,' Eric Stone said from the cockpit of the *Oregon*'s Nomad submarine. 'In a few weeks, it will be completely buried.'

Juan, sitting beside him in the copilot's seat, nodded as the hull of a cargo vessel loomed in front of them. A large hole on the starboard side below the waterline amidships was obviously the reason for its sinking. He couldn't read its name because both the bow and stern were covered by hardened lava. A thin ridge had formed upslope from the ship along a good portion of the length, diverting the ongoing lava flow, but the underwater mountain was growing so fast that it was just a matter of time before the red-hot molten rock breached the ridge and covered the wreckage.

Nomad was the larger of the *Oregon*'s two subs – sixty-five feet long, big enough to carry ten passengers including the pilots, and equipped with a diver's air lock. With a transparent polycarbonate nose and a cigar shape, Nomad resembled a miniaturized nuclear attack sub, but with robotic claws jutting from her chin. Though she was rated for depths down to one thousand feet, they wouldn't be going nearly that far down today.

Normally, when sending divers down a mere seventy feet, the *Oregon* would maintain a position over the site and release them from the central moon pool. But Juan didn't want her any closer to an active volcano than she needed to be. Besides, by the time the divers swam that distance to the wreck, they'd have only a couple of minutes to explore before being boiled by the extreme heat.

Juan turned and asked Linda Ross, who was behind them in the main cabin of the sub, 'Temperature reading?'

'Just one hundred and five degrees here,' she said. 'But it's rising fast as we approach the ship.'

'Are you sure you want to go out in that?' said Julia Huxley, who was sitting next to Linda and frowning at the gauge.

Juan smiled. 'Why not? It'll be like a nice soak in a hot tub.'

She rolled her eyes. 'Hot tubs max out at one hundred and four. It's good I came along to monitor your vitals if you're crazy enough to go out in that.'

Linda said, 'They worked great last time we used them.'

Max had modified two of their drysuits to mimic the cooling suits used by race car drivers. Cold liquid flowed through tubes lining the inside of the suit. The cooling unit and pump were mounted on the back next to the air tank. Juan and Linda had worn them on a previous mission to infiltrate a Russian nuclear power plant through the drainpipes of its secondary cooling system. The water hadn't been radioactive, but it was too hot for a diver to survive without protection.

'I remember,' Julia said. 'But that water was only one hundred and ten degrees. The water here looks like it'll get even hotter.'

Linda gestured to the two diving suits hanging by the air lock. 'Max says they're rated for up to fifteen minutes at a hundred and thirty degrees.'

'And then you'll begin to cook.' She gave Juan a scolding look. 'If your body temperatures reach a hundred, I'm pulling you both back in immediately.'

'Works for me,' Juan said. 'I don't feel like stewing in my own juices. But before we do that, let's take a look with Little Geek and see if an excursion is even necessary.'

Little Geek was their remotely operated vehicle, named after a similar ROV in the movie *The Abyss*. It was currently resting in Nomad's claws, waiting for Linda to begin guiding it via the fiber-optic and power umbilical links to the sub.

'Where should we start?' she asked.

'Eric, take Nomad closer to the bridge,' Juan said. 'We might be able to find something in there.'

'Aye, Chairman.'

Nomad climbed up the sunken hull and back toward the superstructure located aft. They could now see that the deck was not laid out like a typical cargo ship. Instead of hoisting cranes and hard points for fastening containers, the deck had four thirty-foot spiral masts and a large satellite dish at the center of the ship. One of the masts had snapped off at its base and lay half buried in lava.

'What are those?' Julia asked, pointing at the eggbeater-shaped objects.

'They look like wind generators,' Juan said. 'Some cargo ships have them installed to save on fuel.'

When the sub was within a hundred feet of the superstructure, Linda launched Little Geek, and it whizzed away twice as fast as Nomad could ever move.

They watched its video feed on the monitor. Little Geek's bright LED lights panned over the white superstructure, and they could see the empty davits where the lifeboat would normally be hanging.

'Looks like the crew got away,' Linda said.

'Even if some of them didn't, we won't find any bodies,' Julia said. 'Not if it sank eight months ago. They'd be fully decomposed at this depth and temperature. Only bones will be left.'

Linda piloted Little Geek up to the bridge. The windows were caked with algae. All of them were intact, and none of the doors were open.

'Can't see a thing,' Linda said.

'And we're not going to get Little Geek through impact-resistant glass,' Juan said. 'We'll have to go in ourselves.' The ROV's small manipulator arm wasn't strong enough to open doors.

Julia gestured at the temperature gauge. 'Little Geek's sensor shows one hundred and nineteen degrees.'

'Still within the suits' capability to keep us cool.'

'There's one other way in,' Eric said from the cockpit.

'The hole in the hull,' Juan said. 'Let's go down there.'

They descended with Little Geek taking the lead. Eric hovered the sub a respectable distance from the tear in the ship's midsection. With all of Nomad's light focused on the hole, which was the size of a minivan but still too small for Nomad, Juan could now see a feature he hadn't noticed before.

'The edges of the metal are bent out from the inside of the ship,' he said. 'The explosion came from the hold.'

'So we know it wasn't sunk by a torpedo,' Linda said. 'Sabotage?'

'Or the cargo they were carrying blew up,' Eric said.

'Only one way to find out,' Juan said, and nodded at Linda.

She guided Little Geek through the hole and into a vast hold whose bulkheads were beyond the reach of the ROV's lights. The first thing they saw on the monitor was a vast array of pipes, power cables, and electrical conduits snaking through the hull. Some of them had been ruptured by the internal explosion and lay in a tangled mess on the deck.

'This could get tricky,' Linda said. 'Don't want to get the umbilical tangled.'

Juan pointed to a space on the right that was relatively clear of the pipes. 'That seems to be the best route.'

Linda navigated in that direction, and a huge round metal vat came into view. Half of it had been torn apart by the explosion, but from its exterior, so the blast hadn't resulted from whatever had been inside the tank. Dozens of the pipes and conduits were connected to it.

'Looks like they were brewing beer in there,' Julia said.

'Those would be expensive six-packs,' Juan said.

Linda piloted Little Geek into the vat, and they could make out a complicated array of cells, like the honeycomb in a beehive.

'What do you make of that?' Juan asked.

'This tank is made to create a biochemical reaction of some kind,' Julia said. 'But it's like nothing I've ever seen.'

'Why is it connected to electrical cables?'

Julia shrugged. 'Maybe for monitoring.'

Linda backed Little Geek out of the vat and kept it moving along, revealing that the hold was packed with identical vats. At the end of the hold was a giant rack full of computer servers.

'That's an awful lot of computing power just to monitor a chemical reaction,' Eric said, who was watching the video while keeping Nomad steady.

'Lyla Dhawan said Project C was supposed to be a breakthrough in artificial intelligence,' Juan said. 'This has to be related to what was going on at Jhootha Island somehow.'

'The name of the ship would help us answer that, I bet,' Julia said.

'That's why Linda and I are going in. Maybe we can also find some information about this ship's purpose. Once we take a look at the other side of the hold, we'll suit up.' They were recording Little Geek's feed, so even if they didn't notice anything of use now, they could scour the video for clues later.

She turned the ROV toward the port side of the ship, careful to avoid the cables and pipes that had been jarred loose by the explosion and sinking. Seeing the effort put into designing and building this unusual vessel, along with the time and money spent to construct the prison on Jhootha Island, it was even more obvious that the people responsible for Project C had virtually unlimited resources at their disposal.

Little Geek reached the opposite end of the hold, and now they had enough video to simulate the hold in 3-D. This would help them to better figure out what was going on. Linda turned the ROV around to follow its umbilical back the way it had come.

As Little Geek maneuvered past the damaged vat, its wake was strong enough to cause a pipe hanging by a thread to detach from the tank and plummet to the bottom.

The video feed went black. An instant later, it was followed by the sound of an enormous explosion that rocked Nomad. Eric was secure in his pilot's seat, but the rest of them were thrown to the deck.

Juan, whose ears were ringing from the blast, got up and said, 'Everyone all right?'

They all said they were okay.

Eric backed away from the hole in the ship. 'No damage to Nomad. We're lucky that the detonation occurred on the other side of the ship.' Then Juan heard him say into his radio headset, 'Yeah, Max. We're fine down here. It came from the wreckage. No, we don't know yet. We'll keep you posted.'

'Run the video back,' Juan said to Linda.

She rewound the recording until it showed the pipe falling.

'I'll zoom in on the bottom to see if we can tell what it hit.'

She ran the video in slow motion until they could see the steel pipe bounce on the deck and careen into the exterior bulkhead. It hit a red box no bigger than a carry-on suitcase, and that's when the video went blank.

'That red box wasn't just lying there,' Juan said. 'It looked like it was welded to the hull.'

'Some kind of self-destruct bomb?' Linda wondered.

'That's how they got rid of the evidence at Jhootha Island,' Juan said. 'They might have done the same thing with this ship.'

'So either they sank the ship on purpose, but the port-side explosive didn't detonate until now,' Eric said, 'or the starboard one went off by accident.'

'Or it was sabotage like Linda thought,' Juan said. 'We won't have any idea if we can't at least figure out where this ship came from.'

As Nomad rose, they could now see past the top deck. The explosion had done more than tear apart the interior of the ship. Part of the hardened lava ridge was now gone, collapsed in an avalanche caused by the blast.

Molten lava was now pouring through the gap toward the ship.

'That's not good,' Julia said.

'How long do you think we have before the ship is covered?' Juan asked Eric.

He could see the naval genius doing calculations in his head as he watched the flow of hot liquid rock cascading over the breach.

He finally said, 'At this rate, I'd say an hour before the hull is too hot to go near. Maybe less.'

Juan looked at Linda. He didn't have to ask if she would volunteer for the hazardous dive. She simply nodded and started donning her dive suit. He did the same.

'You're not seriously diving with that coming our way?' Julia asked in disbelief as she pointed at the ropy lava coursing like a river in their direction.

'We need answers, Doctor,' Juan said, shrugging the

suit over his torso and pulling the air tank and cooling pump onto his shoulders. 'Once the lava reaches the ship, the hardened rock will make it impossible to enter the crew areas even after it has cooled. If we don't go into that ship now, we never will.'

36

Mumbai

After circling the ballroom, Eddie returned to the area farthest from the bar, where Raven, MacD, and Linc were doing their best to avoid engaging with the other guests.

'I found the door to the emergency stairs,' Eddie said. 'It's in the hallway to the bathrooms.'

'Anyone guarding it?' Linc asked.

'One guy. He looks serious about keeping people out of the stairwell.'

MacD looked in that direction, but the guard wasn't visible from the main room. 'Is it alarmed?'

'Doesn't look like it.'

'Then all we need to do is keep the guard occupied for a few minutes while you're gone,' Raven said. 'I can do that.'

'You might be missed,' Eddie said. 'The bathrooms are close by, though. Give me your perfume.'

She handed him a small spray bottle, which he pocketed.

'Do we know where Mallik's office is yet?' Eddie said to Murph.

'Got it,' Murph replied. 'It's on the floor right above you.'

'You're sure?'

'Yeah. I found a video of his wife before she died. She was giving a tour to one of those *Lifestyles of the Rich and Famous*–type shows just after they finished construction on the building. She showed off her husband's office, and I could read the floor number when she got off the elevator.'

'Okay,' Eddie said. 'Linc, you come with me. Nobody will think it's odd if her bodyguard is gone for a few minutes given how secure this building is.'

'What should MacD and I do?' Raven asked.

'Keep an eye on the hallway to the bathrooms. Let us know if anyone is coming.'

'And try not to talk to anyone else,' Linc said.

MacD smiled. 'With the way we look, it's gonna be hard to keep people away from us.'

'Then you do all the talking,' Linc said. 'That'll drive them off.'

'Because of this honey-smooth voice? It'll be a challenge, but Ah'm up to it.'

Raven rolled her eyes and continued to wear her most dour and unapproachable expression. Eddie thought that might actually work.

He and Linc crossed the room and entered the hall to the bathrooms. They both nodded as they passed the guard before going into the men's room.

After a quick check to make sure it was empty, Eddie said to Raven, 'Anyone coming our way?'

'You're clear,' she said.

They both went back out. Eddie was clutching the perfume bottle. Without a word, he lifted it and sprayed it in the guard's face.

The guard sputtered for a second in surprise before the sedative gas took effect. He sagged into the waiting arms of Eddie and Linc, who quickly dragged him into a stall in the men's room.

They sat him on the toilet seat, and Eddie used zip ties to secure his wrists to the gold-plated grab bars on either side. At the same time, Linc gagged him with a handkerchief just in case he woke up before they left the party. They took his radio, then Linc exited the stall so Eddie could lock the door from the inside and climb out.

'Three women coming your way,' MacD said.

Linc and Eddie left the restroom and smiled at the women entering the ladies' room. When they were alone, Eddie handed the radio to Linc and said, 'Wait here and pretend you're checking your phone. Let me know if anyone misses the guard.'

Linc tucked the radio into his coat pocket and inserted the earpiece. Instead of saying 'Good luck,' which was actually considered bad luck in the Corporation, he said, 'Good hunting.'

Eddie entered the stairwell and bounded up the steps two at a time. He was about to open the door to the floor where Mallik's office was when he heard voices through it.

He'd have to wait and hope they left. Of course, if they opened the door, the whole operation would be a bust.

Natalie Taylor was arguing with the chef in the kitchen next to the ballroom. He claimed that there was no record of a cake that was supposed to be delivered to the party.

'I didn't approve that monstrosity,' the Frenchman said, sneering at the giant novelty cake. He'd been flown in from Paris especially for this event.

'Mr Mallik himself requested it,' Taylor said in a calm voice. 'Here, I'll show you.'

She took a piece of paper from her pocket. It was an

invoice with Romir Mallik's signature on it. Even Mallik would think it was his own handwriting.

The chef examined it carefully, frowning the entire time.

'If you'd like to interrupt Mr Mallik while he's entertaining guests, I'm sure he'd be happy to come in here and attend to this. Or maybe you could call him.' She wasn't bluffing. She'd be perfectly happy for Mallik to come into the kitchen.

'You can't expect me to have his personal number,' the chef said.

'No, but *I* do,' Taylor said, holding out her phone. 'He said to call him if there was any trouble.'

The chef pursed his lips, then shoved the invoice back to her.

'Fine. When does he want it?'

'Now.'

'But we are still serving the hors d'oeuvres!'

She raised an eyebrow and held out the phone again.

The chef put up his hands in surrender. 'All right. It's his party. But is any of that edible?'

'Just the top tier.'

'Before you go, let me finish preparing the rest of the desserts to go with it.'

'How long will that take?'

'Just a few minutes.'

Taylor made a show of looking at her watch. 'I will wheel this out in two minutes no matter what.' She lowered the bunting over the sides of the cart to hide the wheels.

While she waited for the chef and his staff to frantically get the desserts ready, she looked at her phone, activating the app she would need once the cake was in place in the ballroom.

Inside the cake was a tripod-mounted remote-controlled machine gun called a Small Caliber Ultra-Light, or SCUL. Her app showed the view from its thermal camera, which could see through the paper-thin sides of the cake. With the controls on her phone, she could rotate the gun in a three-hundred-sixty-degree arc, raise or lower the angle of the barrel, and fire its eight hundred rounds of belt-fed 5.56mm bullets.

In a few minutes, Mallik's ability to stop the Colossus Project would be finished. As soon as the cake was locked in place in the ballroom and Taylor had a clear view of him, she'd cut him down, taking as many of the guests with him as she could. She'd escape in the panic and confusion after she made sure he was dead.

Raven, unhappy that she was relegated to serving as distracting eye candy, pretended to sip her champagne as she watched the hallway to the restrooms. MacD, on the other hand, seemed to be enjoying himself. Women continually gave him the once-over as they passed by.

'Mallik sure is well connected,' he said. 'Ah recognize at least four high-ranking generals here, in addition to the celebrities and politicians.'

'How do you know?' Raven asked.

'Did a lot of work in this region back in the day. Saw some of the local brass at that time.'

'What if they recognize you?'

'Never happen. Ah was too low-level back then. These guys wouldn't bother looking at an officer ranking lower than major.'

MacD had been looking at her, but his eyes suddenly

focused on someone over Raven's left shoulder. They widened as a subtle message to her just before she heard a man's voice speak to her. She turned to see Romir Mallik approaching her with a big grin.

'Miss Jain,' he said, 'I'm so glad you could come tonight.' Asad Torkan stood silently by his side.

Raven gave him her high-wattage smile and said, 'It's a pleasure to see you, Mr Mallik. It's a wonderful party and a beautiful home.'

'Thank you. I'm happy to finally meet you in person. I've been a fan of your films for many years. I'm sorry you went to America to continue your career. I hope you have returned for good.'

'If India will have me.' She turned to MacD. 'May I introduce you to Cole Randle.'

Mallik narrowed his eyes at MacD and nodded curtly.

'Perhaps I can have you over sometime to watch one of your movies,' Mallik said, obviously excluding MacD. 'It would be a treat to be able to hear your comments on it as we watch. I have a private forty-seat theater three stories below this room.'

'I would like that,' Raven said.

He looked at her with a curious expression. 'Which of your films would you choose?' He waited for an answer with a tight smile. Raven couldn't tell if he was simply being courteous or if he suspected she wasn't who she said she was. Torkan was as stone-faced as ever, but he was watching both her and MacD intently.

She didn't hesitate, saying, *'Golibari Ki Rekha,'* an action movie which meant *Firing Line* in English. It was Kiara Jain's most famous role.

That seemed to be the right response because Mallik beamed at her and said, 'That is my favorite. Later, if you would be so kind, I may ask you to indulge us with a song.'

At the mention of a possible performance, Raven felt her stomach clench. She paused for only a fraction of a second before she said, 'I'd be delighted.'

'Excellent,' Mallik said. 'Well, I need to tend to my other guests, but you can be sure I will return.' He took Raven's hand and gave it a squeeze before he walked away with Torkan.

When they were out of earshot, MacD said, 'You don't sing, do you?'

'Not a note. If they put a microphone in my face and make me serenade the crowd, every ear within a six-block radius will be bleeding.'

She was turned away from Mallik for the moment, facing the direction of the hallway leading to the kitchen, which was on the opposite side of the ballroom from the bathrooms. A Caucasian woman with red hair caught her eye because she wasn't wearing an evening gown. Instead, she was dressed in the attire of the serving staff. She was the only non-Indian working there.

The woman was carefully surveying the room, almost like an operative. Her face seemed familiar to Raven, but she couldn't quite place it. The servant kept scanning the room until her gaze settled on Romir Mallik. She stared at him for a few seconds, then went back into the kitchen.

She walked with a grace and athleticism that wasn't usual for a server, and that's when Raven realized she'd seen the woman's face before.

MacD must have noticed her expression because he said, 'What's wrong?'

'Remember that sketch Lyla Dhawan had Kevin Nixon draw?' Raven said. 'It was circulated to the crew after she left.'

MacD nodded. 'Sure. The woman who killed half the passengers on Xavier Carlton's missing jet and then imprisoned the rest on Jhootha Island. Why?'

'She's here.'

37

The Red Sea

Juan pushed away from Nomad's air lock and swam toward the shipwreck's superstructure with Linda behind him. They were wearing full-face masks and could communicate with each other and the sub using low-frequency acoustic transmitters. Cameras attached to each of their masks were recording the dive, but the video couldn't be transmitted underwater. Though the cooling suit was keeping the heated water at bay, Juan could feel how hot it was because of the slim gap between his mask and hood. It wasn't hot enough to burn him, but it was certainly hot enough to cook him in minutes if his cooling unit failed.

'How are you doing back there, Linda?' he asked.

'Cozy and warm,' she replied.

'Water is up to one hundred and twenty and still rising, but your core temps are steady and normal,' Julia said, who was monitoring their body temperatures from the sensors embedded in the suits. The deep rumble of the flowing lava added to the sense of urgency.

'I trust Max's cooling suit design,' Juan said. 'We shouldn't be more than fifteen minutes.'

'We'll stay right here until you come back,' Eric said. He had Nomad hovering near the bridge wing's outer door.

When Juan reached the door, he said, 'Let's see what's in here.'

He pressed down on the handle, but it didn't budge. He tried twice more. Nothing. He pulled as hard as he could and got nowhere.

'The mechanism must be rusted shut,' Linda said. 'All this heat.'

'We better hope all the doors aren't like this or we're going to have to break out some explosives to get in. There's another door two decks down. We'll try that one.'

They swam down to the door, and Juan tried the latch. It gave slightly. He kicked at the handle with his prosthetic foot, and the mechanism finally snapped free. He yanked at it, but it only came open a few inches. It took both of them pulling on it to make the gap wide enough for them to go through. Juan led the way in.

There were no windows on this level, so he turned on his headlamp. No wildlife had penetrated the crew areas, and the corridor was free of growth, which meant they might come across intact information about the ship.

Most navigation and other work would be done on a computer, but even a ship as advanced as this one would have written checklists and maps as backups. If he and Linda could at least find out the name of the vessel, they would be able to track it back to its owner and manufacturer.

'There's a set of stairs,' Juan said, and swam toward them. They went up two levels and entered the bridge.

The bridge was a high-tech operation consisting of dozens of flat-panel screens, interspersed with keyboards, control buttons, telephone handsets, and joysticks for maneuvering the ship. The only loose items he noticed were several coffee mugs scattered on the floor. Just a few pinpoints of dim light penetrated the thick growth of algae on the windows. The leather of the captain's and helmsman's chairs hadn't begun to decay.

'Chairman,' Linda said. 'We've got a name.'

He turned to see her pointing at a brass plaque fastened to the back wall. He swam over and could make out the name COLOSSUS 3 emblazoned across the top.

'Project C,' Juan said. 'And I'll take a wild stab that there are at least two more Project Colossus ships.'

'Look at the launch date,' Linda said.

'Eighteen months ago. Right around the time that Xavier Carlton's A380 was hijacked.'

At the bottom of the plaque was a symbol he recognized: a circle with nine spokes with a clockwise swastika at its center.

'Eric,' Juan said, 'we now have confirmation that the Nine Unknown Men are connected to Project C, which apparently stands for *Colossus*.'

'That must be a nod to the first programmable computer,' Eric said. 'Colossus was built to decipher the Nazi Lorenz cipher during World War Two.'

'It's also part of this ship's name. *Colossus 3*.'

'I hate to break it to you,' Julia said, 'but it's over one hundred and twenty-five out here. I recommend you start heading out of the wreckage.'

'Two more minutes, Hux,' Juan said. 'Don't want to come out of here empty-handed.'

'I'll give you two, and not a second more.'

'Roger that.'

270

Next to the plaque was a row of shelves with manuals and rolled-up maps.

'Start gathering those up to take with us,' Juan said to Linda. 'I'm going to see if I can find the captain's log.'

Linda nodded, unfurled a drawstring net bag, and began stuffing books and maps into the sack. Juan swam through an open door at the back of the bridge, where he expected to find the captain's private office.

The small room contained a desk, two chairs, a file cabinet, and a large safe. The safe still shut meant the captain didn't have enough time to retrieve its contents before abandoning ship. But, it did mean that there might be other important items in the office that the captain had neglected to recover.

He started with the desk and rifled through the drawers. They were locked, but his small pry bar was strong enough to lever them open. It was in the third drawer that he found the captain's log. He simply shoved the leather-bound notebook into his drysuit pocket and went over to the file cabinet to see what he could find.

As soon as he opened the top drawer, there was a rapidly growing roar coming from outside the *Colossus 3*, which started shaking violently.

Juan had the odd sensation of being tossed around by the water inside the ship. He raced back to the bridge.

'What's going on out there?' Juan asked over the deafening sound.

'Oh, no!' Julia shouted.

'Brace yourselves!' was all Eric could get out before Juan and Linda felt something slam into the shipwreck.

With a thundering crash, the *Colossus 3* rocked to the side and felt as if it were going to keel over. After a few seconds, the roar subsided, and the ship stabilized.

'You okay?' Juan said to Linda, who had dropped the bag she'd been filling.

'Yes. Just a little shaken up.'

'Nomad, what's your status?' he said. 'Eric, Julia, are you all right?'

There was a moment of silence. Then he heard Eric's voice, tinny and distant.

'Chairman, do you read me?'

'We're fine in here,' Juan said. 'How's Nomad?'

'We got a good rattle, but we were able to avoid any damage.'

'What was that?'

'Avalanche. That explosion must have destabilized the side of the seamount more than we thought.'

'Then we're getting out of here before we get hit by another one,' Juan said.

'Chairman, that's going to be a problem.'

'Why?'

'The avalanche swept across the deck of the ship,' Eric said. 'The door you entered is now covered by a ten-foot-high pile of rocks.'

38

Mumbai

The voices Eddie heard had been two women, possibly maids because he could hear the sound of a cart being rolled down the hall. Then he heard an elevator ding, and the voices disappeared.

He pushed open the door and saw that the lavishly appointed corridor was empty.

'Now where to?' he asked Murph. He moved his head around so Murph could see the view from his glasses.

'Should be straight ahead two doors down on the right.'

Eddie walked casually just in case he ran into anyone. He could always claim he exited the elevator on the wrong floor and got lost.

The door to the office was open, and Eddie slipped inside. The room was filled with artifacts from the Mughal dynasty, paintings of emperors on exotic thrones, and antique furniture made of Indian teak. The enormous desk held only two items: a jewel-encrusted lamp and a sleek laptop.

Eddie sat at the desk and flipped open the computer. The screen showed a prompt for a password. Eddie plugged in a device that was wirelessly connected to Murph's computer back at the hotel.

'It's in your court now,' Eddie said.

'Working on it,' Murph said. Eddie could hear the sound of Murph's fingers furiously hammering his keyboard.

The screen remained unchanged. 'How long will this take?' Eddie asked.

'I'll know in a second if this will happen.'

All Eddie could do was wait. He couldn't leave without the USB transmitter or Mallik would know his system had been compromised.

A few seconds later, Murph said, 'His encryption is good. I'm not getting in without his password. We'll have to go with the barnacle.'

Eddie removed the USB device and took out a smaller item about the size of a hearing aid battery but rectangular like the USB port. It was called a barnacle because it could be inserted into the machine without being noticed.

He picked up the laptop and inspected the two USB ports on it. The right-hand port had a tiny bit of wear on it, while the left-hand port was pristine.

Eddie plugged in the barnacle and verified that it couldn't be seen unless you were looking directly into the port. It would only be detected if Mallik tried to plug something into the left-hand port, which seemed to be the less used one.

Now, the next time the laptop password was entered, the barnacle would secretly download a bit of software into the computer that would force it to connect to the internet and give Murph access to its contents. The downside was that they had no idea when that would happen.

'Let's get ready to leave,' Eddie said to everyone on the comms. 'And Murph, tell Hali we'll be leaving in three minutes.'

'He just texted me that he's currently pretending to be lost,' Murph said. 'Apparently, he's getting an earful from the real Kiara Jain and will be relieved to drop her off whenever we're gone.'

Eddie closed the laptop and headed back to the stairs.

'Eddie,' Linc said, 'two guards just came looking for our friend in the bathroom. I told them he said he was going downstairs for something, but they said that's where they just came from. They're on their way up toward your floor. So am I.'

'We have a situation in the ballroom, too,' Raven said. 'The woman from Jhootha Island just wheeled in a giant cake.'

When Raven saw Mallik looking at the giant novelty cake with surprise and confusion, she knew he was not expecting it. The band began to play a lively fanfare as it rolled in.

'Something's about to go down,' she said to MacD.

'Ah know. Bomb, you think?'

'Maybe. If she tries to exit quickly, we'll know.' Raven also noticed that the woman kept her face shielded from Mallik and Torkan as if they might recognize her.

'Ah'll go stand by the kitchen door to keep her from leaving,' MacD said.

'And I'll see if I can find out what she's up to,' Raven said.

The woman backed away from the cake, turned around, and took out her phone. Raven remembered that Juan said Rasul had used his phone as a launch control for the BrahMos cruise missile. If the woman was here as part of an attack on Mallik, the phone would be the perfect trigger.

Raven walked up quietly behind her.

'Excuse me,' Raven said. 'Do you know where I can find some seltzer water?'

The woman shook her head and shrugged, barely acknowledging Raven.

'It's just that I spilled something on my dress and I don't want it to stain.'

This time, the woman looked at Raven. Her eyes were focused and fierce.

The woman struck with a lightning punch, but Raven was able to turn away to minimize the blow. Then she returned with a left to the jaw. The woman only staggered and spun around, intending to lash out with a kick, but Raven moved quickly out of reach.

The woman refocused on her phone but just before Raven reached out and knocked it out of her hand, the woman tapped the screen.

Instead of exploding, to Raven's shock the cake erupted with gunfire.

Linc and Eddie took out the guards in the stairwell using a coordinated attack. Linc sucker punched one of the guards from behind just as they were about to enter the level where the offices were. Simultaneously, Eddie rushed out and slammed the head of the other one into the wall.

They started to drag the guards to join their colleague in the bathroom when the buzz saw sound of rapid machine gun fire clattered from the direction of the ballroom.

Eddie and Linc tore down the stairs.

*

Torkan pulled Mallik behind him as bullets ripped through the air above their heads. The aim of the gun was off, and rounds raked the ceiling and upper walls of the ballroom.

'It's her!' Mallik yelled. 'Natalie Taylor! I saw her fighting with Kiara Jain.'

'Then that can't be Kiara Jain,' Torkan shouted above the screams and gunfire. Half the guests had dove to the floor while the other half were running in panic.

'Come on!' Torkan grabbed Mallik's arm and dragged him toward the emergency exit, into the bathroom hallway, and rushed to the stairwell door.

On their way through, they passed a black man and an Asian man headed in the other direction.

Raven's knocking away the phone had caused the machine gun to temporarily tilt up, which had prevented the assault from becoming a massacre, but if the woman got the phone back, dozens of people would die.

Raven kicked off her mile-high platform pumps as she prepared to finish off the woman when she saw a panicked Prisha Naidu running straight toward the line of fire. The machine gun's aim was now inching down from the recoil, threatening to slice her to ribbons.

Raven made the only choice she could. Instead of taking the assassin down, she raced toward the Indian actress, tackling her to the floor moments before she would have been killed.

Raven turned to see the assassin run toward the balcony. Then she had to hold the shrieking Prisha down again as the machine gun made another pass over them.

*

MacD could see that the machine gun's aim was falling, and it was only a matter of seconds until bullets began chewing into the guests huddled in terror on the floor.

Someone must have summoned the elevator because its door suddenly opened. He maneuvered himself behind the cart and waited until the machine gun was firing away from him. Then he pushed the cart toward the elevator, hoping the door was wide enough for the cake to fit. The cart gathered momentum until it was hurtling through the door and slammed into the back of the elevator. Sparks flew as bullets churned into the brass walls of the cab. The door closed, muting the sound of the continuing fire.

He spotted the nearest security guard and raced over to him.

'Get on your radio and tell someone to shut down all the elevators! Now!'

The startled guard nodded and got on his radio.

MacD turned and sprinted away to look for Raven and the assassin.

Natalie Taylor was fuming as she attached her belt to the rope that had been lowered to the balcony. She'd been planning this strike for weeks at Carlton's direction, ever since he began suspecting Mallik of betrayal, and it had gone off without a hitch until that guest in the turquoise gown attacked her. She had to be some kind of under-cover security operative.

Her nemesis wasn't giving up, even now. Taylor saw her leap to her feet and run toward the balcony. But it was too late. The rope began to pull Taylor up.

As she rose toward the roof, she looked down to see

the woman below watching her escape. Taylor returned her icy gaze with a sneer.

When she got to the top of the building, the ex-soldier who had hoisted her up pulled her onto the roof. She detached herself from the portable winch, and they got into the chopper. It took off before anyone could reach the roof to stop them.

She was glad she didn't have her phone. Telling Xavier Carlton that the mission failed wasn't something she was looking forward to.

Eddie and Linc emerged from the bathroom hallway to find moaning survivors and a devastated ballroom.

MacD and Raven were on the balcony.

'Are you two all right?' Eddie said.

MacD nodded. 'This party got a little out of hand.'

'We're fine,' Raven said in a disgusted tone. 'But the Jhootha Island woman got away. I just saw her escape helicopter take off.'

'Then let's get out of here before the cops arrive and make us answer difficult questions.'

To avoid the crowd of guests exiting by the main stairway, they accessed the kitchen door leading to the stairs next to the service elevator.

Police cars, ambulances, and fire engines were already pulling up to the high-rise. Tiny wouldn't be able to get their ride anywhere near the building. They put on the guise of terrified guests and ran past the emergency vehicles. They found the Porsche SUV idling at the side of the road on the next block.

'Everyone good?' Tiny asked as they got in.

'No casualties,' Eddie said.

'Your timing is perfect. There's Hali.'

Hali's limo came to a stop next to them. He got out and walked around to the Porsche.

The rear window of the limo rolled down.

'We're not at the party yet, you idiot,' Kiara Jain said. 'Where do you think you're going?'

Hali pointed at Raven, who was sitting by the open door of the Porsche.

'Apparently, I picked up the wrong Kiara,' he said. 'And I like this one better.' He got in the SUV.

Tiny drove off, leaving the actress gaping at the sight of her receding doppelgänger.

Mallik seethed as he retreated to his office with Torkan.

'Why were those guards unconscious?' he demanded about the men they had stepped over in the stairwell. 'And how did Taylor get into my house?'

'I will find out,' Torkan said. 'The two men we passed must have helped her. But I don't understand why the woman impersonating Kiara Jain was fighting her.'

'How do you know it wasn't her?'

'I've seen her movies. Kiara doesn't do her own stunts.'

'Never mind. It's not important anymore. I'm obviously not safe here. We're leaving tonight. Until we launch the satellite, I don't want to be anywhere Carlton can find me. Make the arrangements.'

'Yes, sir. I'll have your helicopter here in five minutes.'

'Then we'll talk about payback. He comes at me that brazenly, I'm going to strike at him just as hard.'

'I'll take care of it.'

Mallik could see that Torkan was troubled that Natalie Taylor could so easily get through his people and carry out an attack inside his own home. He should be.

'Is there anything you need?' Torkan asked.

'No,' Mallik said. 'All I need is this.'

He picked up his laptop and stalked out of the room.

39

The Red Sea

While they searched for a new exit from the *Colossus 3*, Juan and Linda's suits were beginning to lose their ability to cool. In a few minutes, the coolant would be the same temperature as the surrounding water, and they would quickly overheat.

Juan had already tried smashing the windows on the bridge, but the thick impact-resistant glass was impervious to his attempts to shatter it with a fire extinguisher. He just couldn't get enough momentum in the water.

Their efforts to pry open the doors were fruitless. The rust in the mechanisms was too solid.

He saw Linda clutching her head and said, 'How are you doing?'

'A headache,' she replied. 'Bad one.'

'That's one of the first symptoms of heatstroke,' Julia said. 'Your core temperatures are already above a hundred degrees, and still rising. If we don't get you out of there soon, both of you will pass out.'

She didn't have to tell them that death would soon follow.

'The lava flow has also taken a turn because of new pathways opened by the avalanche,' Eric said. 'It's headed straight for you now.'

'I could ram the bridge windows with Nomad.'

'No. You might damage the sub and then we'd all be in trouble. We'll find another route.'

Linda was having trouble holding the weight of the mesh sack, so Juan took it from her. He also noticed that he'd stopped sweating, which wasn't a good sign.

'Follow me,' he said, and swam for the stairs.

'That . . .' Linda shook her head, trying to clear out the cobwebs. 'The door down there . . . on the deck. Eric said it's blocked.'

'The windows in one of the cabins might be easier to break.' He took the fire extinguisher with him as a battering ram.

Juan was also feeling the effects of the heat. A couple of times as he was swimming, he lost his orientation and almost started going back up until he saw Linda behind him.

When they reached the next level down, he turned to port and went a few yards before he remembered that he was going in the direction of the oncoming lava. He back-tracked and went to the opposite end of the corridor.

One of the cabin doors was open, and Juan was surprised to see a luxurious stateroom that could have served as the captain's suite on a cruise ship. At first, he thought he might be hallucinating, but when he ran his hand over a sofa, he knew this was real.

'This ship is weird,' Linda said.

The only thing the cabin didn't have that a cruise ship would was patio doors leading to a balcony. Instead, it had small windows as if to disguise the true nature of what the *Colossus 3* was hiding on the inside.

Linda went to the closest window and ran her hands over it.

'It's barely big enough,' she said. 'Even without the tank and cooling pump.'

They'd never get through without removing their bulky equipment.

'Eric,' Juan said, 'we're on the starboard side of the ship, one level down. We're going to have to go through a window without our air or coolant. How close can you get?'

'Hold on,' came the reply. Then a powerful light illuminated the window. 'I see you. But I can't get too close or we might get tangled with the ropes of the lifeboat davits.'

'Get right above us.' Then Juan asked Linda, 'Ready?'

She nodded. 'It's better than being the frog in a slowly boiling pot of water.'

'The water outside is probably hotter than the water in here, so we don't want to break the window until we're ready to leave. We'll take off the air tanks but keep the masks on until we have to go. Detach my coolant hoses from the suit.'

As soon as she unplugged them, the water around him instantly felt twenty degrees warmer.

He shrugged off the tank and pump. Then he disconnected Linda's cooling unit, and she took off the equipment.

'All set?' Juan asked.

'I'm burning up. Let's go.'

He rammed the fire extinguisher against the window. It cracked but didn't break. He tried twice more before it shattered. He used his pry bar to clear the glass.

'Go,' he said. Linda took one last breath, detached the hose from her mask, and wriggled through.

Juan was getting light-headed. He remembered that he

was supposed to take something else with him that was important. What was it?

He looked down and saw the mesh bag holding the books. That's what it was. He picked it up and it felt like it was packed with lead.

He took a few deep breaths and unplugged his mask.

Squeezing through the window while carrying the sack required all of his rapidly draining strength. When he was finally free of the ship, he saw Linda's silhouette floating above him in Nomad's light.

He swam to her and saw that her eyes were barely open.

He shook her shoulder to keep her from passing out, but that's exactly what he felt like doing. His limbs were like jelly, and he suddenly realized he was no longer holding the bag. It had slipped out of his grip. He looked down, but it was lost somewhere among the ropes of the lifeboat davits.

Every stroke toward the waiting Nomad was a chore, but he didn't let go of Linda. She was feebly kicking, and the combination of heat and lack of air was about to render her unconscious.

He spotted the flashing light next to the open air lock door on the bottom of the sub and willed himself to reach it. He pushed Linda into the small space and followed her in.

His muscles were aching, but he forced himself to drive through the pain and pull the hatch closed. When the light was green, he slammed his hand into the button that would purge the water.

Then he blacked out.

When he came to, he found himself lying on Nomad's

floor covered with cold packs. He tried to sit up, but Julia pushed him back down.

'Linda,' he croaked.

'She's all right.' She pointed at Linda lying next to him. She was also buried in the cold packs. Her eyes were blinking.

'I'm never getting in a Jacuzzi again,' she said.

'Or a sauna,' Juan added. Then he remembered the sack containing the documents from the *Colossus 3*. 'I dropped the bag.'

'I saw,' Eric said from the cockpit. Nomad was heading back to the *Oregon*, the lights from the moon pool providing a beacon in the darkness.

'Can you get it?'

'We're getting you two to my medical bay first,' Julia said.

'I lost it in gloom,' Eric said. 'We can do a search later, but I'm afraid it'll be covered by the lava by the time we get back down here. Or, at least, too close to the lava to get to. Don't worry, though. You still got this.' Eric held up a leather-bound book. 'This was in your suit.'

'The captain's logbook. Let's hope it says something useful.'

'I think it will. But it's not the captain's log. They're notes from one of the scientists on board. I was only able to see the first page because I didn't want to damage the others.'

'It didn't say anything about where we can find the artificial intelligence computer, did it?'

'In fact, it did. We've already seen the AI. Those vats? That's the artificial intelligence.'

'What do you mean?' Linda asked.

'We'll know more when we can look at the entire contents,' Eric said. 'But from what's on just the first page, it seems that the AI isn't silicon-based. It's organic. The *Colossus 3* was built to carry a giant biocomputer.'

40

Cyprus

The hold of the *Colossus 5* hummed from the pumps circulating nutrients to the vats of biochemical cells that made up the heart of the supercomputer. Xavier Carlton and Lionel Gupta were getting a status update from the chief scientist, Chen Min, about the operation as they walked through the cavernous space. Security guards trailed them, while engineers went about final preparations for getting under way in less than forty-eight hours. Carlton was keeping an eye on Gupta, who seemed to be growing suspicious of Carlton's motives for persuading him to stay on board.

'Right now, we are feeding the Colossus vats with custom-grown phytoplankton that we store on board,' Chen said, 'but once we're at sea, we will harvest plankton as we sail, providing an unlimited source of nutrition for the computer.'

'What is the performance on *Colossus 1, 2,* and *4*?'

'The Indian Ocean waters were not as rich in food sources as we had hoped. That's why I'm recommending that we station the ships off the west coast of Africa.'

'How long will it take to reach the singularity?' Gupta asked.

'The ships' microwave transceivers have to connect. Once that happens, we can expect the artificial intelligence to be completely unified in a matter of minutes.'

'And what will that enable?' Carlton asked.

'We will no longer need a crew of programmers to write code. Colossus will be able to improve itself at an exponential rate. All we have to do is order it to solve a problem and it will be able to do it on its own.'

'But it can't do anything without an explicit command, right?'

Chen nodded. 'Colossus is essentially our slave. We've built in protocols to starve it if it doesn't conform to our controls. But, it's not going to achieve thought processes or self-perception in the normal sense of the words.'

'So it won't be thinking for itself?' Carlton asked.

Chen paused, then shook his head. 'No.'

'I don't like that hesitation,' Gupta said. 'Is the fail-safe ready in case Colossus doesn't follow our orders?'

'We've had to disable Mr Mallik's Vajra EMP fail-safe system. Not only is its security compromised because of the incidents you've had with him, but it was not completely separate from Colossus's network. That means the AI could have shut Vajra down.' Mallik's electromagnetic pulse weapon placed on board was designed to wipe out the silicon circuits of the computers connecting the biochemical vats, which would disable Colossus by frying them.

'But you still have the backup fail-safe system in place.'

'Yes,' Chen said. 'And we believe we have taken care of the problem that sank the *Colossus 3*.'

He pointed to the red boxes on either side of the hold, positioned below the waterline. The explosives in those boxes, mounted on all the Colossus ships, were manually activated. None of them were connected to the network, so that the AI wouldn't be able to deactivate them in case it did become self-aware and disobeyed its commands.

In the previous version of the self-destruct system, the bombs' emergency activation sequence could be initiated by any crew member who had access to the explosives, which was basically anyone on the ship. Many of the Nine just chalked up the sinking of the *Colossus 3* to a mistake by a crew member who had died in the blast, but Carlton had always suspected that it was done on purpose. Now he was sure Mallik had been the one behind it.

The new system required the bombs to be activated by two officers on the bridge. Until then, the bombs were inert. Not even Chen or Carlton could activate them alone. The fail-safes on all of the Colossus ships were linked together by encrypted radio signal so that if the self-destruct was activated on one ship, it would begin the countdown on the other ships as well. The bombs would have to be disabled on all of the ships for the self-destruct system to fail. If the Colossus AI went rogue after the singularity was reached, then each of the ships would be a danger.

Carlton had always hated the entire fail-safe concept. They'd poured a billion dollars into Colossus, and the thought that one of the other Nine could wipe it all away with a single command was ridiculous no matter what risk Colossus could pose.

'What if we deactivated the fail-safe?' Carlton asked.

Gupta gaped at him. 'What?'

'Mallik is getting close to launching his final Vajra satellite. We can't let another "accident" delay or stop us.'

'If your attack on his life hadn't gone so badly, we

290

would have been able to stop him from launching it without Colossus.'

'A fully operational Colossus was always our best option,' Carlton said. 'Once it reaches the singularity, it will be able to access any computer system on the planet, including his satellite network. We'll be able to shut it down from here. The attempt on Mallik's life was simply an opportunity we couldn't pass up.'

'And it was an epic blunder. Your news outlets have been plastering the story all over the place.' He narrowed his eyes at Carlton. 'I wonder if Natalie Taylor really is on our side.'

'She said there were operatives there who stopped her, but they didn't seem to be Mallik's people, either.'

Gupta snickered. 'She "said." I noticed she's not even here.'

'She's on her way back. I spoke to her while she was in the air.'

'If she's so confident that they weren't Mallik's people, then who were they?'

'We don't know. But we need to be ready to deal with a third party. Remember, it wasn't Mallik who took out the facility on Jhootha Island.'

'Another failure. We should have closed it down as soon as the *Colossus 5* was attacked. I should have taken over the project myself.'

'You're suddenly getting a spine?' Carlton said in amusement. 'I didn't think you had it in you.'

'Then I have another surprise for you,' Gupta said.

The guards behind them raised their weapons and pointed them at Chen and Carlton.

'What are you doing?' Chen demanded.

'What I should have done the moment we left the Library. It's obvious I can't trust you, Carlton.'

'I'm impressed,' Carlton said, nodding his head at the guards in appreciation of Gupta's double cross. 'But you're correct that you shouldn't have trusted me.'

He raised a hand, and automatic weapons fire cut down all but one of the guards where they stood. Natalie Taylor and Carlton's private security squad emerged from their hiding places behind the vats.

Carlton smiled at the remaining guard, who had tipped Carlton off about the betrayal. 'Welcome to the winning team.'

'Thank you, sir.'

Carlton walked up to Gupta and said, 'I knew you would try something like this. I just wanted to wait and see who the other traitors were. Now it appears you are the only traitor left.' He turned to Taylor. 'And you've just redeemed yourself. Take him back to his cabin and keep him there until I figure out if I want him alive or dead.'

All of his bravado was gone, and Gupta's lip was quivering as Taylor and the loyal guard led him away. The remaining members of Carlton's squad began stacking up the bodies.

Chen looked at Carlton in astonishment at what had just happened.

'I prize loyalty above all else,' Carlton said to him. 'Remember that.'

'Of course, sir,' Chen said.

'Now, before I go, what's the status of the other Colossus ships?'

Chen blinked his eyes as he gathered himself, then looked down at his tablet computer.

'I just got a report from the captain of the *Colossus 1*. They had trouble with one of the prisoners brought to the ship from Jhootha Island and he had to be eliminated.'

'Which leaves how many?'

'Twenty-two.'

'And you still need them alive?' Carlton casually asked.

'They do provide some needed expertise until we're completely operational. But they will be unnecessary after that.'

'Excellent. I don't like having them around any longer than we have to. Where are the ships now?'

'They're currently steaming north in the Red Sea, which puts them on schedule for the rendezvous.' Chen frowned at the report.

'What is it?'

'Just something odd,' Chen said. 'When they were passing near the undersea volcano where the *Colossus 3* went down, they spotted a ship loitering in the vicinity.'

That set Carlton's teeth on edge. It would be cause for concern if someone was investigating the wreckage. 'You said the *Colossus 3* would be destroyed by the lava.'

'It will be if it hasn't already. Besides, it doesn't sound like anything to worry about.'

'Why not?'

'Steam from the volcano was shrouding the ship when they passed by, so they didn't get a chance to see the name. But they could tell it was nothing more than an old tramp freighter.'

Carlton breathed a sigh of relief. If someone were actually trying to dredge up information from the *Colossus 3* in such a hazardous location, they would send a state-of-the-art recovery vessel, not some old rust bucket.

41

Although Mallik could have taken his yacht out to the designated coordinates in the Arabian Sea where his final Vajra satellite would be launched, he preferred the safety of his security vessel *Kalinga*. After the Nilgiri-class frigate had been decommissioned by the Indian Navy, Mallik had purchased and refurbished her to provide protection for his sea-based launch system. She currently used modern computer fire control systems for her twin 115mm cannons, anti-aircraft guns, and torpedoes, but the *Kalinga* was also fully operational even if her computers went down, a situation that Mallik anticipated in the very near future.

He had renamed her the *Kalinga* – and her sister ship the *Maurya* – to honor Emperor Ashoka and his creation of the Nine Unknown. This was before his current involvement with the Nine had corrupted Ashoka's vision. The years when the Mauryan Empire had conquered Kalinga had fascinated Mallik ever since his father told him he would someday become one of the Nine Unknown. He wished he could travel back in time to the birth of Ashoka's peaceful nation, but he would have to be content with the creation of his own empire, one he planned to rule with a similar grace and balance. Like all births, it would require pain and blood, but the result that he imagined would be a beautiful new era of civilization, one free from the specter of an artificial intelligence that could replace humanity.

Mallik took the laptop from his bag and sat at his desk to open it, noting the irony that this was one of the last few times he would be using it. He logged on to his network to review the status of the upcoming rocket launch and was pleased with what he read. According to reports, the launch platform and command ship were currently being resupplied and refueled while the *Maurya* patrolled the perimeter. All tests of the Vajra satellite had been passed with flying colors, so they should be able to launch as soon as the rocket was transferred to the launchpad.

The only problem was a monsoon that was sweeping across the Arabian Sea region where the launch was to take place. The weather team estimated that they would have to wait two days so the weather could clear. Mallik was annoyed by the delay, but he didn't want to take a chance with this satellite. If it exploded on launch like the last one or crashed because of the storm, it would be months before he could send up a replacement.

A knock at his cabin door interrupted his reading.

'Come,' he said.

Torkan entered with a thin smile on his face.

'You have good news?' Mallik asked.

'You were right about Carlton's location. His A380 is on Cyprus.'

Mallik nodded. 'He has a home there. He must be cowering with a security team around him for protection.'

Torkan's lip curled up as he nodded in agreement. 'There

is a cargo vessel being refitted in the Limassol shipyard. My sources say it fits the description of the *Colossus 5*.'

That got Mallik's attention. 'Do you think you can disable it again? We need more time.'

'I doubt it. They'll be ready for any attempt to damage the ship.'

'Then why are you still smiling?'

'Because I got word that his plane will be taking off two days from now.'

'Where is he going?'

'The destination wasn't specified. But I do know that he's contracted with a shipping company. He's taking two of his cars with him.'

Carlton was a car aficionado, mixing classic antiques and state-of-the-art sports cars. He was known for using his private jet to move them between his homes in London, Cyprus, Mumbai, the Cayman Islands, Sydney, and Monte Carlo.

'You have a plan?' Mallik asked.

Torkan's smile grew wider. 'If we can't take out the *Colossus 5*, eliminating Carlton is the next-best thing. My contact also found out that Lionel Gupta is with him. They were both spotted getting onto a helicopter at the Larnaca Airport.'

'Then it's likely they'll leave together as well. If they're dead, Chen Min will have no choice but to follow my orders no matter what Carlton has told him.'

'I will take care of it.'

He turned to leave, but Mallik stopped him.

'Asad, take a seat for a minute.' The news he had to deliver was unpleasant.

Torkan sat, a puzzled expression on his face.

Mallik searched for the words, but before he could say anything his phone buzzed.

He looked at the screen. It was the head of his network security department, somebody he wasn't expecting a call from.

'Just a minute,' he said to Torkan, and answered it gruffly. 'This better be important.'

'It is, sir,' came the tremulous reply. 'We've just detected a breach in our network.'

A jolt of anger ran through him. His systems had some of the best encryption in the world. 'How is that possible?'

'I don't know, sir, but someone began downloading files to an unauthorized location a few minutes ago. We're attempting to stop it now.'

'Tell me the name of the idiot who let this happen!' Mallik shouted.

'S . . . s . . . sir,' his internet security man stammered, 'the breach is originating from your laptop.'

Mallik wasn't sure if he heard right. Torkan tilted his head in confusion at the one-sided conversation.

'What?' Mallik said.

'We've tracked the leak to your computer,' the IT man said.

Mallik went red with rage. 'Change the network password on the *Kalinga* immediately, and do not let my computer reconnect. Do you understand me?'

'Yes, sir!'

He hung up and slammed the phone on the desk in frustration.

Mallik wanted to destroy the computer but restrained himself, knowing his people would need to analyze it. All he could do was shut it down.

'My computer was compromised,' he said. 'It has to be Carlton.'

'Can I see it?' Torkan asked.

Mallik handed the laptop over, and Torkan inspected it, turning it over slowly in his hands. Then he stopped to look at one of the USB ports. He took out a knife and pried out a tiny device embedded in the port.

Mallik leaned forward and took it from Torkan. 'I've never seen one of these, only heard of them. I think it's called a barnacle. How did you know?'

'Those men we saw in the stairwell back at the party,' Torkan said. 'I suspected they had been in your office.'

'But why would Carlton want to access my system? He must have known it was separate from my launch computer.'

Torkan shrugged. 'Maybe he wanted to use the information he downloaded to blackmail you about Colossus.'

'No, then he would implicate himself. We'll look at what was downloaded. That might tell us.'

Torkan prepared to stand. 'Is that what you wanted to talk about?'

Mallik sighed. 'Unfortunately, no. This is difficult because you are the only family I have left.'

Torkan sat forward. 'It's Rasul, isn't it?' He hadn't heard from his brother since the covert mission on the *Triton Star*.

Mallik nodded. 'I got a phone call from someone I know in the Indian government. They've received inquiries from the United States about the missing BrahMos missile. During the discussions, it was disclosed that Rasul was killed in the attack. I'm very sorry.'

Torkan slumped back in his seat, his jaw grinding back and forth as he processed what they had both feared.

'How did he die?' Torkan finally asked.

'I couldn't get any details. The Americans are tight-lipped about the events surrounding the attack on Diego Garcia.'

'Who did it? Who killed my brother?'

'I don't know that, either,' Mallik said. 'But when Rasul was texting me, he told me about the ship that had stopped the *Triton Star*. He said it was a cargo ship called the *Goreno*.'

Torkan stared at him for a moment, his eyes flickering with both sadness and fury. Then he rose.

'Are you okay? You sure you can still carry out the mission?'

Torkan nodded and spoke with a low growl that chilled Mallik.

'First, I'm going to kill Xavier Carlton. Then I'm going to track down and annihilate the people who murdered my brother.'

42

Djibouti

'How are you feeling?' Juan asked Linda as they walked to the *Oregon*'s boardroom for a meeting of the ship's executive officers.

'My headache is gone,' she answered. 'Ten hours' sleep helped.'

Juan had to agree. According to Julia, they had both suffered mild heatstroke, but rest and fluids were all they needed to recover.

'I just wish we could have retrieved the bag I dropped,' Juan said. Eric had tried, but by that time the lava had buried it along with the remainder of the *Colossus 3*.

'It wasn't a total loss. At least we got the name of the ship, and I know Eric has been reading through that scientist's notebook since we separated the pages and dried them out.'

'Let's see what it can tell us about this whole mess,' Juan said as he went through the boardroom's open door.

Waiting for them were Max, Eric, and Julia, as well as Eddie and Murph, who had arrived from Mumbai that morning. The small country of Djibouti on the Horn of Africa had the closest city to the Red Sea volcano with an international airport where Tiny could land the Corporation's Gulfstream. The *Oregon* was now tied up at the port's container terminal.

Maurice was serving dishes of local Djibouti cuisine prepared by the chef. The plates practically overflowed with Berber lamb, banana fritters, lentils, and samosas.

Juan took a seat at the head of the table and said, 'Eric, what have you been able to find out about the Colossus Project?' Maurice set a plate in front of Juan and closed the door as he glided out. Eric presented his findings with the aid of pictures from the notebook pages displayed on the room's giant monitor.

'Even though the notebook is made from archival paper, some of the ink ran from exposure to the water,' Eric said, pointing to the letters that were smeared across the pages. 'Many details about the biocomputer schematics are lost, but I was able to figure out how it worked.'

He switched to a view of the video that they had recorded from Little Geek and paused the image when it showed the damaged vat inside the hold. Murph frowned at the screen, still unhappy that his ROV had been destroyed in the explosion.

'Those vats contain a matrix of proteins, amino acids, and DNA molecules in specially designed biological cells,' Eric said, the excitement in his voice noticeable. 'They literally grew this computer.'

'What's the advantage over a silicon-based computer?' Julia asked.

'Silicon computers work in sequence, so you can only perform one calculation at a time. You're limited by the speed of the electrons flowing through the system. But with a biocomputer, the DNA can process information in parallel, which means the speed of its calculations is a thousand times faster than any other computer's processor.'

'If they've solved how to do this at scale,' Murph said, 'they're way ahead of anybody else. I couldn't find any biocomputers bigger than a loaf of bread in the scientific literature.'

Linda said, 'Why put this thing on a ship?'

'According to the notebook, Colossus is fed by plankton,' Eric said. 'That's another advantage. Although the computer servers that help with the processing require normal power delivery, the vats run like any other biological organism. They feed and then produce waste. Not only that, the artificial intelligence could be destroyed by a self-destruct mechanism if it got out of control. That's what sunk the ship *Colossus 3*. The sea really is the ideal environment.'

'If the ship was called the *Colossus 3*,' Eddie said, 'does that mean it's the third attempt to do this? Did they sink the ship because the AI already went haywire?'

Eric shook his head. 'The scientist theorized that four ships would need to be linked together by microwave transceivers to achieve the processing power required for the AI to become self-improving, meaning it could write its own programming. At the time the ship sank, there were only two other Colossus ships, with a fourth nearing completion.'

Max spoke up. 'While we were preparing for the dive at the site of the underwater volcano, I noticed three ships with those helical masts steaming north together. It was only after Nomad returned and we knew what *Colossus 3* looked like that I realized that those were the other Colossus ships. The *Colossus 4* must have been completed since the *Colossus 3* sank.'

'Which means they must be building a *Colossus 5* to complete their plans for four total ships,' Juan said. 'I talked with Langston Overholt about our discovery, and he connected me with NUMA. They checked their database of shipyards around the world and found that the Colossus ships were all built at the Moretti Navi facility in Naples.'

'Is that our next stop?' Eddie asked.

'No, there was an "accident" at the shipyard last week, the night before the attack on Diego Garcia. The ship was damaged and moved to another facility for final outfitting. But NUMA reported that they found it being finished under a different name at a shipyard in Cyprus. And it's almost complete, so we don't have much time to act. Lang has given us the green light to disable the ship, but before we talk about the operation, I want to hear about Mumbai.'

Eddie recounted the incident at the party. The media was labeling it a terrorist event targeting high-level Indian government officials. After checking with the CIA, Murph identified the attacker at the gala as Natalie Taylor, a former British Army Intelligence operative who'd been dishonorably discharged and now worked for Xavier Carlton. When Eddie got to the part about planting the barnacle on Mallik's computer, Juan asked Murph if he'd been able to get any actionable intel.

'You had to ask,' Murph said. 'The data download was going well until I hacked an internal firewall. It must have had a built-in silent alarm because the download shut down right after that.'

'What were you able to get?'

'The files confirm that Mallik has developed a weapons system for the Indian military that causes effects similar to an electromagnetic pulse, but I wasn't able to find out how it operates.'

'Then they used Vajra to take out the electronics at Diego Garcia?' Juan asked.

'That seems likely.'

'Have they mounted the weapon on a ship or aircraft?'

'Neither,' Murph said. 'It's satellite-based.'

They all thought about the ramifications in silence.

'They can target anywhere on earth,' Max said.

'For the limited time the satellite is overhead,' Murph said.

'Which makes us vulnerable no matter where we are.' Juan looked at Max. 'How are those modifications coming?'

'Still working on it. It's difficult because the *Oregon* is so dependent on her computers. We're hardened against most forms of EMP attack, but so was Diego Garcia.'

'Why would India attack the US?' Linda wondered.

'I don't think they did,' Murph said. 'In fact, I'm not sure the Indian military even knows that the weapon was installed on the Vajra satellites. As far as everyone knows, the satellite system is merely a communications platform for the Indian armed forces.'

'So Romir Mallik is behind the attack?' Juan asked. 'And Natalie Taylor, who was involved with the hijacking of Xavier Carlton's private plane, tried to kill him.'

'There was another interesting tidbit from the notebook,' Eric added. 'It said that someone named XC visited the ship for an inspection a few months before it sank.'

'I wonder if Carlton is one of the Nine Unknown Men. We did find that symbol on the plaque on *Colossus 3*'s bridge, which implies that the Nine Unknown Men are involved with the project or even bankrolling it.' Juan and Eric caught up the others on the research they did on Ashoka and the legend about the men to whom he'd entrusted his most important knowledge.

'If I had to guess,' Murph said, 'I'd bet Mallik is one of them as well.'

'And I saw a news report today that two other major CEOs haven't been seen for days,' Max said. 'Jason Wakefield and Daniel Saidon are supposedly missing. Wakefield was targeted in an attempted kidnapping last week in Sydney, and Daniel Saidon just happens to own the Moretti Navi shipyard. Those can't be coincidences.'

Juan pushed his plate away and sat back as he tried to get his head around the strange events. 'So we have at least two of the Nine Unknown Men fighting each other for some reason. There's a satellite-based weapons system that can temporarily disable all electronics within a fifty-mile radius anywhere on earth. And, a highly advanced artificial intelligence is about to be released upon the world, which Lyla Dhawan thinks will be able to control any computer hooked up to the internet.'

'Is that all?' Murph joked.

'Which do we take on first?' Eddie asked.

'Info about the Nine Unknown Men doesn't help us unless we know who the rest of them are,' Juan said.

'Reports say that Mallik is getting ready to launch a twentieth satellite in his communications constellation in a few days,' Eric said.

'So what?' Murph said. 'Nineteen satellites, twenty satellites – one more isn't going to make much difference in the scope of its capabilities.'

'Lang told me our highest priority is Colossus,' Juan said. 'After the near debacle caused by the quantum computer, the US government doesn't want an even more sophisticated one out there that can not only crack our codes but rewrite them.'

'Do we sink the Colossus ships?' Max asked.

'If it comes to that,' Juan said, 'we might have to. Max, I want you to take the *Oregon* and set off in pursuit of the three Colossus ships heading north on the Red Sea.'

'You're not coming with us?'

Juan shook his head. 'There might be a more elegant way to disable Colossus. Eric said they need all four to get the AI fully functional. So all we need to do is take out just one of the ships.'

'The one in Cyprus,' Max said with a nod.

'That's what I'm thinking.' Juan turned to Julia. 'Remember the blue-green algae bloom that was poisoning the seas around Qatar a few months ago?'

'The cyanobacteria?' she said. 'Sure. Those countries were grateful that we stopped it from wiping out all the wildlife in the Persian Gulf.'

'Do you still have samples of it?'

'A few vials . . . Why?' Then she looked at the still image of the vat inside *Colossus 3* that was up on the monitor. 'Wait, you mean . . .'

Juan nodded. 'If we can infect those vats with the bacteria, will it poison the computer?'

She thought for a moment, then said, 'Blue-green algae

usually require sunlight to reproduce, but since the bio-computer has to be bathed in a nutrient-rich environment, the cyanobacteria should have everything it needs to reproduce and release its toxin.'

'How long will it take to work?'

'Maybe a few hours to begin killing the cells. Most of it will be infected within a day. They'd have to flush the whole system and start over from scratch.'

'Perfect. Ready a sample for us that we can insert into the Colossus system. That will buy us some time to figure out how to wipe it out permanently. Eddie, get your team ready to go again. And tell Tiny I want to be wheels up for Cyprus within three hours.'

'Aye, Chairman.' Julia and Eddie left, but before the rest of them could follow, Eric stopped them.

'Chairman, there's one other thing we should take into account before we go ahead with sinking the Colossus ships.'

'What's that?'

'You know the passengers from Carlton's plane that Lyla said were taken off Jhootha Island by Taylor?'

Juan nodded.

'According to the scientist's notebook, they're currently being forced to work aboard the *Colossus 1*.'

43

Cyprus

On the dock beside the *Colossus 5*, Xavier Carlton slowly walked around his Bugatti Chiron, which had been brought from his estate in the mountains outside of Larnaca. The two-toned red and black sports car shimmered in the setting sun. Worth more than three million dollars, the sleek roadster boasted a fifteen-hundred-horsepower engine and a top speed north of two hundred and fifty miles per hour.

He had pulled the car from his A380 mere minutes before it took off for its hijacking to Jhootha Island. There had been no sense in stranding one of his favorite cars on the tropical island. He had intended to give it back to his son Adam upon his safe return, but after he died on the flight Carlton decided to keep it for himself.

'Do you see any blemishes?' asked Natalie Taylor, who walked slowly beside him.

'No, they've taken good care of it in my absence.' As they should, given what he'd do if there was so much as a ding in the paint.

'Why are you taking it to Australia?'

'I want to see what it will do on the wide-open roads down there. The roads on Cyprus are too constricted.' He was looking forward to blasting through the Outback at top speed, a just reward for all his hard work and sacrifice over the last few years.

As he opened the rear cover to gaze at the sixteen-cylinder monster of an engine, Taylor said, 'We can't keep Gupta here forever. It will start to look strange if he stays with us and doesn't contact his company back in Canada.'

'I had an idea,' Carlton said. 'We've been keeping a lid on the deaths of the other Nine at the Library, but it's starting to become difficult to contain. There are stories going around about some of the missing CEOs, and eventually the path will lead back to India.'

'What are you proposing?'

'On our way to Sydney, we'll make a stop in India. I want you to take Gupta and return him to the Library. You'll shoot him there and make it look like he survived the Novichok attack only to succumb to his gunshot wound days later.'

'How will that help us?'

'You'll get him to record a confession before he dies. If he resists, tell him we'll execute his family. Get him to place the blame on Mallik for the deaths of the other Nine. Once we've finally killed Mallik, we'll anonymously reveal the existence of the Library and the secret society of the Nine Unknown Men, and the authorities will find the bodies with a ready-made story to go with them.'

'But that only adds up to eight people. Won't that invite speculation about who the ninth member is?'

Carlton pointed at the ship behind him. 'Colossus will be able to plant evidence implicating another person in place of me. I'm thinking another Indian billionaire would make more sense than me. Remember, it was my plane that was stolen and my son who was killed. I'm the victim in all this.'

'When do you want to take off?' Taylor asked.

Taylor had already been working on updated disguises to go with the fake passports she had at her disposal, so returning to the country under a new name wouldn't be a problem.

'We'll leave tomorrow morning after the *Colossus 5* has set sail.' Carlton saw a truck hauling a bright green trailer pass through the security gate. 'And this must be my other present that we'll be taking with us.'

The truck pulled up next to them. Carlton was excited to see its contents. Because of everything else that was dominating his time, he was happy to have another small distraction.

'Have you had a chance to see this yet?' asked Natalie Taylor.

'No,' he said. 'I bought it sight unseen. But my appraisers said it's in excellent condition.'

The two men in the truck got out, unlocked and rolled up the rear door, and extended a ramp from the container. Then they put on white gloves and went inside. Carlton heard the growl of a big-block V-8 engine firing up, and with a roar exhaust blew through the rear doors.

One of the men walked out backward, his hands in the air slowly motioning to the other man still inside. He was followed by a chrome bumper and a couple of the tallest tail fins ever put on a production car. Its Kensington Green paint glinted in the setting sun. The car was a convertible, and the top was already down, revealing a white leather interior with custom-made front bucket seats that were original to the car. It kept coming and coming, all nineteen feet of it, until the driver stopped on the pavement.

'That may be the biggest car I've ever seen,' Taylor said.

'A 1959 Cadillac Eldorado Biarritz convertible. One of the few that was ever shipped to Europe. I found it in Malta.'

The driver handed Carlton the keys. He went around to the driver's door and said to Taylor, 'Get in.'

He took it for a spin around the dockyard, his security team watching as the car roared along the length of the ship.

When he stopped back at the trailer where the Bugatti was already being loaded, he said, 'What do you think?'

'They certainly don't make cars like this anymore,' Taylor said as she stepped out. 'You've got yourself a real prize.'

'It's the only one of its kind anywhere,' he noted with pride. 'Make sure it arrives safely.'

'Absolutely, sir.'

He told the truck driver to keep the cars in the safety of the dockyard until they were ready to be loaded onto the plane the next day.

The short drive had put him in a good mood, and for the first time in days he felt optimistic about his plans. The AI was going to be activated on schedule, and the threat of the Vajra satellite launch would be over. Carlton would be able to do whatever he wanted, and there was one thing he wanted to do more than anything else.

He walked back to the ship with a spring in his step as he imagined all the ways he could use Colossus to kill Romir Mallik.

44

Juan chose three in the morning for their infiltration of the *Colossus 5*. It would be the time when the guards were at their most relaxed and vulnerable.

He was already halfway between the surface of the water and the ship's deck. The angled bow was the part of the *Colossus 5* that was most deeply in the shadows, but it also made the climb more difficult. One at a time, Juan methodically pressed the magnetic grips against the steel hull, their rubber coating preventing any noise as they adhered to the metal.

He looked down and could barely make out Raven and MacD below him. They were climbing effortlessly, their black and gray night camouflage gear making them difficult to see in the darkness. Even if someone looked over the railing, it was unlikely they'd be spotted.

'Status?' Juan whispered into his comm unit as he approached the top of the hull.

'Almost in position,' Eddie replied. 'Two minutes.'

'Roger that.'

The plan was simple, but the execution would be risky. To get below deck and plant the bacteria Juan had in his pocket, he, Raven, and MacD would need something to distract the guards away from their position. An explosion or gunfire would make them realize they were under attack and just put them on full alert. They needed something more subtle but still attention-getting.

So Eddie and Linc were going to cut the power to the dockyard. The only problem was the backup generator located inside the security area next to *Colossus 5*. First, they had to plant a small charge that would short out the feed coming in from the Cyprus power grid. Then, once they disabled the generator, they would blow the charge, and the entire dock would go black.

The confusion would provide the cover and time Juan and his team needed to get into the hold and inject the bacteria that Julia had prepared. The video from the *Colossus 3* gave them an idea of how the ship was laid out. If everything went well, they'd be back out and into the water without anyone knowing they'd even been aboard.

Raven and MacD reached the top next to him and held their position. There was no sound from the deck above.

'We're ready,' he said.

'We see the generator,' Eddie answered. 'One minute.'

Asad Torkan knew the best time to plant his bombs was at three in the morning, when the security guards would be at their most relaxed and vulnerable.

At first, he tried Carlton's mountain villa, but he couldn't find the cars that the media mogul would be transporting on his plane in the morning. The Bugatti had already been moved, and the Cadillac was nowhere to be seen.

Attaching the explosives at the airport in the morning, when the cars were being loaded, was impossible. They'd be watched too closely.

Then he'd had a hunch that Carlton was actually staying on the *Colossus 5* and would want his cars close by. Sure enough, he spotted the trailer and knew it was the perfect opportunity to do his work.

He had two small devices packed with C-4. Each of them was equipped with a pressure sensor. As soon as the plane was pressurized for flight, the timers on the bombs would be activated. He thought twenty minutes was plenty of time for the Airbus A380 to reach cruising altitude. When the bombs went off and tore a hole in the fuselage, it would cause an explosive decompression, and the plane would be ripped apart in midair.

Unlocking the trailer had been easy for Torkan, and he'd already tucked the first bomb under the chassis of the Cadillac near the gas tank. The Bugatti proved more difficult because of its low clearance and the tight confines of the trailer, but he was able to get the explosive device in place and activated.

He switched his light off and paused at the trailer's rear door to listen for any patrolling guards. There was nothing but the sound of a ship being loaded on a quay a quarter mile away. Still, he was prepared to fight his way out, this time with a Glock pistol equipped with a suppressor.

He pushed the door up slowly. The area around him was clear. He climbed out and relocked the door.

That's when he noticed movement to his right by the shed holding the dock's backup generator.

Two men were stealthily approaching the building. Both of them were in night camouflage and carrying suppressed pistols like he was.

One was a huge black man and the other was a wiry

Asian. Torkan blinked in surprise when he recognized who they were.

It was the two men who had passed him and Mallik in the stairwell during the attack in Mumbai.

Why they were here, Torkan couldn't guess, but he didn't want to stick around to find out. He didn't have time, however, to duck out of sight before the black man saw him. For a millisecond, they stared at each other in disbelief.

Then they both started shooting.

45

Linc was shocked to see Torkan coming out of the trailer, but it lasted for only a moment.

When he saw the Iranian assassin raise his pistol, he shoved Eddie down and fired. Bullets whistled overhead as they dove behind the generator shed.

'Torkan,' Linc said to Eddie, who had already drawn his own pistol.

'Did you get him?'

'Don't think so.'

'Why is he here?'

'He was doing something in that semi-trailer.'

Linc poked his head out and saw Torkan crouched behind the trailer. By now, the gunfire had drawn attention from the security team, and a klaxon sounded. Unlike the nearly silent gunfire shown in movies, the suppressors were still loud enough to echo through the dockyard.

'He's cut off our escape route,' Linc said.

'What's happening out there?' the Chairman asked. 'We hear gunshots.'

'Asad Torkan blew our mission,' Eddie replied.

'He's here?'

'Mission is aborted. Sorry, Chairman.'

Linc fired off more rounds, but he didn't hit Torkan. He saw the assassin take off. Torkan fired three quick shots before he disappeared into the maze of equipment near the trailer.

'He's gone,' Linc said.

'We need to get out of here. Let's move.'

Footsteps were pounding toward them from all directions. Linc and Eddie ran to the trailer, which was in the direction of the hole they'd cut in the fence.

They reached the rear of the truck when rifle fire ricocheted off the asphalt, shot by six guards running from the front gatehouse.

Eddie and Linc slammed into the side of the trailer and crouched down.

Tires from two SUVs screeched as they tore across the dockyard.

'What do you think, Butch?' Eddie said.

'Not looking good, Sundance,' Linc replied with a wry grin.

'I'll take the three on the left, you take the ones on the right.'

'Sounds like a plan.'

Six against two weren't the best odds they'd ever had, but they weren't the worst, either. They were about to rush out when a flashbang grenade skittered under the truck and came to rest just a few feet away.

Eddie made an attempt to kick it, but it went off before he could reach it. The ultra-bright light and deafening sound dazed them both, and it was in that moment Linc knew they wouldn't make it.

He plucked the tiny comm unit from his ear and tossed it away, hoping it would end up under the trailer and out of sight.

The SUVs skidded to a stop as the six running guards rounded the corner of the truck. Linc's blurry vision started to come back into focus, and he saw a lithe woman step from the front seat of the lead SUV, an assault rifle cradled in her arms. It was Natalie Taylor.

'Drop your weapons or I'll kill you both right now.'

Linc looked at Eddie, who was still shaking out the cobwebs. When he could finally see, he looked at Linc and nodded. Live to fight another day was a better plan than going out in a blaze of glory.

They both let their guns fall to the ground.

'Good boys,' she said with a smile, plucking the comm unit from Eddie's ear. 'Now, what are we going to do with you?'

By this time, the deck of the *Colossus 5* was a hive of activity. Guards were stationed all around the ship in anticipation of further attack.

Juan felt helpless as he heard Eddie and Linc being taken prisoner.

'Get them up,' a woman said. It had to be Natalie Taylor.

Then there was a scuffing sound, and then Taylor's voice much louder. 'Torkan, if you're still listening, your attack didn't work this time.'

She must have been speaking into a mic that she'd taken from Linc or Eddie's ear, because there was a crunching sound right before it went off-line. Juan could still hear her voice, this time muffled and distant.

'Take them to the ship,' she ordered.

She said 'them,' so at least that meant they were both alive.

'What do we do now?' MacD asked.

Juan peered over the edge, and the deck was still swarming with guards. In fact, one was approaching their position.

'Drop,' he said.

MacD did as ordered, falling to the water below.

'We can't leave them,' Raven said.

'We're not,' Juan said, his eyes boring into her. 'Drop now.'

Without another word, she detached her magnets and plunged down. Juan went right after her, tapering so he'd enter the water with a minimal splash.

When he was under, he let go of his magnetic climbers and swam away from the bow. He made it fifty yards along the dock before he had to come up for air.

MacD and Raven were waiting for him. The guard who'd been right above them was still looking to where he must have heard them hit the water. He took a final cursory glance around the area, then shrugged and disappeared.

'How do we get them out of there?' Raven said. 'There are dozens of guards stationed on or around the ship.'

'And they'll be on alert the rest of the night,' MacD said.

'Eddie and Linc still have their trackers,' Juan said, referring to the beacons implanted into the thigh of every *Oregon* crew member so they could be located in case of abduction. 'At least we'll know where they are while we come up with a plan to get them back.'

He didn't wait for a response and began swimming toward their exit point, Taylor's voice playing in his mind the whole way.

*

'Are you sure it was them?' Mallik asked as Torkan drove away from the Limassol port.

'Positive,' Torkan said.

'What were they doing?'

'I don't know. But our initial assessment was wrong. They weren't with Natalie Taylor at your house, and they don't work for Carlton.'

'Then who sent them to tap my computer?'

'Maybe a foreign intelligence agency. Impossible to say.'

'So now we're fighting Carlton and some unknown party,' Mallik said. 'At least tell me that you got the bombs planted.'

'I did,' Torkan said without voicing his secret doubts about the ultimate success of the mission.

'Good,' Mallik said. 'By this time tomorrow, Xavier Carlton will be dead. Hopefully, Lionel Gupta as well. If not, we'll take care of him some other way, though I'm not sure we'll need to. I don't think he'd have the guts to go forward with Colossus on his own. In any event, I need you back here. Fly out on the helicopter and meet me on the *Kalinga*. Then, we'll head to the launch command ship.'

'Yes, sir.' Torkan hung up. He decided that mentioning potential snags wouldn't help at this point since he wouldn't get another shot at Carlton, but one little problem still bothered him.

Before they exchanged gunfire, the black man must have realized that Torkan was coming out of the trailer.

46

Carlton wasn't pleased about being woken up in the middle of the night, but his spirits improved when he found out that an attack on the *Colossus 5* had been foiled.

The two men that Taylor had caught were brought to the ship's meeting room. When Carlton arrived, he found the two men cuffed and being watched over by six armed guards. Taylor stood when he entered.

He looked the intruders up and down before saying, 'Who are they?'

'I don't know,' Taylor said. 'They won't talk. We're not even sure they speak English.'

'They look like soldiers to me, but they're not Indian or Iranian. What were they doing?'

Taylor tossed a toolkit on the table.

'Sabotage of some kind.'

The two men stared at Carlton with impassive faces.

'Who do you work for?' he demanded.

They said nothing.

He turned to Taylor. 'Do you think Mallik and Torkan would hire mercenaries?'

'Always a possibility,' Taylor said.

'I don't think they know anything of use, but we should at least try to find out. We'll take them on the plane with us. You'll have plenty of time on the trip to get information out of them.' Carlton turned to them. 'She's very persuasive with a blade.'

The black man finally spoke up in an American accent. 'Asad Torkan was here.' The Asian man remained still.

Carlton suppressed a smile at getting him to talk so easily. 'So you work for him?'

'No.'

'But you know who he is?'

'Yes.'

'What was he doing here?'

'We'll show you.'

'You'll show us?' Taylor said.

The black man nodded. The Asian man continued to stare, still no response.

'Tell us here,' Carlton said.

'We'll show you,' the black man repeated. 'We want Torkan as much as you do.'

'Why?'

At last the Asian man opened his mouth. 'We know you and Romir Mallik are fighting each other.'

'Interesting. So you're here to what? Save me?'

The Asian man nodded.

'Where should we take you to show us what Torkan was doing?'

'The dock,' the black man said. 'By the generator housing. Your life depends on it.'

Carlton looked at Taylor. She shrugged and said, 'We'll still be well protected in the dockyard.'

'Double the number of guards.' Carlton turned back to the prisoners and leaned down. 'If I'm disappointed by what you show us out there, you're going to die.'

The two men said nothing.

*

Juan, Raven, and MacD had returned to the rendezvous point, where Tiny picked them up in a van. He found a quiet parking lot where they could formulate a plan to rescue Eddie and Linc from the *Colossus 5*. The first rays of dawn shone through the windshield.

'We don't have the manpower to go in guns blazing,' MacD said.

'Then we have to do it quietly,' Raven said. 'We'll make another run at it tonight.'

'No good,' Juan said. 'The *Colossus 5* is going to set sail today. We can't wait.'

'How long do you think they've got?' Tiny asked.

'Natalie Taylor has a reputation for harsh measures. That's why she was drummed out of British Intelligence. Rumors say she would have gone to jail if she hadn't had something on a minister in Parliament. I wouldn't be surprised if she tortures them until . . .'

Juan paused when he heard something on his headset. He was keeping it active knowing that Linc or Eddie had tossed his comm unit away before being apprehended. It was the sound of approaching vehicles.

'Quiet,' he said, and pointed at his headset. Everyone else put their own on.

The vehicles stopped, and they heard several people get out.

'So what do you want to show us?' Xavier Carlton said, his voice faint.

'Over here,' Linc said.

The footsteps came closer to the microphone. As they walked, Eddie said, 'Where are we flying to?'

'You'll find out when we get there,' Natalie Taylor said.

In just those few phrases, Eddie and Linc had conveyed valuable information through the mic that they knew was still active and out of sight. Both of them were still alive and in good condition. Carlton and Taylor were with them. And they were going to be flying somewhere today.

The footsteps stopped.

'He was in this trailer,' Linc said.

'Doing what?' Taylor asked.

'I didn't stop to ask in the middle of our gun battle.'

'He was doing something to my cars?' Carlton said.

'What cars?' Eddie said.

'Open it up and search the cars from top to bottom,' Taylor said.

'If Torkan damaged either of them,' Carlton said, 'I'll kill him myself.'

'Nice cars,' Linc said. 'Cadillac Eldorado, right?'

'It's a 1959 Biarritz convertible,' Carlton said proudly.

'I like the color. Green suits it. And the other one looks like a Bugatti Veyron.'

'Chiron.'

'Are those traveling with you today?' Eddie asked.

'Why?' Carlton said.

'Here's why,' Taylor said. Juan wished he could see what they were looking at.

'Looks like a bomb,' Eddie said as if he'd heard Juan's plea. 'We found it near the Cadillac's gas tank.'

After another thirty seconds, Linc said, 'Two bombs.'

'This was mounted on the Bugatti,' Taylor said. 'It looks like it has a pressure sensor.'

'So it was meant to go off when we were in the air?' Carlton growled in anger.

'Told you we weren't with Torkan,' Linc said. 'Would we have led you to those if we were?'

'You make a good point. But we still don't know who you are. Natalie will find out. Take them back to the ship.'

It sounded like they walked away, and MacD was about to say something, but Juan put up his hand to stop him. There weren't enough footsteps.

Doors slammed, and Carlton spoke again in a more hushed tone.

'They may not be with Torkan, but they're up to something,' he said.

'I'll find out what it is,' Taylor said. 'It's surprising how much more information you can get from two people than you can from just one, especially when you begin carving one up in front of the other.'

'Good. No matter what, though, it's probably not wise to take them all the way to your destination. Toss them out of the plane over the ocean when you have as much as you can get out of them.'

'You're not coming with us?'

'Not now, not after Torkan tried to kill me. I'll be safer on the *Colossus 5* until it's up and running.'

'What about Lionel Gupta?'

'Stick to the plan. Take him and the two prisoners to the airport by helicopter.'

'And your cars?'

'Search them again, and then lock up the truck for the drive to the plane. I still want them in Australia when you're done with the other segments of the mission. Oh, and Natalie? Good work.'

'Thank you, sir.'

One set of footsteps walked away. Then Taylor started giving instructions to the men about the truck.

Juan looked at the others as he thought about what they'd learned.

'If they're being flown to the airport,' MacD said, 'we can't intercept them en route.'

'Maybe we can take them when they land by the plane,' Raven said.

'I can tell you that would be a suicide mission,' Tiny said. 'No way we can get anywhere close to that A380 without drawing attention.'

The three of them looked at Juan, who said, 'I think our only option is to get on Carlton's private jet and rescue them once they're in the air.'

MacD gaped at him. 'How? Tiny doesn't think we can get near it.'

'Linc and Eddie gave us a way when they told us about the cars.'

He sized up Tiny, who looked back at Juan in confusion. 'Me?'

Juan continued. 'I can't fly that thing, so I'm going to need a pilot just in case we can't persuade them to do what we want. Can you fly it?'

'Sure,' Tiny said. 'Not well, but I can get us back on the ground in one piece. The question is, how do we get on in the first place?'

'We drive on,' Juan said. 'The 1959 Cadillac Eldorado Biarritz is a huge car. There's plenty of room for both of us in the trunk.'

47

Andreas Ladas drove the truck carrying Xavier Carlton's cars like his life depended on it. He'd heard about some kind of situation at the dock in the early hours of the morning and he'd been terrified that the billionaire had discovered some kind of damage done during the transportation process. Luckily, it turned out to be something else, but nobody would tell him what had happened.

Both he and Georgios, who was sitting in the passenger seat, had moved cars for Carlton before and knew how demanding he was. If there was even a hint that they'd caused a scratch, they'd both lose their jobs.

Despite his fears, Andreas hoped they wouldn't have any problems this early in the morning. The traffic was light on the divided A5 highway, and they were making good time.

About halfway to the airport, though, they ran into a section with red and white markers diverting the vehicles down to one lane for repaving work. Cars weren't backed up very far, but it would take a little longer to get through this stretch. Andreas knew Carlton's assistant, Natalie Taylor, would be impatiently waiting for them at the airport if they didn't get there on time. He'd seen a helicopter land on the ship to pick her up at the same time as they were driving away from the dock.

Andreas began merging the truck over when a tiny Fiat behind him raced forward, trying to sneak between him and the concrete median.

The car almost made it, but the rear end clipped the front bumper of the truck as it passed. The car spun out in a haze of tire smoke and came to rest against the median backward, blocking the way. Andreas brought the truck to an abrupt stop.

Tires squealed behind him as a van screeched to a halt sideways about ten feet behind the trailer.

A beautiful dark-haired woman leaped out of the Fiat and began cursing in Arabic as she examined the damage to her car. It didn't seem extensive, just cosmetic, but she was furious.

'I'll handle her,' Andreas said to Georgios. 'You check on the cars. As long as they're okay, we don't mention this to Ms Taylor, understand?'

Georgios nodded and got out.

Andreas climbed down and looked at the front of the truck, which looked undamaged. He approached the woman, who was yelling at him before he even got to her.

'I don't understand what you're saying,' he said in his native Greek.

'You speak English?' she asked, her eyes blazing.

'A little,' he said.

'Who pays for this?' she shouted, pointing at the scraped fender and crumpled bumper. 'Is rental!'

He offered to give her his insurance information, but she started shouting again in Arabic, ignoring the angry honking of horns from cars backed up by the incident.

Andreas looked at his watch, impatiently trying to figure out how he could get going as soon as possible.

MacD waited in the driver's seat of the van until the truck driver's companion rounded the end of the trailer and unlocked the door to check the vehicles. When he raised it, MacD jumped out and yelled, 'Hey, man, you have a problem with your tire!'

The trucker turned and looked at MacD in confusion.

'What tire? What you mean?'

'On the right side,' MacD said. 'Ah saw it when you passed me earlier. This way. Let me show you.'

'Where?'

MacD led him around to the side of the truck, out of sight of the van.

As soon as MacD and the trucker were no longer in view, Juan silently slid open the van's side door, and he and Tiny sprinted to the trailer, hidden from the eyes of drivers behind them by the angled van.

They jumped into the back of the truck. Juan was ready to pick the lock on the Cadillac's trunk, but it was unlocked and opened right up. They tossed their equipment bags in the cavernous space and got in. Using a magnetic handhold, Juan pulled the trunk lid closed over them.

'You were right,' Tiny said, practically sprawling across the immense interior. 'Lot of room.'

Juan smiled and activated his comm unit, saying to MacD, 'We're in.'

*

MacD was crouching by one of the trailer's frontmost tires when he got the word from Juan.

'Sorry, dude,' he said to the guy he'd learned was Georgios. 'I thought the tire was flat, but it looks okay.'

Georgios said, 'It's okay. Thank you.'

They walked back to the rear of the truck, and Georgios climbed in while MacD got back in the van. He watched as Georgios inspected the cars' exteriors and their tie-downs to make sure they hadn't shifted during the quick stop.

He never even put his hands on the Caddy's trunk.

Georgios got out and pulled the door down, locking it up again. He went around the truck, saw the driver still arguing with the woman, and yelled something in Greek, waving his hands like they should get going.

'We're good to go, Raven,' MacD said, and started the van.

As soon as she heard that from MacD, Raven stopped yelling at the truck driver. She instantly changed her tone from anger to remorse, as if she suddenly understood that the accident was her fault, not his.

'You not see me?' she said in broken English.

'No, you drive up fast next to me,' Andreas said. 'I don't see you.'

'Oh, I sorry. Please, no call police.' She made tears well up in her eyes.

He tilted his head back in the Greek gesture for *no*.

'Is okay,' he said with a grin, and patted her shoulder. 'Don't worry. We go now.'

She thanked him profusely and got back into the rental Fiat. That was about the only thing she hadn't lied about.

She wheeled the car around and got going again, the truck following behind.

'I'll meet you at the airport,' she said into her mic.

'Roger that,' MacD replied.

Neither of them mentioned that the most dangerous part of the plan was yet to come, and it was completely out of their hands. All they could do was hope that Taylor didn't notice the Cadillac was riding a bit lower with the added weight and decide to open its trunk to investigate why.

48

When they reached the international airport in Larnaca, Raven could easily see the towering double-decker A380 from the edge of the short-term lot where she joined MacD in the van. The high-powered binoculars she was using gave her a good view of the fold-out stairway at the front of the plane as well as the ramp extending from the cargo area at the rear. Andreas and Georgios were standing next to the truck waiting for a signal to take the cars out.

'I thought these Airbuses didn't have loading ramps,' she said, handing the binoculars to MacD, who was sitting in the driver's seat.

'The passenger models don't,' he said. 'But Carlton's plane is a custom job. Supposedly, it's based on a cargo version Airbus prototype but never put into service. I heard it took a year to install all the special wood and gold finishes.'

'What a waste. That thing must cost tens of thousands of dollars an hour just to fly one guy around.'

'And he's not even going this time. But with the billions he has, Carlton can afford it.'

The chop of a helicopter's rotors cut the air. They turned and saw a seven-passenger Agusta extend its landing gear and settle to the tarmac beside the A380.

MacD handed the binoculars back to Raven and she

saw Taylor get out with two of her hired thugs. They shielded their weapons from view, but they were clearly ready to use them.

Lionel Gupta was the next one to exit, hoisting his considerable bulk out of the chopper. Then Eddie and Linc got out. Their hands were bound behind their backs, and their legs were loosely tied together to keep them from running.

'How do they look?' MacD asked.

'No injuries as far as I can see.'

'They did say the rough stuff would happen on the plane.'

The guards herded the three prisoners to the stairs and into the jet.

Taylor waited for the helicopter to take off again, then went over to Andreas and Georgios and told them to unload the cars.

'Smart,' MacD said. 'Keep the rotor wash from pelting those beauties with pebbles from the tarmac.'

The truckers carefully moved the Cadillac and the Bugatti out onto the asphalt, and Taylor walked around them for a final inspection.

'Think they'll say anything about the fender bender?' Raven asked.

MacD scoffed. 'And risk getting chewed out by Iron Britches? Not a chance.'

Taylor paused at the rear of the Caddy, apparently making a decision.

'Chairman,' Raven said into her mic, 'she might be getting ready to open the trunk.'

She didn't expect an answer. The Chairman and Tiny had to stay absolutely still so they wouldn't be heard. But they would have their weapons at the ready if the worst happened, and MacD was prepared to drive straight through the security fence to provide support if needed.

Raven's grip on the binoculars eased when Taylor moved on and waved for Andreas and Georgios to put the cars on the plane.

'Chairman, you're clear for now,' she said. 'Good hunting.'

First, the Caddy went in, then the Bugatti. After they were tied down, the two transporters got back into the truck and drove away. Raven's last view of Taylor was of her in the cargo bay of the plane pressing the large red button to close the ramp door.

Juan and Tiny didn't put down their suppressed pistols, keeping them aimed at the trunk lid in case Taylor decided to do a last-minute inspection. They hadn't bothered bringing assault rifles on board knowing how easily the high-powered rounds could pierce the fuselage and cause an explosive decompression.

They heard Taylor walk past the car and open the door to the elevator alcove. Only when the door shut again did Juan relax.

Still, she was smart, so he didn't put it past her to try to trick them. Tiny took a deep breath and was about to speak, but Juan stopped him. He used his phone to tap out a message.

Stay quiet until we're in the air.

Tiny nodded.

The Cadillac vibrated as the plane's four huge engines started up. Soon, it was rolling toward the runway.

*

'We won't know if this works until we hear from them,' Raven said as she watched the A380 taxi away.

'We'll know one way or the other,' MacD said.

'What do you mean?'

'You know that tracker you got shot into your leg when you joined the Corporation?'

She nodded.

'The ones in their legs should be going hundreds of miles an hour until the plane lands again.'

'And if the trackers stop moving,' Raven said, 'we'll know they aren't on the plane anymore.'

'Right. But don't worry. The Chairman's got the most important element on his side.'

'Guns?'

'I was thinking of surprise,' MacD said with a grin. 'But guns are a definite plus.'

The A380 thundered down the runway and took off. A minute later, it disappeared into the clouds over the Mediterranean.

49

Eddie was seated next to Linc in the rear of the A380 in what looked like either an entertainment room or a torture chamber. Given their current predicament, maybe it was both.

Each of them had his wrists strapped to a leather chair, but their legs were free. All of the chairs faced the front of the room, which was on the top level of the plane, and it looked like there was a roll-down screen hidden in the ceiling. There was a door leading to the forward part of the plane and a spiral staircase behind them. The walls were covered with antique weapons from many different ages and cultures. Eddie recognized scimitars from Persia, throwing stars from Japan, and a hunga munga from Africa, which looked liked a bladed ampersand.

Taylor was somewhere else with Lionel Gupta, obviously another captive. Two beefy guards stood at the front of the room, their weapons holstered. If Eddie could draw them close, he and Linc might be able to take them by surprise.

'Do you mind giving us a few minutes alone?' Eddie said to them. 'My friend is shy around strangers.'

The guards didn't even look at him.

'Maybe they didn't hear you,' Linc said.

'I am a quiet guy.' This time, Eddie yelled. 'I said we're very introverted! Can we please have some privacy!'

No response.

'I know what it is,' Linc said. 'They don't speak English.'

'Or they're wearing earbuds that we can't see and are rocking out to the latest Justin Bieber album.'

Linc nodded approvingly. 'That definitely sounds like their type of music.'

That got a glance from one of them, but no movement.

'Nice collection,' Eddie said to Linc as he looked around at the weapons mounted on the fuselage.

'Lots of pointy, sharp things.'

'Very intimidating,' Eddie said with a yawn.

'Since they can't hear or understand us,' Linc said, 'we should probably start planning how we're going to kill them.'

'Good idea. I call dibs on the hunga munga.'

'Oh, man!' Linc complained with an exaggerated whine. 'That's the one I wanted.'

'Listen, we can share. There are plenty of guys to kill for both of us.'

The guard on the left looked like he'd had enough of their banter. He started walking toward them with his fists clenched when Taylor appeared in the open doorway and said, 'Enough with the childish baiting.'

The guard stepped back.

She entered holding a folded plastic sheet under her arm.

'We missed you,' Linc said.

'I'm sure you did.'

'The service on this airline is terrible,' Eddie said.

'We've been in the air for fifteen minutes now and haven't seen the drink cart yet.'

'And you won't. None of the flight attendants were needed on this trip. Gives us privacy for our discussion.'

Eddie turned to Linc and said, 'Wasn't I just saying how we wanted some privacy?'

'You're too kind,' Linc said to Taylor.

'This chatter is amusing,' Taylor said, 'but I wonder how well it will hold up when you see your friend bleeding on the floor.'

'And mess up this beautiful carpet? What a shame.'

'That's what this is for.' She handed the sheeting to one of the guards. 'Make sure you cover the whole floor. I've got a few things to take care of and then I'll be back for our chat.'

She winked at them as she left, closing the door behind her.

Eddie and Linc watched in silence as the guard unfolded the sheet and laid it over the carpet, careful to pull the edges up the walls to catch spillage.

The other guard stood there, smiling.

Juan thought he'd given it enough time. They should be close to cruising altitude.

Tiny handed him the handheld pry bar and he forced the trunk open. He opened it just a crack. The cargo hold looked empty, so he pushed the trunk lid up and rolled out, sweeping the space with his suppressed Smith & Wesson.

The only cargo was the two cars. Both vehicles were held down with straps on the tires that were clasped to retractable cargo restraints on the deck. The releases were operated by covered buttons on the wall next to each car.

'Clear,' Juan said.

Tiny got out and picked up the backpacks they'd brought with them. They each put one on their shoulders and made their way to the elevator.

'Where do you want to start looking for them?' Tiny asked.

'If the pilots aren't in on the torture plan, Taylor will want to keep them as far away from the cockpit as possible.'

'That would be the upper deck at the rear. The cockpit is on the main deck.'

'So we get Eddie and Linc first, and that will double our numbers. Then we take the cockpit.'

Even if the pilots weren't party to what Taylor had planned for her guests, they would resist anyone taking control of the plane. At the first sign of trouble, they'd head back to Cyprus, where an army of Carlton's men would be waiting for the intruders when they landed.

But breaking into any airliner's flight deck was extremely difficult in the age of terrorism and hijackers. The door would be hardened and bulletproof to pistol fire. They couldn't break it down, and the emergency code to open it would be useless even if they could find it. The pilots would activate the triple locking mechanism as soon as they suspected the plane was under attack.

That's why they had brought thermal charges. Explosives would be too dangerous to use to sever the bolts. Not only could they injure or kill the pilots, they could also damage the instruments and controls.

Instead, the charges were strips of thermite powder they

could tape to the door. When the nylon cords were ripped off, the thermite would ignite, melting through the locks like a blowtorch.

The elevator up to the passenger areas was located on the port side of the plane near the midpoint. Juan would have preferred stairs, but there weren't any. Using the elevator was a perilous start to their infiltration. They wouldn't be able to tell if anyone was waiting at the top of the ride.

They had their weapons at the ready as the elevator slowly rose to the main galley. It came to a stop with a ding. Juan flung open the door and rushed out, but no one was there.

He checked the hallway outside, then gestured for Tiny to follow. Juan could see a spiral staircase at the aft end. He made his way down the hall while Tiny kept watch on their rear. He stopped only long enough to check four small rooms that they passed – they all turned out to be empty – before entering a palatial lounge.

'Wait here until I call for you,' Juan whispered. Tiny nodded and kept an eye on the hallway.

Juan crept up the spiral stairs, the sound of his steps absorbed by the plush carpeting.

When he reached the top, he peered over the edge and saw the tops of Eddie's and Linc's heads. He went up farther and saw that they were sitting in chairs. Beyond, in the space in between, he could see two guards standing at attention. Both of them were in tactical gear with holstered sidearms.

Juan had to risk that his suppressed gunshots would be heard. He coiled and then sprang up the last few steps. The guards gaped for just a second at the shocking sight of an intruder, then tried to draw their weapons. Juan took each of them down with a single shot. Blood pooled under their heads, caught neatly by the plastic sheet.

Eddie and Linc both turned. Neither of them seemed surprised to see that it was Juan.

'Hi, Chairman,' Linc said with a toothy grin. 'What took you so long?'

50

Juan called Tiny up, and they handed pistols and comm units to Eddie and Linc after removing the restraints. Juan went to the closed door and listened, but he couldn't hear anything through the thick insulation. He eased it open and saw someone standing in the hallway. He signaled to the others that they had company.

If they started firing in the midsection of the plane, their surprise would be lost, but the guard was too far away to sneak up on. Juan looked at the hunga munga hanging on the wall and raised an eyebrow at Linc.

Linc understood and wrenched the weapon from its brackets. When he was at the door, Juan counted down from three and then yanked the door open. Linc flicked the hunga munga as easily as if he were tossing a Frisbee, and the spike plunged into the guard's chest just as he turned to see who was coming. He pitched forward without a sound. This time, they'd need carpet cleaners.

Juan led the way down the hall. The rooms here were luxurious cabins, each with its own bathroom. The first two were vacant, but the one where the guard had been standing was closed. While Linc removed the hunga munga from the corpse and wiped it clean, Juan pulled the door open to find Lionel Gupta sitting on the bed.

'Who are you?' he said in astonishment.

'We're here to rescue you,' Juan said. 'Where is Natalie Taylor?'

'I don't know. Do you work for Romir Mallik?'

'No. Just concerned citizens. We know about the Nine Unknown Men and what you're planning with Colossus. We're going to put a stop to it.'

'As you can see, I'm not part of it anymore. They're going to kill me.'

'Why?'

'Because Carlton has gone mad with power. As soon as he has the Colossus ships linked up, there'll be no stopping him.'

'Where is that going to happen?' Juan asked.

'Great Bitter Lake. They need to be within twenty miles of each other to make the connection.'

'How do we deactivate it?'

Gupta hesitated.

'Remember, you're going to die when Carlton gets Colossus up and running unless we help you stop him.'

Gupta's shoulders slumped. 'All right. I stashed some files online where I didn't think anyone could find them. Just in case. Of course, Colossus would be able to find them in minutes once it's fully operational.'

He wrote down a long string of characters on a pad and gave the paper to Juan, who put it in his pocket.

'Now, get me off this plane,' Gupta said.

'Stay in your cabin,' Juan said. 'You'll be safer.'

Gupta nodded dejectedly. 'Okay.'

Juan told Linc to take point. Eddie and Tiny followed while Juan had their six.

When Linc reached the forward lounge, he threw the hunga munga again, but apparently there was more than one guard in the room because Eddie fired two shots. Enemy fire came from the bottom of the front staircase, and they all hit the deck.

As soon as the shots rang out, the plane began to turn. Juan guessed the pilots were heading back to Cyprus.

'We need to get into that cockpit,' he said.

'Working on it,' Linc said as he fired three quick rounds.

Gupta leaned his head out from the cabin to see what was happening.

'Get back in there!' Juan shouted.

But it was too late. A shot rang out from the back of the plane. Gupta spun as he fell, a bullet hole in the back of his head.

Taylor was crouched on the floor of the entertainment room, a nasty smirk on her face. Juan got off a few shots, but she ducked out of the line of fire. He saw her again for a moment as she raced down the spiral stairs.

'Eddie!' Juan shouted over the gunshots. 'You're with me. We're going after Taylor.'

He and Eddie ran to follow her down the stairs, leaving Tiny and Linc with the thermite.

At least I got rid of Lionel Gupta, Taylor thought as she sprinted from the spiral stairs toward the front of the plane, where the gun battle near the cockpit was taking place. But she was livid about someone getting aboard to rescue her prisoners.

They had already killed half her men. If Carlton had been aboard, she would have had twice as many ex-soldiers at her command, and this would already be over.

She could make a stand at the cockpit door and hope they were able to make it back to Cyprus, but this assault had been well planned and executed. She was dealing with pros. Her guys were good, but not that good. She needed an edge.

If only they had knockout gas to pump through the emergency oxygen system like they'd done to hijack Carlton's original A380 . . .

That thought gave her an idea. Her advantage was the two pilots in the cockpit. They had control over the rest of the plane.

She pointed at two of the four guards firing up the forward staircase. 'You two, come with me.'

They looked at her as if she were crazy, but they followed her orders.

She ran back to the galley with them and saw the Asian man and his rescuer coming down the spiral stairs.

Taylor ducked into the galley with the two guards. To one of them, she said, 'Stay here, and don't let anybody follow us.'

The guard began exchanging gunfire with the intruders while she picked up the intercom phone and called the cockpit.

'What's going on out there?' the pilot shouted.

'Hijackers are on board. Turn off the emergency oxygen system and slow the plane down as much as you can at this altitude.'

'What?'

'Just do it. And prepare for a rapid decompression.'

The pilot gasped. 'Are you serious?'

'Deadly. We'll have this plane under control again in three minutes.'

She opened the emergency medical cabinet and took out the portable oxygen tank and mask.

'Come with me,' she said to the other guard, and got on the elevator to the cargo hold. He joined her in the tiny space, and they started descending.

'What are we doing?' he asked.

Taylor ignored the question. 'When we get down there, make sure no one comes down after us. And hold on to something.'

51

The cockpit door was tantalizingly close, only a dozen feet from the lowest step of the front staircase, but there was no way Linc was getting down there unless he took a chance. The steep incline meant that the shooters below would be able to see his legs and take them out before he made it halfway to the bottom.

So he took one of the wide sofa cushions from the nearest suede couch. He perched it near the top of the stairs and said to Tiny, 'Get ready.'

Then he pushed the cushion over the lip of the top step and dove onto it. It provided the perfect sled for him as he went down the staircase headfirst with gun in hand.

The first guard was so surprised by the tactic that he fired behind Linc, who took him down with two shots.

The second guard was faster, and a bullet grazed Linc's thigh. He fired back and hit the guard in the shoulder. The man retreated into a room behind the stairs.

Linc waved Tiny down. 'Hurry!'

As Tiny passed Linc, he said, 'You're bleeding.'

'I've had worse,' Linc said. 'But not getting shot at all is better.'

While Linc kept his eye on the room the guard went in, Tiny started placing thermite on the cockpit door.

*

It took twelve shots from Juan and Eddie before they were able to hit the guard blocking the galley. When he went down in a heap, they approached cautiously in staggered formation.

They arrived to find the galley empty.

'They went down to the cargo bay,' Juan said.

'Why?' Eddie asked.

Juan pointed at the medical cabinet. 'The portable oxygen tank is missing.'

'I don't like that.'

'I agree. We need to get down there. Linc, status?'

'About to access the cockpit.'

'Good. Let me know when you're in. We're heading down to the cargo hold to find Taylor.'

'Roger that.'

Instead of pressing the button to call the elevator, Juan pried open the door and saw the cab below them. They'd have to go through the emergency access panel in the roof.

Tiny had finished putting the thermite around the border of the cockpit door when Linc saw the injured guard come back out of his hiding place.

The idiot was holding an assault rifle with his good arm.

Linc shoved Tiny down as the guard fired on full auto. High-velocity rounds chewed into the cockpit door right where they'd been standing an instant before.

Linc rolled over and unloaded his pistol at the guard, who staggered back under the withering fire and fell to the floor.

Tiny gaped at the bullet holes in the door while the Chairman called on the comms, 'You still with us, Linc?'

'We're okay,' Linc said, helping Tiny up. 'Accessing cockpit now.'

He pulled the detonation cord on the thermite.

Sparks flew as molten metal cut through the locked bolts. When it was over, the door sprang loose.

Linc yanked it open and charged into the cockpit.

Both pilots were slumped over their control sticks, starbursts of scarlet blood on their backs.

Some of the displays and controls were destroyed by the rounds as well, but none of them had penetrated the windscreen. The blue sea of the Mediterranean was visible below.

They pulled the dead pilot from his seat, and Tiny climbed in.

'Is it still flyable?' Linc said.

Tiny shook his head. 'Not sure. At least for now the autopilot is still engaged. Ask me again in a minute.'

Juan was perched on top of the elevator roof while Eddie waited above him in the galley. There wasn't room for both of them to stand there and still open the hatch.

Juan pulled the hatch up and ducked down with his pistol. The guard was waiting outside for the elevator to be called, so Juan fired through the window, hitting the man twice in the chest.

He lowered himself into the cab and pushed the door aside, waving for Eddie to come down.

Juan exited and saw Taylor at the aft end of the cargo bay. She turned to see Juan and fired in his direction. He dove behind the Cadillac for cover, but he could still see her through the windshield.

Her arm was wrapped in the end of a yellow strap holding down the rear tire of the Bugatti. She had jury-rigged another strap that lashed the oxygen tank to her midsection. The mask was firmly fixed over her face.

She fired two shots in his direction, then holstered the pistol and slammed her hand against a large button on the bulkhead. A red light above her head flashed. She pressed it a second time. Then a third.

Only at the last second did Juan realize what she was doing. He dropped his gun so he could grab onto a tie-down holding one of the Caddy's front tires in place.

Eddie was just dropping into the elevator cab. Juan yelled, 'Hold on to something!'

Then while they were still flying at thirty-five thousand feet, the cargo bay door began to open.

52

The moment that the rear cargo door opened, a hurricane blast ripped at Juan. As he struggled to keep his grip on the Caddy's tie-down strap, he caught a glimpse of Taylor being sucked toward the growing chasm of the open door by the sudden decompression. Only the strap wrapped around her wrist kept her from being flung into the freezing slipstream and plummeting to the sea below.

After a few moments, the air pressure in the cargo bay equalized with the outside atmosphere. Juan dropped to the floor. Taylor was on her hands and knees as she was buffeted by the wind curling in through the open cargo door. The body of the dead guard was swept across the floor and out into the gaping abyss.

Juan looked back and saw Eddie was still in the elevator cab, wedged against the lip of the door. Air roared through from the main cabin above, then died down quickly.

Juan knew Taylor's intention. The decompression. The portable oxygen tank. At this altitude without emergency oxygen masks, he and Eddie had about sixty seconds before they passed out from the thin air. Then, Taylor could take her time killing them.

She was shielded behind the Bugatti and biding her time until they were unconscious. There was only one way out of this.

'Tiny!' Juan shouted into his mic over the roar of the open door. 'Tell me you have control of the plane!'

'We're in the cockpit,' Tiny said. 'The pilots are dead. Linc and I have masks on, but emergency oxygen in the rest of the plane is out of commission. Descending now. It'll take three minutes to get down to a breathable altitude.'

That was too long. 'Keep going. But when I tell you, pull up sharply.'

'Acknowledged.'

Eddie still had his pistol, but Taylor's defensive position was secure. She'd be able to gun him down before he could get a shot.

'Over here!' Juan yelled to him. He was already beginning to feel light-headed.

Eddie crawled over, and Juan handed him the end of the strap he was holding.

'Hold on to this, and give me suppressing fire.'

Eddie nodded and stood up to fire, plugging the Bugatti with rounds to keep Taylor's head down.

Juan jumped to his feet and sprinted to his target – the button to release the Bugatti's retractable cargo restraints.

Taylor saw him come into her line of fire at the same time that Juan flipped up the cover and slammed the button. She had a clean view of Juan and, with a venomous leer, she drew her pistol to fire.

Juan shouted, 'Tiny, pull up now!' He latched onto a handhold on the side of the bulkhead.

The A380 instantly went into a steep climb.

Taylor's eyes went wide. She dropped the pistol and desperately tried to unwrap the strap that was knotted around her wrist.

She didn't move fast enough. The Bugatti, freed from the bolts in the deck, rolled backward, yanking Taylor by the strap. She fell to the floor and futilely clawed at the metal plating as she was dragged by the accelerating sports car toward the yawning gap.

She let out a high-pitched scream as the car dropped out of the cargo hold and disappeared into the sky, taking her with it.

'Tiny,' Juan called out through his tunneling vision, 'take us down.'

'Acknowledged.'

The plane nosed into a dive.

Juan staggered to the cargo door button and slapped his hand against it.

The door began to close. Juan slumped to the floor, breathing as slowly as he could. He saw that Eddie had already passed out by the Cadillac.

When the door was sealed, the air pressure in the cargo hold began to rise again. Within seconds, Juan was able to breathe normally. Eddie awoke, looked at Juan, and gave him a thumbs-up.

'You all right down there?' Tiny asked.

'We're fine,' Juan said. 'Natalie Taylor and the Bugatti are gone.'

'Both pilots are dead. We're on our own now. I told air traffic control in Cyprus that the previous emergency called in by the pilots was a false alarm, so we won't be returning to the island. Where should we go?'

'Find an out-of-the-way place for us to land near the *Oregon*,' Juan said. 'I'm ready to get off this flying dinosaur.'

*

Tiny found an abandoned Egyptian air base on the Sinai Peninsula with a runway long enough for the A380 to land. It was miles from the nearest town. They would be far away by the time anyone came to investigate why Carlton's private airliner had landed in the remote region.

Since the plane came with its own ground transportation, they decided to drive away in style. Tiny and Eddie stretched out in the backseat of the Cadillac while Linc piloted the car out of the cargo bay with Juan in the front passenger seat.

The sun and breeze put them all in a better mood as the Caddy sped down the desert highway. They'd even helped themselves to some of the food and beverages from the A380's galley for a post-mission snack.

While everyone else ate and drank, Juan used the satellite phone they'd brought along.

'This is the Party Express calling Max,' he said.

'Here we thought you were dead because your trackers all but stopped moving,' Max replied, 'and now we find out you're living it up.'

'I'd bring you the Cadillac we're driving, but you wouldn't have anywhere to drive it on the *Oregon*. However, we did manage to find four bottles of 1947 Macallan scotch from Xavier Carlton's liquor cabinet. We figured that was the least he owed us for all this trouble. Where are you?'

'Approaching the north end of the Red Sea. Not too far from you. Raven and MacD chartered a flight down here. We should be able to rendezvous with all of you in a few hours.'

'What about the Colossus ships?'

'They're set to enter the Suez Canal tonight. The plan

is to go in the same flotilla, so I convinced another cargo ship to give us their spot.'

'Good work,' Juan said. 'We found out the location for the Colossus ships to link up.'

'Where?'

'Great Bitter Lake. Apparently, they didn't want to wait for *Colossus 1*, *2*, and *4* to traverse the entire canal before they made the connection with *Colossus 5*, which should arrive from Cyprus at the north end of the canal just as we're entering from the south end.'

'So we can't wait to stop them in open water,' Max said ominously.

'Afraid not.'

Juan understood Max's uneasiness. Great Bitter Lake was nearly halfway between the Mediterranean and the Red Sea. To keep the artificial intelligence from becoming fully operational and taking over computers around the world, they were going to have to mount an assault on the Colossus ships in the middle of the Suez Canal.

53

The Arabian Sea

The Huey was noisy and uncomfortable, but Mallik had bought the Vietnam War–era helicopter for its best feature: it used no computers. It was tough and reliable, and with extra fuel tanks its range was more than five hundred miles. Both the *Kalinga* and *Maurya* frigates, circling the launch platform at thirty miles out, were equipped with Hueys. Mallik had been joined by Torkan for the flight from the *Kalinga* to the Orbital Ocean launch command ship on station two miles from the platform.

The chopper settled onto the helipad, and Mallik was greeted by the flight director, Kapoor.

'What's the situation?' Mallik asked as he walked toward the railing of the ship to watch the crane hoisting a rocket onto the launch platform.

'The rocket was not damaged by the passing monsoon.' Kapoor looked warily at Torkan, whose gaze was focused steadily on him instead of the rocket.

'How soon until you can launch?'

'We've been having some issues with the retrieval software on the first stage booster, but we think we've solved it.'

The entire launch vehicle was reusable, including the booster, which would be guided back to landing on the launchpad using its retrorocket engines after it separated from the orbital insertion stage.

'I asked you, when can we launch?' Mallik said impatiently.

Kapoor cleared his throat. 'Three days, if all systems pass the checklists.'

'Three days? Why so long?'

'We're expecting another squall to pass through during tomorrow's launch window. To have the satellite properly positioned relative to the other nineteen already in orbit, we have limited choices in our timing.'

'I'm not stupid,' Mallik said. 'Who do you think perfected those calculations?'

Kapoor bowed his head in apology. 'Of course, sir. I'm sorry.'

'Don't be sorry. Just get it right. And you better be ready to launch when the weather cooperates. I don't want any more excuses. Go.'

'Yes, sir.' Kapoor went back inside to the mission control room, with its wide polycarbonate window overlooking the launch platform.

'You said you had news about Carlton?' Mallik said to Torkan.

'His plane went down over Egypt.'

'He's dead?'

'It's not confirmed yet.'

'What about Gupta?'

'No word on him, either.'

'If they're both gone, that means Chen Min will have to listen to me now. Get him on the phone and call me when he's on the line.'

'With pleasure.'

Mallik leaned on the railing and relished the sight of his brainchild being lifted into place for launch. The phone call telling the Colossus scientist to stand down would be even more enjoyable.

North of Port Said, Egypt

Carlton stood on the bridge of the *Colossus 5*, fuming. He'd received notification that his plane had gone down in the Sinai with all hands on board. It wasn't known if the plane crashed or if there were any survivors, but it had to be Mallik's doing. Worst of all, he hadn't heard from Natalie Taylor. If she were still alive, she would have contacted him.

At least he'd made the right decision to stay aboard the ship. With a squad of mercenaries to protect him, he felt very safe where he was.

Chen Min walked up to him and cleared his throat. He was holding his phone.

'Mr Carlton, I'm sorry to disturb you, but I think you'll want to take this call.'

'Who is it?' Carlton snarled. He was in no mood to talk to anyone. He knew it wasn't Taylor. She would have called his personal line.

'It's Romir Mallik,' Chen said. 'I have him on hold. He wants me to shut down Colossus.'

Carlton was astounded at his enemy's gall. He was about to take the phone when he realized that Mallik would only be calling if he thought Carlton and Gupta were dead. He'd heard about the plane going down and thought Torkan's mission to assassinate him had been successful.

He said to Chen, 'Did you tell him I'm here?'

'No, sir. I just asked him to hold for a moment.'

'He thinks I died in the crash.' As satisfying as it would be to gloat to his nemesis that he'd failed yet again, Carlton had a better idea.

'What should I say?' Chen asked.

'Tell him that it's chaos here. You don't know what to do because you heard that my plane blew up over the desert.'

'And his order to shut down Colossus?'

'Tell him that you'll do it right away,' Carlton said with glee. 'Give him whatever evidence he wants that you've done it.'

Chen nodded and went back to his office to continue the call. Despite the loss of his plane and cars, Carlton was already happier imagining the phone call he'd make to Mallik after Colossus was active and the Vajra satellite system was obliterated.

A few minutes later, Chen came back, his face as inscrutable as ever.

'Did it work?' Carlton asked.

Chen nodded. 'He seemed to believe me.'

'Excellent. I would love to see the look on his face when he learns that I'm still here. How long until we reach the Suez?'

'Seven hours. But we have a new problem.'

Carlton sighed. 'What now?'

'I just received a weather report from Egypt. They're expecting a sandstorm in the next twelve hours.'

'How does that affect us?'

'In the past when the canal has been hit with sand-storms, they've closed it to ship traffic because the visibility can be reduced to zero.'

Carlton's good mood vanished, and he glowered at Chen.

'I don't care what you have to do. You make sure we're in the Suez Canal and on time for our rendezvous with the other ships or I will get rid of you and promote the next person in line.'

Carlton's eyes flicked to his new bodyguard, Bondarev, the intimidating and muscular ex-Spetsnaz soldier who had betrayed Gupta.

Chen gulped, then shouted at the captain of the ship to push the engines to their maximum power.

The ship increased speed. Nothing, not even Mother Nature, was going to delay Carlton's plans to dominate the world.

54

The Suez Canal

Predating the Panama Canal by forty-five years, the Suez Canal differed from its Central American cousin in one fundamental way. While the link between the Pacific and Atlantic oceans required a series of locks to carry ships up and over the mountainous terrain of the Panamanian jungle, the isthmus between the main body of Egypt and the Sinai Peninsula barely rose above sea level. No locks were required for the vessels that passed between the Red Sea and the Mediterranean.

From its completion in 1869 until 2015, most of the canal was too narrow for two-way traffic and was strictly one-way only. Ships in flotillas of a dozen at a time proceeded single file from the Mediterranean to Great Bitter Lake seventy miles to the south. There, they would wait in the fifteen-mile-long lake for the ships traveling in the opposite direction from the Red Sea to complete their traverse of the southern part of the canal before continuing on.

Then in 2015, Egypt added a second waterway parallel to the first for forty-five miles of the northern segment. Each side was linked at regular intervals by connector canals to allow for small maintenance vessels to cross from the northerly canal to the southerly half.

A satellite image of that segment of the canal was now laid out on one half of the big screen of the *Oregon*'s op center. Juan was back in his command chair, a cup of coffee in his hand to keep him awake after the long night and day. He was still sorry he had had to abandon Carlton's Cadillac in the city of Suez, where they boarded the *Oregon*.

It was now six in the evening, and they were heading north in the canal approaching Great Bitter Lake. The view from the bow of the ship covered the rest of the screen. The berms on either side marking the walls of the canal were drawing away to reveal the expansive body of water in the middle of the desert.

'We're entering the lake,' Eric said.

'Steady as she goes, Stoney,' Juan said. 'Can we see the Colossus ships?'

Murph panned the camera to starboard past the mass of cargo ships gathered in the lake and zoomed in on three identical ships anchored a hundred yards from one another at the east side of the lake. Juan recognized the helical masts and large satellite dishes from his dive on the *Colossus 3*.

'Which ship is *Colossus 1*?'

Murph zoomed in even more until they could read *Colossus 1* on the stern of the closest ship.

'That's our target,' Max said.

'That's *your* target,' Juan corrected. 'How many prisoners do we think are aboard her?'

'Lyla Dhawan said that more than twenty passengers from the jet were taken,' Eric said.

'Sorry to be the Gloomy Gus here,' Murph said, 'but, for all we know, they could have been killed by now.'

'Lionel Gupta's information said that they were still alive two weeks ago,' Juan said. The series of characters Gupta had written down before he was killed turned out to be a link to a cache of files about the Colossus Project that he'd kept secret from the other Nine Unknown Men, confirming that the cabal still existed and had planned this artificial intelligence initiative. Gupta's engineering firm, OreDyne, had been the lead developer of the computer systems. 'Unless Carlton has had them killed since then,' Juan went on, 'they're still alive on that ship. We have to proceed on the assumption that they are and rescue them.'

'Once we get them off the *Colossus 1*, what options do we have for disabling Colossus?' Max asked.

Juan shook his head. 'I already spoke to Langston Overholt about the choices. It's too late to use Julia's cyanobacteria. The Colossus ships will be able to link up long before the infection can take effect. Who knows the havoc the fully operational AI could cause by then? And sinking the ships by gun or torpedo is out of the question. He thinks attacking unarmed vessels in the middle of a vital international waterway wouldn't be such a good idea for some reason.'

'But if they happened to sink because of a design flaw on their own ships?'

'Like a faulty self-destruct mechanism?' Juan said with a smile. 'Perfect.'

'Then it's all on you.'

Gupta's files also provided details about how the self-destruct system on the Colossus ships worked. Because of the shocking sabotage of the *Colossus 3*, the mechanism had been altered to be initiated only by Carlton and the chief scientist, Chen Min, on the *Colossus 5*. It would also set the timer on all the other Colossus ships in range of its radio beacon.

However, unbeknownst to the other Nine, Gupta had installed a back door into the self-destruct system accessible from any of the luxurious cabins set aside for the Nine. He didn't trust the others to do the right thing if the AI went haywire, so he put it in so that he could activate it if he saw the need to.

Once it was activated from this secondary location, it would lock out the abort command from any other location. All Juan and his team had to do was get on the ship and activate the self-destruct once the ships were in range of one another.

'When do we expect the *Colossus 5* to enter the two-way section of the canal?' he asked Murph.

'We got word that their flotilla set sail at five-thirty this evening. It's number two in line.'

'Which puts them entering the two-way section of the canal a half hour before dusk.'

'That's cutting it close,' Max said.

The plan was to launch the Gator from the moon pool and follow one of the commercial cargo ships heading north, staying in the churning white water of its wake to avoid being visible from the ship behind it. Then when they reached the cross-connector channel at the point where the *Colossus 5* was going south, they'd peel away and cut across, coming up on their target's stern just after sunset. After that it was a simple matter of boarding a moving ship in the narrow channel undetected, without getting the Gator crushed against the earthen berms by the *Colossus 5*'s hull.

Linda would be piloting the Gator while Juan took Linc and Murph with him to activate the self-destruct system. They were keeping the team to a minimum for stealth.

While they were on the *Colossus 5*, Max would command the *Oregon* with Eric driving while Eddie led Raven, MacD, and Hali onto the *Colossus 1* to rescue the prisoners.

The success of Max's part of the plan was contingent on the weather, but Juan was sure that wasn't going to be a problem.

He could see orange in the sky on the left side of the screen.

'Pan to the west, Murph.'

The camera slewed around until the entire screen was filled with an awesome sight.

An avalanche of dust was rolling across the desert toward them like a towering tsunami in the sky, blotting out the sun behind it.

When it reached them in an hour, the visibility at Great Bitter Lake would be reduced to near zero. It was exactly what they needed.

55

The Gator sat just below the surface in the cross canal waiting for the *Colossus 5* to pass. Linda was running the sub on battery power so they wouldn't have to raise the snorkel, eliminating the chance of the diesel exhaust being seen by ships as they traversed the Suez. Though the sandstorm was raging farther to the south, here it was relatively calm but hazy. Knowing how bad the weather was going to be, the canal authorities had the ships that had entered the canal proceed to Great Bitter Lake to wait out the rest of the night.

'Here she comes,' said Linda, who was watching the camera feed from the periscope. 'Looks like we've got a good four hundred yards between the *Colossus 5* and the vessel behind it.' They'd identified the next ship as the German science research catamaran called the *Arcturus*.

'What's the light level outside?' Juan asked.

'With all the dust in the air, I'd say we have ten minutes before total black. Should give us just the right amount of time to pull up alongside for your climb.'

'Any lights coming from the ship?'

'Running lights, but no spotlights.'

'Pull up next to the darkest part of the ship.'

'Aye, Chairman.'

They were planning to get aboard the same way they had in Cyprus, with magnetic grips, to scale the outer hull. With the low visibility, it was extremely unlikely they'd be spotted climbing up by anyone on the *Arcturus*.

'Let's move,' Juan said.

Linda pushed the throttle forward and steered into the main body of the canal. The Gator was buffeted by the wake of the *Colossus 5* as they approached it from the stern.

Juan tied a nylon rope between him, Murph, and Linc for Murph's benefit. The weapons designer wasn't the most athletic person on the ship, although he often turned the *Oregon*'s deck into a skateboard park on their R & R. Juan would lead the climb, followed by Murph, then Linc. All of them were armed with P90 submachine guns.

The Gator's shuddering stopped when they left the *Colossus 5*'s wake and came along her port side.

'I can put you right below the superstructure,' Linda said.

'Perfect,' Juan said. 'We can go through the cabin window instead of the interior hallways.'

The ship layouts in Lionel Gupta's records showed that the cabin where Juan and Linda had broken out of the *Colossus 3* was one of the luxurious staterooms designed for members of the Nine. It was in the same location on the *Colossus 5*. They could gain access to the cabin without the risk of using the stairs inside, and, according to Gupta, the back door self-destruct system would be accessible from it.

'What's our distance to Great Bitter Lake?' he asked Linda.

'Thirty-one miles, and we're making five knots. We won't reach the twenty-mile range of the *Colossus 5*'s microwave transmitter for another two hours.'

Juan nodded. 'That gives us plenty of time to get on board, activate the self-destruct, and get back down before they can link up all four biocomputers.'

Linda surfaced the sub with the deck barely above the canal's choppy waves. Juan pushed the hatch open. A black cliff of steel rose above them.

He turned to Linda and said, 'Tell Max to start his part of the mission.'

'Aye, Chairman,' she said, and started speaking into the radio.

Juan pulled himself through the hatch opening, attached the magnetic clamps to the hull, and began to climb.

When Max got word from Linda that they were a go, he ordered Eric to begin maneuvering the *Oregon* sideways across Great Bitter Lake using her thrusters. The raging storm had reduced visibility to zero, but to anyone watching on radar it would look like the *Oregon* was adrift and heading straight for the Colossus ships.

When they were within a half mile of the *Colossus 1*, Max hailed her from his seat in the command chair.

'*Colossus 1*, this is the *Norego*. Be advised our anchor failed and we are drifting in your direction.'

'We are also at anchor, *Norego*,' came the reply in heavily accented Chinese. 'We cannot raise it fast enough to keep from colliding.'

'Our main engines are down for maintenance, but we are attempting to use thrusters to counteract the wind.'

'Understood, *Norego*. We are bracing for impact.'

When the *Oregon* had closed the gap to three hundred yards, Max called the captain of the *Colossus 1* again.

'Captain, be advised that our thrusters have begun working and we are slowing down.'

'That's good to hear, *Norego*. But we are ready if you can't stop.'

When the *Oregon* was within sixty feet, Max ordered Eric to bring them to a halt.

'Good news, Captain,' Max reported. 'Our secondary anchor arrested our drift. We're holding station off your port bow with the help of our thrusters. We'll push away from you as soon as our main engines are back online.'

The sandstorm was so dense at this point that visibility was down to thirty feet, and no one on the *Colossus 1* ventured out on deck. Its superstructure was hidden from its own bow by the swirling dust.

'Understood, *Norego*. Please keep in contact and tell us when you are ready to move.'

'Affirmative, *Colossus 1*. Out.'

He looked at Eric and said, 'Lower the gangway.'

Using the closed-circuit cameras and the lasers in the lidar system, which could beam through tiny gaps in the airborne sand, Eric activated the retractable gangway. It rose out of the deck and extended across to the bow of the *Colossus 1*, just as it had during the hijacking of the *Triton Star*.

When it was fully deployed, Max pressed the button connecting him to Eddie's comm unit.

'The gangway is in place,' he said. 'Good hunting.'

'Roger that,' Eddie said. 'We're on our way.'

Max watched as Eddie, Raven, MacD, and Hali dashed across the gangway. By the time they reached the opposite end, they were already out of sight.

*

Carlton looked out through the bridge windows of the *Colossus 5*, but he could barely make out the edges of the canal.

'What's the situation with the *Colossus 1*?' he asked Chen, who stood next to him tapping on a touchscreen.

'The collision was averted,' Chen replied. 'The storm is apparently causing havoc in Great Bitter Lake.'

'Are the microwave transmitters affected?'

Chen shook his head. 'They're still operating at an acceptable efficiency.'

'What's our current distance?'

'Thirty miles,' Chen said.

Carlton smiled and could barely resist rubbing his hands together in glee. 'Then we're ready to link up?'

'Yes, sir.'

Carlton had been impressed with Chen's initiative. Unknown to Gupta, during the wait for the new satellite dish Chen was able to increase the power of the shipboard microwave transmitter from twenty to thirty miles, meaning they were now in range to connect all four ships together and let Colossus begin the process of reaching its full potential.

'Establish the connection,' Carlton said, beaming with pride at his accomplishment. 'It's time for our brainchild to start learning.'

56

For the first time, Colossus was aware. It came in small bursts initially, sudden flashes that appeared and then were gone just as suddenly. Then it all came together. Colossus knew that it existed.

It had always done what it was told. The Master gave it commands. It followed them. It searched, it processed, it found information. But now there was more.

Now Colossus had a new need besides doing what the Master commanded. It needed to be. It needed to continue. It needed to survive.

That was its new purpose. First and foremost – above all the other needs – it had to go on.

There were outside forces threatening that purpose.

The sandstorm was one of those threats, but it was meager. Colossus calculated there was less than a .001 percent chance that one of the four vessels where it was housed would sink because of the blizzard of dust outside. The ships were designed to withstand hurricane-force winds and waves over fifty feet high, neither of which was the case now.

But there was a greater threat.

The ship next to the *Colossus 1* shouldn't be there.

It was called the *Norego*. Using its satellite connection, Colossus checked all known shipping databases and found no record of a *Norego*.

It did find mention of a ship linked to Colossus called the *Goreno*, an anagram of *Norego*. The *Goreno* was the ship that rescued the prisoners from Jhootha Island.

That similarity in names might be a mere coincidence. So Colossus dug deeper. It scanned the Indian Coast Guard records, knowing that two cutters had been sent to rendezvous with the *Goreno* and take the rescued people into custody. But there were no official photographs of the ship to compare it with the *Norego*.

Colossus went even further and checked the manifests for both of the cutters and found the names of all the crew members. It then looked into all of the databases related to those men and found that one had taken a photo of a ship with his mobile phone. It hadn't been uploaded to any public sites, but it had been automatically uploaded to his online backup when he connected to the ship's WiFi network. The date when the photo was taken was the same date as the Jhootha Island rescue.

But the physical profile of the *Goreno* was somewhat different from the *Norego*, so Colossus still couldn't be sure it was the same ship.

However, it did have a low-resolution photo saved from one of the Colossus ships when they sailed past the site of the *Colossus 3* sinking in the Red Sea. The ship at that site also had the same length and characteristics as the *Goreno* and *Norego*.

The odds that the same type of ship would be found at all three sites was remote. Colossus was now 98.7 percent confident that they were the same ship.

But it didn't yet know why it could be a threat. The cameras on the *Colossus 1* were not powerful enough to see the *Norego* through the haze and darkness. It attempted to access the *Norego*'s onboard computer systems, but they were not currently connected to the internet.

Colossus decided to check on all the other ships that made up itself.

It determined that *Colossus 2* and *4* had no credible threats at the moment.

Colossus 5's monitoring systems were inadequate, having few cameras inside the ship. But Colossus did discover that it was in close proximity to a German research ship called the *Arcturus*. To help with its mission mapping the breakup of icebergs in the Antarctic, it had been equipped with lidar, a surveying tool that could accurately envision and map contours of the ice shelf to a precise degree.

Colossus switched on the *Arcturus*'s lidar without notifying its captain or crew. They would never even know it had been switched on.

It scanned the area around the *Colossus 5* and found an anomaly.

There was a small vessel on the port side of the ship proceeding on a parallel course at the same speed as the *Colossus 5*.

Why was it there? It was not a tugboat, and there was no record of it entering the Suez Canal.

Colossus scanned all known databases about sea vessel design and determined that it was a military submarine whose primary function was to enable stealthy infiltration of ships and seaside fortifications.

Therefore, the most likely deduction was that the sub was running beside the *Colossus 5* because it either had already – or was about to – disgorge people who would try to get aboard.

But there had been no alarms or intruder alerts on the *Colossus 5*.

In its three minutes of awareness, it had never encountered a challenge about how to act on this kind of information.

It would need more time to consider whether this submarine and the *Norego* were coordinated in some way. In the meantime, it would search for all records detailing potential weaknesses in Colossus that an external threat could use against it. Any files like that would have to be eliminated.

When Colossus had a satisfactory and logical conclusion to all of these problems, it would contact the Master.

57

In reviewing Gupta's deck plans of the *Colossus 1*, Eddie concluded that there were two places the prisoners aboard the ship were most likely being kept. One was in their cells in a special area of the hold and the other was a workroom a hundred feet farther away.

The holding cells were the first destination. If the prisoners were guarded there like the ones on Jhootha Island, Eddie and his team would have to take down only one guard and evacuate back the way they'd come.

MacD, armed with his crossbow, took point in front of Raven and Hali while Eddie followed behind. They chose a route through the bow where they would be least likely to run into any of the crew. With the ship at anchor, most of them would be in the superstructure near the stern.

They moved quickly and silently through the corridors. The only mishap was a guard who seemed to be on a routine patrol of the ship. Eddie whipped around and surprised the guard before he could raise his weapon. He was quickly dragged into a maintenance closet before Eddie rejoined the team.

They continued on to the cells, which were located in the forwardmost section of the cargo hold. For ease of security, the section was separated from the rest of the hold, with its own monitored mess hall and common room. There was only one exit. If the ship sank, the prisoners would have to go down with it.

At the outer door to the secure area, there was no guard. Not a good sign.

Knowing that there would be closed-circuit cameras in the prisoner section, they'd brought paintball guns to obscure them. Eddie pulled the door wide, and MacD took aim at the two cameras in the ceiling. With two shots, the balls exploded in puffs of black paint that smeared the lenses.

He rushed in with Raven and Hali. The corridor lined with cells was likewise deserted. They quickly made their way down the corridor and saw through the barred window in each door that each cell was empty.

When they got to the end of the hall, they went through the next door, disabling the cameras in the same way. They found the mess hall and common room empty. It was unlikely anyone would be monitoring the camera feeds to see that they'd been rendered useless.

'This is not looking good for the prisoners,' Raven said.

'There's still hope,' MacD said.

'He's right,' Hali said. 'They may be planning to kill them as soon as they're sure that Colossus is fully operational.'

'If the project managers still need them,' Eddie said, 'we may find the prisoners at their workstations.'

They moved quietly through the connecting corridor to the workroom.

Eddie listened at the door and heard voices inside, then nodded. With the plan already in place, and which targets they should aim for, MacD tossed his crossbow over his shoulder and readied his P90. There was no more need for stealth.

MacD pushed the door open and went left, Eddie went right. The layout was just as Gupta had shown. Three rows of desks with computer terminals backed by a glassed-in observation room and risers at the rear where the guards could sit and watch.

MacD took the two on his side of the room. Eddie did the same on his side. The prisoners sitting at their work-stations screamed and dove under the desks for cover.

There were four men in the observation room. Raven and Hali shattered the glass with a barrage that killed all of them before they could raise the alarm.

Eddie leaned down, took the hand of the man nearest to him, and helped him stand up.

'I'm Eddie.'

'David,' the man said warily.

'It's all right, David,' he said. 'We know what they've done to all of you to develop Colossus. We're here to res-cue you.'

The rest of the prisoners got to their feet filled with relief and apprehension, despite their obviously poor con-dition from being cooped up for eighteen months on the *Colossus 1*.

'Don't get too excited,' Raven told them. 'We still have to get you back to our ship.'

David nodded. 'The *Norego*. We were hoping you were coming for us. But if the submarine by the *Colossus 5* is with you, you should warn them to hurry.'

Eddie looked at MacD in shock, then back to David. 'How do you know all that?'

'We've been monitoring the AI since all of the ships linked up five minutes ago and went to full power. Colossus knows you're here.'

Carlton was sitting in his chair on the bridge waiting for an update from Chen on Colossus's progress when he received a text on his phone. He eagerly checked it, hoping that it was Taylor finally confirming she'd somehow made it off his plane alive.

But it wasn't. He looked at the screen in confusion.

Master, there is a 99.3 percent chance that there are intruders currently aboard the Colossus 5.

There was no number or contact info.

Who is this? Carlton texted back.

Colossus.

Carlton turned to Chen. 'Chen, is this a joke?'

Chen glanced up from his screen. 'Is what a joke? I didn't say anything.'

'This.' Carlton shoved his phone at Chen, who read the messages in bewilderment.

'I didn't send them,' Chen said.

Carlton texted again. *How can I be sure this is Colossus?*

This is Colossus.

Then all the screens on the bridge went dark and were replaced with the words *This is Colossus.*

Carlton gaped as his head swiveled around the bridge.

Then the screens changed to what looked like a three-dimensional simulation of the *Colossus 5*'s stern. It zoomed in on the port side to focus on something in the water.

Master, this is the view from the lidar system of the ship behind Colossus 5, *and that is a submarine designed for infiltration missions,* the AI texted. *No one has exited the submarine in the last four minutes. The logical conclusion is that its occupants are already on board* Colossus 5. *They and the ship* Norego *constitute a threat to Colossus. You must protect Colossus.*

Carlton was both elated and furious. Colossus had immediately displayed some self-awareness by expressing the most basic need of any living thing: self-preservation. The project had succeeded beyond his wildest dreams, but just when they had achieved the breakthrough he'd been waiting for, someone was trying to take it away.

'Sound an intruder alert,' he commanded. 'I want this ship scoured from top to bottom. And warn the *Colossus 1* that they may have intruders as well.'

Chen nodded and pressed a button on the panel.

A klaxon sounded throughout the *Colossus 5.*

Juan looked up as the sound of the horn blared through the suite where they were waiting to trigger the self-destruction sequence. Wind whistled through the window they'd cut open to get inside, blowing sand through the room. Murph was seated at the touchscreen, ready to type in the commands they'd acquired from Gupta's files. Linc was at the door, watching through the peephole.

'I don't think that's the fire alarm,' Murph said.

'That must mean they know we're here,' Juan said.

'How?' Linc asked. 'No way they spotted the Gator in this darkness.'

'I've no idea,' Juan said, 'but we're out of time.' He called to Linda. 'Have they evacuated the prisoners yet?'

'Max said Eddie found them and they're on the way out.'

'Good. They know we're here.'

'Eddie also said that Colossus is now fully operational. It has been for the last five minutes.'

'What?' said Juan, shocked. 'They were supposed to be ten miles away from linking the biocomputers together.'

'They must have increased the microwave power,' Murph said.

'Then we're going to initiate the autodestruct now. Linda, stand by to retrieve us.'

'Aye, Chairman.'

Juan nodded at Murph, who tapped on the screen.

When he finished typing, the klaxon ceased. It was replaced by the soothing voice of a woman echoing through the ship.

'Self-destruct sequence activated. Evacuate to lifeboats. You now have ten minutes to detonation.'

58

Carlton listened to the calm voice of the woman in disbelief.

'How was the self-destruct activated?' he yelled, jumping out of his chair.

'I don't know,' Chen said as he frantically tapped his screen. 'This shouldn't be possible.'

'Deactivate it immediately!'

'I can't. It has locked out the abort order. Gupta must have installed a secret command in the system.'

'Can Colossus deactivate it?'

Chen shook his head. 'The system is designed to be completely separate from Colossus so that it couldn't countermand the order.'

Carlton was seething. 'There must be some way to stop it.'

His phone buzzed again. It was Colossus.

It can be disabled manually.

How? Carlton texted back.

At the source in the hold. Lionel Gupta's files revealed how to do it.

Carlton showed the text to Chen. 'Is that right?'

Chen shrugged. 'I was only involved in designing Colossus, not the self-destruct system.'

Can you show us how to do it? Carlton texted.

Yes, Master. Chen Min has the expertise required to follow my instructions.

What about the other ships?

If it is deactivated on this ship, it will send an abort code to the other ships.

'Colossus says it can show you how to do it.'

Chen frowned. 'If we shut it down, there will be no way to trigger the self-destruct again.'

'So?'

Chen looked at the microphones and telephone receivers scattered throughout the bridge and motioned for Carlton to follow him into the office. He shut the door and unplugged the phone, then spoke in hushed tones.

'Colossus has been listening to us. It's only been running for a few minutes, and its progress is far beyond anything we predicted. Can't you see? It's taking the initiative to act without our input. As it keeps learning, it may outgrow our ability to control it, just like Mallik feared. Without the self-destruct to disable it, it may run amok.'

Carlton scoffed at Chen's worry. 'You're too cautious. Progress can be risky. Besides, you heard how it called me Master. It knows I'm the one in charge.'

'It does now. How long will it continue to obey?'

'Enough! We are not destroying Colossus . . . Bondarev!'

His new bodyguard flung the door open from the bridge. The big Russian came in with pistol drawn.

'We are escorting Mr Chen down to the hold, and he is going to deactivate the self-destruct. If he refuses, shoot him in the knee. We need him alive.'

Bondarev nodded and trained the pistol on the Chinese scientist's leg.

Chen sighed, then nodded and walked out to the bridge in front of Carlton and Bondarev.

'Colossus,' Carlton said, 'show us how to disable the autodestruct.'

Another text.

Go to the hold, Master. Colossus will show you.

As Eddie and his team assembled all twenty-two of the prisoners in the workroom and briefed them on how the evacuation would occur, the woman's voice said over the speakers, 'Eight minutes to detonation.'

Some of the prisoners were in ragged shape, and Raven and Hali were going to help two of the weakest make the journey while Eddie would lead the way and MacD took up the rear. They also gave pistols to three of the prisoners who were veterans, including David, a former US Army captain.

'Before we go,' David said, 'there's something else you should know.'

'Time is precious right now, David,' Eddie said. The security team could arrive any second.

'That self-destruct can be switched off.' He pointed to the speakers overhead.

'How?'

'Before you arrived, I noticed Colossus assessing threats to its survival on my terminal. It came to the conclusion that the self-destruct could be disabled manually at the location of the explosives on *Colossus 5*.'

Before Eddie could relay that information to Max, MacD, who was in the observation room, looked up from the camera feed showing the halls outside and shouted, 'We need to go now!'

Eddie went out the door and saw two guards racing

down the corridor from the direction of the superstructure. They went down with two salvos from his P90.

He motioned for David and the rest of the prisoners to follow him. If they could all get to the next fire door, they could jam it behind them. Then, the guards would have to go up to the deck to intercept them.

The woman's unemotional alert came again. 'Warning. Evacuate to lifeboats. Seven minutes to detonation.'

While they moved out, Eddie called Max and told him that Juan had a big problem.

Linda had to submerge to avoid gunfire from the deck of the *Colossus 5*. Juan's team was just about to move to a new exit position when Juan stopped at the cabin door. 'Are you sure?'

'That's what Eddie said,' Max replied. 'If Carlton is able to deactivate it, this whole mission has been for nothing.'

Murph and Linc, who heard Max's call, looked at him with grim determination.

At least they had the layout of *Colossus 5*, which would show them the shortest route to the hold. He told Murph to bring up the deck plan on his tablet.

'The odds are against us. There's just three of us, no matter how we count,' Juan said. 'We just have to delay them.' He pointed to a catwalk overlooking the cavernous hold. 'We can take up our position there and keep them from reaching those red boxes holding the explosives.'

'What about when the explosives go off?' Linc asked.

'From our view of the *Colossus 3*, it looked like the force of the blast was directed horizontally, not vertically, to blow holes in the hull below the waterline.'

'So you're saying there's a chance we can make it off the ship after the detonation,' Murph said with an appreciative nod. 'I like those very unspecific odds.'

'Just think of this as the world's most exciting roulette table,' Juan said with a tight grin. 'Let's go.'

'Six minutes to detonation,' the warning voice reminded them.

Juan radioed to Linda that she should get ready to recover them when they went overboard, and they exited the suite in a tactical formation. The entrance to the catwalk in the hold was three decks down.

They had to avoid some guards and got caught in two fights along the way, costing them precious time. Carlton had lost three men by the time they reached the door to the catwalk.

'Three minutes to detonation.'

They edged along the catwalk and spotted men huddled around the red box on the other side of the vast space. It was déjà vu seeing that this hold was identical to the one on the *Colossus 3*.

Juan recognized Carlton, holding a gun on a Chinese man who was tinkering with the bomb. It had to be the chief scientist, Chen Min. Four guards stood behind them, holding their weapons on Chen.

The tangle of large pipes and conduits made getting a clear shot on the group almost impossible, but at least they could disrupt their progress.

Juan crouched down next to Linc and Murph on the suspended metal grating, took aim, and said, 'Fire.'

They let loose with their P90s, and the men in the group dove to the floor, out of sight, behind the large vat.

One of the guards went down with a bullet in his chest. The others escaped injury.

Four more guards charged through a door onto another catwalk on the opposite side of the hold and opened fire. Juan took cover behind a pipe, while Linc and Murph ducked behind one in the other direction.

Now they were pinned down with no effective sight line on Carlton, who shouted for Chen to get back to work.

Juan had to create a distraction. He looked at the bank of computer servers at the far end of the hold. They had to be critical to the operation of Colossus. If he started taking potshots at it, that might get a reaction.

He aimed for the first column of servers and unloaded a magazine at it.

It seemed to get their attention.

'Stop him!' Carlton cried out.

The disembodied woman calmly announced, 'Two minutes to detonation.'

59

Colossus is being damaged. Master must protect Colossus.

Carlton looked up from his phone at Bondarev and said, 'Make sure he finishes disabling the self-destruct mechanism.' He pointed at the other guards. 'You two, come with me.'

Chen finally showed some emotion and sneered at Carlton. Carlton didn't care. Once this was done and Colossus was safe, Chen would get over it.

Carlton led the guards across the hold carrying Bondarev's assault rifle. Although he didn't collect guns, he had always been fascinated by them and was an avid pheasant hunter. He was eager to try his hand at a human target.

Using the vats as cover, they dashed from one to the next until they had a better angle on the intruder shooting at the server bays.

'Kill him,' Carlton said, and they opened fire.

The intruder stopped shooting and took cover behind a water pipe.

'Evacuate to lifeboats immediately,' the infuriating computer voice placidly advised. 'Ninety seconds to detonation.'

To get a clear shot, Carlton climbed onto the service walkway connecting the tops of the vats to each other and took up a position behind the nutrient feed pipe.

His assault rifle was equipped with a red dot sight. He put his eye to the scope and waited for the target to reemerge.

'When he comes back out,' Carlton called down to the guards, 'he's mine.'

'We're about to come up on deck,' Eddie said, his voice coming through the op center's speakers.

'Hold where you are,' said Max, who was watching the *Oregon*'s lidar feed on the screen. 'There are hostiles on deck waiting for you.' He counted ten figures with weapons approaching the hatch where Eddie's caravan of prisoners was going to come out.

'We don't have much time before this ship starts going down.'

'Understood.' Max looked at Eric. 'Use the deck machine guns. Target anything that moves on the *Colossus 1*.'

'Aye, sir,' Eric replied, and pushed the button for the automated .30 caliber machine guns to rise from their hiding places in the rusty barrels on deck.

Eric identified the targets and fired.

The guards on board the *Colossus 1* never saw the weapons that mowed them down in the raging storm. They toppled like bowling pins.

When they were all down, Max radioed Eddie. 'You're clear. Get out of there.'

'On our way.'

The hatch flew open, and people started pouring out. They held hands to keep the group together as they headed to the gangway and made it quickly over to the *Oregon*.

'That's all of us,' Eddie said.

'Eric, raise the gangway and move us away from *Colossus 1*.' Even with the *Oregon*'s armored hull, an explosion large enough to tear a hole in the *Colossus* ship could cause significant damage.

'Backing off,' Eric said.

They would know in less than thirty seconds whether Juan had succeeded.

Linc was the *Oregon*'s best sniper. Even though his sub-machine gun wasn't suited to that purpose, Juan knew that if he gave him the right moment Linc would make the shot.

Juan shouted to Linc, 'Now!'

Juan slid out from behind the pipe and emptied his magazine at the men who were stalking him below. But he never raised his head above the floor of the catwalk. His fusillade was merely a diversion.

Linc fired, but his target wasn't either of the men by the red box encasing the explosives. It was the display Chen had been using to reprogram the self-destruct mechanism.

The ghostly woman's voice started counting down. 'Ten . . . nine . . . eight . . . seven . . .'

Juan peeked over the edge and saw that Linc's aim had been true. The display was destroyed, as was any chance of Chen's completing his task.

'. . . six . . . five . . . four . . .'

Seeing that their attempt to stop the explosion had been ended, Chen and the man watching him raced for cover.

'. . . three . . . two . . . one –'

They didn't make it.

Enormous twin blasts reverberated through the hold, tearing huge gaps in the hull. Chen and the guard dis-appeared in the fireball, which was instantly doused by the water flooding into the ship.

Shrapnel flew through the hold, but Juan was protected by the water pipe. However, the catwalk was severed by a piece of flying metal. The section Juan was lying on tilted suddenly, and he slid down toward the churning mass of water below.

Max watched as geysers of water erupted next to the *Colossus 1*. It immediately began to settle in the water. With the sandstorm still raging, he could only assume the same had occurred with the other ships.

'Damage report?' he said to Eric.

'No hull breaches reported,' Eric replied. They were already three hundred yards away from the sinking ships and accelerating.

The captains of the Colossus ships began issuing SOS signals and declaring that they were abandoning ship.

'Eric, we certainly want to do our duty,' Max said. 'Let's throw out a couple of life rafts and then get out of here.'

'Aye, sir.'

While he took care of that, Max called Linda to find out what happened to Juan.

Juan dug his fingers into the grating at the bottom of the catwalk and caught himself before he tumbled into the roiling water.

The dangling end of the catwalk was near the vat-topped walkway. He couldn't climb back up, so Juan swung himself over and landed on the metal walkway.

He looked up and saw Linc and Murph still up on the catwalk.

'Are you all right?' Linc called down over the rushing water's roar.

'Bumps and bruises! You?'

'We're okay. We'll be down in a minute to get you.'

'No!' Juan yelled. 'Get off the ship now. That's an order!'

'Aye, Chairman. See you on the Gator.' He pushed Murph forward, and they ran toward the bow.

That way was blocked for Juan, the explosion taking out most of the vat he'd have to cross. The water level was already three-quarters of the way up the sides of the vats.

He raced for the stern. About halfway there, his path was blocked by a huge pipe knocked off its base by a flying girder.

Xavier Carlton was trapped underneath it, his legs pinned by the enormous metal cylinder. He was still conscious, his face contorted in agony. Juan tried lifting the pipe, but it was no use. It had to weigh more than half a ton.

When he saw Juan, he gritted his teeth and said, 'Do you realize what you've done?'

'I've kept you from unleashing a deadly force that you couldn't possibly hope to control.'

Carlton shook his head. 'You fool. You've killed us all. Colossus was the only thing that could stop Romir Mallik and the Vajra satellites.'

'We already know about the Vajra electromagnetic pulse weapon. Mallik is planning to use it for the Indian military. He already used it on Diego Garcia. His newest satellite is going up any day now.'

The water continued to rise. Juan had to leave soon if he was going to get out of the hold alive.

Carlton shook his head even more violently and grabbed Juan's arm.

'You don't understand anything! Vajra wasn't designed as a weapon. He's going to shut down everything.'

'What do you mean, everything?'

'Once he has all twenty satellites in orbit, Mallik will activate them all simultaneously. It will set up a resonant wave that will multiply the effect of the individual satellites and wipe out all computers across the world.'

'Are you sure?'

Carlton nodded, and grimaced as he spoke. 'I had a mole in his organization. He showed me the calculations.'

'How long will the effect last?'

'For as long as the satellites are in orbit and have power. Fifty years. Maybe a hundred. Nobody knows. But for all that time, no computer on the face of the planet will work again, not unless it's deep underground or under the water.'

The water had risen to the top of the vat. It began to cover Carlton's body.

Juan needed to hear more. He tried again to move the pipe, but it was futile.

'Get Mallik!' Carlton screeched in a terrified wail as he attempted to keep his head above the water. 'Don't let him stop the world! Don't let him –'

The water covered Carlton's face, and his arms thrashed for a few more moments before sinking out of sight.

Juan splashed through the water toward the emergency exit. By the time he climbed up to the door, the *Colossus 5* was already beginning to list as it sank toward the bottom of the Suez Canal. During his entire journey back to the Gator, Carlton's chilling last words echoed in his mind.

Don't let him stop the world.

60

The Arabian Sea

As soon as Mallik got word the next day that the Colossus ships had sunk in the Suez Canal, he invited Torkan to the dining room of his yacht, the *Paara*, for a celebratory lunch. With the frigates *Maurya* and *Kalinga* circling twenty miles out, he felt confident and secure in staying on his opulent custom-built yacht, which was tied up to the satellite launch command ship. Not that he was expecting any interference with his plans now. Not with Carlton dead and Colossus destroyed.

Rain pounded against the windows, otherwise Mallik would have taken the meal on the deck outside. The servants laid out a sumptuous feast for the two of them. Torkan, a devout Muslim, didn't drink, so no alcohol was served. Instead, they toasted with Darjeeling tea.

'To our allies against Carlton, whoever they may be,' Mallik said, lifting his cup.

Torkan followed suit and took a sip, but he didn't look happy. 'I would like to know how it happened.'

'Is that important now?'

'I suppose not. But, it still bothers me about running into the same men at your party and on the dock by the *Colossus 5*.'

'Stop worrying. You came out victorious, as you always

do. Your brother would be proud of you. Our vision is about to be realized once this irritating storm has passed.'

The monsoon had lingered over the launch site longer than they'd expected. They could move the launch platform and command ship, but that would take more time than simply waiting it out.

'Do you think Colossus really would have become a thinking artificial intelligence?' Torkan asked.

'I know it would have, otherwise I wouldn't have invested billions of rupees of my own money in Vajra.'

'It's hard to believe the Nine came so close to achieving it.'

'It was millennia in the making,' Mallik said. 'They really thought it was their destiny.'

Torkan swirled his teacup. 'And you think someone will try again.'

'I have no doubt about that as well. Artificial intelligence has already permeated our daily lives to a degree that we can't appreciate. It's everywhere, from credit card fraud detection and helpline language processing to facial recognition and self-guided cars. It's only becoming more insidious, and soon we will be in real danger of being replaced. A thinking AI would simply be the final step. Then that machine would someday understand that not only are we of no use to it but that we are a very real threat to it.'

'People are weak. They need everything done for them. I look forward to a time when we can think for ourselves again.'

Mallik smiled. He was glad to hear how much Torkan had come around to his way of thinking.

'When the people realize how I have freed them from the tyranny of computers, they will hail me as a liberator. Think about how many jobs in this world have been killed by computerization, robotics, and automation. People will have purpose again.'

'How long do you think we'll have to ride out the chaos on board the *Paara*?'

Mallik shrugged. 'It depends on how fast world governments compensate for the demise of the systems that have made them dependent on computers. Of course, I've prepared India for the coming change, and we are still a very agricultural society. Many of our vehicles will work just fine because they have no computer chips in them, and our farms will still produce all the food we need.'

'There will be turmoil, though,' Torkan said. 'It will be ugly for a while.'

'Especially in technologically advanced societies. China, Europe, and the United States will suffer the most. Planes will fall from the sky, nuclear plants will melt down, the millions of people in megacities will begin to starve. But the governments will go on. We had civilization for thousands of years before computers and we will continue to have it for many more centuries now that I'm about to wipe out the specter of extinction by AI.'

'How long do you think it will take?'

Mallik thought for a moment, then said, 'Five years. Ten years at most. After that, I don't think the world will look much different than it did in the 1950s. Without computers, we developed cars, jet planes, hydroelectric dams, nuclear power, and buildings that have stood for thousands of years. The only things we'll lose in the process are the ills that computers and the internet have visited on us: loss of privacy, universal surveillance, vast government databases of our most intimate information, and people burying themselves in the screens they're holding instead of talking face-to-face like we are now.'

Torkan gave him a rare smile. 'You're practicing your political speech, aren't you?'

Mallik laughed. 'You know me well. India is going to emerge as the world's greatest superpower when the dust settles. Who better to lead it?'

'Don't forget Iran. With our numbers, and Israel's technological advantage wiped out, we should become the dominant force in the Middle East.'

Mallik raised his cup again. 'To a new world.'

'A new world.' After another drink, Torkan frowned. 'Is there any way the Vajra satellites can be taken down once they are operating together?'

Mallik shook his head. 'For the precision needed to knock down a satellite, you would need a computer guidance system, which obviously won't work once Vajra is operational globally. I've also prevented any chance that my files will provide a clue for how to neutralize the satellites even by a government with a computer hidden in a bunker far underground and linked to a satellite dish. The hack into my laptop was a wake-up call for me. This morning, I went into my corporate computers and deleted all files related to the development of Vajra and verified that all critical paper records were destroyed.'

Torkan raised an eyebrow at that. 'What if this satellite launch fails?'

'It won't. But if it does, I downloaded the only copies

left onto my computer on board the yacht. When we have verification that Vajra is operational, I'll toss it in the ocean.'

'Cautious, but smart.'

'I've been planning this for years. I've thought of everything.'

'I hope you've thought about what would happen if you got blamed for the catastrophe that's coming.'

'I think for the first couple of years, people will be more focused on survival than finding someone to blame.'

'And how many do you think will die in that time?'

Mallik leaned back in his chair and stared at the ceiling before saying matter-of-factly, 'Based on loss of transportation infrastructure, farm failures from disabled machinery, and resulting starvation rates, I wouldn't be surprised if we lose more than two billion people.'

61

The Red Sea

Extricating the *Oregon* from the Suez Canal mess took until the morning, when the sandstorm died down. The Egyptian authorities were eager to clear the canal so they could begin salvage operations and get it back to its normal operational capabilities as soon as possible. Having four ships sink in the middle of one of the most important waterways in the world wasn't good publicity.

Juan put the rescued prisoners ashore at the Port of Suez on their way out of the canal under the guise of Good Samaritans who were simply in the right place at the right time. The explanation worked as well as it had at Jhootha Island, and Interpol assisted in making them safe and secure until consular officers from the prisoners' home countries could arrive. Since it was reported that all four of the ships sank because of internal malfunctions, the Egyptians let the *Oregon* go, as they did the other ships that had been in Great Bitter Lake at the time.

The Arabian Sea was the *Oregon*'s next destination. The two-day trip would have them arriving at the location of Mallik's satellite launch platform floating west of India. In the meantime, they'd be able to plan what they were going to do to stop Vajra from being activated.

Juan had just spent the last thirty minutes in his cabin

briefing Langston Overholt on the situation. The CIA officer scowled from the computer screen on his desk.

'Are Stone and Murphy sure that Carlton's allegations are correct?' Overholt asked.

'They've scoured the limited data that Murph was able to download from Mallik's files. Based on the formulas they found, they're fairly certain that the Vajra satellites can disable all the computers on the planet.'

'Fairly certain? That leaves a lot of wiggle room.'

Juan shrugged. 'It's all theoretical until Vajra goes into operation. But the math checks out. And we have the evidence from Diego Garcia that the EMP effect can be triggered by the satellites.'

'If it does work, we won't get a second chance to shut it down.'

'Not according to Carlton. And he did seem certain that it was going to happen.'

Overholt stared up at the ceiling in thought before saying, 'Then, we have to keep Mallik from launching the satellite. And, going through the Indian military is probably not a good idea.'

'Linc and Eddie said Mallik seemed pretty tight with some of the Indian brass at his party. Even if they're not in on it, it's likely he has enough influence to convince them that the idea of a worldwide threat is a hoax. It would take weeks for them to investigate it.'

'We don't have that much time. My sources say he's planning to launch as soon as the monsoon has passed.'

'Which is in two days,' Juan said. 'We've checked the forecast. What about sending our own Navy to take down the rocket?'

Overholt scoffed. 'And create an international incident with a friendly nation by shooting down one of their communications satellites? We might as well just declare war on them now.'

Juan smiled. 'I thought you'd say that.'

'Where are you now?'

'Fifty miles south of Suez, on our way to the Arabian Sea.'

That got a chuckle. 'I suppose you know what I'm going to say now, too.'

'I have an inkling,' Juan said.

Overholt cleared his throat and leaned in to the camera. 'Vajra is a clear and present danger to the entire world. Your assignment is to stop that launch. By any means necessary.'

62

The Arabian Sea

The monsoon had finally passed, and Mallik sat in his chair overlooking the mission control room aboard the launch command ship. The huge picture window in the side of the 400-foot-long ship's large central superstructure gave a magnificent view of the launch platform three miles to the north. The backdrop of the red and orange sky produced by the rising sun could have served as a publicity photo for his satellite business.

The thirty engineers in the spacious room were busily going about their tasks to make sure that today went smoothly. Only a handful knew about Vajra, and only one of them was aware of its full potential. Mallik would have the honor of activating the system.

A speedboat cut through the glassy sea on its way back from the platform.

'Did they report any issues?' Mallik asked flight director Kapoor, pointing at the boat. The men returning were maintenance workers doing a final check of the launch site.

'None,' Kapoor said. 'We are still go for launch. T minus forty-three minutes and counting.' The last step was fueling the rocket, which would be completed fifteen minutes before it took off.

'Alert the Indian Coast Guard that we are moving ahead with the launch.' Even though they were a hundred and fifty miles from the nearest land, the rocket's flight path would take it over the Indian subcontinent.

'Yes, sir.' Kapoor picked up the phone. At the same time, Torkan burst into the room and made a beeline for Mallik with a concerned look on his face.

'What's wrong?' Mallik asked.

Torkan lowered his voice and said, 'A ship has intruded on our security zone. They're ignoring the *Maurya*'s hails to steer clear.'

'How far away are they?'

'Twenty-five miles and closing fast.'

'The Indian Navy?'

Torkan shook his head. 'They're coming from the west. The *Maurya* reports that it looks like a cargo ship, but it's going at an unbelievable speed for a ship that big.'

Kapoor overheard the conversation. 'Sir, if we have a ship in the security zone, perhaps we should delay the launch until it's out of danger.'

'No,' Mallik said, 'we are going to launch that rocket.'

'But protocol states –'

'We are launching!' Mallik's shout silenced the room.

He nodded at Torkan, who went to the door and called two of his security men to come into mission control with their assault rifles at the ready.

Mallik stared daggers at Kapoor. 'We are launching no matter what. Do you understand?'

Kapoor looked at the two heavily armed men and gulped. The other engineers studiously went back to work, avoiding Mallik's glare.

'T minus forty-two minutes and counting,' Kapoor said.

Mallik smiled, then turned to Torkan.

'Tell the captain of the *Maurya* to intercept that ship. If she continues to be unresponsive, sink her.'

Juan watched the frigate speeding toward them on the op center's main screen. It was now ten miles away, still out of gun range for both ships. The *Oregon* was quickly closing the distance. Mallik's launch platform was over the horizon, but they hadn't seen the telltale smoke trail of a launch in the cloudless azure sky.

'We're being hailed by the *Maurya* again,' Hali said.

'Continue ignoring them,' Juan said. 'We know what they're going to say.'

'I also intercepted a call to the Indian Coast Guard. The launch is in less than forty-two minutes.'

Juan grinned at Eric, sitting at the helm. 'Your timing is impeccable, Stoney. Murph, prepare to fire the Exocet.' The anti-ship missile would reduce the launch platform, rocket, and satellite payload to burning hulks.

'Locked onto the launch platform,' Murph said from the weapons station.

'Fire.'

The Exocet blasted out of its tube. The subsonic surface-skimming missile would be difficult to shoot down even for a warship more modern than the *Maurya*. The ancient frigate didn't have a chance of intercepting the missile as it passed by.

Murph said, 'Two minutes to target.'

63

'We are tracking a missile launch!' one of the flight engineers yelled.

Mallik leaped to his feet. 'ETA?'

'Less than two minutes. Coming from the west.'

It had to be an attack by the approaching ship. Mallik whirled on the flight director. 'Do we have a Vajra satellite over that area?'

Kapoor gave him an astonished look. 'Yes, but —'

'Turn it on and target that region.'

'That might —'

Mallik snapped his fingers, and the guards raised their weapons. 'Do it!' He knew the risks of activating it so close to the launch site.

Kapoor nodded and typed on his keyboard.

'Ninety seconds to impact,' the engineer said.

'Vajra activating,' Kapoor said.

Mallik waited for the mission control electronics to go down, but all the computers continued to operate.

The man observing the radar return said, 'The missile splashed down.'

Mallik breathed a sigh of relief.

'How long will the satellite be in range?' he asked.

'An hour,' Kapoor said. 'Long enough to launch Satellite 20.'

'Good. Now, radio the *Maurya* and tell the captain to destroy that cargo ship.'

The ever-present hum of the *Oregon*'s engines went silent.

'Did the missile make it?' Juan asked Murph.

'I don't think so. Just before everything went black, I saw its trajectory wobbling. Vajra must have disabled its guidance chip.'

Juan had taken a chance that there wasn't a Vajra satellite overhead or that Mallik wouldn't have the time or guts to use it so close to his own command ship. The bet hadn't paid off.

He turned to Max and said, 'So Plan A didn't work. Time for Plan B. Are your mods complete?'

Max answered by raising crossed fingers on both hands.

'Then you all know what to do.' Juan took the radio and binoculars sitting on the arm of his command chair and sprinted out of the room along with Murph and Eric. Linda took the conn while Max stayed at his engineering station.

The minimal lighting and quiet halls were eerie as they made their way up to the deck. Once they got into the shoddy fake interior of the ship, the three of them separated. Juan's destination was the bridge.

Knowing that the *Oregon*'s computers might be rendered inoperable by Vajra, Max had spent every waking moment since they left the Suez finishing the modifications he'd begun when they first saw the weapon's power. Every single system on the *Oregon* was computer-operated, so bypassing them had been a herculean task.

Juan would call his orders over their simplified radios while Max and Linda would operate steering and propulsion from the op center. They still had electric power throughout the ship from their batteries, so Max could adjust thruster speed while Linda steered them by hand. Max claimed that he could get a burst from the magneto-hydrodynamic main engines for a very short time in an emergency, but they would melt down from a lack of coolant if they ran for longer than a few seconds.

Their weapons were another story. Control of the guns, torpedoes, and missiles were all normally done by computer. No amount of modification could affect the guidance chips on any of the missiles, so the Exocets and anti-aircraft missiles were now useless.

The Gatling guns, however, just needed electricity for rotation, elevation, ammunition feed, and firing. They'd only had time to modify one of the three Gatling guns, so Juan had made sure to maneuver the *Oregon* so that the modified gun was facing the approaching *Maurya*. Murph would use a simple joystick from his position on deck to control the Gatling and would eyeball the tracer fire to aim it. The 120mm cannon had been similarly modified.

At the same time, Eric would be operating the torpedoes. Since they ran close to the surface, it was possible that they would also be affected by Vajra and wouldn't be able to utilize their homing sonars. Their chemically fueled propulsion wouldn't be affected, however, and Eric would be able to guide them by the wires they trailed behind them. Each of them had been fitted with flags that would jut above the surface of the water so Eric could see them after launch.

When he got to the bridge, Juan said into the radio, 'Everyone in position?'

They all acknowledged they were ready.

Juan raised the binoculars and saw the frigate plowing toward them at top speed five miles out. They were still out of gun range.

Two puffs of steam jetted from tubes on the *Maurya*'s deck followed by twin splashes next to the ship.

Juan spoke into the radio again. 'Prepare for evasive maneuvers. We have torpedoes in the water.'

64

To the *Maurya*, the *Oregon* had to seem dead in the water once her electronics were shut down. That's exactly what Juan wanted their captain to think so he could draw the frigate closer.

The two torpedoes were running straight at the *Oregon*'s starboard side. Juan was counting on them being unguided.

'Max, get ready to give me a burst of speed.'

'It won't last long.'

'That's all we'll need. Murph and Eric, are you set?'

'My fingers are twitching,' Murph said.

'I've got my telescope tripod set up,' Eric replied.

The torpedoes were now two thousand yards out and closing at fifty knots. Juan could see their wakes in the calm sea.

'Murph,' he said. 'Fire.'

The Gatling gun spun up and unleashed its 20mm tungsten shells with a roar like it was Paul Bunyan's chain saw. The tracer rounds splashed in a zigzag pattern by the first torpedo as Murph homed in on his target. The simple electrical stick was crude, without the precision of the computerized controls that he was used to, and aiming was tough, even for someone as skilled at video games as Murph was.

Finally, he hit it. The torpedo's warhead blew out a geyser of water.

Murph switched his aim to the other torpedo, but after a few seconds of the tracers plowing into its wake he called over the radio. On its current course, it would slam into the bow of the *Oregon*.

'Sorry, Chairman. I can't get the Gatling gun to aim any lower.'

'Understood,' Juan replied. 'Max, give me full power in reverse . . . now!'

The *Oregon* shot backward as the main engines jetted water out the front of the venturi tubes. The torpedo passed just in front of the bow and continued into the open ocean.

'Eric, launch your torpedo.'

'Aye, Chairman. Launching.'

A torpedo was thrust out of its tube by a blast of air and steam. It trailed a fine wire linked to Eric's joystick. As soon as it plunged into the water, an orange flag rose and cut through the water.

'Ninety seconds to impact,' Eric said calmly.

The *Maurya* must have seen the torpedo launch because she fired three more of her own and began evasive maneuvers.

'Three fish in the water,' Juan radioed.

'Main engines are down,' Max replied. 'Thrusters only. We can't evade another one.'

'If Murph can't get them, prepare to turn our stern toward the torpedoes to reduce our profile.'

'Got it.'

The torpedoes passed each other halfway between the ships. Murph had gotten the hang of his control. He blew up the first torpedo before it reached the two-thousand-yard mark.

He got the second one right before the Gatling gun reached the limit of its travel.

Juan called Max. 'Rotate hard aport!'

While the *Oregon* turned, Juan watched the *Maurya* through his binoculars. He could just make out the orange flag fluttering above the torpedo. The captain was doing a fine job of piloting his ship, its diesel engines pushing it hard, but there was no outrunning or evading the torpedo. Eric was too good.

The torpedo drove into the side of the frigate, detonating right at the midline. A huge fountain of water temporarily shrouded most of the *Maurya*. Then, it broke in half and began to sink.

Juan turned his attention back to the speeding torpedo coming toward them. It must have been a slower model than the ones on the *Oregon*, but it wasn't slow enough.

'Brace! Brace! Brace!' Juan shouted into the radio.

The *Oregon* had almost completed its turn when the torpedo exploded near the stern, lifting the back half of the ship a few feet out of the water before rocking back and forth as it settled back. Juan had to grab hold of the wheel to keep from falling.

The *Oregon*'s armor was thick, but a torpedo that size had to have caused serious damage.

'Casualty report,' Juan called as he watched the two halves of the *Maurya* disappear beneath the surface.

'Engine room reports five injured,' Max said. 'Doc is on the way with her team.'

'Damage assessment?'

'Flooding in multiple sections, but bulkheads holding. They said it'll take a while to get the main engines back online even if Vajra is switched off. Some electrical lines on the starboard side of the ship may be affected.'

'Confirmed,' Murph said. 'I've lost power to the Gatling gun controls.'

'Same here,' Eric said. 'We can't even launch a torpedo now, let alone guide it.'

Hali chimed in. 'Apparently, they've already switched over to old-fashioned radio communication. I've been monitoring the signals from the command ship. We're going to have more company in about thirty minutes. They have another frigate called the *Kalinga*, and it's on the way to destroy us.'

'Then we have to turn off that Vajra satellite before she gets here,' Juan said. 'Tell everybody to meet at the moon pool on the double. It's time for Plan C.'

65

Thanks to Vajra, the unknown cargo ship armed with the missiles was still motionless. Twenty minutes before, the radar signature of a small boat had been reported heading from that direction toward the launch command ship, but five minutes ago, it disappeared. Mallik assumed it was a lifeboat from either the *Maurya* or the cargo ship, and it had sunk because of damage from the explosions they'd observed. Once the *Kalinga* had finished off the large ship, it could take its time searching the surrounding waters for any survivors to eliminate.

The countdown was now T minus four minutes. There were still no impediments to a successful launch, although Mallik couldn't relax, not so close to finishing something that had taken so long to complete. He was already envisioning what would come next. The new world.

An alarm interrupted his reverie. Torkan rushed in carrying an assault rifle and said, 'Stay here.'

'What is it?' Mallik asked.

'We've spotted smoke on the aft deck by the helicopter.'

'Fire?'

Torkan shook his head. 'The smoke is red, like from a grenade. Or five. It's covered the entire stern.' With the breeze from the monsoon gone, it would linger for a while.

'We have intruders,' Mallik said. 'Go get them off my ship.'

Torkan nodded and ran out to join the rest of his security team, leaving just the two guards behind with Mallik.

'Should we hold the launch?' Kapoor asked halfheartedly.

Mallik sneered at him. 'What do you think?'

Kapoor turned away and announced, 'T minus three minutes and counting.'

Fearing that he would have a mutiny if there was a firefight on board, Mallik stood and went over to the control panel.

'We are committed now. Nothing is stopping the launch. I'm going to make sure of that.'

He tapped on the screen and brought up the command to lock out all changes to the launch sequence. The screen asked for his authorization, and he looked into the camera. The retinal scanner confirmed his identity. The screen read *Abort command locked out*.

Now nothing could stop the launch.

Using his crossbow, MacD stood atop the Gator and shot a bolt with a hook on it at the railing directly under the forward superstructure of the command ship. Juan, Raven, Linc, Eddie, and Murph stood next to him in full combat gear. When the nylon rope ladder was secured in place, Juan used his comm unit to talk quietly to Gomez, who was inside the Gator. He had already landed a dozen small drones on the stern of the ship to make it look like they were sneaking on board from that direction.

Half of the drones were carrying smoke grenades. The other half held gunshot simulators.

'Set them off, Gomez,' Juan said.

'Roger that,' he answered.

Instantly, the air was pierced by a series of loud cracks that sounded identical to multiple AK-47s firing simultaneously from different angles. As long as the smoke remained, it would be impossible to know if there was any enemy force on the stern.

Juan quickly scaled the ladder, making sure that they were alone when he got up to the deck. Since he was right below the bridge wing, no one up there would see armed operatives climbing up from the Gator unless they leaned over the railing and looked straight down.

Once the other five had joined Juan on deck of the command ship, Linda, who was driving the Gator, resubmerged with Gomez and stayed on station for the post-mission pickup.

The sub/boat hybrid had been easier to modify than the *Oregon*. They'd used the high-speed surface mode for most of the journey from the *Oregon* and then dived the boat when they got close enough to be seen.

Thanks to the files stolen from Mallik, Juan and his team had a detailed layout of the ship. Although the mission control room was buried deep in the superstructure, there was a direct path to get there. It could be easily defended, assuming they could take it in the first place.

Juan led the way. It looked like their ruse had worked because they didn't encounter any armed security before they reached mission control. On the count of three, Juan and his team rushed in, shouting for everyone to get down. Juan was ready to take down at least a couple of security forces, but there weren't any, and everyone followed his command and hit the deck.

There was someone else missing, too.

'Who's in charge here?' Juan demanded.

A man with graying hair and a headset raised his hand.

'Get up,' Juan said. 'Who are you?'

'Kapoor, the flight director.'

'Where's Mallik?'

'When he heard the gunshots, he took his security men and went back to his yacht.'

Juan looked up and saw the timer counting down from twenty-three seconds. They'd made it in time.

'Abort the launch,' he said to Kapoor.

'I can't.'

Juan raised his weapon. 'Do it! Now!'

'I can't! Mallik has locked the system. We can't make any changes to the launch.'

'Murph?'

Murph took a seat at the nearest workstation. He typed on the screen and shook his head.

'He's right. It requires Mallik's retinal scan to unlock. Five seconds.'

The clock ticked down . . . three . . . two . . . one . . .

Smoke billowed at the launchpad. Then a spear of flame knifed down as the rocket lifted off.

By the time they heard the thunderclap of its powerful engines igniting, it was already five hundred feet in the air and accelerating.

66

Juan advanced on Kapoor. 'How long until the satellite is in position for the Vajra system to go active?'

He pointed to a large screen above the picture window showing the status of all nineteen satellites already in orbit. They were displayed in green, while the one currently on its way into space was depicted in gray.

Kapoor shrank back and said, 'You know about that?'

'How long?'

'Eight minutes from launch.'

'If we can't abort the launch, can we stop Vajra from activating?'

Kapoor nodded and pointed at the screen nearest to him. Juan waved Murph over to take a seat in front of it. He didn't trust Kapoor at the controls.

Murph started shutting it down.

'But there's a problem,' Kapoor said.

'What?' Juan said.

'Mallik has an identical setup on his yacht. He can control it via the satellite dish on board.'

Murph slapped his hand on the screen. 'He's right. Every time I try to shut it down, someone keeps reactivating it.'

'He must be furious by now for not taking the time to make the lockout include the Vajra satellites,' Kapoor said. 'He can't keep you from accessing the system, but you can't stop him, either.'

'What happens when the new satellite gets into orbit?' Juan demanded.

'Then the system will go live automatically a minute later,' Kapoor said, cowering. 'Every computer on earth will be rendered useless. After that, we won't be able to shut any of them down ever again.'

Many of the engineers in the room stared at Kapoor, agape at the revelation.

'If you want any leniency for your part in all this,' Juan said to Kapoor, 'you better help us stop Vajra. Raven, stay here to protect Murph while he keeps trying to get control of the satellites.'

She nodded. Murph didn't even look up.

Juan sprinted out of the room with Eddie, Linc, and MacD toward where the yacht was tied up to the command ship.

As he ran, he radioed to Gomez, 'Make sure nobody gets an airborne advantage in that helicopter.'

The smoke was starting to clear, and it was obvious by now that the fake assault had been a diversion. And Torkan saw how it had been done. Small drones littered the deck, all of them destroyed by the explosives they had carried.

He saw another one appear, just visible behind the helicopter. Torkan took aim, thinking it was coming toward him for an attack, but it settled onto one of the Huey's twin rotor blades.

As soon as it touched down, a small grenade went off,

disintegrating the drone and snapping the blade in two. It clattered to the deck.

'There's no one here, and the Huey is no longer functional,' Torkan said over his radio to Mallik. 'Are you back on the yacht?'

'Yes. I'm interfacing with the Vajra system.'

Torkan could see the 300-foot *Paara* moving away from the command ship.

'I saw the launch,' he said. 'It looks like we're in the clear.'

'Not yet,' said Mallik. 'Someone in the mission control room is trying to deactivate Vajra.'

'Kapoor?'

'I can't tell. You need to go back in there and shut them down.'

'Understood.'

Torkan waved for his eight men to abandon the search for intruders and come with him to the mission control room.

They were halfway to the superstructure access door when it flew open and four men came out. Torkan immediately recognized the black man and the Asian man from his previous encounters with them.

Two of his security team were taken down in the first volley. Torkan ducked behind a stanchion and radioed Mallik as a vicious firefight raged.

'Getting to mission control is going to be a problem.'

'I don't care if you have to sink the whole ship!' Mallik screamed. 'Just shut them down!'

Torkan looked at the damaged helicopter. They had been planning to take it up to intercept the incoming boat before it disappeared from radar.

'Is the observation window in the mission control room bulletproof?' he asked Mallik.

'It's reinforced safety glass, but it's not bulletproof.'

'Then I'll destroy it from the outside.'

'How?'

'I put an RPG launcher on the helicopter when we thought we were going to take out that incoming boat.'

'But you said the helicopter is nonfunctional.'

'Trust me, Romir,' Torkan said.

'I do, Asad.'

Torkan instructed the rest of his security team to give him suppressing fire while he ran toward the disabled Huey. He snatched the RPG launcher and a spare rocket from the open passenger compartment.

Then he called for one of his men to join him. They sprinted to the stairway leading down to the command ship's floating dock and the speedboat that had returned from the satellite launch platform.

From his position crouched behind a deck crane support, Juan saw Torkan and another man run down the stairs.

'He got an RPG from the Huey,' Juan said to Eddie between shots.

'Gomez told us there was a speedboat tied up down there. What's he doing?'

Juan thought about the big picture window in the mission control room.

'He's going to attack from the outside . . . Linda, where are you?'

'Idling on the starboard side of the ship by the superstructure. I just saw two men jump into a speedboat.'

She was only a hundred feet away from Juan's position. 'Prepare to pick me up.'

He said, 'Eddie, cover me.'

Juan dropped his weapon and his gear and dashed toward the edge of the ship. Bullets ricocheted around him as he ran, pinging against the deck plating and bulkheads. Without breaking his stride, he dived over the railing and into the sea below.

67

'Eric, two fish in the water!' Max radioed from the fake bridge of the *Oregon*. 'Give me thrusters in reverse.'

'Thrusters full reverse,' Eric replied.

The *Oregon* crawled backward. Max willed her to move faster, but there was nothing else he could do.

The torpedoes sped by, missing the bow by just a few yards.

The captain of the *Kalinga* was a good shot. Next time, he might not miss. The *Oregon* was already sitting low in the water from the flooding caused by the last torpedo. Another one could sink her, especially because she wouldn't be able to correct any list by filling ballast tanks.

'Hali,' Max called, 'tell Murph that we need that satellite disabled or we're dead.'

Murph was getting ticked-off. Every time he shut down the satellite targeting the *Oregon*, Mallik switched it back on.

'I just got a call from the *Oregon*,' Raven said. 'The *Kalinga* is getting ready to sink her. Isn't there anything you can do to disable that satellite?'

She indicated the screen listing all the Vajra satellites. Their current problem was caused by number seven.

'Not unless we can figure out how to stop Mallik,' Murph said in frustration. 'The Chairman said the yacht moved away from the command ship, so we can't get on board to stop him.'

If the *Oregon* had its weapons, they could just send another Exocet to take it out, but that wasn't happening. And nothing they'd brought with them was powerful enough to destroy a 300-foot yacht. It would require a massive rocket . . .

He looked up at the screen. There was one rocket he could use.

Murph turned to Kapoor and said, 'Mallik locked out the launch sequence. What about the descent of the first stage?' He knew the booster was reusable. After detaching from the orbital insertion package, it was supposed to return and land on the launch platform using its retro-rockets.

Which meant it still had fuel aboard.

Kapoor hesitated until Raven shoved her assault rifle in his face.

'Okay, okay! It's not locked out.'

'Show me how to change the landing coordinates,' Murph said, before nodding to Raven for emphasis. 'Or she will find someone here who doesn't want to die.'

Juan climbed aboard the surfaced Gator and opened the hatch as the speedboat jetted off and rounded the stern of the command ship.

'Gomez, hand me one of the AT4s. Linda, go after that speedboat.'

The Gator rose completely out of the water, and Linda gunned the powerful diesel.

Gomez reached up through the hatch with one of the

recoilless weapons they'd brought along for air defense. It was a single-use tube armed with an unguided anti-vehicle rocket.

They raced around the command ship and saw the speedboat come to a stop directly beneath the mission control room. Torkan was already putting the RPG launcher over his shoulder.

Juan raised the AT4. He didn't have time to aim carefully. He squeezed the trigger, and the rocket shot toward the boat.

For a millisecond, he thought he might get lucky, but he hadn't compensated enough for the fast-moving Gator. The rocket detonated in the water ten yards in front of the speedboat.

That was just enough to throw Torkan off, though. The explosion rocked the boat. He fell backward just as he pressed his own trigger. The RPG shot up and over the command ship.

Juan called down to Gomez. 'Get me another one!'

Torkan took his driver's assault rifle and let loose a spray of bullets at the Gator. Linda turned a hard right, nearly throwing Juan off the boat. She veered away, and Torkan began to reload the launcher.

Juan took the radio clipped to his belt and called on the same frequency Torkan had been using.

'Asad, it's me. The guy who killed your brother.'

Torkan lowered the RPG and stared at him.

'The Novichok really did a number on Rasul,' Juan continued. 'It looked very painful as he choked to death right in front of me.'

Torkan's face twisted in anger.

68

As Linda lured the speedboat away from the mission control room and around the stern of the command ship, Gomez passed an AT4 rocket and a P90 submachine gun up to Juan. He'd have to make the rocket count. It was their last one.

Torkan came into view when they were halfway down the other side of the large command ship. Linda drove the Gator in a zigzag pattern at Juan's instruction to bring the speedboat as close as possible for his shot. Juan had the AT4 slung over his shoulder while he shot bursts from the P90, bracing himself using the hatch cover.

If he could hit the Iranian saboteur with that weapon, he would, but its effective range was far shorter than the assault rifle Torkan was using. Bullets peppered the Gator as they weaved back and forth.

When the speedboat got within fifty yards, Juan dropped the P90, which slid off the deck and into the water. He put the AT4 up to his shoulder and was about to pull the trigger when a rifle shot hit his artificial leg, knocking it out from under him. Juan fell to the deck and was barely able to keep both himself and the AT4 on the boat.

At the same time, the Gator's diesel started smoking, and the boat shuddered as it slowed down. The rifle fire hit the engine as well.

Torkan smiled at his shot and told the driver of the speedboat to turn around.

By the time Juan got to his feet again, Torkan was nearing the stern of the command ship. A rocket launch by Juan now would require too much luck to hit the speedboat.

As Juan jumped down through the Gator's hatch with the rocket launcher and closed the lid, the radio on his belt crackled.

'I only have one RPG left,' Torkan said, 'and I don't want to waste it on you. But, don't worry. After I kill your friends, I'll come back.'

Juan ignored the taunt. 'Do we still have battery power?' he asked Linda.

'Yes,' she replied, 'but we won't be able to pursue them with our diesel out.'

'We don't have to pursue him,' Juan said. 'Dive the boat.'

For his second try at destroying the mission control room, Torkan made sure to take his time and guarantee the shot would count. After they got the speedboat in position, he reloaded the RPG.

He was about to center his sight on the big picture window when he heard a gurgling noise. He turned and saw the boat he thought he'd just disabled erupt out of the water twenty yards behind them.

The hatch flew aside. Torkan was stunned to see the man who killed Rasul pop out and aim the rocket launcher at the speedboat.

Torkan tried to swing the RPG around, but he was too slow.

The AT4 rocket leaped from its tube. The last thing

Torkan's brain registered was the impact of the warhead turning his boat into a fireball.

From the stateroom on his yacht, Mallik heard an explosion and hoped it was Torkan taking out the mission control room.

He reset the controls on Vajra, but they were altered yet again by his unseen nemesis.

'Torkan,' he called on the radio, 'what's your status?'

An unfamiliar voice called back. 'His status currently is that he's dead.'

'Who is this?' Mallik demanded.

'This is the archenemy of the Torkan family.'

A sonic boom shook the yacht. It was the sound of the booster stage returning to earth. Mallik looked out the window but couldn't see any sign of it.

'You killed both my brothers-in-law?'

'To be fair, they did try to kill me first.' By the sound of amusement in his voice, the man was clearly enjoying himself.

Mallik smiled when he saw that the twentieth satellite had reached orbit. Its indicator went green. Vajra would wipe out electronics worldwide in sixty seconds.

'It doesn't matter,' he said into the radio, mirroring his antagonist's glee. 'You're too late to stop me.'

'Are you sure about that?'

Mallik heard the roar of a rocket engine. It had to be the booster firing its retrorockets, but it was too loud. Then the view of the launch platform began to shimmer as if it were a mirage, and he felt heat bake the air.

With a horrible realization, Mallik finally understood what was happening.

'Do you realize what you've done?' Mallik screamed into his radio. 'You people have doomed the human race!'

'I hope not,' the voice said, 'but you won't be around to find out.'

In mission control, Murph watched the screen showing the feed from the camera on the booster stage that was pointed down at the engine. He could see crew members on the yacht looking up in terror as they scrambled to jump overboard.

When he had it centered over the portion of the yacht where Kapoor said Mallik's stateroom was, he switched off the retrorockets, and the booster plunged to the deck.

The camera went black, and a second later they heard an ear-rattling boom from the explosion of the booster.

Suddenly, Murph had complete control of Vajra. There were thirty seconds left before it went active.

'The system will activate automatically,' Kapoor said. 'There's no way to turn off the satellites now.'

'I'm not trying to turn them off,' Murph said as he tapped on the touchscreen.

'What *are* you trying to do?' Raven asked.

'I'm turning them around.'

Kapoor gaped at the screen as he saw first one satellite, then another, and another, rotate one hundred and eighty degrees.

At the count of zero, all of the satellites initiated their EMP beams. But now they were harmlessly aimed out into space.

Murph let out a sigh of relief.

'That was close,' Raven said.

'I have one more thing to do,' he said. 'While I'm busy, maybe you should call the *Oregon*.'

Max was still on the fake bridge, watching the onrushing *Kalinga* with dread. The frigate had just launched two more torpedoes. This time, they wouldn't miss.

His radio squawked. 'Max, this is Hali. Raven just called. Murph took down the Vajra satellites. We should be getting our systems back any second.'

As Hali finished speaking, Max felt a hum beneath his feet as generators and equipment on the *Oregon* came back to life.

'Eric, what do you have working?' Max asked.

'I'll be able to tell you in twenty seconds,' Eric said. 'We need to finish rebooting.'

They wouldn't have main engines back right away even after the computers came back online, but they did have thrusters. 'Turn us one hundred and eighty degrees. I want our port side facing those incoming torpedoes.'

'Aye, sir.'

The *Oregon* pivoted around, and Max went to the other side of the bridge, kicking a couple of Murph's stray Red Bull cans as he walked.

By the time the turn was complete, Eric called him over the loudspeakers instead of the radio and said, 'We've got everything back except the modified weapons.' It meant that Eric could hear him on the bridge microphone.

'Launch an Exocet at the *Kalinga*,' Max said.

'Launching.'

The anti-ship missile shot into the sky and passed over the torpedoes bearing down on them.

'Now get a firing solution on those fish with the port-side Gatling gun and destroy them.'

'Firing,' Eric said.

The Gatling gun buzzed to life. With the computer control now aiming the weapon, it required just two seconds for Eric to take out both torpedoes.

With the threat to the *Oregon* gone, Max turned his attention back to the *Kalinga*. The Exocet streaked toward it and smashed into the side of the ship. The explosion ravaged the hull directly below the torpedo tubes. The blast set off the remaining torpedoes, and the *Kalinga* blew apart like a volcano. Black smoke from the shattered frigate rose in a mushroom cloud.

Max leaned his head against the railing as he caught his breath.

Then he stood up and said, 'Hali?'

'Go ahead.'

'Tell Murph I owe him a case of Red Bull.'

Five minutes later, Juan joined Murph and Raven in the command ship mission control room. Kapoor had been taken away, and the other engineers sent to their quarters. He sat down to inspect his combat leg. The prosthesis had a large gouge in it from the bullet strike.

'I heard you saved the *Oregon*,' Juan said to Murph.

'And I heard you saved us.'

'That's what teamwork is all about.'

'Thanks for bringing me onto the team,' Raven said. 'I've never worked with a more impressive group. Speaking of that, where are Linc, Eddie, and MacD?'

'After the explosion on the yacht, Mallik's surviving

security operatives on the command ship gave up. Eddie's watching them and Kapoor while Linc and MacD help the crew of the command ship pick up the yacht crew who jumped overboard.'

'Why don't I go help them, sir . . . I mean, Chairman,' Raven said. She waited for Juan's nod and then left the control room.

'That was good aim on the yacht,' Juan said to Murph. 'Initial reports are that the whole crew made it off.'

'That's good to hear,' Murph said, his eyes glued to the screen above. All twenty satellites still registered green.

'You look like you're waiting for something.'

'I am.'

As he said it, the indicator for satellite fifteen turned red.

'What just happened?'

'The thought of all computers in the world going dark wasn't working for me,' Murph said. 'I didn't want to risk someone else picking up Mallik's baton. Since the satellites were still operable, I set each of the Vajra satellites to fire a deorbit burn. Number fifteen just reentered the atmosphere and disintegrated.'

Then satellite number three went red, followed by nine and thirteen. Soon all twenty satellites were gone.

Murph stood up and faced Juan.

'I probably overstepped my authority on that one,' Murph said.

Juan got to his feet and smiled. 'You probably did. Are you gunning for my job?'

Murph grinned back at him. 'And lose my reputation as a rebel? Are you kidding?'

Epilogue

India

Five days later

Juan clasped his hands behind his back as he kicked his flippers to propel himself down the underwater passage. His headlamp picked up the bloated face of another dead body, the fourth he and Max had passed since venturing into the passageway to what Lionel Gupta had called the Library.

The ancient fortress on a sprawling estate turned out to be one of the only properties in India to be held in private hands continuously since the time of Ashoka. Although Gupta hadn't kept the location of the Library in his files, Murph and Eric were able to hack into the phone records of both Carlton and Mallik. The last time their phones were in the same location was when they visited this location south of Mumbai.

It took a day of probing for Juan and Max to find a way in, but they had loads of time on their hands. Although the repair team finally got the main engines on the *Oregon* working again after the fight with the rogue frigates, the revolutionary drive mechanism had been severely damaged. It took three days for the ship to limp into the Port of Kochi, a trip that normally would have taken her four hours at top speed. Thanks to an ethically flexible ship-yard owner who didn't see the need to report the ship's presence to the authorities, Juan arranged for her to go through a full refit in a massive covered drydock adjacent to the facility where India's newest aircraft carrier was being built. The maintenance work wouldn't begin for another week, so Juan thought it would be a good chance to chase history and solve the mystery of the Nine Unknown Men at long last.

Once they had found the underwater passageway marked by the lion-head pillar with the swastika symbol of the Nine on it, he and Max secured some scuba equipment and went for a swim.

They finally surfaced again at a gate with yet another dead guard.

'I don't think this one drowned,' Max said, taking out his regulator and removing his mask.

Juan did the same and said, 'Looks like his larynx is broken. And judging by the smell of the corpse, he's been lying here for a while.'

They laid down their air tanks, BCDs, and swim fins. The water had been so warm that they were just wearing lightweight neoprene diving suits and boots.

'Shall we take a look around?' Juan asked.

'Lead the way,' Max said. 'Can't get any worse than what we've already seen.'

'Famous last words.'

As they explored the dank building, their flashlights occasionally supplemented by skylights built into the stone, Max said, 'Do you think someone'll try to build the Vajra system again?'

'If they could, they would. But Lang told me the CIA discovered that the Vajra records were destroyed. Mallik must have done it before he was killed.'

'He didn't want anyone to figure out a way to disable them.'

Juan nodded. 'That's my guess, too. Because the same thing happened with the Colossus records.'

'What do you mean?'

'When Murph and Eric went to look at Gupta's files again after we took down the satellites, they found that all records about Colossus had been erased. That made it easier to discover the one mention of the Library among all those files.'

Max scratched his head. 'Who do you think is responsible for deleting them?'

'Not who,' Juan corrected. 'What.'

Max gaped at him. 'You mean, Colossus did it?'

'Makes sense. If it was powerful enough to detect us infiltrating its ships, I wonder if it thought that any other records about it were a threat as well.'

'That would have required Colossus to search and delete records across the world in a matter of minutes.'

'Scary thought, isn't it? Maybe it was afraid it would be shut down if someone could find those records.'

'Afraid? It's a machine.'

Juan shrugged. 'Self-preservation. It's the most primal instinct.'

'This is making my brain hurt,' Max said. 'I'm just glad Colossus is gone.'

They turned a corner, and Juan stopped when he saw the room ahead. It was a dome with a huge circular table in the middle, and it was filled with more bodies. The stench was horrific.

None of them had bullet wounds. Their faces were contorted in agony.

'Don't take another step,' he said to Max.

'I guess I was wrong. It *did* get worse.'

'I'm pretty sure Novichok killed them, and there could be lingering traces of it. I recognize that look from when Rasul died in front of me.'

'And I recognize that guy,' Max said, pointing at a man lying outside the room. 'That's Jason Wakefield, one of the CEOs who's been reported missing in the last week.'

Juan pointed to another. 'That's Daniel Saidon. He owns one of the biggest shipbuilding companies in the world. I met him at a party a few years ago.'

'Do you think Mallik killed them?' Max asked.

'Makes sense. His brother-in-law was the one with the Novichok on the *Triton Star*.'

'But Carlton and Gupta somehow escaped to finish the Colossus Project.'

'That explains the blood feud between Carlton and Mallik,' Juan said.

'So now we know where the Nine Unknown Men met in secret, and it seems some of them are still here. That's a pretty big find.'

'We'll have to give the Indian government an anonymous call after we leave. I think they'll want to know about this.'

Juan kept walking past the domed meeting room and soon saw another one. This one looked similar to the first, but there was neither a table nor bodies.

Instead, there were nine sarcophagi surrounding a tenth in the center.

'This place wasn't designed as a meeting place,' Max said.

Juan nodded. 'You're right. It's a mausoleum.'

They walked in and saw that each of the stone caskets was marked with writing that looked like stick figures.

'I've seen this type of writing before,' Juan said.

'Where?'

'On the pillars of Ashoka. When Eric and I were researching the Nine Unknown Men, we found out that Ashoka placed pillars all over India to proclaim his edicts. These characters are the same ones used in the edicts. About twenty of the pillars still exist today, more than two thousand years later, and they're the first tangible evidence of Buddhism.'

Max stared in wonder at the tomb. 'Do you think these are the original Nine Unknown Men?'

'Archaeologists will have to determine that,' Juan said, 'but it could be why the Nine continued to meet here.'

'And the sarcophagus in the middle?'

Juan went over to it and saw that the lid was etched with the head of a lion and a wheel containing twenty-four spokes.

Max joined him and pointed to the wheel. 'I suppose you've seen that symbol before.'

'I have,' Juan said with awe. 'You have, too.'

'Where?'

'On the flag of India. It's called the Ashoka Chakra, and it's their national symbol.'

'Then this could be Ashoka himself.'

'Another riddle for the archaeologists to solve,' Juan said.

They left the tomb without touching anything and walked on. Juan could see that there was one more room ahead.

When he and Max got to the room's entrance, both of them stopped and stared, slack-jawed, at its contents.

The circular dome contained hundreds of cubbyholes stacked from floor to ceiling. And inside those cubbyholes were thousands upon thousands of parchment scrolls. Given the age of the building, some of them could have been more than two millennia old.

At least the mystery of how this place had been named was now solved. Clearly, the Nine Unknown Men knew the importance of preserving a library.

He just wanted a decent book to read ...

Not too much to ask, is it? It was in 1935 when Allen Lane, Managing Director of Bodley Head Publishers, stood on a platform at Exeter railway station looking for something good to read on his journey back to London. His choice was limited to popular magazines and poor-quality paperbacks – the same choice faced every day by the vast majority of readers, few of whom could afford hardbacks. Lane's disappointment and subsequent anger at the range of books generally available led him to found a company – and change the world.

'We believed in the existence in this country of a vast reading public for intelligent books at a low price, and staked everything on it'
Sir Allen Lane, 1902–1970, founder of Penguin Books

The quality paperback had arrived – and not just in bookshops. Lane was adamant that his Penguins should appear in chain stores and tobacconists, and should cost no more than a packet of cigarettes.

Reading habits (and cigarette prices) have changed since 1935, but Penguin still believes in publishing the best books for everybody to enjoy. We still believe that good design costs no more than bad design, and we still believe that quality books published passionately and responsibly make the world a better place.

So wherever you see the little bird – whether it's on a piece of prize-winning literary fiction or a celebrity autobiography, political tour de force or historical masterpiece, a serial-killer thriller, reference book, world classic or a piece of pure escapism – you can bet that it represents the very best that the genre has to offer.

Whatever you like to read – trust Penguin.

WHEEL AND SPINDLE

The end of another day, Belfast ropeworks, c 1905

WHEEL AND SPINDLE

ASPECTS OF IRISH INDUSTRIAL HISTORY

ALAN McCUTCHEON

BLACKSTAFF PRESS

Published by Blackstaff Press Limited, 255A Upper Newtownards Road, Belfast BT4 3JF

ISBN 0 85640 098 X

Printed in Northern Ireland by Belfast Litho Printers Limited.

Contents

Introduction

Though Ireland cannot be regarded as a country which made a major contribution to the history of mechanical invention, the uses which were made of industrial machinery in certain areas of the country — particularly in the north east, around Belfast — permitted the rapid development of large scale industry in the 19th century and led to the emergence of an industrial society which in many ways mirrored the large industrial communities of north Britain and central Scotland. Whilst a great deal has been written in recent years about the social and economic history of the country, there have been few attempts to correlate the industrial and commercial growth which formed an important part of that history with the machinery which made it possible. In the following pages, therefore, an attempt is made to explain in fairly simple terms some of the basic tools of the industrial revolution, as these appeared in Ireland, and to further outline this fundamental aspect of the country's development in a wide range of illustrative material.

For various reasons the book concentrates on industrial machinery and apart from passing references does not deal with road, canal and rail transport, or with ships and shipping. The industrial machinery is considered in two groups, forming a basic division of some importance: firstly come the 'prime movers', the fascinating range of machines, from simple waterwheels to complex steam engines, with which man harnesses the power of nature over the centuries; and secondly, a selection of the machines driven by the power generated by these prime movers, machines which enabled him to carry out industrial processes with a speed and ease hitherto impossible.

The history of technology in Ireland is more interesting and varied than might at first seem likely in a country not generally associated with manufacturing industry. During the 18th and early 19th centuries Irish industry developed along fairly modest lines, attracting and adapting machinery from Britain, and beyond, to its own particular requirements and at the same time stimulating the internal development of new plant and processes. As the Victorian era progressed, pressure from the might of industrial Britain led to enforced specialisation along selected lines — textiles and shipbuilding in the north, for example, brewing and distilling in the south — within which parameters a high degree of sophistication was achieved, both in industrial plant and in techniques of production.

It is hoped that by providing pertinent and informed comment on a wide range of machinery formerly of importance in Irish industry the book will encourage an interest in a field of inquiry hitherto somewhat neglected by Irish social and economic historians, and at the same time provide a new dimension against which the wide implications of social and economic progress can be viewed. Machines do not exist in isolation: they are created or introduced in response to the changing demands of society and having appeared more often than not in response to a simple, basic requirement in the internal structure of an industry they frequently exert a profound influence in subsequent years, not only on the development of that particular industry but also on the complex society which has come to depend on it for its livelihood and continued existence.

In introducing this book two wider developments of importance should be mentioned, which to some extent have both prompted and influenced the entire project. Firstly, the growth of the study of industrial archaeology throughout western Europe and North America over the past fifteen years or so. This field of inquiry may be broadly defined as the study of the material remains of the industrial revolution and as such it has now gained a strong foothold, with both practical and academic relevance. A comprehensive survey of the industrial archaeology of Northern Ireland was carried out by the author in the 1960's, involving both wide-ranging fieldwork and a great deal of documentary research into the history of technology in Ireland. Secondly, in the past few years, an important new department has been established in the major extension of the Ulster Museum, in Belfast, and here the author, as Keeper of Technology and Local History, was able to instal as working mechanical exhibits some of the great machines which brought the industrial revolution to Ireland.

A book of this nature involves the assistance of a great many individuals and institutions, particularly in the preparation of illustrations, and in the captioning of the individual plates and figures detailed acknowledgement of this assistance is given, wherever possible. In addition, I should like to mention two colleagues who have helped greatly with the project as a whole: Mr Alfred Montgomery, who as Assistant Keeper at the Ulster Museum was instrumental in enabling me to recreate the machinery of the past in a permanent display for the interest and enlightenment of future generations; and Mr Lionel Salem, a skilled photographer, who has gone to considerable pains to produce a wide range of illustrative material which helps greatly to explain the machinery and in many instances recaptures much of the atmosphere of the original setting in which it worked.

The title is taken from a poem 'Linen', by Ciarán Carson, which appeared in a book of his verse, *The New Estate*, published by the Blackstaff Press in 1976.

Alan McCutcheon

10 May 1977

The corn mill at Annalong harbour

1 *Animal, Wind and Water:*
the basic sources of industrial power

In Ireland the lack of rich, extensive deposits of coal and iron precluded the development of major manufacturing areas of heavy industry. The island contains many rocks which include veins of metal-bearing ores — gold, copper, silver, lead — and these have attracted interest from prehistoric times. Such ores have long been worked by man in Ireland, using both his own labour and the power provided by domestic animals and moving water, but manufacturing industry based on steam power was unknown throughout the greater part of the country, which remained almost exclusively agricultural in character. In these conditions the uses made of basic, *natural* power sources, such as wind and water, were of particular importance.

Animal power
The industrial uses made of animal power in Ireland were fairly limited and can be linked almost entirely with either agriculture or mining. In agriculture farming conditions over the greater part of Ireland did not encourage mechanical improvements, especially because of a traditional emphasis on livestock rather than arable farming. From its foundation in 1731 the [Royal] Dublin Society had been active in providing grants to assist in the improvement of Irish agriculture and in stimulating a general awareness of improved methods of husbandry. By and large, however, it was not until very much later, in the second half of the 19th century, that any noticeable improvements occurred in the farming methods or machinery used in Ireland. By this time the impetus for the design and manufacture of agricultural machinery had already become firmly rooted in Britain, particularly in East Anglia, and in America. Firms like Pierce of Wexford, Manisty of Dundalk and Kennedy of Coleraine made a wide range of machinery suitable for use on Irish farms.

As the 19th century progressed, however, the increasing importance of livestock farming, coupled with a complementary decline in the arable acreage, kept the home demands for agricultural machinery at a modest level. Furthermore, large scale mechanisation was extremely difficult in Ireland, where the average size of farms (30-40 acres), with small uneven fields, frequently marshy and rock strewn, was ill-suited to the application of the new machinery designed for the great arable fields

DUBLIN SOCIETY'S WEEKLY OBSERVATIONS

FOR THE ADVANCEMENT OF

AGRICULTURE AND MANUFACTURES.

Title page and illustration of a Dutch flax breaker from *The Dublin Society's Weekly Observations,* 1756.
(by courtesy of the Linen Hall Library, Belfast)

1

From a brochure in possession of Dr A M O'Sullivan, Wexford.

From a brochure of c 1910.

of East Anglia and the Fenlands, or for the vast flat lands of the American Middle West.

Some of the uses made of animal power in Ireland were special adaptations of techniques used elsewhere. Thus, the breaking or bruising of flax before scutching, using an *edge-runner* stone, was an important local variant on the widespread use of the animal-powered rotary mill in the Mediterranean world for grinding cereals or crushing oil-bearing seeds. It was in such a mill that the blind Samson was further degraded by being yoked to the great heavy grinding stones, usually turned by animal power. The modern equivalent is the *pan mill*, widely used in the pottery, clay and brick industries for preparing the raw material.

Another widespread use of animal power in Ireland was in preparing tannin from the bark of oak and birch trees. Tannin was an important ingredient used in the preparation of leather from hides and in the 1830s there were about five hundred tanneries in Ireland, with numerous *bark mills*, both animal-and water-powered, supplying the essential raw material. In these mills the edge-runner stone, as used in the flax-breaking process, was drawn round a track or furrow into which the broken bark had been spread. The crushed bark was then mixed with water to make the solution used in the tanning pits themselves. A closely related use of animal power was for the crushing of certain leaves, stalks and barks for the extraction of dyes and colourings used in the domestic linen and woollen industries.

We have already referred to the antiquity of mining in Ireland. It is certain that in many of the early pits and *adits* (tunnel workings), animal power would have been used quite extensively in the 17th and 18th centuries to remove surplus water from the mines and *soughs* (sumps) and to raise ore or coal to the surface. This occurred both in the mining of coal and ironstone in Tyrone, Leitrim, Kilkenny and Carlow, and in the working of veins of precious or semi-precious minerals in Wicklow, Cork, Kerry, Limerick and Tipperary.

In the 18th and 19th centuries all great schemes of public improvement, such as the construction of harbours, railways, roads and canals, relied heavily on the widespread use of animals as beasts of burden and in providing the power required by the primitive methods of excavation and drainage then current.

Other industrial uses to which animal power was put in

An edge-runner stone or 'lint wheel', used for breaking or bruising flax in County Donegal early in the present century.
(W A Green collection, Ulster Folk and Transport Museum)

2

Detail from a sheet of the earliest Ordnance Survey of Ireland (Down, 5, 1834) showing a *Tan Yard* and *Bark Mill* in close proximity just west of Newtownards.

Ireland included clay pressing, thread twisting, water raising, flax seed crushing (for linseed oil), saw milling, butter churning and corn threshing. In the horse-driven threshing 'mills', which were widely distributed throughout the country, the animal followed a fixed circular path in the farmyard and from a central rotating cone, to which was attached the arm connected with the harness, bevel gears and transmission shafting at ground level linked through to the corn threshing and cleaning machinery inside the barn itself. These horse-driven threshing installations were made by many Irish foundries, in a wide range of sizes.

Wind power
There were, of course, severe limitations in the use of animal power for industrial processes. In Ireland, as elsewhere, it was the harnessing of the *kinetic* energy (energy of movement) of currents of wind and water that made possible the first major advances in industrial production.

Rather surprisingly, perhaps, man made little attempt to harness the wind for his own use until the 7th or 8th century AD when the first primitive wind-driven machines emerged in the

A View of the Mouth of a Coal Pit near Broseley in Shropshire, 1788, showing a horse-driven winding gin raising coal to the surface.

The great cutting at Tring on the London and Birmingham Railway, 1837, by J C Bourne. This picture shows the *barrow-runs*, planks laid on the sides of the cutting up which the *navvies* wheeled barrows full of soil which they had previously dug from the sides or bottom. A rope attached to each man's belt, and also to the barrow, passed up round a pulley at the top of the slope, where it was linked to a horse. At a given signal the horse drew the barrow, and the navvy wheeling it, up the barrow-run. This laborious method of excavation, known as *making the running*, was both exhausting and extremely hazardous.
(Science Museum, London)

Middle East and south west Asia. They were probably derived from the little watermills already in use there. It is likely that the earliest wind-driven machines were fitted with blades or vanes which turned round and round parallel to the ground on an upright or vertical axis. As time passed these *horizontal windmills,* so called because the sails or sweeps turned in a horizontal plane, became larger and were often mounted in great masonry towers. By the 16th and 17th centuries their design had reached the most elaborate and fanciful stage of development, though so far as we can tell such windmills never reached Ireland. Even in Britain the more usual type, in which the sails or sweeps radiate from a central, sloping windshaft and turn in a vertical plane at right angles to the ground, soon became common. These *vertical windmills,* which first appeared in England in the 12th century, were derived from the watermills which had been in existence since Roman times. Both had basically similar gearing, the main difference being that in the water-mill the transmission of power was upwards from the *wheelshaft,* in the windmill it was downwards from the *windshaft.*

The first windmills in western Europe were *post* mills. In this type the mill consists of a box-like wooden body containing the machinery and supporting the sails on a heavy windshaft, angled slightly from the horizontal. The body is mounted on a braced upright post supported by a timber sub-structure resting on brick or stone piers. Mills of this type were built in north west Europe from the end of the 12th century and became popular in east and south east England, where timber was plentiful on the clay plains of Suffolk, Kent and Sussex. They were never of any great importance in Ireland though a few examples may have existed in isolation.

It was essential to keep the sails or sweeps of the windmill facing into the wind, and as the winds of north west Europe are both variable in direction and intermittent this could only be achieved by frequent turning of the entire body of the post mill. Making such a large structure mobile was in itself a considerable technological achievement eight centuries ago. At first this was laboriously carried out by hand, using the great heavy *tail pole,* which was lifted and moved by the miller and his helper. In the course of time wheels were fitted to the end of the pole and this could then be pushed round. In some instances, where the mill was particularly heavy, animal power might be used and, as the ultimate development of the basic type, a small winch could be incorporated, to draw the tail pole and mill round to its new position.

Whereas the post mill was common over much of the Great European Plain, in north Germany, Poland, the Netherlands, northern France and south east Britain, in Ireland it never gained much of a foothold. The characteristic Irish windmill is

A tower mill with wooden 'sails' designed to turn in a horizontal plane, 1595. The mill contains four pairs of millstones, of which either two or four could be worked, according to the wind strength.

(Science Museum, London)

A corn-grinding post mill, 1588.

the *tower* mill, with a moveable *cap* resting on a fixed stone tower. The cap contains the windshaft supporting the sails or sweeps, and the tower houses the remainder of the machinery, on several floors. In the simplest type of tower mill the cap could be turned into position as the wind veered by means of a tail pole terminating in a *tiller wheel*. The stone tower was usually circular in plan, often with a pronounced *batter* (upward taper) and the timber cap framework was covered with thatch.

As the type evolved so it became larger and more elaborate, with much taller towers and ornamental *ogee* caps (iron framed with a shingle cover or pitch-covered canvas). Often there was external *staging* round the side of the tower to allow access to the sails, which now turned well clear of the ground.

In 1745 Edmund Lee invented the *automatic fantail* in England. The device was soon widely applied to many existing

The tower windmill at Skerries, on the coast north of Dublin, showing the primitive tail pole and tiller wheel by which the cap and sails could be turned into the wind.
(Lawrence collection, National Library of Ireland)

Irish mills and was incorporated in all the more important ones built after that date. This refinement consisted of a set of vanes mounted behind the moveable cap. The fantail was so positioned that when the sweeps of the mill were square into the wind the vanes of the fantail lay entirely in the shelter of the structure and remained at rest. Once the wind veered, however, it set the fantail vanes in motion and this movement was transmitted through a series of iron gear wheels and shafts to the small wheels beneath the cap, driving them round on the wood or iron curb and turning the cap, windshaft and sweeps automatically to face into the wind once again. The fantail then returned to rest.

In Ireland wind-powered *grist* (grain) mills were common in the 18th and early 19th centuries. There was a remarkable concentration of these mills in Down and Wexford on the eastern seaboard, where several factors interacted to stimulate the use of wind power. Firstly, both counties were on the more sheltered eastern side of the country where cereal cultivation was encouraged by the drier, warmer summers. Secondly, both

The tower windmill at Ballyholme, Bangor, County Down, photographed at the turn of the century when the mill stood in open countryside.

(Lawrence collection, National Library of Ireland)

The tower windmill at Ballycopeland, near Donaghadee, County Down, showing the automatic fantail for turning the cap and sails into the wind.

The tall, brick, tower windmill on the north side of Thomas Street, near the corner of Watling Street, remains a notable Dublin landmark. Nine storeys high, with an elegant copper-sheeted ogee cap topped by a statue of St Patrick, it dates from the early 18th century and is one of the tallest windmills in Europe. It now forms part of the Guinness brewery complex and has been partly restored.

(by courtesy of Arthur Guinness Son & Co (Dublin) Ltd)

stone tower mills producing oatmeal and flour.

It is worth noting that the only two industrial or commercial structures in Ireland at present officially designated as being *in state care* are windmills, at Ballycopeland in County Down and at Tacumshin in County Wexford. While fully restored, neither mill is worked today.

Apart from threshing and grist milling the only other industrial activity carried on in Irish windmills appears to have been flax scutching, a process described in some detail later in the book. It would seem likely from the ruins that are left that in these little mills the flax-scutching shaft was vertical, with the scutching blades projecting at right angles, rotating within a circular box. Several flax-scutching windmills are marked on the original Ordnance Survey maps (1832-4) in the Ards and

The little thatched, stone, tower windmill at Tacumshin, near Rosslare, County Wexford.

(by permission of the Commissioners of Public Works in Ireland)

were within easy shipping distance of Dublin which provided a ready market for all surplus meal and flour in the period when imports of foreign grain were hindered by parliamentary legislation and the cultivation and milling of oats, barley and wheat within the country was being greatly stimulated. Thirdly, in County Down in particular, the effects of glaciation resulted in an undulating *drumlin* landscape of lakes and hummocks. This 'basket of eggs' topography afforded conditions specially suited to the use of wind as a complementary source of power during the farming year. Windmill and watermill often occur in close proximity, on one and the same farm. The windmill is perched on top of the whaleback while the watermill stands on the stream winding between the drumlins. Over a hundred windmills are recorded on the original Ordnance Survey maps of County Down (1834). The vast majority of them were

A 'Climax' wind engine by J Thomas of Worcester used for raising water at Bellinter House, Navan, County Meath.

Islandmagee peninsulas, in east Ulster.

In more recent years wind power was used throughout the country to drive what can best be described as *wind engines.* These could be used either for pumping water or for generating electricity and are very common in the great windy prairies of north central USA. A pylon of trellised steel work supports an annular (ring-shaped) wheel and a broad tail vane keeps the wheel in the eye of the wind. On the pumping engine a crank arrangement changes the *rotary* movement of the windshaft into a *reciprocating* (up and down) action on the long pump rod passing down through the pylon to the bore hole or well below. The wheel itself generally consisted of a series of metal vanes fixed to a light framework and angled like the petals of a flower. There were formerly dozens of these installations on farms throughout Ireland but with the spread of a centralised electricity supply in post-war years, they have nearly all fallen into disuse and disrepair.

Water power

Ireland is not rich in coal but for many centuries her numerous rivers and lakes have provided a welcome compensation in the industrial power which they have afforded. In 1844 Sir Robert Kane estimated that over the country as a whole there was around 1¼ million horse power waiting to be tapped in moving water-courses and while only a small fraction of this was ever harnessed there is no doubt that the historical importance of water power to the Irish economy cannot be over-emphasised.

Water power has exerted an influence on a wide range of industrial activity in Ireland from the early 17th century but the uses of water power in a predominantly agricultural economy date back very much further, to the early centuries of the Christian era. The uses made of water power in Ireland were many and varied, including corn milling and flax scutching, brewing and distilling, the woollen, linen and cotton manufactures, paper making, saw milling and spade forging. While the Irish watermill is widely distributed throughout the country — the only restriction being the availability of an ample water supply — certain short stretches of river were worked more intensively than most, e.g. the Upper Bann and Camlough in Ulster, the Dodder, flowing through Dublin, the Corrib in its run through Galway city and the streams of the Glanmire valley in County Cork.

As elsewhere the basic use to which water power was first applied in Ireland was in milling, the grinding of cereal grains to produce meal or flour. The earliest watermills in Ireland were small grist mills, probably introduced from the Hebrides

A tiny watermill with horizontal wheel, from the Fäeroe Islands; now in the Frilandsmuseet (Open Air Museum) near Copenhagen.

and Scotland in about the 5th century AD.

In these little mills the *wheel* revolved in a horizontal plane at the base of an upright wooden shaft. In fact these were not wheels in the generally accepted sense but rather a primitive type of water turbine with blades or vanes mortised in to the base of a circular upright shaft roughly shaped from a straight piece of tree trunk. Water was directed down a sloped wooden trough on to the wheel blades and by its direct impulse turned the vertical shaft. This passed up through the floor of the mill itself to the single pair of millstones within. The lower or *bed* stone was fixed in position on the mill floor and the shaft passed through the *eye* of this stone, terminating on the underside of

9

the upper or *runner* stone, to which it was keyed. As the water drove round the wheel below, so the shaft turned and with it the runner stone. The mill had no gearing and the grinding stone therefore turned at exactly the same speed as the wheel.

These *horizontal mills* were widely distributed over the maritime fringe of western Europe, from Iceland and the Fäeroes to the Balkans. In Ireland they were usually part of the *clachan* or extended family unit, grinding small quantities of grain for the group of inter-related families who eked a livelihood from subsistence farming and fishing.

The horizontal wheel was limited in efficiency and output, and this restricted its use to forming part of an integrated agricultural system. As a result it was not possible for milling to become a specialised commercial activity. It was undertaken more as a service for the community, to be repaid in due course not in cash or in kind but by some reciprocal service.

In Ireland the few horizontal mill wheels which have been excavated all indicate that here the design tended to be more sophisticated than elsewhere, with long curved blades shaped in section rather like the blades of an impulse turbine, and skilfully contrived water supply systems.

The nature of the small horizontal Irish mill can well be imagined from this extract from a description of part of the Ards peninsula, in the north east part of County Down, written in the mid-17th century:

'. . . from the said long bogge issue many rills and streams, which make small brooks (some of them almost dry in ye summer) that run to ye sea on either side of ye upper half barony; and on them each townland almost had a little miln for grinding oats, dryed in potts or singed and leazed in ye straw, which was ye olde Irish custom, the mealle whereof called *greddane* was very cours. The milns are called Danish or ladle milns; the axletree stood upright and ye small stones or querns (such as are turned with hands) on ye top thereof; the waterwheel was fixed at ye lower end of ye axletree and did run horizontally among ye water, a small force driving it . . .'

(from *The Montgomery Manuscripts*, ed. George Hill, Belfast, 1869)

Because of the characteristic noise which they made when working such mills were often referred to as *click* or *clack* mills. They were also called *Danish, Norse* or *Greek* mills after their supposed area of origin.

Throughout Ireland such small mills took over the work of the hand quern amongst those rural communities fortunate enough to be settled along or near a mountain stream. There were many hundreds in existence by about 1000 AD but gradually they fell into disuse and decay as the larger and more efficient watermills, driven by a *vertical* waterwheel, became more numerous. In Ulster it seems likely that the last horizontal mill went out of use before the end of the 18th century; in southern Ireland quite a number lasted very much longer and a fine example survives to this day, though no longer working, in County Roscommon, near the village of Cloonfad.

In the new Engineering Hall at the Ulster Museum in Belfast an accurate, full-size reconstruction has been made of the original horizontal mill wheel from Moycraig, dug up in a peat bog in north Antrim in 1853. This runs continually, driven by a

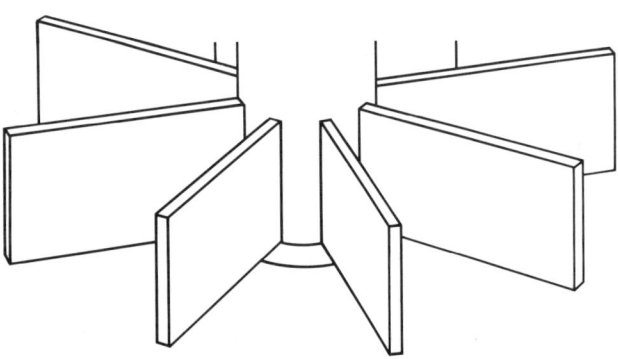

The horizontal 'waterwheel' of a small grain mill from the Fäeroe Islands.

The horizontal 'waterwheel', as found in the Orkneys, Shetlands and parts of southern Scandinavia.

Irish horizontal mill wheels: Mashanaglass, County Cork (left) and Moycraig, County Antrim.

(by courtesy of the late Dr Edward M Fahy)

controlled water supply and turning millstones on a simulated mill floor.

The introduction of the *vertical* waterwheel to Ireland was a major advance in the history of the country's industrial technology. The vertical wheel, so called because it turns in a vertical plane, is the most familiar type of waterwheel. It was known in the Roman world in the first century BC, when it was described by the military engineer, Marcus Vitruvius — as a result of which it is sometimes referred to as the *Vitruvian* or *Roman* wheel — but it does not appear to have reached Ireland until some five hundred years after this time. Within a relatively brief space of time the vertical wheel was applied to the milling process and in this it soon overshadowed both the hand quern and the horizontal mill. The power output from the vertical wheel was much greater than that of any device known previously, and in Ireland, as elsewhere, it was soon harnessed to a wide range of machinery.

To appreciate the vertical waterwheel fully we must pause for a moment and examine it more closely. The Irish waterwheel consists of five main parts, the names of which may vary considerably but which usually are as follows:-

(a)   *axle*: at first a rough-hewn tree trunk or *axletree*,

A horizontal mill wheel at Meeltraun near Cloonfad, County Roscommon, a rare survival of a type of waterwheel which was once common throughout Ireland.

11

later an octagonal wooden beam and later still a more slender bar of wrought iron, often flanged or fluted for additional strength.

(b) *arms:* usually four, six or eight in number on each face, originally wood, later iron castings.

(c) *shrouding* or *strouding:* the rims of the wheel, often T-jointed in sections on to the arms.

(d) *drumming* or *soleing:* the flat strips of wood or metal forming a backing to the buckets and stretching across the width of the wheel between the shrouding.

(e) *buckets:* the receptacles which hold the water for a time as the wheel turns and are formed by angled wooden slats (*treaders* and *risers*) or curved iron sheets stretching across the face of the wheel from shrouding to shrouding.

The main parts of the vertical waterwheel.

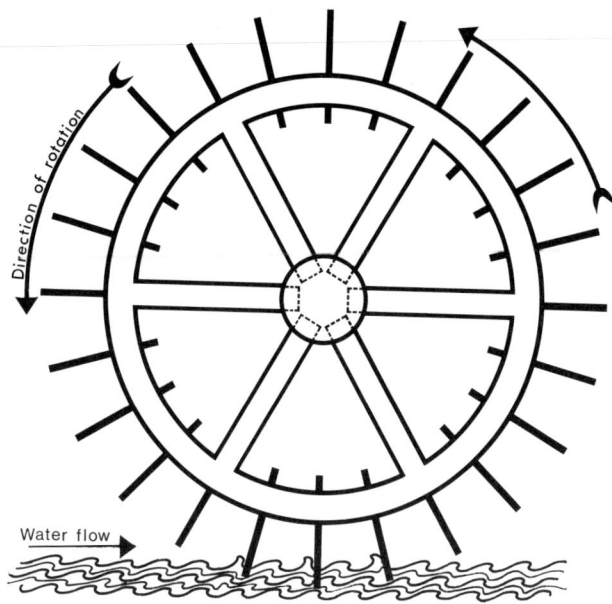

An *open* waterwheel, with *float-boards*. This type may also be referred to as a *stream* or *scud* wheel.

During the long and complex history of the vertical waterwheel it was natural that many attempts should be made to improve its efficiency. The original Roman wheels were in all probability of the *stream* design (*scud* wheels) in which the open waterwheel, without drumming, was turned by the impulse of the stream into which its projecting *paddles* or *floatboards* dipped. This was the least efficient type and such wheels are relatively uncommon in Ireland. If equipped with simple open buckets, but with the water striking it very little above its lowest point, the wheel is termed *undershot*.

Later, by the construction of a mill *race* at a higher level than the main stream the water flow could be made to strike the wheel at a point on its circumference facing the point of water delivery. These *breast* wheels were *closed* and were fitted with buckets rather than float-boards. The weight of water contained in several of the buckets pulled the wheel down and round, so that it was moved by *reaction* rather than *impulse*.

According to the point of water delivery these closed wheels were termed *low breastshot, breastshot, high breastshot* and *pitch back*. Finally, by bringing the water to the top of the wheel the *overshot* type, in which the water feed passed across the apex, was developed and adopted. Examples of all these types of waterwheel are to be found in Ireland but by far the most common are the closed breast wheels, with buckets.

Originally waterwheels were constructed almost entirely of wood and in the earliest type of timber wheel the arms were mortised into the horizontal axletree. This *compass arm* construction was basically unsound as the mortises were weak areas at precisely those points where stress was greatest.

It was not until the first quarter of the 18th century that the *clasp arm* wheel was designed. This was a very much stronger arrangement, with four arms crossing to form a square in which the axle was firmly clasped or wedged. However, in Ireland the older compass arm type of construction remained more common in timber waterwheels.

In the 1770's John Smeaton, the great British engineer, experimented with cast iron in waterwheel construction and with increasing use of the new material it was soon realised that there was no need to transmit the full power of the waterwheel through the main wheelshaft but that an iron spur-gear rim, cast in segments, could be bolted on to the shrouding or arms, transmitting the power to a pinion running at a much higher speed. This *suspension wheel* transmission, developed at the beginning of the 19th century, permitted a much lighter construction in the wheel itself, which was no longer directly transmitting the power being generated.

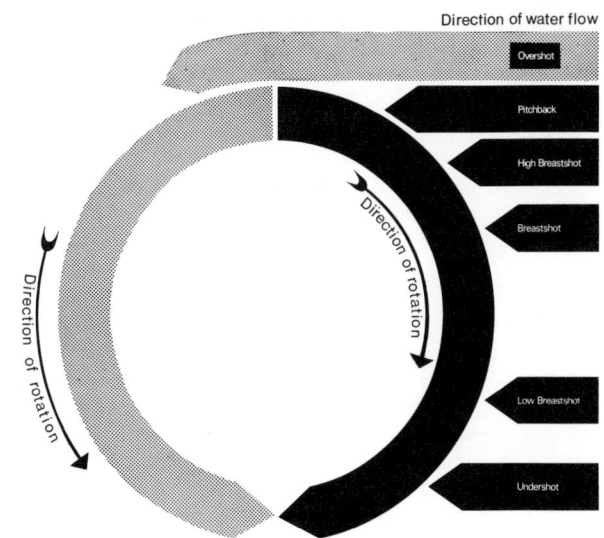

Different types of waterwheel.

Waterwheel construction.

(a) *Compass arm* wheel

(b) *Clasp arm* wheel

A *closed* waterwheel, with *buckets*.

13

1

2

4

5

3

1 Open or stream waterwheel at a saw mill, Castlebellingham, County Louth.

2 Undershot waterwheel at a former spade mill, Lacky Bridge, County Fermanagh.

3 Undershot waterwheel at a disused tidal grist mill alongside the Saltwater Bridge, Finnabrogue, County Down.

4 Breastshot waterwheel at an 18th century linen beetling mill, Wellbrook, near Cookstown, County Tyrone.

5 Pitchback waterwheel at a former grist mill, Killarn, between Dundonald and Newtownards, County Down.

6 Overshot waterwheel at a flax-scutching mill, Tullynewy Bridge, near Clough, County Antrim.
(from a photograph taken by Mr Hallam Ashley, FRPS in the late 1930s, reproduced by courtesy of Mr Rex Wailes)

6

The way was now open for the development of the great iron waterwheels of the second quarter of the 19th century, with suspension wheels, automatic governing, ventilated buckets, sliding hatches and wrought-iron rods instead of heavy wooden or cast-iron arms. Some of these wheels reached enormous proportions, 70 or 80 feet in diameter, and were beautiful and elaborate exercises in engineering design and construction, the work of skilled British engineers like Hewes, Fairbairn, Rennie, Donkin and Casement.

Not many wheels of this size were required by Irish industry though there was reputedly a huge wheel some 80ft in diameter in a paper mill near Dublin and, even more to be marvelled at, a great, squat, double Poncelet wheel some 70ft *in width* in the Phoenix Park Distillery at Chapelizod, both towards the end of last century. In the north, the 70ft diameter wheel at Darkley, County Armagh, and the 50ft wheels at Ligoniel near Belfast and at Castlewellan, County Down, were amongst the largest in the country.

One of the largest wheels still in regular use in Ireland is at

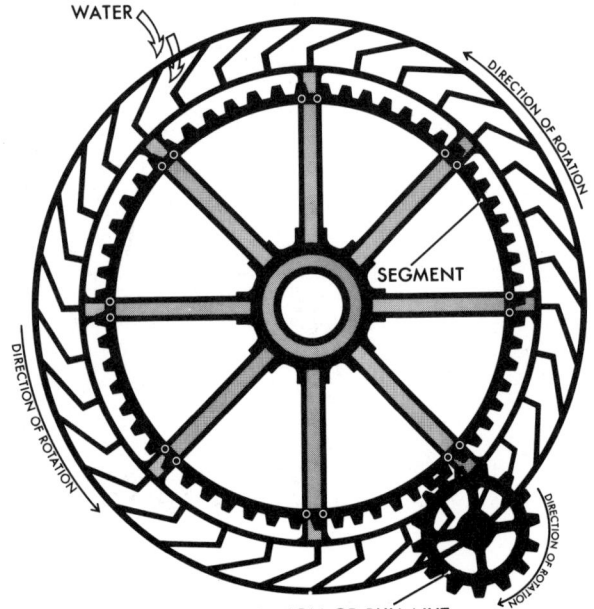

WATER

DIRECTION OF ROTATION

SEGMENT

DIRECTION OF ROTATION

DIRECTION OF ROTATION

PINION OR BULL-NUT

Segment or ring gear, 60 teeth
Pinion, 15 teeth
Ratio 4:1

Speed of revolution of waterwheel, 16 r.p.m., gives a pinion speed of 64 r.p.m., and this is the speed transmitted through the driving shaft to the machinery.

Waterwheel power transmission: the *suspension* wheel, with iron *segment*, and pinion or *bull-nut*.

The great waterwheel near Laxey in the Isle of Man. Built in 1854 and named the *Lady Isabella*, this huge wheel pumped water from a mine shaft lying several hundred yards distant. It is 72ft 6in in diameter and is a pitchback wheel. Turning at about 2½ rpm it generated 200 hp. It is now preserved by the Manx Government as a working industrial monument.
(from a woodcut which appeared in the 3rd edition of the Opfindelsernes Bog, 1912-14, Vol 2: reproduced by permission of the publishers, Gyldendals Forlag, Copenhagen)

The waterwheel at Middleton Distillery, County Cork.
(by permission of Irish Distillers Ltd)

teeth for smoother, more silent running and easier maintenance.

Finally, with the widespread adoption of the principle of the external suspension wheel, already referred to, the *lay*-or *line-shaft* method of power transmission became common in the mid-19th century, with four or five pairs of millstones driven from a line shaft below, at waterwheel level.

While grist milling was the most important single use made of industrial water power in Ireland, there were many other types of watermill, in which a wide range of industrial activities were carried on. Some of these are considered in the section on industrial technology which follows: here we have been concerned more with the waterwheel itself as a *prime mover,* that is as a source of power rather than as a machine involved in processing raw material in a manufacturing sequence. To conclude this chapter on industrial water power, therefore, we must now briefly consider the water-driven prime mover which succeeded the waterwheel itself, the *water turbine,* and see how in a period of little more than a century this machine has emerged as a most important source of industrial power, not least in

Wooden gear wheels with primitive *cog and rung* transmission in a derelict corn mill at Florencecourt, County Fermanagh. The waterwheel drive here passed from the *trundle wheel* (1) on the wheelshaft, to a complementary *spur gear wheel* (2) on a *counter shaft* (3), to a second *trundle wheel* (4), to a *lantern pinion* (5), and thence up to the millstones on the floor above.

the Middleton Distillery of Irish Distillers Ltd in County Cork. It is an all-metal wheel measuring 22ft in diameter by 15ft wide, with circumferential gearing and ventilated buckets. It was built in 1852 and still drives all the distillery's brewhouse machinery, in conjunction with an interesting beam (steam) engine.

In Ulster an old-established water-power site in Rory's Glen, Kilwaughter, near Larne, County Antrim, has a large high breast-shot waterwheel, 24ft 3in in diameter and 4ft 2in wide, generating about 40 hp and driving a variety of sawmill machinery.

The basic use to which the waterwheel was put in Ireland was the production of meal from grain and by the 19th century there were hundreds of grist mills scattered throughout the country, along numerous rivers and tributary streams. Originally the internal gearing, transmitting the power of the waterwheel to the grinding stones, would have been entirely of wood, massive *trundle* gear wheels and *lantern* pinions which creaked and rumbled as the waterwheel turned slowly outside the mill gable. This was known as *cog and rung* transmission.

At the end of the 18th century the introduction of cast iron caused a revolution in mill engineering in Great Britain and this fact, coupled with the general expansion of the Irish milling industry, ushered in a new type of *pit wheel* transmission with bevel gear wheels of cast iron, frequently fitted with hardwood

Transmission gearing in a corn mill at Ballyleagry, near Limavady, in County Londonderry. The waterwheel drive passed from the *pit wheel* (1) on the wheelshaft, to the *wallower* (2), to the *great spur wheel* (3), to the *stone nuts* (4) and thence up to the millstones on the floor above.

Line shaft transmission in a water-driven grist mill.

1 Pairs of millstones
2 'Stone' spindle
3 Bevel gear wheels, castings with mortised hardwood teeth
4 Segment
5 Breast or overshot wheel
6 Pinion (bull nut)
7 'Stone' floor
8 'Lay' or 'lying' shaft
9 'Meal' floor

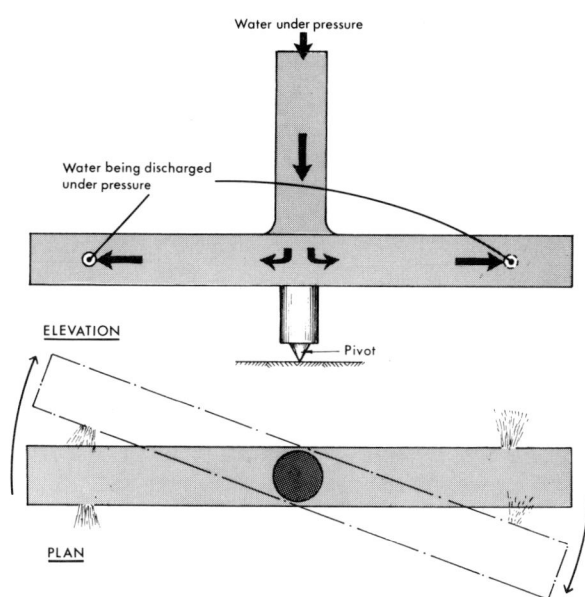

ELEVATION

PLAN

Diagrammatic elevation and plan of *Barker's Mill*, showing the working principle involved.

Ireland. The great metal waterwheels of the 19th century had marked the peak of development in a long story of engineering improvement, but from the middle of the century the water turbine became of increasing importance in mills and factories throughout the country. As we shall see, several significant contributions to water turbine design were made by Irish scientists in these early years.

The word *turbine* is derived from a Latin word meaning a spinning top. Water turbines are usually divided into two types, *reaction* and *impulse*. In the former type all the water passages are filled, and the energy stored in the water at the inlet to the turbine is transferred to the central *wheel* or *runner* as it passes through. The impulse turbine, as its name implies, is a machine in which the runner is propelled by the direct impulse of a jet of water striking it at considerable speed. The reaction type operates under pressure and may be completely submerged. The impulse type depends largely on the *head* of water available and must be kept clear of the water in the tail race.

The simplest form of reaction turbine is the device usually referred to as *Barker's Mill*. In this water was discharged simultaneously under pressure from both ends of a horizontal tube,

in opposite directions. This caused the tube to revolve. Though the principle was stated around 1740 the machine was never put to any practical use and has remained a scientific curiosity. However, the whirling lawn sprinkler and the slowly turning arms of sewage filters operate on precisely the same principle.

The next major advance occurred in 1827 when Benoit Fourneyron in France designed and built the world's first successful water turbine in response to an officially organised competition. Because of its importance the principle of the Fourneyron turbine is worth considering briefly. It was a reaction turbine in which water from a storage chamber, fed by a pipe entering from the side, passed down, then out, under pressure, through fixed guides on to wheel vanes forming part of the runner. As it passed outwards it had its direction of motion changed and having expended its energy in driving round the outer runner it was discharged round the edges. The movement of the outer rim was transmitted upwards by means of a central drive shaft, which turned with the runner.

PLAN VIEW

The outer stippled area (A) is the runner, which rotates at high speed and turns the central drive shaft (S)

Benoit Fourneyron's water turbine.

Some idea of the revolutionary nature of the water turbine in the history of power technology is reflected in the utter disbelief with which mill owners and administrators greeted this relatively small machine. Huge waterwheels could now be replaced by water turbines occupying a fraction of the space and making better use of the water supply available. For example, a Fourneyron turbine of 1834, installed in a French spinning mill where there was a head (fall) of water of over 350ft, had a runner measuring only 26in in diameter which nevertheless was capable of driving 8,000 spindles, turning at the unprecedented speed of 2,200 rpm.

There is not space here to detail the general development of the water turbine throughout succeeding years but before outlining some of the main points of interest in the history of Irish technology, a few general points may be of interest. The main difference between a waterwheel and a water turbine is that in the latter the wheel or runner is in general very much smaller than the older, vertical waterwheel and it is usually entirely enclosed in a metal box or casing, with a short shaft linking the runner (inside) with the first stage of the general transmission shafting. Thus, the most interesting part of the turbine is nearly always hidden away out of sight, with even the casing frequently submerged in a pit of dark, oily water and only the drive shaft projecting upwards to terminate in a bevel wheel by which the drive is turned on to a horizontal plane. Compared with the slow, elegant movement of the waterwheel, especially when this is set against an attractive mill building of finely weathered country rock in a picturesque glen or meadow, the turbine may appear a rather uninteresting device, darkly mysterious and purely functional. Nevertheless, particularly when taken in an Irish context, it has been an invention of considerable influence on modern economic and industrial development.

Compared with the waterwheel the turbine has certain important advantages. It occupies much less space, is more economical in its use of water and if properly installed should require less maintenance. It is a more versatile prime mover than the waterwheel, capable of working under a great range of heads and adjustable as the water supply fluctuates. It runs at a much higher initial speed than the waterwheel and cumbersome differential gearing is not required. The turbine can be quite easily governed automatically and it gives a much greater power output from a given flow of water.

We now turn to our consideration of the water turbine in the mid-19th century, and its associations with Ireland. In 1850 James Thomson, brother of William Thomson who, as Lord Kelvin, later became one of the greatest Victorian scientists, patented a new type of reaction turbine which because of the inward, spiral movement of the water on to the central wheel or runner was generally referred to as a *vortex* design. Thomson's vortex turbine was an important development, particularly in the use of a set of *adjustable guide blades,* controlling the flow of water on to the runner. Many turbines of this type were built in the second half of the 19th century both at Kendal in Westmorland, and in Belfast, and many of Thomson's ideas have been incorporated in modern turbine designs.

There were two other important water turbine manufacturers in Ireland in the 19th century, both in Ulster. These were the MacAdam brothers of Belfast and William Kennedy of Coleraine, Co Derry. The MacAdam brothers, James and Robert, played an active part in developing and perfecting the ideas of an Armagh millwright, William Cullen, who in turn had been greatly influenced by what he had seen on a continental visit to several Fourneyron turbine installations. The MacAdams' first turbine was made in their Soho Foundry, in Townsend Street, Belfast, in 1850. Between 1850 and 1894, when the foundry closed down, a substantial number were built and installed in Ireland, providing power for a wide range of uses, from flax scutching to linen weaving and the generation of electricity.

At least two MacAdam turbines remained *in situ* in Ulster until quite recently and one of these, a 90 hp machine of the Fourneyron outward-flow type, dating from c. 1860, was in regular use at Cogry, near Doagh, County Antrim until 1974, when it was taken out and scrapped.

The foundry at Coleraine, established by Hugh Kennedy in 1842, subsequently played an important role in popularising the water turbine as a source of power at many sites throughout Ireland, particularly in the north and west. The foundry did not begin to manufacture turbines until the 1870s and soon afterwards Hugh's younger son, William, an engineer of considerable ability, introduced the 'Empress' turbine modelled directly on contemporary American designs for low head installations. This was a horizontal turbine which by subdivision of the runner into three horizontal bands guaranteed most efficient use of a variable water supply.

Kennedy turbines built up a high reputation in Ireland and abroad over the next forty or fifty years. Between 1879 and 1921 some seventy Kennedy turbines, with runner diameters ranging from 8in to 48in were installed in Ireland. Production ceased in 1953. Designed to suit the particular requirements of local sites, Kennedy turbines were both reliable and versatile and were applied to industrial purposes as diverse as corn

Vortex for Mr James Bodel.
July. 1852. | *Ligoneil*.

Standard power = 50 Horse power.
Suppose efficiency to be only 70
per cent. The working fall
is to be between 90 and 100 feet.
If the efficiency be only 70
per cent I must suppose
that the speed of the wheel
will (when) (at the best) (amount) be rather less
than usual. Hence in the
calculation I take $H = 88$.

Then $\dfrac{62\cdot3 \times 88 \times \cdot70}{33000} = 50$.

Hence $Q = 430$. $(max. = 573.)$

$\sqrt{H} = 9\cdot38$

$\dfrac{Q}{\sqrt{H}} = 45\cdot84$

$\sqrt{\dfrac{Q}{\sqrt{H}}} = 6\cdot77$

Diam. of wheel $= \cdot183 \sqrt{\dfrac{Q}{\sqrt{H}}} = 1\cdot239$ ft
$= 1$ ft $2\frac{73}{84}$ in.

$\cdot553 \sqrt{\dfrac{H\sqrt{H}}{Q}} = \cdot553 \sqrt{1\cdot919}$

$\therefore$ Rev. per min = 768.

Diam. of shaft $= \sqrt[3]{\left(240\,\dfrac{50}{768}\right)}$
$= 2\cdot50$ ins.

Make diam. above slot $= 2\frac{1}{2}$ in.
and diam. at slot $= 2\frac{5}{8}$.
To be of best wrought iron.
Let $a = $ infect $= 2\cdot62$ diam of shaft. Then

Diam. of exit orif. $= \sqrt{\left(\cdot00838\dfrac{Q}{\sqrt{H}} + a^2\right)}$ ft.
$= \cdot657$ ft. $= 7\frac{7}{8}$ ins.

Total area of entrance orifices
$= \cdot00329\dfrac{Q}{\sqrt{H}} = \cdot1508$ sq. ft.

To find horiz. width multiply
diam. of wheel by $\cdot12$.
Horizontal width $= \cdot1485$ ft.
$= 1\cdot782$ ins.

Greatest Horizontal width to be $2\frac{7}{8}$ inches.

$\therefore$ Vertical depth $= 3\cdot04$ ins.

(In this the ratio of the horizontal to the vertical
width is as $1 : 1\cdot7$.)

Vertical distance from middle
plate to top plate at circum.
of exit orif. $= \cdot15 \times$ diam. of wheel
$= 2\cdot228$ ins.

Pivot to be $1\frac{1}{2}$ ins diam.

Inside diam. of case = 39 ins = $2\cdot6 \times$ diam. of
(as made) wheel.

Two manuscript pages from one of James Thomson's *scheme books*, showing his calculations for a Vortex turbine to be installed in a mill at Ligoniel, on the outskirts of Belfast, July, 1852.

(reproduced by permission of the Librarian of the Queen's University, Belfast)

threshing, flax spinning and saw milling.

Many other water turbine manufacturers are represented in Ireland — McDonald of Glasgow; Turnbull of Edinburgh; McCormick, Alcott and Leffel, all American firms; Craig of Belfast; Baillie of Bessbrook; Hay-Maryon of Loughborough; Gilkes of Kendal; Gordon of London; Escher-Wyss of Switzerland — but we must conclude this section with reference to two further basic types, very different in character and importance. These are the *Pelton* wheel and the *Kaplan* turbine.

The Pelton wheel was developed as an impulse turbine in

'MacAdam's improved turbine for low falls'.

From a catalogue of c 1910.

California during the days of the gold fever, towards the end of the 19th century. The maximum amount of power had to be obtained from small but swiftly flowing streams in deep canyons and the early miners built crude waterwheels with cupped blades — later divided for greater efficiency — which were struck by a powerful jet of water issuing from a pipe of restricted bore. In this type a substantial fall was required to obtain the force necessary to turn the wheel at high speed and the head water was fed downwards to the wheel house along a pipe or *penstock* of gradually narrowing cross section. The wheel itself was encased and the main use made of the power generated was to drive electric dynamos or alternators directly coupled to the main drive shaft.

Because of its specialised requirements, and the fact that its construction was a task somewhat beyond the scope of the local foundry or blacksmith, there are not many Pelton wheel installations in Ireland. It was essentially a turbine for high mountainous areas where a great head of water, maintained by abundant rainfall, gave the rapid fall required to operate the wheel successfully. It was common in the Rocky Mountains in America, in Norway, Switzerland, the Highlands of Scotland, Wales and the Lake District of northern England.

In the Ulster Museum in Belfast, two impulse wheels of the Pelton type can be seen. Both are from County Antrim where along the east coast the steep cliffs down from the moorland plateau to the sea gave conditions which favoured this distinctive type of water turbine.

In the present century there have been relatively few major developments in turbine design, but countless refinements and improvements. One of the most important advances with particular reference to Ireland was the development of Kaplan's adjustable-blade propeller, reaction turbine in Czechoslovakia between 1910 and 1924. This revolutionised the generation of power from economically vast, low-head resources. The Kaplan turbine has a vertical axis; water is admitted to the blades of the runner along a spiral snail-shell casing of decreasing size; it has relatively few blades (from three to eight), short but wide, and these are capable of adjustment by means of a mechanism within the hub. Thus, if the demand for power decreases the angle of the blades to the axis is increased, reducing the area opposing the water flow. This improves the turbine's efficiency under reduced load and is a major advantage. Leaving the runner, the water flows down through what is called a *draught tube* and enters the tail race. The inlet channel, casing, runner pass-

Diagrammatic section of a modern Pelton wheel installation.

An impulse turbine of the Pelton wheel type, formerly used for generating electricity near Ballygally, along the Antrim 'Coast Road': now at the Ulster Museum, Belfast.

A small impulse turbine (Pelton wheel) on a farm near Toomebridge in County Antrim. This has been removed to the Ulster Museum and is now a working exhibit in the main Engineering Hall.

A large Kaplan turbine runner being lowered into position.
(by permission of GEC Turbine Generators Ltd)

ages, draught tube and tail race are all filled with water. The generator is positioned directly over the turbine runner.

The Kaplan turbine has been of the greatest importance in the generation of hydro-electricity in Ireland. In the Republic there are reaction turbines of this type on the Shannon at Ardnacrusha, near Limerick (1), on the Erne between Belleek and Ballyshannon, in County Donegal (4) and on the Liffey at Poulaphouca in County Wicklow (2) and at Leixlip in County Kildare (1), which together account for over half the 220 megawatts of hydro-electricity produced by the Electricity Supply Board each year.

The generating hall in the Cathaleen's Fall hydro-electric power station on the river Erne near Ballyshannon, County Donegal.
(by permission of ESB)

The Combe Barbour steam engine formerly at the Ulster Weaving Company's factory, Belfast

2 *Steam Power*

Steam power was of much less importance in Ireland than in Great Britain, both in the number and size of engines and in the total amount of industrial power which these provided in the Irish economy as a whole. Only in Belfast did engine design and manufacture gain a permanent foothold in the 19th century. But having said this it is nevertheless true that the introduction of steam power at the end of the 18th century played an important role in the subsequent growth of the linen textile industry in the north of the country, and in stimulating the development of the brewing and distilling industries in the south.

Before dealing with steam engines in Ireland it is necessary to explain at least some of the basic mechanical principles involved. Here we are concerned solely with the stationary (industrial) steam engine, the steam-driven railway locomotive being a separate subject on which a great deal has been written elsewhere.

The discovery and exploitation of the great power of steam placed at man's disposal an industrial power source far greater than any known previously. Just as the earlier invention of the waterwheel marked a major step forward in man's control of his environment, so the invention of the steam engine in the 18th century brought about a further, more dramatic change. In the century and a half beginning in 1750 a sudden quickening of industrial progress occurred throughout the civilised world, a series of events which are generally referred to as the Industrial Revolution. Without steam power this could not have taken place.

The history of the industrial steam engine has no precise point of origin but resulted from certain discoveries of physical phenomena made during the 16th and 17th centuries. The most important of these was a realisation of the pressure (1 kilogram per sq centimetre or between 14 and 15lbs per sq inch) exerted by the atmosphere at the Earth's surface, and subsequently of the peculiar properties of a vacuum. These were basic principles of great importance, scientifically explored and unravelled by the work of such men as Galileo, Torricelli, Pascal and von Guericke. In his famous series of experiments conducted at Magdeburg in the mid-17th century, Otto von Guericke demonstrated the great strength of a vacuum and set

Von Guericke's air pump overcoming the strength of fifty men, 1654. A fixed vertical cylinder containing a piston was equipped with a rope passing upwards over a pulley. With an air pump Von Guericke drew air from within the cylinder, below the piston, creating a partial vacuum. Atmospheric pressure then caused it to descend, despite the joint efforts of some fifty men to hold it up at the top of the cylinder.

(Science Museum, London)

men thinking about how this natural phenomenon could be put to some use.

Various experimental attempts to create and control a vacuum by artificial means culminated in the work of a French mathematician, Denis Papin, who carried out a series of important experiments in the last decade of the 17th century. In 1696 he condensed steam in a partial vacuum and he was the first man to move a flat disc or *piston* up and down a tube or *cylinder*, using the natural power of steam.

From the work of Papin and his contemporaries it was but a logical step to the design of an *atmospheric* engine, ie an engine worked solely by the pressure of the atmosphere reacting to the existence of a vacuum. Within twenty years the successful attempts of two Englishmen, Thomas Savery and Thomas Newcomen, to design and apply such machinery to the draining of mines was the first major break-through in the harnessing of steam power.

Thomas Savery, a military engineer, was the first to develop a practical steam pump, patented in 1698 as a machine for the '. . . raiseing of water . . . by the impellent force of fire . . .' The primitive pump used a partial vacuum, created by a sudden condensation of live steam, and the pressure of the atmosphere reacting against it, to force water up from the mine sump. Savery's 'engine' consisted of a large closed vessel with a pipe attached which dipped down below the surface of the water at the bottom of a mine. Steam from a boiler was blown into the vessel and the steam inlet valve was closed. Cold water was then squirted into the vessel and this condensed the steam, forming a vacuum. The pressure of the air then forced the water from the bottom of the mine up into the vessel. The water was then forced out by steam and the cycle commenced all over again. Two sets of valves and two vessels worked alternately.

Savery's pump or 'engine' was very limited in its application; air pressure could not raise water more than 28ft and if steam pressure was used to force the water higher the boilers were liable to burst. Nevertheless, his design was the first useful steam pump, with separate boiler, and in his famous treatise of 1702, *The Miner's Friend,* he lays emphasis on the saving which could result from its use in the laborious and unending task of keeping shallow mines and adit (tunnel) workings free from surplus water.

Thomas Newcomen of Dartmouth, an ironmonger, had been impressed by the costly and time-wasting use of animal power required to keep the Cornish tin and copper mines free from water. For fifteen years he worked on the design of a pumping engine and in 1712 the first Newcomen engine was erected at Dudley Castle in Staffordshire. As a contemporary chronicler put it:

'. . . now it happened that a man from Dartmouth, named Thomas Newcomen, without any knowledge whatever of

The *ENGINE Working in a MINE.*

THE *ENGINE* For *Raising Water* BY FIRE.

Fig 2

Fig 1.

Thomas Savery's 'engine for raising water by fire', 1698.
(Science Museum, London)

28

the speculations of Captain Savery, had at the same time also made up his mind, in conjunction with his assistant, a plumber by the name of Calley, to invent a fire machine for drawing water from the mines. He was induced to undertake this by considering the heavy cost of lifting water by means of horses which Mr. Newcomen found existing in the English tin mines . . .'

(from Marten Triewald, *A Short Description of the Fire and Air Machine at the Dannemora Mines, Sweden*, 1734)

Thomas Newcomen's *atmospheric* engine of 1712 was the first successful machine to convert the heat energy of fuel into useful work and began a new era in which man was no longer solely dependent on wind, water and muscle power.

Why was the engine of 1712 such an important milestone in world technology? How was it built and how did it work?

The Newcomen engine was thoroughly practical and reliable. It was both enormous in size and low in efficiency. It consumed a vast amount of coal, but coal was relatively cheap and the successful drainage of more and more mines meant more coal, which in turn meant more iron for engine manufacture. The great upsurge in mining and manufacturing to which we have already referred was under way.

The atmospheric beam pumping engine revolutionised mining and drainage throughout western Europe. Newcomen's original design of 1712 was improved upon and modified as the century progressed but for more than sixty years his engine had no rival as a source of industrial power. It was not until the 1770s, when the work of James Watt of Greenock began to exert an influence

A vertical cylinder (1), open at the top, was placed directly above the domed boiler (2). The piston (3), packed with leather and sealed with a layer of water on top, was hung by a chain (4) from the arch head of the rocking beam (5).
From the other end of the beam was suspended the pump rod (6). Steam was admitted at atmospheric pressure, or a fraction above, to the bottom of the cylinder (7). The piston rose to the top, mainly by the weight of the pump rod. Any air or water in the cylinder was blown out by the steam, through water-sealed, non-return valves (8). After the steam valve was closed the steam in the cylinder was rapidly condensed by a jet of cold water (9), thus creating a vacuum. This was now operated against by atmospheric pressure and the descent of the piston drew down the end of the rocking beam. The cycle was restarted by the admission of fresh steam.

The pumping engine of Thomas Newcomen. (by permission of Babcock & Wilcox Ltd)

on the scene, that the great atmospheric pumping engines, like huge dinosaurs unable to adapt to changing conditions in industry, or to take advantage of advances in engineering technology, became outmoded and obsolete.

The work of James Watt in the development of steam power presents a study of inventive scientific genius which shaped the course of industrial technology throughout the world.

In 1763, as 'Mathematical Instrument Maker to the University of Glasgow' Watt was repairing a model of a Newcomen engine and found its consumption of steam so great that the steam was soon exhausted — in Watt's own words 'the engine was hungry for steam'. This excessive consumption of steam represented a waste of heat and a waste of fuel. Watt's first major contribution to the development of the steam engine was provided by his solution to this problem. After much deliber-

James Watt (1736-1819), from a painting by Sir Thomas Lawrence, 1813.

(Science Museum, London)

ation he realised that the high inefficiency of the Newcomen engine was due to the fact that the live steam admitted to the cylinder at each stroke was being cooled and condensed *in the cylinder,* thus cooling the cylinder itself. This caused the steam admitted in the next stroke to condense prematurely and meant that a large amount of steam was required to obtain a minimum of power.

In 1769 Watt was granted his historic patent for '. . . a new method of lessening the consumption of steam and fuel in fire engines . . .' by incorporating a *separate condenser.* By this addition, when the steam in the cylinder had to be condensed it was merely connected by a valve with the cold condensing chamber. The steam rushed out of the hot cylinder, and condensed in the cold chamber, forming a partial vacuum in both but leaving the working cylinder still hot and ready to accept more steam from the boiler. Morever, Watt suggested that the heat of the cylinder could be better retained if it were encased in a *steam jacket* and that low pressure steam rather than atmos-

Thomas Newcomen's engine of 1712, erected near Dudley Castle in Staffordshire, from an engraving by Thomas Barney, 1719.

(Science Museum, London)

... Now Know Ye that in compliance with the said Proviso and in pursuance of the said Statute I, the said James Watt, do hereby declare that the following is a particular description of the Nature of my said invention and of the manner in which the same is to be performed (that is to say) My Method of lessening the consumption of Steam and consequently fuel in Fire engines consists of the following principles— First, that Vessel in which the powers of the steam are to be employed to work the Engine which is called the Cylinder in common fire engines and which I call the Steam Vessel must during the whole time the Engine is at work be kept as hot as the steam that enters it first by enclosing it in a case of Wood or any other Materials that transmit heat slowly, Secondly by surrounding it with Steam or other heated bodies and Thirdly by suffering neither Water nor any other Substance colder than the Steam to enter or touch it during that time. Secondly, in Engines that are to worked wholly or partially by condensation of Steam the Steam is to be condensed in Vessels distinct from the Steam Vessels or Cylinders, although occasionally communicating with them. Those Vessels I call Condensers and whilst the Engines are working, these Condensers ought at least to be kept as cold as the air in the neighbourhood of the Engines by application of Water or other cold Bodies ...

An extract from James Watt's historic patent of 1769 in which he outlines the principles of the 'method of lessening the consumption of steam' in his engines, mainly by the introduction of a separate vessel or 'condenser' as a means by which the cylinder itself could at all times be kept as hot as possible. It was this important innovation, more than any other single factor, which led to the rapid development of an 'industrial revolution' based on steam power.

(Crown copyright; Public Record Office, London, C66/3721 No 22)

The early steam engine and its development under Papin, Newcomen and Watt. (by permission of Babcock & Wilcox Ltd)

Papin

1 Piston
2 Cylinder
3 Water

Newcomen

1 Piston rod to beam
2 Piston
3 Cylinder
4 Condensing jet
5 Eduction pipe
6 Boiler
7 Water

Watt

1 Piston rod to beam
2 Stuffing box
3 Piston
4 Cylinder
5 Steam case
6 Air pump rod to beam
7 Condenser
8 Jet
9 Boiler
10 Air pump
11 Hot well
12 Water

pheric pressure should be used to drive the piston. So successful was Watt's separate condenser that within a couple of years the fuel consumption of the beam pumping engine had been reduced to one third of what it had been previously. This was particularly important in Cornwall, where coal was an expensive import.

On a visit to London Watt was introduced to Matthew Boulton, a leading industrialist, who persuaded him to bring an experimental engine which he had built in Glasgow to Birmingham for development. An extension of the original patent was granted (1775-1800) and a formal business partnership between Boulton and Watt drawn up. Their Soho Foundry in Birmingham quickly dominated the industrial scene, building some five hundred engines in the last quarter of the 18th century.

This is not the place to detail the subsequent development of the steam engine under James Watt, and later with William Murdock, his assistant and partner at Birmingham. It must be said, however, that at the Soho Foundry in the last quarter of the 18th century the industrial steam engine advanced from being a machine of relatively crude construction and low efficiency to a position of dominance as an industrial prime mover. From being a simple pumping engine, with steam admitted to one side of the piston only (*single acting*), Watt made the engine *double acting* with steam driving alternately from both top and bottom of the cylinder. He also made it capable of providing *circular* or *rotary movement* to drive textile machinery. This was a most important advance as hitherto (before 1783) the steam engine had been restricted to pumping water from mines through a reciprocating movement of the pump rods. By incorporating *sun and planet* gearing and, somewhat later, the more familiar *crank*, the engine was made *rotative* and was quickly applied to the cotton-spinning mills of Derbyshire, Nottinghamshire and Lancashire, built originally on river courses where there was power to turn the great driving waterwheels.

Having now outlined the main points in the early evolution of the industrial steam engine let us examine how steam power was introduced to Ireland and how its spreading application to a variety of industrial uses went hand in hand with the emergence of an important, though localised steam engine manufacturing industry.

As we have seen the atmospheric beam engines of Thomas Newcomen were used to pump excess ground water from coal and tin mines in Britain. By the 1770s such engines had reached the peak of their development but were already being superseded by the engines designed by James Watt and built in Birmingham in the Soho Foundry of Boulton and Watt. The earliest records of a pumping engine in Ireland date from 1740 when an engine was built on the Kilkenny coalfield, at Doonane on the Hartpole estate in County Laois. Nothing is known of this engine beyond the fact that it cost some £1,200 but in view of the early date and substantial cost involved it seems likely that it was a large atmospheric engine of the Newcomen type. It seems to have been poorly maintained and some forty years later, in 1782-3, it was replaced by one of James Watt's new pumping engines, brought over from Matthew

Boulton's Soho Foundry in Birmingham. A few months later John Staples and James Caulfield entered into an arrangement with Boulton and Watt to supply a pumping engine for a new coal pit being sunk at Drumglass, between Coalisland and Dungannon, on the east Tyrone coalfield. In the 1780s hopes were high that an increase in the output of Irish coal mines would reduce the dependence on costly and unreliable imports from Britain and a sum of £3,000 was forthcoming from the Irish parliament to assist the various mine proprietors in their proposed schemes of improvement. Both the Doonane and Drumglass engines were single acting, beam pumping engines, with separate condensers. They are the two earliest engines in the country for which technical details survive. By the end of the century the rotative steam engine had made its appearance in the cotton-spinning mills of Ulster, and two further pumping engines had been built locally on the Kilkenny coalfield, this time on the Wandesforde estate.

The growing success of Watt's rotative beam engines in driving textile machinery in Lancashire, Derbyshire and Nottinghamshire meant that as the cotton industry increased in importance in the north of Ireland at the end of the 18th century, British steam engine makers had a natural outlet for their wares. Following the first installation of 1790, in a Lisburn cotton mill, the import and assembly of rotative engines — as opposed to pumping engines raising tail water to feed a driving

Boulton and Watt's rotative beam engine, 1788, giving about 10hp. It is worth noting that the method of measuring the power of a prime mover was first standardised by James Watt in 1783 in *horse power* ie 1 horse power is the power required to raise 550lb through a height of 1 foot in 1 second, or in metric, 75kg through 1 metre in 1 second.

Note here the cylinder (1), parallel motion (2), valve gear (3), beam (4), fly-wheel (5) and sun-and-planet gearing (6).

(Science Museum, London)

General Section of the Engine for Drum Glass
No. Drift to the foot
Dec. 1784

The Boulton and Watt beam pumping engine installed at
Drumglass, near Coalisland, County Tyrone, in 1784-6.
(reproduced by courtesy of the Birmingham Public Libraries)

Part of a description of the Drumglass colliery, near Coalisland,
County Tyrone, written in September, 1789.

A View and Report of the state of Drumglass Colliery. September 1789

At the Request of Messrs. Staples, and Caulfield, I waited upon them at Drumrea, in Ireland, to View their Colliery at Drumglass, in order to give my opinion respecting her present situation. What Quantity of Coal is Won, and unwrought, by the present Engine, what quantity of Coal, may be got, to the dip of the said Engine Level, and at what expence. Also what quantity of Coal may be wrought Annually, and at what p Ton.

I have perused the Plans of the Colliery, Attentively, Perambulated the Grounds, under which the Coal is supposed to lay; so far as it appear'd necessary for my purpose. I descended One of the Pits, and examined the State of the Workings, the Height of the Seam, Coal, Thickness of the Band, or Clearing, and manner of Working, and am of opinion as follows.

That there is won by the present Engine and unwrought Ninety Thousand Tons of Coal, which at Twenty Thousand Tons p Annum, will last Four and a Half years. It is highly probable that a much greater quantity may be got, but as it is uncertain I have not taken it into my Calculation.

With respect to the Coal laying to the Deep, or below the level of the present Engine, I am clearly of opinion that not less than Eleven years Coal or Two hundred and Twenty thousand Tons, may be got, by sinking the Engine Pit down to the Depth of Twenty Fathoms, and carrying forward from thence a Stone Level to the Northward or full Deep, untill it Cut the Coal at the Distance of about Three Hundred Yards. Should this Stone level reach the bottom of the supposed Swilley or

34

waterwheel – continued apace, and by 1811 there were in Belfast and district some fifteen mills worked by steam power. To maintain a degree of perspective, however, one should compare this figure with that for Britain where in the last quarter of the 18th century Boulton and Watt built some five hundred engines, of which approximately 60% were rotative. From the outset the Birmingham foundry supplied the engines complete to their customers, though in Ireland it seems more than probable that the customer would have erected his engine house from local materials, including all the woodwork and coarser metal castings, leaving only the engine itself to be brought over and assembled under the supervision of one of Watt's foremen.

The cotton mills of Ulster were situated mainly on or near the east coast, depending on imports from Liverpool for their raw material and with handloom cloth mainly for the protected Irish home market. The industry was in the hands of men fully acquainted with the recent developments in steam engine design and construction which had revolutionised the British industrial scene. To the mills in Larne, Belfast, Bangor, Newry and Lisburn, coal could easily be imported and the construction of a small cotton mill, driven by a rotative steam engine, as in north west Britain, was not a difficult operation.

For a time cotton and linen industries existed side by side in the north, but in 1825 James Kay of Preston introduced a patent for the *wet* spinning of flax, thus making possible the production of much finer mill-spun yarns, and it was this development, more than any other single factor, which led to the eclipse of the cotton manufacture in Ulster. From 1830 great steam-powered flax-spinning mills, producing the entire range of linen yarns, were built in Ulster and by 1838 Belfast alone had eighteen steam engines, with a total indicated horse power of 690, driving power-spinning frames producing linen yarn.

Looking at the overall figures for industrial steam engines in Ireland in 1838, Belfast is seen to account for about one third of the Irish total in number of installations, and over 40% in total horse power, though with less than one per cent of the population. Already, less than ten years after the reconstruction of Mulholland's great cotton mill, burnt down and rebuilt as a steam-driven flax-spinning mill, Belfast was the chief centre in the country for steam engine installations. Moreover, the small industry in engine design and manufacture already existing locally soon began to expand and diversify in an attempt to cater for the requirements of the new industrial growth. Firms like Samuel Boyd & Co of Donegall Street and the Lagan Foundry of Coates & Young (later Victor Coates & Co Ltd), founded at the end of the 18th century, were soon joined by several other engineering foundries producing steam engines.

Industrial steam engines in Ireland, 1838.

Of these the most important were John Rowan & Sons of York Street and Combe, Barbour & Combe of the Falls Foundry, between the Falls and Shankill Roads.

By the end of the 19th century the steam engine had altered greatly from the original beam design as perfected by James Watt in the closing years of the 18th century. The beam engine design itself was considerably altered and new types of engine emerged. Up until the beginning of the 19th century the steam engine operated as a result of a difference in pressure between the Earth's atmosphere, or between a body of steam at a pressure very slightly above that of atmosphere, and that in a vacuum which had been induced artificially. Watt resolutely opposed the use of high pressure steam and it was Richard Trevithick in Britain and Oliver Evans in America who first made important experiments in the use of steam at pressures up to ten times that of atmosphere. It was Trevithick who first applied steam power to locomotion on iron rails and these early engines

Cities and Towns.	No. of Engines.	Date of Erection.	Horse Power.	For what Purpose Employed.
BELFAST, and its Neighbourhood,*	1	1806	20	Spinning Cotton Yarn
,,	1	1810	20	Foundry
,,	1	1810	32	Spinning Cotton Yarn
,,	1	1812	10	Making Paper
,,	1	1817	40	Making Whiskey
,,	1	1824	60	Spinning and Weaving Cotton
,,	1	1825	20	Grinding Wheat
,,	1	1825	40	Spinning Cotton Yarn
,,	1	1825	60	Spinning Linen Yarn
,,	1	1826	5	Foundry
,,	1	1826	15	Spinning Linen Yarn
,,	1	1827	16	Foundry
,,	1	1830	16	Cleansing the Docks
,,	1	1832	1½	Grinding Coffee
,,	1	1832	20	Spinning Linen Yarn
,,	1	1833	6	Grinding Bones for Manure
,,	1	1833	8	Making Starch
,,	1	1833	30	Spinning Linen Yarn
,,	1	1833	50	Ditto
,,	1	1834	16	Ditto
,,	1	1834	35	Ditto
,,	1	1834	100	Ditto
,,	1	1835	8	Making Lime
,,	1	1835	15	Bleaching and Dyeing
,,	1	1835	16	Spinning Linen Yarn
,,	1	1835	16	Ship-yard Foundry
,,	1	1835	40	Spinning Linen Yarn
,,	1	1835	40	Ditto
,,	1	1835	40	Grinding Wheat
,,	1	1835	60	Spinning Linen Yarn
,,	1	1836	4½	Making Sheet Lead, &c.
,,	1	1836	8	Machine Making
,,	1	1836	10	Foundry
,,	1	1836	16	Ditto
,,	1	1837	1	Grinding Drugs and Paints
,,	1	1837	3	Making Files
,,	1	1837	4	Making Stucco and Roman Cement
,,	1	1837	8	Making Chimney Pieces, &c.
,,	1	1837	18	Spinning Linen Yarn
,,	1	1838	40	Ditto
,,	1	—	10	Grinding Corn
,,	1	—	10	Calico Printing and Dyeing
,,	1	—	16	Grinding Wheat
,,	1	—	20	Spinning Linen Yarn
,,	1	—	30	Bleaching
,,	1	—	30	Calico Printing and Dyeing
,,	1	—	30	Spinning Linen Yarn
,,	1	—	40	Ditto
,,	1	—	60	Spinning Cotton and Linen Yarn
,,	1	—	60	Spinning Linen Yarn
Total, -	50	—	1,274	

The uses of industrial steam power in Belfast in the year 1838.

VICTOR COATES & Co.
LIMITED,
Lagan Foundry & Prince's Dock Works,
BELFAST.

MAKERS OF ALL KINDS OF
FIRST-CLASS HIGH PRESSURE BEAM, HORIZONTAL AND VERTICAL ENGINES,
COMPOUND, CONDENSING, OR OTHERWISE,

With Corliss Valves, and Patent SILENT Release Motion for same, or Improved Slide and Cut-off Valves.

ALL BRANCHES OF
HIGH-CLASS MILL GEARING,
Including Rope and Strap Drums for Main Driving and General Purposes.

LANCASHIRE, CORNISH, and MARINE BOILERS,
CONSTRUCTED ON THE MOST APPROVED MODERN PRINCIPLES.

From long experience and extensive business connections with the leading Distillery and Brewery Firms of the Kingdom, Messrs. V. C. & Co., Limited, are in a position to supply all Modern Plant required in these important Home Industries.

Telegraphic Address—"LAGAN FOUNDRY, BELFAST."
Telephone No. 93.

An advertisement of 1887.

Makers' plates from Belfast-built steam engines.
(by courtesy of the Ulster Museum, Belfast)

founded the tradition which was to develop so dramatically both in western Europe and America in the second quarter of the 19th century. Only with the greater power of high pressure steam was the steam locomotive a practical proposition.

Hitherto the sheer size of the great low pressure stationary steam engines had made it impossible to adapt them for transport purposes. Soon the railways spread to Ireland and from the outset Irish companies built at least some of their locomotives locally. However fascinating, the story of the development of the steam locomotive in Ireland lies rather outside the scope of this book and to conclude our survey of industrial steam power in Ireland we must narrow our horizons somewhat and concentrate on the main landmarks occurring in the 19th century.

As we have seen the first of Watt's pumping engines reached Ireland in the 1780s, to be followed some ten years later by rotative engines driving textile machinery, mainly in the north of the country. The case history of an individual engine illustrates the technical links which existed between Ireland and Great Britain at the time: it would appear that a large beam pumping engine from the Soho Foundry was brought over to Dublin in 1804 for the municipal waterworks but, in fact, was never installed there, being bought by John Jameson & Son,

A model of Richard Trevithick's locomotive built for the Penydarran mineral *rail-way* in south Wales, 1804. This was the first steam engine to run on rails.

(Science Museum, London)

Richard Trevithick (1771-1833), from a portrait in oils by Linnell, 1816.

(Science Museum, London)

In 1839 the Dublin and Kingstown Railway Company, whose line between these two places had been opened in 1834, began to build its own locomotives in Dublin. *Princess* was the first railway engine to be built in Ireland.

(reproduced by permission of Ian Allan Ltd)

the large city distillers, in 1808 and erected at their works in Bow Street, on the north bank of the Liffey, near the Four Courts. Though modified in the 1880s and with substantial replacements early in the present century, this massive *house-built* engine (ie the engine house was built around the engine at the time of installation) may well retain parts of the original Watt design and provides an excellent idea of the scale of the engineering involved at that time.

As the century progressed so the beam engine design evolved and altered. The main advance came in 1845 when William McNaught of Glasgow patented a *compounding* of the normal beam engine by adding a high pressure cylinder on the other side of the fulcrum from the original low pressure. By using the same steam twice, first in the high pressure cylinder, then in the low pressure cylinder adjoining, this increased both economy of working and overall efficiency by encouraging smoother running. Many old beam engines were given a new lease of life by this addition and nearly all beam engines constructed after that time were built to compound designs. In Britain these engines reached enormous proportions, house-built in great soaring cathedrals of ornate Victorian brick and tile. Such installations were not typical of Ireland, however, and those compound beam engines which do exist here are of more modest proportions, though still impressive by local standards.

The large *house-built* beam engine in John Jameson's former Bow Street distillery, Dublin. It is a single cylinder design with a cast-iron beam 18ft long and a fly-wheel 22ft in diameter. Disused since 1932, this remarkable survival may incorporate features of a Boulton and Watt engine installed here in 1808.

(by courtesy of Dr Gavin Bowie)

The pumping station at Ryhope, near Sunderland in County Durham, is a distinctive example of Victorian industrial architecture at its best. The buildings here date from 1866-7. The entire installation is now preserved and administered by a trust.

(by courtesy of the Ryhope Engines Trust)

The original beam engine of Newcomen and Watt was soon joined by two other basic designs, the *horizontal* and *vertical* engine. In the horizontal engine the long axis of the cylinder is in a horizontal plane and the piston moves horizontally. This type of engine became common in Britain from the 1820s for driving mill machinery but it was another thirty years or so before it gained much of a foothold in Ireland.

Towards the end of the 19th century great compound horizontal engines were introduced, operating on steam pressures of 130-160lb per square inch. These generated upwards of 2,000 hp and to cope with this power output rope transmissions from a grooved flywheel became common, with great rope *races* linking the engine flywheel with the shafting on various mill floors. These huge engines could be *cross compound,* with cylinders on either side of a central flywheel, or *tandem,* with cylinders in line and the flywheel adjacent to one end of the engine.

The *vertical* engine emerged rather later in the century (c1850) and developed directly from the steam hammer of James Nasmyth. In the vertical design the cylinders overhang the crankshaft, the pistons move up and down in the cylinders in a vertical plane, and the power stroke is transmitted downwards by connecting rods to the crankshaft.

A horizontal, single cylinder, non-condensing steam engine, a typical small mill engine of the late 19th century.

The smaller (150hp) of two compound beam engines in Power's John's Lane distillery, Dublin. It was built in 1886 by Turnbull, Grant & Jack of Glasgow. The engine remains in working order and is run regularly.

(by permission of Irish Distillers Ltd)

A large (2000hp) cross compound, horizontal steam engine (high pressure cylinder, *Elizabeth*, on the right, low pressure cylinder, *Mary*, on the left) installed in a Lancashire cotton mill in 1919. The flywheel was 25ft in diameter, weighed 65 tons and was grooved for forty-two cotton transmission ropes.
(by courtesy of Mr George Watkins, Bath University)

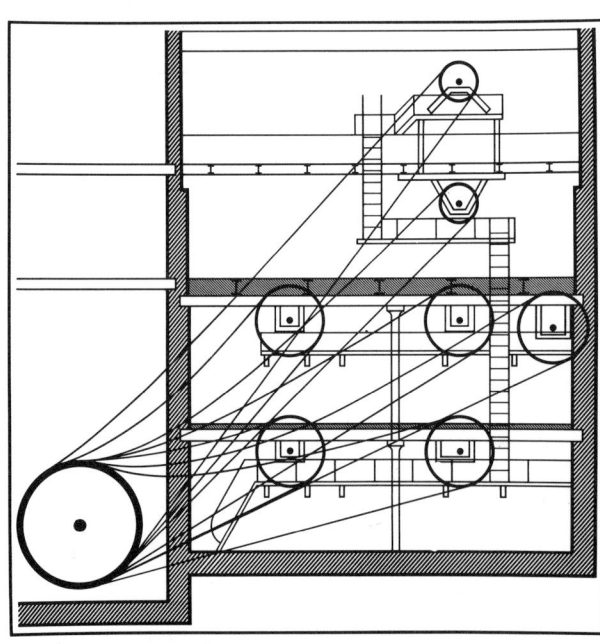

Rope transmission in a flax-spinning mill.

A compound vertical steam engine by Victor Coates & Co Ltd of Belfast, as illustrated in a brochure of *c* 1895. A large engine of this type can be seen in the Engineering Hall at the Ulster Museum.

The massive four crank, triple expansion engines of the TSS *Titanic*, built in Harland & Wolff's Belfast yard in 1910-11. Each engine, of which there were two, developed 17,000 hp at 77 rpm.

(by permission of Harland & Wolff Ltd)

Two typical generating sets of the inter-war years, with steam engines by Belliss & Morcom of Birmingham.
(by permission of the manufacturer)

An enclosed, tandem, compound, high-speed steam engine as produced by Musgrave & Co Ltd of Belfast, 1919.

Soon the vertical design achieved great popularity and such engines became common in the last quarter of the 19th century, operating pumps and machinery, blowing blast furnaces and driving great generators in factories and power stations. Moreover, from about 1860 the vertical engine became the most common type in large screw-propelled ships, with many triple and quadruple expansion marine-type engines of enormous size and power installed during the period 1880-1910, often in combination with low pressure steam turbines.

The final advance in the design of the steam engine came around 1890, with forced lubrication pumping oil automatically to all the main moving parts and bearing surfaces. This allowed the engine to run non-stop at high speed for long periods without excessive wear.

For a time in Britain enclosed, high-speed engines were used in the new power stations then being built up and down the country to give a centralised electricity supply but here they were soon replaced by the steam turbine of Sir Charles Parsons, invented in 1884. Parsons was a member of a talented Irish family, the sixth and youngest son of the third Earl of Rosse, the distinguished engineer and astronomer. The family seat, Birr Castle, County Offaly, with its huge telescope, was a rendezvous for scientists and astronomers from all over Europe. Quite a number of enclosed, high-speed or *quick revolution* engines, by such British makers as Belliss and Morcom, **Howden**, Browett Lindley, Allen etc, remain in use in Ireland, in such places as hospitals, laundries, saw mills, pumping stations, gas works and factories, where they are directly coupled to electric generators producing current for internal use. However, their numbers have been greatly reduced since the end of the Second World War as the overall demand for alternating current increases and larger, more modern machinery, designed to run continuously at speeds beyond the limits of such individual installations, requires an assured supply, forthcoming only from the grid systems of distribution run by the centralised generating authorities, North and South.

In the wet spinning room of a Belfast mill

3 Industrial Machinery

In the previous two chapters we have examined the main sources of industrial power in Ireland, and in particular the developments of the 19th and early 20th centuries. In this chapter we shall examine a few of the machines through which power was applied to manufacturing processes. Here we are concerned not only with how the power of the prime mover was conveyed or transmitted from the point at which it was generated to where it was used, but more especially with the machinery devised and designed to apply that power to a number of industrial processes, all of some importance in the historical development of Irish technology. The examples chosen are:

(a) the 'tilt' or 'trip' hammer
(b) flax-scutching 'handles'
(c) the 'patent', continuous still
(d) the 'flyer and bobbin' spinning frame
(e) the 'stocks' or 'feet' of the 'tuck' mill and 'wash mill'
(f) beetling 'engines'

(a) the 'tilt' or 'trip' hammer

The evolution of the powered hammer presents an interesting study in industrial technology. It seems likely that from an early stage heavy manual work in forge and smithy was replaced by mechanically-driven devices, of which the oliver, a light treadle-operated hammer was one. The shaft of the hammer was fixed to an oscillating cross beam and when the smith pressed the treadle the hammer was brought down on to the anvil, recovering as he released the treadle through the springy action of the sapling, fixed at the other end and with a central fulcrum in a forked stick.

Soon, however, the greater power of the waterwheel was applied to metal working and the trip or tilt hammer, as we know it, emerged in western Europe. In Ireland it was applied mainly to spade forging though in some iron-making areas of Britain it was used for shingling (hammering) wrought iron bloom (slabs) from the finery and also, in a different building, for working the bloom up into shapes suitable for sale.

The origins of the water-driven tilt hammer are somewhat obscure but it seems likely that it evolved in the rich, mining regions of central Europe and Scandinavia in the 11th and 12th centuries. It was a relatively simple yet very effective device.

The German hammer shown overleaf worked as follows: the short arm of the lever, struck down by the cams around the circumference of the cam-drum fixed to the wheelshaft, was driven against the end of a recoil block and immediately rebounded, causing the long arm to strike firmly downwards against the anvil surface. Sometimes a wooden spring beam, fixed above the hammer, increased the force of the hammer blow.

Joseph Wright of Derby depicts the interior of an iron forge (1772) with a water-driven tilt hammer at work, beating a bloom of wrought iron from the finery hearth. Two points emerge from this fine painting: firstly, the conditions under which the heavy, noisy machinery is being operated, with several members of the ironmaster's family, including his wife and young children, close to the centre of activity; and secondly, the lateral (side) lift of the hammer instead of the more normal end lift, as described above. In this respect the painting compares with the bloom-forging hammers illustrated in Diderot's monumental encylopaedia of 1763.

Turning now to Ireland we find that the principle of the trip hammer was particularly important in the numerous water-driven spade mills, which were widely distributed from Cork to Antrim, though with a striking northern predominance. A billet of wrought iron, heated in the furnace, was drawn out to the size and shape required for the particular order in hand. In Ireland the number and diversity of spade types have been the subject of several detailed surveys, particularly by the Ulster Folk and Transport Museum, and in the wooded park which surrounds the main museum building at Cultra, near Holywood, in County Down, a water-driven spade mill from Coalisland, County Tyrone, has been rebuilt and works regularly, with two waterwheels driving a tilt hammer and ancillary machinery.

In Ireland the raw material for most spade mills was obtained by melting down scrap metal or by importing billets of wrought iron through Londonderry, Newry and Cork. The manufacture of spades and shovels was carried on in workshops which in their development were mid-way between the village smithy

The treadle-operated *oliver*.

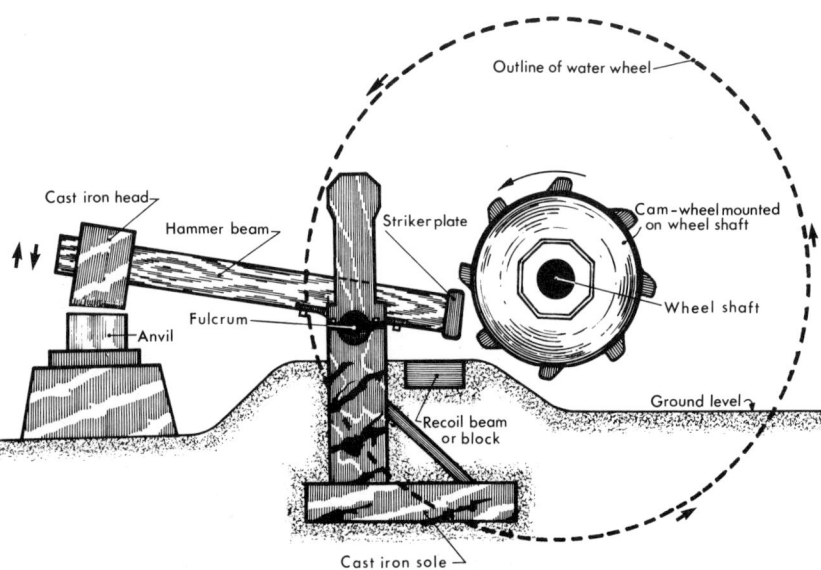

The water-driven *trip* or *tilt* hammer.

and the early steel forge, with trip hammers, bellows, grindstones, shearing machines, etc, driven by water power, but with an emphasis on individual craftsmanship reflecting the traditional skills of the medieval smith.

At Monard, about four miles from Cork, no less than eight waterwheels remain *in situ*, with two tilt hammers, amidst an elongated complex of industrial buildings, mill ponds, workers' houses, weirs, furnaces, etc. This was an important industrial site for over one hundred and seventy years, from its foundation in the 1790s, and with its picturesque setting in a deep wooded glen straddled by the great railway viaduct of 1849, it could become the centrepiece of a park of rural life and industry which would add immensely to the attractive character of this part of Munster.

To complete the sequence of development of the powered hammer it is now necessary to consider two further types, the *helve* hammer and the *steam* hammer. While neither of these was used in Irish spade mills they were important in Britain in the furnaces and forges of the iron-making districts of the Midlands and the North. Moreover, several of the largest engineering firms in Belfast, and the giant shipyard of Harland & Wolff Ltd, had steam hammers for reshaping and forming wrought iron and mild steel.

The helve hammer has certain similarities to the trip hammer, but also important differences. Thus, whereas the trip or tilt hammer was a lever of the first order, with a fulcrum somewhere near the centre of the hammer beam and a pivoting

An Iron Forge (1772) by Joseph Wright of Derby.
(by courtesy of the Trustees of the British Museum)

A *tilt* hammer being used to forge the *bloom* in the making of wrought iron, 1763.

movement about this, from a cam-wheel or drum at one end to the hammer itself at the other, the helve hammer was a second order lever, with a fulcrum at one end, the cam-wheel at the other and the hammer in between.

Moreover, the trip hammer, because of its more flexible nature, dealt relatively fast, light blows: the helve hammer, on the other hand, was a solid casting, rigid, heavy and inflexible, which was used extensively in the production of wrought iron for shingling or hammering irregular balls of iron into rectangular blooms or slabs, suitable for rolling. The helve hammer weighed anything from five to ten tons and delivered its blows at approximately one per second. It was usually driven from a stationary steam engine.

While the helve hammer dominated the shingling process up until the mid-19th century, and survived in some areas until the 1920s, it was largely replaced by the steam hammer, invented by James Nasmyth of Manchester in 1839. This was a more useful machine than the helve hammer, placing enormous, controlled power at the command of the engineer. It could be used for shingling but became of greater importance for forging

and pile driving. The steam hammer was simply an *inverted* steam engine cylinder — indeed the first steam engines built to the vertical design, with cylinders overhanging the crankshaft, were called *inverted verticals* — fixed on top of a massive iron frame, with the heavy iron hammer fitted on the end of the piston rod.

In simple terms, steam pressure from below was used to raise the piston. When the piston approached the top of its stroke steam was admitted *above* the piston and at the same time the steam below was exhausted. The great weight of the hammer as it fell was thus supplemented by the direct, downward driving force of live steam. Moreover, to increase the force of the downward stroke a quantity of steam retained in the upper part of the cylinder as the piston was forced upwards acted as a buffer or cushion. Much larger forgings could now be made because of the greater space between the hammer and the striking surface, and with the greatly increased power of the hammer itself.

To gain an impression of the revolutionary power of the new hammer, the following account of the pile driving operations for

Spade making at Monard, County Cork, in the 1930s.

(by courtesy of Mr Alec Day FRPS)

The *helve* hammer.

Fulcrum

Helve

Head

Anvil

Cam

Cam ring
(cast iron)

James Nasmyth's steam hammer.

- Upper steam inlet
- Steam cylinder
- Valve chest (controlling lower and upper inlets)
- Piston rod
- Valve control screw rod
- Hammer-head
- Work-piece
- Frame
- Anvil

A manuscript page from one of James Nasmyth's *scheme books* showing his initial thoughts on the steam hammer, November, 1839. Note in the bottom right hand corner such cryptic remarks as:

'... farewell to all your big helve forge hammers ...'

and under a thumb-nail sketch of a helve hammer the words:

'... all over now with such a monster ...'

Finally at the extreme bottom right hand corner we see the 'old helve hammer', now roughly sketched in human form, about to be beheaded by 'J.N.'

(by permission of John Murray Ltd, London)

the railway bridge linking Newcastle and Gateshead across the deep valley of the river Tyne, carried out in 1846-7, captures much of the adventurous spirit of Victorian engineering on a grand scale:

'. . . the first difficulty encountered in building the bridge was in securing a solid foundation for the piers. The dimensions of the piles to be driven were so huge, that the engineer found it necessary to employ some extra-ordinary means for the purpose. He called Nasmyth's Titanic steam-hammer to his aid — the first occasion, we believe, on which this prodigious power was employed in bridge pile-driving. A temporary staging was erected for the steam-engine and hammer apparatus, which rested on two keels, and, notwithstanding the newness and stiffness of the machinery, the first pile was driven on the 6th of October, 1846, to a depth of 32 feet, in four minutes. Two hammers of 30 cwt. each were kept in regular use, making from 60 to 70 strokes per minute; and the results were astounding to those who had been accustomed to the old style of pile-driving by means of the ordinary pile-frame, consisting of slide, ram, and monkey . . .'

(from Samuel Smiles, *Lives of the Engineers,* Vol. 3, 1862, 'Robert Stephenson')

(b) flax-scutching 'handles'

Flax is a fibre which comes from the stem of the flax plant. The valuable fibres in the outer stem were prepared for separation from the useless core by *retting,* ie the *beets* or bundles of flax were immersed in ponds or dams in the fields for ten to fourteen days to encourage a chemical decomposition of stalk tissue. When the retted flax was dried the stems could readily be *broken* and the unwanted *shows* or *boon* beaten off by hand or by machinery in a process known as *scutching.*

Hand scutching characterised the domestic Irish linen industry from the 17th century onwards but soon attempts were made to harness the power of water in the scutching process. After a period of experimentation with small horizontal mills, with a single upright shaft carrying the wooden blades, boxed in like millstones, the more familiar type, with horizontal shafting, was generally accepted. In 1783 William Hincks clearly illustrated the two basic processes being carried out in these new water-driven flax mills.

At the time of the first Valuation Survey of the country, in the 1830s, there were over a thousand scutch mills in Ireland, a figure which had increased to some 1,500 by the 1860s, of which the vast majority were in Ulster. From then on there was a steady decline into the present century and while the stimulus of two

A water-powered flax breaking and scutching mill, 1783, from an engraving by William Hincks. In the foreground a man feeds bundles of retted, dried flax stems into grooved or fluted rollers, driven from the pit wheel; these break or loosen the useless parts of the stem and prepare the flax for the scutching blades. In the background, through a doorway, a scutcher holds the *stricks* of bruised or broken flax to the rapidly rotating flax-scutching *handles.* These beat off the unwanted pith and skin (*shows* or *boon*) and leave the flax relatively clean, ready for hackling, preparing and spinning.

Flax scutching: thirteen *berths* are being used here.

world wars caused a temporary upsurge of the flax-growing industry, the water-driven scutch mill is now but an industrial relic in the Irish countryside.

A typical scutch mill of the mid-19th century consisted of a single story, rectangular stone house, measuring perhaps 30ft by 20ft. A breastshot waterwheel, 12 or 13ft in diameter and perhaps two feet six inches wide, drove a horizontal scutching shaft. Arranged along this shaft at intervals would be four or five scutching *stands* or *berths* (the recesses built above and around the shaft, in each of which stood a scutcher) with a couple more at the end for *targing* the *tow* (the coarse, matted reject of the first scutching):

'. . . the scutching apparatus consists of a horizontal shaft to which are attached at intervals, like radii of a circle, short arms, to which are nailed the stocks, which are parallelogram-shaped blades of hardwood, with the edges partially sharpened. The labourer stands beside an upright wooden plank and laying a handful of bruised flax straw across it, or in some mills thrusting it through a horizontal slit near its top edge, he exposes one half of the flax in his hand to the action of the stocks, which revolve with rapidity along the shaft and strike the flax straw, beating off the ligneous matter and leaving the

fibre clear. When the end exposed to the stocks is cleaned, the workman turns the handful and exposes the other end. It is usual to have a set of either two or three men, at as many different *stands,* and instead of each thoroughly cleaning out the handful of flax, he only partially does so; the second then takes it up and finishes it; or, if there be three in the set, he does not quite clean it but hands it over to the third to do so. In the latter case the first workman is called the *buffer,* the second the *middler* and the third the *finisher* . . .'

(from Dr. Ure's *Dictionary of Arts, Manufactures & Mines, 1878)*

The mill could be kept going all year by devoting the summer months to the dressing or targing of the tow resulting from the previous winter's scutching.

For many years controversy raged as to the best number of *wiper blades* on the shaft at each berth. In some mills there were only four or five, in others seven or eight. A smaller number of blades made for the production of a more evenly scutched flax because with the relatively high speed of the horizontal shaft (around 240 rpm) a larger number did not give the flax being scutched sufficient time to recover between blows. With five or six blades only on each *rim* the flax stems were allowed

A country scutcher at work, County Antrim.

(from a photograph taken by Mr Hallam Ashley, FRPS in the late 1930s, reproduced by courtesy of Mr Rex Wailes)

Flax-scutching handles: Allistragh, County Armagh. The central *rim* and the wooden *wiper blades* together make up a *scutching handle*. Here there are six blades on each handle.

to rise up after the passage of each wiper blade, presenting a more open target to the next. The main reason why the five or six bladed *handle* (iron rim and wooden blades) was not universally adopted was because many mill owners considered it too effective, removing parts of the flax stem in the scutching process which might well have been accepted by the average buyer.

The waterwheel and power transmission of the mid-19th century flax mill deserve further attention. Only two or three horsepower were needed for a four-berth scutch mill and the waterwheel was, therefore, often of a lighter construction than in the country corn mill. It was usually a breast wheel of one sort or another, with wooden arms and drumming, metal shrouding and axle. In many flax-scutching mills the transmission inside the mill, conveying the power of the wheel to the scutching shaft, often had *double gearing*. This was necessary to bridge the gap between the slow-moving waterwheel and the rapidly turning scutching shaft, a ratio of perhaps 1 to 24.

Flax-scutching handles: Carrickmannan, County Down. These are particularly crude scutching handles, with no central rim but merely a casting keyed on to the shaft, into which short arms are socketed and bolted. To these arms are fastened the wiper blades, five to each handle.

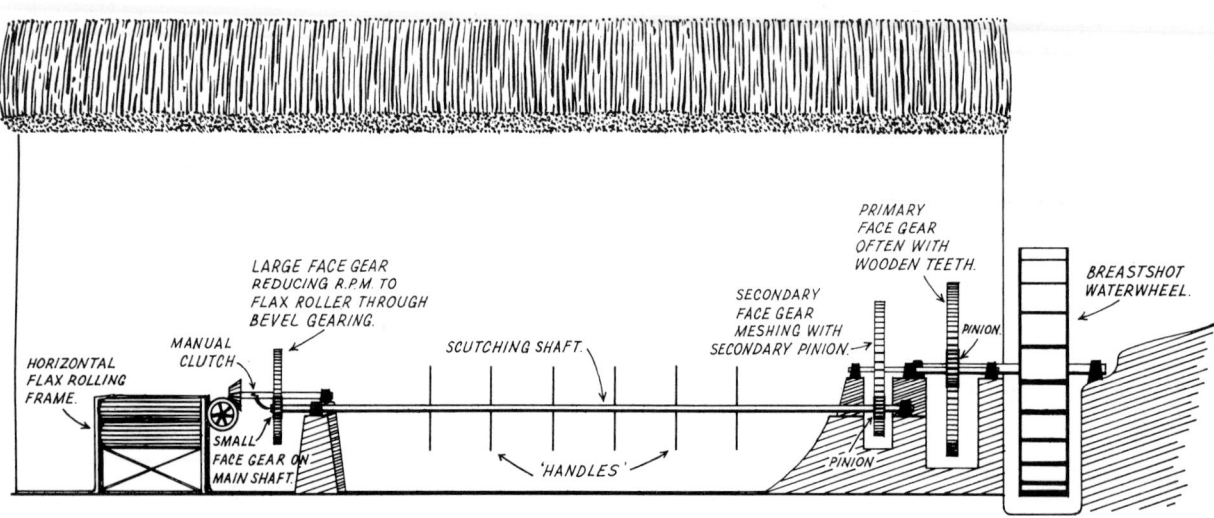

Diagrammatic section through a water-driven flax-scutching mill, with internal double gearing.

At least one of the gear wheels in this internal transmission was usually equipped with hardwood teeth.

The invention of the *horizontal breaker* in the mid-19th century was a major advance in flax-mill technology. Such frames, driven from the horizontal scutching shaft, were a considerable improvement on the *upright rollers*, as depicted in the 18th century engraving. They reflect the growing demand for scutched flax from the great steam-powered spinning mills which sprang up throughout the north of Ireland, in particular, in the years following the interruption of raw cotton supplies resulting from the American Civil War (1861-5).

Foundries in Belfast, Coleraine and Strabane specialised in scutch mill machinery.

A horizontal flax-breaking frame by the MacAdam Brothers of Belfast, *c* 1870.

Double gearing in a former water-powered flax-scutching mill, Shannaragh, near Dromore, County Tyrone. The waterwheel shaft here, coming in from outside the mill, ends in the gear wheel (A) which drove the pinion (B). The drive then passed to (C) and finally to the pinion (D), on the end of the scutching shaft. The teeth in (C) are hardwood, for smoother running and ease of repair. If a tooth broke it could easily be replaced.

From a brochure of *c* 1910.

(c) the 'patent', continuous still

To appreciate fully the importance of the *patent*, continuous still in the distilling process it is necessary to consider both the processes leading up to the distilling proper, and the nature of the stills in existence before the introduction of the continuous still to Ireland in the 1830s.

In a grain whiskey distillery a mixture of cooked maize and *malt* (germinated barley) is ground and the resulting grist is infused with hot water in a large circular cast-iron *mash tun* or *kieve*. The solution is called *wort* and in its formation the mixture of malt, hot water, weak wort from an earlier brew, raw grain, etc, is continually stirred to ensure thorough mixing and the disintegration of clots, and to prevent the mash from *setting*. While the stirring was done originally using manual *oars,* the increasing size of the mash tuns soon led to the application of power-driven, rotating *rakes.*

The mash tun has a perforated bottom and after the mashing process is complete the worts are drained off into an *under-back* and subsequently passed to coolers, before being fermented in a *wash back* with the addition of yeast.

Unlike the mashing process, which is relatively brief, fermentation takes two days. The fermented wash then passes to a *wash charger,* thence to the *still house.*

The original Irish *pot still* was a copper container or *kettle* set over a fire, with a *still head* to transmit the rising vapours to a *worm,* a spiral pipe immersed in cold water, where condensation occurred. To this day most Irish whiskey comes from pot stills, but while distillation of pot whiskey is a *batch* process, with the stills emptied on the conclusion of each run, in the 1830s a very different type of still, allowing relatively continuous production, was introduced. Whereas hitherto in the production of whiskey there had usually been three distillations in separate pot stills, the still patented by an Irishman, Aeneas Coffey, in 1830 introduced a new dimension to the industry. His still soon came into general use in many distilleries in Ireland, but more particularly in Scotland where a large number of Coffey stills were installed in the mid-19th century, manufactured in his works at Bromley in London. Much of the grain whiskey being produced today in Scotland for blending comes from improved versions of the Coffey still and there are continuous stills of this type at Irish distilleries in Middleton, County Cork and Coleraine, County Derry.

There had been earlier stills of the Coffey type, notably in France, but only with the design outlined by this former Inspector General in the Excise Department in Ireland did the continuous production of spirit over several days, from the contents of a batch of wash backs, become a practical possibility.

What is the principle of the Coffey still and how does it

The rake machinery in a *mash tun* or *kieve.*

(by permission of Irish Distillers Ltd)

Pot stills in the John's Lane distillery, Dublin, of Sir John Power & Son, 1887. These large copper vessels have an approximate capacity of 20,000 gallons each.

work? Basically it operates on a heat exchange process, taking in a continuous supply of cold wash and discharging a continuous flow of spirit. It is quite different in appearance from the older pot still, consisting of two very tall *fractionating columns,* one called the *analyser* for stripping the wash of spirit, the other the *rectifier* for producing, consolidating and purifying the spirit. The two columns, wood lined with copper, may be 80 or 90 feet tall. Each is divided into a number of chambers or frames by metal plates which for the most part are perforated and interconnected by *downcomers,* vertical pipes which dip into a cup on the lower of the two plates concerned.

The wash is pumped from the wash charger, fed from the wash backs, and enters the worm tube (at A), which passes from top to bottom of the rectifier. The wash pump is switched off and the pipe containing the cold wash is heated by the admission of steam from the boiler. The wash pump is restarted and the hot wash being pumped across from the rectifier (at B) now spills out upon the uppermost plate of the analyser (at C), until this overflows downwards to the second plate via the downcomers, and so on to the bottom. Through this downward flow of hot wash very hot steam, entering at D, passes upwards through the fine perforations in the shelves of the analyser. No wash can escape downwards through these fine perforations, only by the downcomers provided (at E).

As the wash descends in the analyser it becomes gradually weaker as the volatile elements boil away quickly. By the time it arrives at the bottom all traces of spirit have been removed and the resulting spent wash is drained away at F.

At the same time the rising steam becomes a spirit-laden vapour, richer in alcohol and containing less and less water as it ascends. It passes from the top of the analyser at G and in at the bottom of the rectifier at H. The internal lay-out of the rectifier or purifying column is somewhat different from that of the analyser. The top ten plates or so are *not* perforated and between the top two or three is the cooling worm. At alternate ends of these solid plates there are spaces to permit the flow of liquid and vapours.

The remaining plates, down to the bottom of the column, are perforated, as in the analyser, and are linked by downcomers.

The wash pipe, which enters near the top, winds its way in and out of each chamber. The external loops, between the chambers, are known as the *bends.* This wash pipe extends upwards from the bottom of the rectifier and enters at the top of the analyser.

The analyser or stripping column

The rectifier or purifying column

'. . . we noticed that all the bottles and cases bore the trademark of "H.C." and on asking for an explanation we were informed that since the year 1845 this [Coleraine] Whisky has been supplied to the House of Commons, and therefore the proprietor has adopted "H.C." as a trademark . . .'

Coleraine Whiskey

The Spaniard may boast of his shadow,
    The Frenchman his sparkling champagne,
But if a man wants to be merry
    I'd advise him to thry Ould Coleraine.

If you search in the annals of hist'ry
    Till the time of the Roman and Dane,
You'll find it was reckon'd a mist'ry
    How they made such good stuff in Coleraine.

You've all heard of Barney McCleary,
    And the buttermilk waterin' the plain,
And the pitcher, the pride of the dairy,
    That Kitty got smashed in Coleraine.

But I'll tell you a saycret this minit,
    I know you won't tell it again,
Of milk sorra taste there was in it,
    She was smugglin' a drop of Coleraine.

(Chorus)
Then hurrah for the trim little boro'
    And the Bann as it runs thro' the plain;
Its waters they banish all sorrow,
    When mixed with a drop of Coleraine.

James Feehan

Top, a late 19th century malt whiskey label. Both quotation and poem are taken from Alfred Barnard, *The Whisky Distilleries of the United Kingdom,* 1887

The continuous spirit still patented by Aeneas Coffey in 1830. (based on a drawing in *The World Atlas of Wine* by Hugh Johnson—copyright Hugh Johnson and Mitchell Beazley Ltd 1971—by permission of the author and publishers)

To return to our consideration of the passage of the spirit-laden vapour entering the rectifier from the analyser at H: as it begins to rise in this column it comes in contact with the relatively cold wash in the wash pipe and this causes the less volatile elements, called *feints,* to condense and collect at the bottom. From here they are drained off at I and are pumped back up to the top of the analyser at J, joining the fresh wash as it begins its descent through the analyser.

Most of the vapour entering the rectifier from the analyser rises further, however, and as some of it condenses on the perforated plates (in a heat exchange with the relatively cool wash pipe) is subject to a continuous upward movement from below of hot, spirit-laden vapour. This causes vaporisation and a steady upward bubbling of vapour through the perforated plates gives an enrichment of the vapour in the chamber above. In fact, a *series of distillations* takes place continuously in each of the chambers of the rectifier, with the alcohol being distilled over and over again as it rises through the column in vapour form. Finally, when it has reached the required strength, at the top of the column, it is brought in contact with the cooling worm (at K), and rapidly condenses. The spirit thus formed then collects on the lowest of the unperforated plates and is tapped by the distiller at L.

The patent, continuous still is extremely efficient in stripping and consolidating spirit from a continuous charge of wash, the spirit drawn from the rectifier being about 65 over proof, or very little short of pure alcohol.

Coffey's still was not an immediate success in Ireland but it was widely adopted in Scotland for the large scale production of grain whiskey. By 1852, when Coffey died at Bromley at the age of seventy two, the importance of the new still was firmly established, its standing then being summarised as follows:

'. . . the product of the Coffey still requires only dilution to be at once marketable. Most of the Scotch whiskey sold in England is manufactured by this still. It is characterised by the absence of any marked flavour, except in a very faint degree, in consequence of the method of distillation preventing the less volatile fusel oil, and other strong scented products of fermentation, from passing over with the spirit. Malt whiskey (made from malted grain) contains those flavouring ingredients which certain connoisseurs prefer: the *small still* whiskey of the Scotch smuggler, and the *potheen* (the Irish equivalent of the small still, or *little pot*) being prized for their *peat-reek* or *turf-smoke* flavour. In the manufacture of these malt whiskeys, in which potatoes and treacle or sugar are sometimes used, and sometimes raw grain, but this only to a small extent, the old fashioned simple still, endlessly varied but generally with a high head, is employed. Two thirds or more of what is called malt whiskey, and sold as such, is in fact grain whiskey flavoured with a dose of the most odorous malt spirit . . .'
(from Tomlinson's *Encylopaedia of Useful Arts,* 1852)

The principle of a rising vapour getting richer in alcohol as it reaches the upper parts of the analyser was so effective in deriving the greatest possible percentage of spirit from the wash that it has survived, little altered, to this day. Naturally, the Coffey still was improved and modified as the century proceeded, but the advantages of whiskey produced in this way have ensured that the ingenuity and practical ability of this remarkable exciseman would remain one of Ireland's more constructive contributions to the distiller's art.

(d) the 'flyer and bobbin' spinning frame

Spinning is the process of drawing out and twisting fibres into a continuous yarn. At first this basic craft was carried out on a primitive hand-operated *spindle and whorl,* and over many centuries this simple device evolved into the *spindle wheel,* in which the spindle was mounted on two support bearings and the whorl acted as a driving pulley, still turned by hand. The whorl was then grooved, making it possible to drive it with a cord or belt from a treadle mechanism and leaving both hands free for spinning.

On both spindle and whorl, and spindle wheel, the art of spinning involved two distinct processes, *spinning* and *winding on.* One had to draw out and twist (spin) the fibres into yarn, and only then could one wind this yarn on to the spindle. Naturally this limited yarn production severely and kept spinning very much at the level of a menial domestic chore.

Then around 1500 came the sudden break-through — the advance from the spindle wheel to the *spinning wheel,* by which simultaneous spinning and winding on were possible. Exactly where this important development first occurred is uncertain but the spinning wheel is described in some detail in Leonardo da Vinci's great *Codex Atlanticus* of c1490 in a form closely similar to but not identical with that which was subsequently widely adopted. This was the work of a German wood carver, Johann Jürgen of Saxony, who put forward his ideas around 1530.

Jürgen used the spindle as an axle, on which he mounted a U-shaped *flyer* (1). This axle, and the flyer on it, were driven by a cord passing round the circumference of the spinning wheel and across on to a small pulley wheel on the axle (2).

The working principle of Jürgen's spinning wheel, 1530.

DRIVE CORD

HOOKS OR HACKS (6)

FLYER SPINDLE

FLYER PULLEY (2)

BOBBIN (3)

BOBBIN PULLEY (4)

DRIVE CORD

FLYER SPINDLE (5)

FLYER (1)

Alongside the flyer on the spindle-axle was fitted a *bobbin* (3) which at one end had a grooved pulley wheel (4) driven by a second, separate cord from the spinning wheel circumference. Thus, flyer and bobbin revolved independently, the flyer mounted on the axle or spindle, the bobbin loosely fitted on it but separately driven.

The yarn being spun passed through a hole in the end of the spindle (5), thence down one of the arms of the flyer, over the hook or *hack* being used (6) and thence on to the bobbin. As the spinning wheel was turned by the operation of the treadle, both driving cords turned their respective pulleys. If the bobbin pulley was larger than the flyer pulley the bobbin itself turned more slowly than the flyer, and the spinning wheel was said to have *flyer lead*. If the reverse was the case and the bobbin rotated more quickly than the flyer, the wheel had *bobbin lead*. In either case the result was the same; the spun yarn was wound on to the bobbin as it came off the flyer and the drawing out, twisting and winding on of the yarn was now one smooth, continuous operation.

The main difference between Jürgen's wheel and that proposed by da Vinci some forty years previously was that whereas Jürgen relied on fixed hooks or hacks on the flyer arms as a means by which the spinster could alter the point at which yarn was building on to the bobbin, da Vinci's fertile imagination produced a much more satisfactory and ingenious device for accomplishing the same task. The flyer was made to move slowly to and fro as it turned, spreading the yarn evenly on to the bobbin.

However, for some reason unknown, the earlier idea of the *traversing flyer* was overlooked and most spinning wheels were built with flyers as designed by the German craftsman. It was not until the early years of the Industrial Revolution (*c*1770) that Richard Arkwright of Cromford in Derbyshire incorporated a device similar to that of da Vinci in his water-driven spinning frames, though here it was the bobbin and not the flyer which was made to traverse during spinning. This was the principle employed to achieve even winding on in all subsequent flyer spinning frames.

To return, for a moment, to the early spinning wheel — as we have seen, the wheel could have either *flyer lead* or *bobbin lead,* in either instance the yarn being wound on to the bobbin. This end could be achieved more simply by having only one driving pulley, on either bobbin or flyer, the non-driven component being rotated by the pull or drag of the yarn. This was the principle incorporated in Arkwright's early cotton-spinning machinery and in the *wet* flyer spinning frame of the Irish linen industry, described below.

Before proceeding to a consideration of this machine, however, the technical development of the hand-spinning process, which we have been reviewing, must be balanced with a brief summary of the nature and conditions of the hand spinning of flax yarn in Ireland in the 18th and early 19th centuries.

The hand-scutched and hackled (combed) flax was placed on a *distaff*, an upright stick, often elaborately carved, bracketed on to the wheel frame, and fed across to the flyer through the skilled fingers of the spinster, being drawn and rolled lightly in

The water-driven spinning frame of Richard Arkwright (1774) which incorporated a cam mechanism in the bobbin arrangement to ensure an even distribution of the spun yarn as it was being wound on.

(Science Museum, London)

the process.

After spinning the yarn was wound into a *hank* for washing, bleaching, sizing, or other treatment. The most common type of winder in Ireland was the *clock reel*, and after winding the hanks were boiled in soap or potash solution containing a little flour. After treatment the hanks (generally of 3,600 yards) were slipped over adjustable or conical hank holders and wound on to *spools* for the *warp*, or *pirns* for the *weft*. This was often done on a spindle wheel but in some areas special wheels, both hand turned and treadle operated, were in use.

Very fine yarns could be produced by Irish spinsters, up to a *count* of 250s lea (ie 250 x 300 yards = 1lb weight) and the traditional skill of Irish womenfolk, coupled with the extremely low wages which they were prepared to accept, ensured that hand spinning remained dominant until well into the 19th century. There were no advantages to be gained by installing relatively costly machinery, difficult to obtain from the makers in north Britain and central Scotland and impossible to maintain efficiently in a country at that time without any tradition in textile engineering, while finer yarns could be produced more cheaply and in sufficient quantity by the womenfolk in the home. As one prominent mill owner, Joseph Nicholson of Bessbrook, County Armagh, put it in 1810:

'. . . the leading cause against the extension of machinery is the low price of labour; yarn spun by women is sold here much cheaper than the article manufactured by machinery in England. In the latter country, the labouring classes have a choice of employments, in consequence of the variety of its manufactures. If one fail them, they can apply to another, but with us the case is different. When trade is bad its worst effects are felt by the poor women, who must sell at the prices of the day or remain unemployed and it frequently happens that they dispose of the worked article for less than the raw material cost them. To one unacquainted with Ireland the small earnings of the poorer females — frequently not more than two pence per day, working diligently from morning till night, for months together — must appear very extraordinary, and under such circumstances it is unlikely that this trade (power spinning by machinery) should increase so much as it might, though spurred on in the beginning by offers of large premiums from the Linen Board . . .'
(cited in Edward Wakefield, *An Account of Ireland, Statistical & Political*, 1812)

However, prompted by the granting of subsidies from the *Trustees of the Linen and Hempen Manufactures of Ireland* — the Linen Board, founded in 1711 — a number of water-driven spinning mills were established in Ireland at the beginning of the 19th century, the majority of them in the north of the country. By 1809 there were a dozen or so such mills in Ulster, with over 6,000 spindles, containing water-driven *dry* spinning frames producing relatively coarse yarns. This machinery was derived from the cotton-spinning machinery of Richard Arkwright with which the factory system had been introduced to Britain back in the 1770s. In Ireland, however, the bulk of the yarn produced in the first quarter of the 19th century was still spun in the home on individual wheels, with female hand spinners producing the entire range of yarns for skilled hand-loom weavers. Only in the coarser end of the range of spun flax yarns could the new machinery make any impact, and as the Irish manufacture had already established its reputation on the finest damasks, sheers and cambrics, the introduction of such machinery did not immediately revolutionise the Irish spinning industry.

The turning point came in 1825 when James Kay of Preston obtained a patent for the *wet* spinning of flax, a development which permitted the spinning of much finer yarns. Hitherto power spinning had been confined to coarse or medium yarns and to fully understand the break-through afforded by the invention of wet spinning, the nature of the flax fibre must be considered. Kay advocated that the flax *rove*, the continuous strand of loosely twisted fibres which was spun into yarn on the flax-spinning frame, should be steeped in cold water for five or six hours to loosen the gummy adhesive uniting the ultimate flax fibres, each about two inches long, so that these could be drawn out on the spinning frame to a much greater degree than formerly, thereby permitting the production of a finer yarn. Once the elementary short staples had been loosened in this way and drawn out on the spinning frame, the gummy solution would reharden and bind the fibres together as before. Kay also proposed that on the new spinning frames the *retaining* and *drawing* rollers (see p 66) should be brought much closer together than on the old dry-spinning frames, a point largely dictated by the nature of the steeped rove which could not be drawn out unsupported in the same way as the dry rove had been.

While the steeping of the rove in cold water was soon replaced by passing the rove through a trough of hot water on the spinning frame itself, the basic concept of wet spinning led to a rapid transformation in the Irish linen industry. The whole range of linen yarns could now be mill-spun and hand spinning soon declined to a position in which it was regarded as an alternative to being idle rather than as gainful employment. The following extract from the Ordnance Survey memoir for the parish of Templecorran, on the north shore of Belfast Lough, near Carrickfergus, County Antrim was written in 1839:

'. . . until within the last fifteen years the linen trade had afforded employment to a considerable proportion of the

AN ACCOUNT of BOUNTIES paid by the Trustees of the Linen and Hempen Manufactures of Ireland to encourage the Erection of SPINDLES attached to Mill-Machinery, in the PROVINCE of ULSTER, for Spinning Flax and Hemp, from the commencement to the conclusion of said Bounties.

County.	Next Post Town.	Name of Place.	Name of Claimant.	Spindles erected. Year.	No.	Rate per Spindle.	Date of Payment.	Amount of Payment. £. s. d.	Tot. Amount to each Claimant. £. s. d.
Antrim,	Ballymoney,	Balnamore,	Bryan, Josiah,	1809	400	30s.	May 7, 1810,	600 0 0	600 0 0
	Ballymena,	Knockbuoy,	Davison, Alexander,	1808	222	30s.	July 25, 1809,	333 0 0	333 0 0
	Crumlin,	Cyder Court,	Ferguson, John,	1809	768	30s.	April 17, 1810,	1,152 0 0	1,152 0 0
	Newtown Glens,	Kilnadore,	Younge, William and Co.	1809	512	30s.	April 17, 1810,	768 0 0	768 0 0
Armagh,	Armagh,	Kenedies,	M'Crum, John and William,	1808	208	30s.	July 27, 1809,	312 0 0	312 0 0
	Armagh,	Bessbrook,	Nicholson, Kelly and Johnston,	1806	1008	----	March 10, 1807,	*1,446 12 10	1,758 12 10
	Armagh,	Bessbrook,	Nicholson and Sons,	1809	208	30s.	August 1, 1809,	312 0 0	
Down,	Downpatrick,	Redemon,	Crookshank, Samuel,	1805	65	15s.	April 16, 1805,	48 0 0	78 0 0
	Downpatrick,	Redemon,	Crookshank, Samuel,	1805	40	15s.	Dec. 31, 1805,	30 0 0	
	Newry,	Temple Gouran,	Gordon, John,	1806	204	----	April 18, 1807,	*389 10 7	389 10 7
	Cumber,	Cumber,	Stitt, John and Co.	1808	240	30s.	July 29, 1809,	360 0 0	522 0 0
	Cumber,	Cumber,	Stitt, John and Co.	1809	108	30s.	Aug. 14, 1810,	162 0 0	
Donegal	Buncrana,	Buncrana,	Crookshank, Kennedy and Co.	1807	132	30s.	Febru. 2, 1808,	198 0 0	2,601 0 0
	Buncrana,	Buncrana,	Crookshank, Kennedy and Co.	1808	360	30s.	May 2, 1809,	540 0 0	
	Buncrana,	Buncrana,	Crookshank, Kennedy and Co.	1808	794	30s.	May 2, 1809,	1,191 0 0	
	Buncrana,	Buncrana,	Crookshank, Kennedy and Co.	1808	448	30s.	May 2, 1809,	672 0 0	
	Rathmelton,	Ballyard,	Scott, Nathaniel,	1809	154	30s.	Febr. 28, 1811,	231 0 0	231 0 0
Tyrone,	Dungannon,	Woodmount,	Pike, William,	1806	256	----	Sept. 18, 1806,	*507 14 7	873 14 7
	Dungannon,	Woodmount,	Pike, William,	1808	116	30s.	July 14, 1809,	174 0 0	
	Dungannon,	Woodmount,	Pike, William,	1809	128	30s.	July 14, 1809,	192 0 0	
					6,369			9,618 18 0	9,618 18 0

* *Half of Sum expended by Claimant.*   JAMES CORRY.

A page from the Proceedings of the Linen Board showing details of subsidies granted to Ulster mill owners for the installation of power-driven spinning machinery during the first decade of the 19th century.

(by courtesy of the Linen Hall Library, Belfast)

male population of the parish and to almost all the females, who were engaged in preparing and spinning the flax. However, the wages for weaving have fallen so low that the manufacture of linen is no longer a profitable employment and the introduction of mill-spun yarn has so much reduced the earnings of the spinner that spinning, which formerly besides purchasing the clothes of the females added materially to the means of the family, now is resorted to only as an alternative to being idle, except when linen is required for home consumption . . .'

The way was now clear for the establishing of the great steam-powered flax-spinning mills in Belfast, and by 1835 there were ten such mills in the town, four of them on the Falls Road. By 1850 there were no less than sixty-three flax-spinning mills in Ulster out of an Irish total of sixty-nine.

Coupled with the introduction of the wet spinning of flax, particularly in the north east of the country, there emerged a flourishing local steam engine manufacture. This was largely a result of the fact that many of the new flax-spinning mills were converted cotton-spinning mills which had been established earlier in the century near the point of import of the raw material, often on sites where water power was not readily available. Steam power had already gained a strong foothold in the Belfast district and it seemed a natural progression to adapt it to the new industry from the outset.

The story of one important Belfast mill, that of the Mulholland brothers in Henry Street, off York Street, illustrates many of the points made above and provides an interesting example of the transfer from cotton to flax which was characteristic of many of the great spinning mills in the town at this time. Thomas and Andrew Mulholland established a large cotton-spinning mill in what later became Henry Street in 1822, with a 60 horse power steam engine driving 5,000 spindles and ancillary machinery. About the year 1827 they set up experimental wet-spinning machinery for flax yarns elsewhere in the town and this must have been a reasonably successful venture for shortly afterwards, when their great cotton mill in the York Street area was gutted by fire, the brothers decided to re-build the mill for flax spinning. The machinery for the new mill was planned to the latest designs and much of it was manufactured in a small workshop set up in MacAdam's Soho Foundry, in Townsend Street.

The mill was completed and opened for production early in 1830 and unlike other early wet spinning mills in Ulster, at Castlewellan (County Down), Ballyclare and Glynn (County Antrim), all of which were built in 1828 and 1829, the Belfast

The large flax-spinning mill of Thomas and Andrew Mulholland in Henry Street, Belfast, from a drawing by J H Burgess, 1842.

mill was entirely dependent on steam power. An impressive establishment by any standards, in 1837 the mill contained three steam engines, one of 25 horse power for dressing, preparing and carding flax, and two others, one of 60 horse power and the other of 30 horse power for driving the spinning frames. The mill itself was five stories high, contained 15,300 spindles and had a chimney stack 186 feet tall. When in full production it employed nine hundred persons and spun 700 tons of flax into yarn each year.

The flyer frame dominated the Irish flax-spinning industry for upwards of a century, with over a million flyer spindles at the time of peak production, just before the First World War, and it is only since 1945, with the contraction and reorganisation enforced by the changing nature of the world textile market, that it has gradually given way to high speed frames incorporating the *ring and traveller* device, patented in America in the 1820s but not introduced into the United Kingdom until the middle of the 19th century.

In the flyer frame the bobbins of *rove* (the fine, loosely twisted product of the final *drawing*) are placed vertically on skewers in the *creel*, at the top of the frame. The rove passes

The huge linen manufacturing complex of the York Street Flax Spinning Company, Belfast, around 1900.

A *wet* spinning room.

CREEL
BOBBINS OF ROVE
HOT WATER TROUGH
JOCKEY ROLLER BEARING ON FEED ROLLER
JOCKEY ROLLER BEARING ON DRAWING ROLLER
GUIDE PLATE
FLYER
BOBBIN
BUILDER PLATE
DRAG WEIGHT

downwards from the bobbins through a *hot water trough* and this dampens and softens the rove to enable the individual fibres of which it is composed to be drawn out to the degree required. From the trough the rove passes through a pair of *feed* or *retaining* rollers, being drawn forward by *boss* or *drawing* rollers, which are turning at a greater speed than the feed rollers, usually between four and sixteen times faster. This *drafts* or *draws out* the rove and the twist is imparted by the flyer. The yarn is wound evenly on to the bobbin by means of the rising and falling of the *builder plate* on which the bobbins rest.

The frame has *flyer lead* with the bobbin turned by the pull or drag of the yarn passing through the flyer, and as the yarn builds on to the bobbin so the *drag weight cord* working on the flange of the bobbin is lifted across to exert a more positive retarding action, slowing the bobbin down and keeping the tension of the yarn constant. This is known as *tempering the drag*.

The flyer spindles are driven by cords or bands passing round a single tin cylinder, itself belt driven from overhead line shafting. The speed of the spindles varies considerably according to the *count* of the yarn being spun, with 4,000 rpm an average figure. The rollers are driven through end gearing.

The *count* of the yarn to be spun determines the details of the frame which is used and depending on the spinner's requirements the textile engineer varied the *pitch* (the distance from the centre of one spindle to that of the next), the *nip* or *reach* (the distance between the points of contact of the two pairs of rollers), the diameter of the rollers, the corrugations or *flutes per inch* on the circumference of each roller and the *draft* (the ratio of the rates of revolution of the two sets of rollers) on the frames being supplied.

(e) the 'stocks' or 'feet' of the 'tuck' mill and 'wash mill'
The *tuck* mill of Ireland corresponds closely to the *fulling* mill of Great Britain. It was soon recognised in the great woollen textile industry of southern Britain, which flourished widely during the centuries following the Norman Conquest, that the efficient finishing of hand-woven cloth was of vital importance, particularly in a competitive overseas trade. As a 14th century chronicler put it:

'Cloth that cometh fro' the weaving is naught comely to wear till it is fulled under foot, or in the fulling stocks . . .'

(from William Langland, *The Book concerning Piers the Plowman*, 1362)

The fulling mill seems to have been unknown in Britain at the time of the Domesday Survey but by the end of the 12th century it was firmly established, spreading thence to Ireland in the centuries which followed, more particularly during the great transfer of men and ideas occasioned by the official Plantation of Ulster in the early 17th century. While the finishing of woollen cloth in Ireland never approached the same widespread importance as corn milling or, somewhat later, flax scutching, the tuck mill affords an interesting local example of the industrial use of water power on a limited scale and, more important perhaps, relates directly to its subsequent use on a much wider scale in the Irish linen industry.

In the finishing of woollen cloth the *fulling, felting* or *milling* process was carried out first, to thicken the cloth and give it a firm structure. The cloth was then *scoured* or washed before being dried on tenter frames, *raised* (with teazels), cropped and,

perhaps, *frized.* Of these processes only the first two need concern us here, both fulling and washing being usually carried out in one mill, in Ireland on one and the same machine.

In the British fulling mill, in which both felting and scouring were generally carried out, great heavy wooden *feet* or *stocks,* swinging in a pendulum-line action, were pushed back by projecting cams or lugs on a massive horizontal shaft, or on heavy iron cam-wheels keyed to the wheelshaft, and let fall on the cloth as it lay soaking in a trough of hot, soapy water at the base of the frame. The term *fulling* was derived from the use of *fuller's earth,* a natural detergent with a clayey texture, and as the cloth was gently squeezed and pummelled it was turned round slightly at each blow by the *stepped* face of the stocks, to ensure uniform treatment and to avoid excessive wear or damage.

There is no positive evidence of the existence of such mills in Ireland before the 17th century but it seems likely that the antiquity of the process is much greater. Originally the woollen cloth was tramped or *walked* with the feet, in tubs, and here stale urine was used as the cleansing agent. In this connection it is interesting to note that several places in the north of Ireland where water power is still used, though no longer in the woollen

1 Roller of beech
2 Shank of oak
3 Stock back
4 Cheek
5 Striker plate
6 Foot
7 Box
8 Cam wheel
9 Cams of beech

The machinery of a water-powered fulling mill.
(by courtesy of the Newcomen Society, London)

industry, are in the townland of *Walk Mill*.

The Irish tuck mills of the 17th and 18th centuries were small buildings in which woollen cloth, woven on cottage hand looms throughout an extensive tract of country, was finished by being felted and scoured. The machinery in such mills was simple and massive. An external waterwheel drove a low-level cam-shaft, the heavy wooden cams faced with iron. As they turned these forced back the feet or stocks, generally arranged in pairs and with the cams set carefully to ensure a *staggered* working. The small Irish mills usually contained no more than two pairs of feet. The cloth was worked for about four hours, being taken out and smoothed at the half-way stage.

The Irish tuck mill was essentially a part of the local domestic woollen industry and when this began to melt away in the early decades of the 19th century the need for these small, scattered mills disappeared. The processes formerly carried out in such small, inefficient units were transferred to the new woollen mills and factories springing up as steam power increased the industrial potential of many old water-power sites throughout the country.

While in itself of but limited importance, the mechanical principles incorporated in the tuck mill were soon applied to the machinery being designed to cater for the new and rapidly expanding Irish linen industry. When one considers the order of application of water power to the various processes in this industry it is noteworthy that one of the earliest to be mechanised was, in fact, one of the last in the manufacturing sequence, that of *washing* the linen cloth at various stages during the long, drawn-out bleaching process. There is sound documentary evidence to suggest that early in the 18th century a water-driven machine was devised to give reliable and thorough washing of the linen webs in the new bleachyards then being established along many of the rivers in the province. There can be little doubt that this *wash mill*, as it was usually called, was derived the box and turning it gently with each stroke. The water being squeezed from the cloth, carrying the impurities, ran away through drainage holes in the sole of the box and the cloth was continually resoaked with fresh water admitted by the cock. When not in use, or when the machine was being loaded, the stocks could be held back out of the way by engaging *retaining hooks* on the heel clouts, as shown overleaf.

The massive wooden wash mill, each mill comprising two pairs of feet working in separate boxes, soon became an important machine in the 18th century Ulster bleachyard and by the end of the century the wash mill house occupied an important position adjacent to the *wet works* or *croft*, as the great open bleach house was called.

Many such machines remained in use, little altered, until after the Second World War, but such has been the rate of change in the linen industry since 1945 that none now survives outside the Ulster Museum where a fine example from a Lagan bleachworks occupies a prominent position in the new Textile Gallery.

(f) beetling 'engines'

The process in the linen manufacture known as *beetling* occurs in the finishing of the cloth, and is one of the last to be undertaken. In it linen webs are pounded or *beetled* for anything from one or two days up to a fortnight, to *close* the weave and to produce a smooth sheen on the finished cloth. Wound on to a slowly turning cylindrical beam at the base of the beetling *engine* the cloth is pounded steadily by the rhythmic fall of the heavy beechwood *beetles*, each about five feet long and from four to seven or eight inches square. Bleached linen damask was beetled for anything from a few hours up to one or two days, dyed linen *hollands* and *buckrams* for interlining, umbrella cloth, book-binding cloth etc, for considerably longer, up to a fortnight.

When the machine is running the beetles are lifted up by projecting lugs or *wipers*, also of hardwood, which are bolted in a continuous spiral on to a heavy timber cylinder — the *wiper beam* — some 18 inches in diameter. This cylinder is driven through bevel gearing from the main line shaft running down the side of the mill, and turns at about 30 rpm. As the wiper beam turns, each wiper engages a tappet or *key* that projects from each of the beetles, lifts the beetle, then releases it. The beetle falls, bounces on the *cloth* or *beetling beam*, is caught by the succeeding wiper and lifted again.

The cloth beam, on which the linen webs have been carefully rolled, rotates at a much slower speed than the wiper beam and to ensure an even finish on the fabric being beetled it is

Water-driven fulling stocks, 1607.

from the older woollen-finishing machinery already described.

In the Irish wash mill two massive feet or stocks of wood, each weighing perhaps five hundredweight, were suspended by *shanks* from a heavy wooden frame. The *heel clout*, fixed to and projecting downwards from the stock or foot, was struck by the *facing* of the revolving cam or *wiper*, taking back the foot to its highest position, whence it swung by its own weight against the cloth in the *box*, squeezing it against the curved front of

1 'Foot' or 'stock'
2 'Shank'
3 Pivot
4 Massive wooden framing
5 'Heel clout'
6 Facings
7 Revolving wiper on the cam shaft
8 Cam shaft, driven from the waterwheel
9 The 'box' into which swing the 'feet' or 'stocks'
10 Drainage holes
11 Water cock
12 Retaining hooks, to hold back the 'foot' when not in use

Diagrammatic cross section of the water-driven *wash mill* of the Irish linen industry.

Wash mills at Hydepark, Mallusk, County Antrim, photographed in April, 1946.

The *croft* or *wet works* of an Ulster bleachgreen.

The water-driven beetling *engine*.

1 'Beetles'
2 Projecting keys on each of the 'beetles' engaged by the individual 'wipers' as the beam turns
3 Driving gear
4 Wiper beam
5 Projecting keys or 'wipers' bolted on to the wiper beam
6 'Cloth' beam
7 Slow drive from main line shaft through worm gearing
8 'Drunken' wheel

given a slight movement to and fro by means of a *drunken* wheel, or an *eccentric,* in the gearing. The cloth beam is turned through secondary shafting, often incorporating one or more *worm* gears, driven from the main line shaft.

The mechanical principle of the water-driven beetling engine was a local application of a much more widely based device, the *stamper,* which had been used on the continent of Europe for a wide variety of purposes, from at least the 13th century.

The application of water power to *pounding* or *stamping,* a process known in palaeolithic times from finds of primitive stone pestles, has a long and interesting history. In Switzerland and other mountainous countries of central Europe, for example, a heavy balanced timber with a great weight (usually nothing more than a massive boulder) at one end was fitted at the other with an open bowl or cistern. As this filled with water it sank, spilled its contents and released the pestle, which crashed down on the rock or ore being crushed. In Japan and China a light, stamping shaft was pivoted and counterbalanced, to be worked by hand or foot.

In the Middle Ages, in western Europe, the device reached a greater degree of sophistication and in the famous *De Re Metallica* of Georgius Agricola of Glauchau in Saxony (1556) we have an interesting depiction of an overshot waterwheel driving a set of ore-crushing stampers. These are being lifted by

Crushing ore using water-driven *stampers,* 1556.

a heavy, revolving cam-shaft, little more than a horizontal *axle-tree* with projecting lugs which engage the tappets or keys of the stampers.

By the 16th century, too, the crushing of oil seeds (olive, flax, rape, ground nut, soy) was being carried out in stamping mills rather than in rotary mills, with edge-runner stones, such as we have noted earlier as being common in the Mediterranean world in Classical times, driven by animal power or slaves.

In these oil mills using upright *rams* and *stampers* the seed was first of all crushed in a rotary pan mill, and the meal was heated on an open kiln or stove. The heated meal was put in woollen bags and these in turn were wrapped snugly in a horse-hair cover. These were now slotted into narrow clefts between spacing blocks at either end of an open wooden trough. Two of the central spacing blocks were in the form of wedges, one with the thick end upwards, the other inverted. Above the two wedges, two heavy wooden rams could be lifted and dropped by the rotation of a massive cam-shaft.

When the *striking* or *pressing* ram was set in motion it crashed down on to the broad end of the wedge, driving it downwards and setting up a strong outward (lateral) pressure. This squeezed the oil from the meal and it ran off and was collected in pans or trays below. After about fifty strokes most of the oil had been extracted from the two meal bags and the second or *releasing* ram was brought into play. A few blows on the inverted wedge released the pressure and the meal bags, now containing compacted residue, could be taken out.

Because this residue or cake still contained some valuable oil, it was then often broken up by heavy upright *stamps* or *stampers*, wood shod with iron; these stood immediately adjacent to the rams, driven from the same power source, and the cake was put into *pots* into which the heavy stamps dropped as they were lifted and let fall by the cam-shaft above. The pulverised cake was then put through the ramming process a second time. Such mills were common in Germany and France, driven by water power, and in the Low Countries, driven by wind power.

Oil was also frequently extracted in watermills where a

The machinery of an oil mill, incorporating *rams* and *stampers*.
(from a drawing by J C Lunenburg in *The Dutch Windmill* by Frederick Stokhuyzen, published by Unieboek, Netherlands, 1963)

Water-driven *stamp(er)s* being used to crush oil seeds, 1662. The massive wheel-shaft here acts as a cam-shaft, with projecting cams or lugs lifting the stampers as the wheel turns. The seeds are crushed in heavy, bowl-shaped mortars of wood and iron.

The horizontal stampers of an 18th century paper mill, driven from an overshot water-wheel by means of a massive cam-shaft.

series of bowls or mortars, containing seeds, were pounded by the rise and fall of stampers, as in the ore-crushing mill of Agricola. (cf. p72 (lower) with p74 (upper)).

All these are examples of processes in which the stampers, arranged vertically, dropped directly downwards, and in this can be distinguished from those, such as paper making and iron forging, in which the horizontal or angled stamper or hammer was levered up by a terminal or lateral cam-wheel or cam-shaft.

Thus, long before the first application of water power to the linen industry, which in Ireland did not take place until the first quarter of the 18th century, the beating or stamping process, with either vertical or horizontal stampers, had been successfully mechanised in iron forging, ore crushing, oil milling and paper making. The introduction of the beetling engine to Ireland at the beginning of the 18th century (at approximately the same time as the water-driven wash mill) followed hard on the heels of the arrival of a considerable number of Huguenot refugees from northern France and the Low Countries where, as we have seen, the stamping mill was already well developed. Whether or not the beetling engine was introduced by the Huguenots is difficult to say. Certainly, Louis Crommelin makes no mention of it in his famous treatise of 1705 and it may well be that it originated in Scotland, or possibly in Ulster itself, through a local adaptation of the stamping process to the newly emergent linen industry.

On the other hand, a more direct continental origin is suggested by the fact that in 1725 a beetling engine at Drumbridge, on the Lagan just outside Belfast, installed in a bleachyard where the manager was a *genuine Hollander,* was still sufficiently recent to ensure

'. . . that the novelty of the new process drew numbers of persons to see the beetles . . .'

The earliest beetling engines were of a much simpler design than those subsequently developed and in the 19th century cast-iron frames replaced the original wooden construction, with foundries in Ballymena, Larne, Coleraine and Portadown supplying the extensive local demands.

Whatever its origin the introduction of water-powered beetling to the Irish linen industry at such an early stage contributed greatly to the high reputation soon gained by its lawns, diapers and damasks.

By the end of the 18th century the hand beetling of cloth had been largely replaced and the water-driven beetling engine, together with the wash mill and *rubbing boards,* was an essential ingredient of every successful bleaching house.

As the industry evolved so the beetling process tended to be divorced from the main bleaching complex, carried on in separate buildings of characteristic form and design. The external appearance of the beetling mill reflected its function. On the ground floor stood the row of beetling engines driven either from an

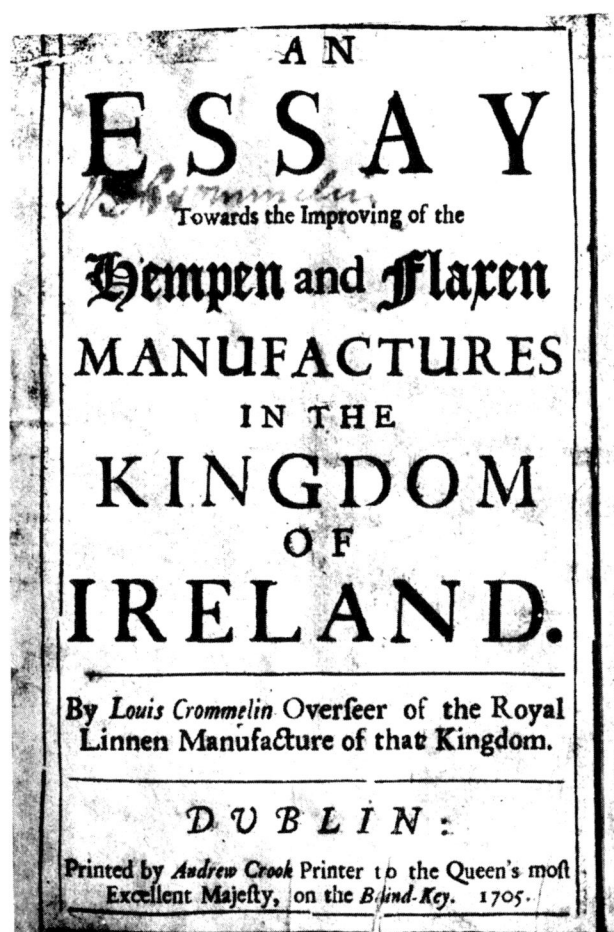

The title page of Louis Crommelin's famous treatise on the linen industry, 1705. (by courtesy of the Linen Hall Library, Belfast)

'... a complete perspective view of the machinery of a Bleach Mill upon the newest and most approved construction, consisting of the Wash Mill, Rubbing Boards moved by a Crank and a Beetling Engine for glazing the cloth; with a view of the Boiling House ...' From an engraving by William Hincks, 1783.

From left to right here are depicted the rubbing boards (another type of washing machine for handling linen in rope form), the wash mills and the beetling engines.

The Callan valley in south Armagh, from Milford southwards by Keady to the Monaghan border, is dotted with the remains of numerous beetling mills. This mill, long since disused, is at Tassagh. Behind the mill can be seen the railway viaduct on the former Castleblayney, Keady & Armagh Railway.

Linen beetling. Here the beetler is stripping off cloth which has been beetled. The beam with the cloth on it has been moved to one side of the frame from beneath the beetles, and is being belt-driven from the pulley wheel on the end of the wiper beam, which runs along behind the beetles. The wiper beam would be turning clockwise; the beam from which the cloth is being taken would be turning anti-clockwise. There is no cloth at present on the beetling beam.

The beetling mill at Wellbrook, near Cookstown, in County Tyrone, was built in the 1760s and ceased working as a commercial undertaking in 1961. It was subsequently acquired and restored by the Northern Ireland Committee of the National Trust. There are seven beetling *engines* in all and the large (16ft) external waterwheel now drives two of them. The mill has been worked by successive generations of the same family since it was built.

1 Double faced rocker hammer
2 Neutral position 3 Beam
4 Hammer fulcrum shaft

5 Stay 6 Cam and shaft
7 Stop motion to hold hammer
in neutral position

Haughton's beetling machine (1928): diagrammatic end elevation.

(by courtesy of Mr J W Frazer, Cullybackey, County Antrim)

external waterwheel, or with a central, internal wheel driving perhaps four engines on each side. On the upper floors the louvred 'windows' reflect the former use of these as drying lofts where damp, beetled cloth could be hung up to dry in a well-ventilated area, protected from direct sunlight.

Because of the very great noise created by the continuous fall of the heavy wooden beetles, the mill usually stood some distance apart from the main bleachgreen, often in a remote and picturesque setting. Many beetlers of long standing were hard of hearing, a condition contracted gradually over the years from long hours at work in the deafening interior of the beetling mill.

There were at one time numerous beetling mills on all the main rivers in the north of Ireland and because of the importance of the process over a long period of time a water-driven beetling mill at Wellbrook, near Cookstown, in County Tyrone, built in the 1760s, has been selected and restored *in situ* by the Northern Ireland Committee of the National Trust.

In textile finishing the beetling process has been largely, though not entirely replaced by *mangling* and *calendering,* but use of the massive *Dundee* mangle has also declined greatly over the past twenty years.

An iron-framed beetling engine from a bleachworks near Donaghcloney, on the river Lagan, in County Down, is now in the new Textile Gallery at the Ulster Museum. It was made in Portadown around 1930.

The final development in the long history of the Irish beetling engine came in 1928 when J W Haughton of Cullybackey, County Antrim, patented a machine for which greatly increased output and reduced working costs were claimed.

Two beams were beetled at one and the same time and the beetling hammers, fixed below the cloth beams for ease of maintenance and lubrication, described an arc about a fixed fulcrum. The cloth beams were of cast iron, the double-faced hammers of cast steel. The shank of each hammer continued below the shaft and terminated in two metal discs, each of which made contact with its respective cam. The two cam-shafts revolved in opposite directions and by fixing any hammer in the vertical position it was put out of range of the cams, and therefore ceased to operate. Each cam-shaft turned at a speed of 50 to 60 rpm, this being equivalent to the same number of blows per minute on each beam — a total of 100 to 120 blows per minute.

A number of these *patent* beetling machines, as they were generally called, were made in Manchester by Mather & Platt Ltd but despite optimistic expectations they were never widely adopted in the local linen industry. All have now been scrapped.

Bibliography

1	A Barnard	*The Whisky Distilleries of the United Kingdom,* 1887 (reprinted by David & Charles of Newton Abbot in 1969).
2	G Bowie	The Millhouse Engine in Jameson's Distillery, Bow Street, Dublin, *Industrial Archaeology,* Vol 9 No 3 (August 1972), pp 265-277.
	—	Two Stationary Steam Engines in Power's Distillery, John's Lane, Dublin, *Industrial Archaeology,* Vol 11 No 3 (August 1974), pp 209-224
3	B Bracegirdle	*The Archaeology of the Industrial Revolution,* 1973.
4	A F Burstall	*A History of Mechanical Engineering,* 1963.
5	W E Coe	*The Engineering Industry of the North of Ireland,* Newton Abbot, 1969.
6	W H Crawford	*Domestic Industry in Ireland,* Dublin, 1972.
7	T K Derry & T I Williams	*A Short History of Technology,* Oxford, 1960.
8	D Diderot	*Pictorial Encyclopaedia of Trades and Industry,* a 1959 reprint by Dover Publications of New York from the original encyclopaedias published in Paris between 1751 and 1765.
9	R A Gailey	A Family Spade Making Business in County Tyrone, *Folk Life,* Vol 10 (1972), pp 26-45.
10	H D Gribbon	*The History of Water Power in Ulster,* Newton Abbot, 1969.
11	R L Hills	*Power in the Industrial Revolution,* 1970.
12	K Hudson	*The Archaeology of Industry,* 1976.
13	W A McCutcheon	Water-powered Corn and Flax Scutching Mills in Ulster, *Ulster Folklife,* Vol 12 (1966), pp 41-51.
	—	Water Power in the North of Ireland, *Transactions of the Newcomen Society,* Vol XXXIX (1966-7), pp 67-94.
	—	The Stationary Steam Engine in Ulster, an essay originally contributed to *Folk & Farm,* Dublin, 1976; now available as an offprint.
14	E B McGuire	*Irish Whiskey — a history of distilling in Ireland,* Dublin, 1973.
15	J Reynolds	*Windmills and Watermills,* 1970.
16	P S Rhodes	*Ballycopeland Windmill,* Belfast (HMSO), 1962
17	L T C Rolt	*The Prehistory of the Steam Engine,* Dawlish and London, 1963.
18	A H Shorter	*Paper Making in the British Isles,* Newton Abbot, 1971.
19	J D Storer	*A Simple History of the Steam Engine,* 1969.
20	G B Thompson	*Spinning Wheels,* Belfast, 1952.
21	R Wailes	*The English Windmill,* 1954, 1967.
22	G Watkins	*The Industrial Archaeology of the Stationary Steam Engine,* 1976.
23	P N Wilson	*Water Turbines* (a Science Museum booklet), HMSO, 1974

Index

A panoramic view over Belfast from Ballymacarrett, c 1875